Garden
of her
Heart

HAVE YOU EVER WONDERED HOW BOOKS ARE MADE?

UCLan Publishing is an award winning independent publisher. Based at The University of Central Lancashire, this Preston-based publisher teaches MA Publishing students how to become industry professionals using the content and resources from its business; students are included at every stage of the publishing process and credited for the work that they contribute.

The business doesn't just help publishing students though. UCLan Publishing has supported the employability and real-life work skills for the University's Illustration, Acting, Translation, Animation, Photography, Film & TV students and many more. This is the beauty of books and stories; they fuel many other creative industries! The MA Publishing students are able to get involved from day one with the business and they acquire a behind the scenes experience of what it is like to work for a such a reputable independent.

The MA course was awarded a Times Higher Award (2018) for Innovation in the Arts and the business, UCLan Publishing, was awarded Best Newcomer at the Independent Publishing Guild (2019) for the ethos of teaching publishing using a commercial publishing house. As the business continues to grow, so too does the student experience upon entering this dynamic Masters course.

www.uclanpublishing.com
www.uclanpublishing.com/courses/
uclanpublishing@uclan.ac.uk

Garden of her Heart is a uclanpublishing book

First published in Great Britain in 2024 by
uclanpublishing
University of Central Lancashire
Preston, PR1 2HE, UK

978-1-916747-04-3

1 3 5 7 9 10 8 6 4 2

Set in Kingfisher by Becky Chilcott.

A CIP catalogue record for this book is available from the British Library.

Printed and bound in Great Britain by Clays Ltd, Elcograf S.p.A.

Zoë Richards

Garden of her Heart

uclanpublishing

To my nana for everything she taught me,
including a love of reading.

To anyone who has ever struggled with their mental health –
may you find some comfort in Holly's time at Pinewoods Retreat.

Grow with love
Cook with love
Eat with gratitude

Part One

JOURNAL ENTRY
Wednesday 26th May

HOW I FEEL: 3/10

SLEEP: Three hours tops

WEATHER: Sunny, hot and humid, barely any breeze

WEARING: Old tea dress – forgot I even had it

1

PERIOD HOMES & OVERWATER VILLAS

HOLLY'S eyes circle around the water ring left by Tasha's mug on the coffee table – once, twice, three times, four – as she waits for Tasha to speak. The silence that hangs between them is well beyond pregnant. What is Tasha even doing here? She's been in touch precisely three times in the last five months. That's all. Not that Holly's counting, but when it's only three times, you notice these things. The first time was when Holly was in hospital; the second, a phone call a week after she was discharged, to find out when she'd be back in work; the third, an email last week telling her that Tasha would be 'popping by for a chat'.

And here she is, in Holly's front room in her South Liverpool terraced house where she'd lived with her grandparents from the age of sixteen until she inherited it a couple of years ago. Tasha is perched on the edge of Holly's sofa in a pair of tighter-than-skintight jeans and too-high heels, resting Holly's least favourite mug on her knee. Not that Tasha knows Holly's feelings towards that particular mug.

Tasha clears her throat and opens her mouth to speak,

before closing it again and wiping beads of sweat from her pumped-up top lip. She surveys the room. Holly's eyes follow Tasha's, seeing it as her ever-critical manager might. Ancient TV in the corner that only gets five channels; threadbare suite that Nan acquired a lifetime ago; rickety sixties coffee table that must be back in fashion by now; bookcase full of Holly's favourite books, from Jane Austin classics to Emily Henry romances. The room is hardly *Period Homes and Gardens*, but Holly likes it this way: just how Nan and Grandad left it. Could she get away with calling it shabby chic? As Tasha finishes her inspection, Holly imagines a sneer of 'hardly chic, girl, more full-on shabby' – being harsher on herself than Tasha would ever be. Crimson Aunt-Sally-circles break out across Holly's cheeks as she silently berates herself for her unkind thoughts.

"Bloody hell, Hols, it's warm in here," Tasha says, glancing at the drawn curtains. She coughs and takes a sip of her tea. The words hang between them. Sure, it's cosy, just how she likes it – since the attack, at least. It's comforting. A warm, safe hug around her, like one of Nan's cuddles.

"It's like this, Hols." Tasha clears her throat. "Look. I know it's not easy, what you've been through, but you've been off work for five months and . . ." Tasha pauses to dab her brow with a tissue. "Well, the company's making cuts. A full-time member of staff for our branch, and reduced hours for everyone else. And, well, right now, with you being off," more throat clearing, "that's it." Tasha gives Holly one of those smiles of hers, her eyes not bothering to join in, despite winged eyeliner giving them a helping hand.

No, no, no. Tasha's sacking her? Holly bites her top lip. And then her bottom one. She can't lose her job. Really, she can't. Holly's skin prickles and she closes her eyes, fighting the urge to crumple. She wants to hide her head in her hands, but knows she can't let Tasha see how upset she is. Nan would say not to make it easy for Tasha. So, trying to channel her inner Nan, Holly swallows – with some difficulty, like there's glass stuck in her throat – and looks back at Tasha.

"Don't make this more difficult for me than it needs to be, Hols."

Holly's heart hammers hard against her rib cage and she rests her hand on her chest, as if holding her heart in place.

"We're letting you go."

Now Holly isn't even sure if she's breathing.

Tasha shuffles dangerously close to the edge of the sofa. "I had no choice."

Out of all them, Tasha has decided that it's her who is being made redundant. Not Tony, not Jane, Joel or Cat, not even Donna, who changes her scheduled days so often you'd be forgiven for thinking she no longer works for Out of the Ordinary Travel – OO-TO Travel as it had become known over the years.

Blood roars in Holly's ears. "I-I . . . I mean, why?"

Tasha tuts and rolls her eyes. "Isn't it obvious? You've been off sick for five months." She shrugs. "It's the sensible decision."

Holly gives her head one of her customary little shakes, like her counsellor suggested she should do in stressful situations. It does nothing to calm her or slow down her breathing, nor does it change her thinking. She gives it another little shake.

"I know this is difficult to take in, Holly. It's very hard for me too, you know. Just think what it's like having to tell someone they're losing their job."

"Please, don't do this. I – can't I – I'll come back to work. I'm ready," Holly blurts out. "Next week. I'm sure I can manage it." Her hands are damp with sweat.

"You've been off sick for months, Holly. For a little cut on your cheek."

Holly swallows the gasp that is desperate to escape. She grabs hold of her plait, wishing she'd left her long auburn hair to fall in front of her face and hide the scar. *Little cut on her cheek?* Is that what Tasha thinks it was? She went through major surgery after the attack. And now therapy for the PTSD. She sighs, deeply and slowly, trying to calm her breathing. 'You can't calm the storm, so calm yourself', that's what her counsellor says.

"Cat was back in work after ten days off," Tasha continues, filling the silence. "And let's not forget, the attacker was her ex. How do you think *she* felt? Dreadful. Embarrassed as hell at the fuss she caused the company. But she came back to work straight away. Let's face it, you've strung out your sick leave, Holly. It has to be you that we let go. Anyway, I've already told head office."

"But I need my job." She stares down at her hands, now clasped in a white-knuckle grip. "What will I do?" Don't cry, Holly. Do. Not. Cry. Not in front of Tasha. Holly lets her eyes travel around her hands to the cuffs of her sleeves, in the hope she can distract herself. There's a loose thread. She'll need to snip that off before it unravels. She wraps the thread around her little finger, unwraps it, and wraps it around her ring finger.

"If I'm honest –" when has Tasha ever been anything but brutally honest? "– it was between you and Tony. He's a complete waste of space, we all know that."

"Uh-huh."

"But at least he's in work." Tasha glares at Holly. "You're not. You see how difficult you made this for me, Holly. You brought it on yourself."

"What do I do now?" The words going around Holly's head escape without her intending them to.

"Well, you can't sit here in the dark for the rest of your life." Tasha stands up and strides over to the window. "Let's start with these." She grabs hold of the drab curtains and yanks them apart, letting sunshine flood the room.

"Don't do that!" Holly flinches as Tasha opens the window, pushing her nose out into the air, and takes in a deep breath.

"It's nothing to do with me, I know. But honestly, Holly, you've got to get on with your life. You can't live day-in, day-out, cooped up in this place. It's airless." Tasha turns and faces Holly, hands on her hips. With the sunlight streaming in behind her, she's a dark, menacing silhouette.

Holly's chest tightens, her breathing labours, her pulse quickens, her skin tingles down her spine. All the signs are there – a panic attack is threatening to come on.

Breathe, Holly. You can't calm the storm, so calm yourself.

Tasha returns to sit on the edge of the sofa. "There's paperwork," she says, pulling a thick envelope out of her oversized tote bag. "And head office have said I can offer you gardening leave, if you like."

"What's that?"

"You can choose to finish straight away, as soon as the paperwork's all signed. And we pay you your notice period on top of your redundancy pay. With your annual leave that you're due as well, you'll get a tidy sum. It's more than six months' pay. You'll have plenty of time to work things out, get another job. You'll be fine."

Fine? Is that what Tasha thinks? Holly's had enough of her manager being in her home. She channels more of her inner Nan as she forces herself to her feet, steadying herself as she holds the living room door open.

"I'll take it – the gardening leave."

"Very sensible." Tasha smiles one of her smiles again. "One more thing. You know the free holiday that OO-TO Travel offered you? You need to use it in the next month, or you'll lose it. The company has been very generous – it was a big gesture from the regional manager to help you get over the attack. Honestly, I don't understand why you've not taken it yet."

"Sorry." Holly looks down at Tasha's shoes. Bright yellow patent leather.

"Get something booked this month. Cat used hers at Easter. Went to St Lucia."

Holly's never been one to fight for the best freebie breaks the staff get offered. Holidays are just not her thing – odd, she knows, for someone working in a travel agency. A three week, all expenses paid, trip abroad has been the last thing on her mind; it's not what she'd choose to help herself get better.

Now that she's losing her job, she'd like to tell Tasha where to stick the holiday. She stares at the rug she bought last year in a failed attempt to cover up the threadbare carpet. *Now's your chance, Holly. Stand up for yourself, you can do it.*

"I-I don't want ... I-I'll get it booked," Holly mumbles. Pathetic.

Tasha sighs and purses her lips. "Get it booked this week. Up to three weeks, anywhere in the world. Won't cost you a penny. Just think of the places you can go on your holibobs." Urgh, that word. "The Maldives, that's where I'd go, one of those overwater villas. Or Sri Lanka. New Zealand, even!"

Holly wants – needs – Tasha to leave. The tell-tale threat of the looming panic attack is still building. "Fine, I'll book somewhere. Goodbye."

"Right. OK. Yes." Tasha drops the envelope on to the sofa and grabs her tote bag. "I'll leave all the redundancy paperwork for you. If you could just sign it in your own time and get it back to me in the next week, that'd be great."

Finally, Holly closes the front door and slides down to the floor. Sobbing in gulps, the panic attack takes over.

Thursday 27th May

HOW I FEEL: 1/10

SLEEP: Two hours, then another hour later

WEATHER: Raining, warm

WEARING: Baggy shorts, old T-shirt, once-white pumps

It's not fair.
I've lost my job.
And it's raining.

2

SAGE NODS
& TREE HUGS

THE counsellor nods, sagely. He glances down and writes something in his notebook. What is it he finds sufficiently interesting? Because from where Holly's sitting, much of what she says is boring and, if she's honest with herself, complete and utter drivel. Still, he seems to find plenty to jot down during their sessions together.

Holly's been seeing her counsellor for four years, and there are times when she asks herself why she still comes to see him every month. Nan had persuaded her that she needed help, and Holly agreed to attend counselling to please her. Now she keeps coming for the same reason, even though Nan died over two years ago.

Each month, the counsellor gives her tips and suggestions that she tries out – once or twice at least. But, in truth, she's not sure what any of it's doing for her. She's still anxious, still has panic attacks, still struggles to sleep at night. And since the attack it's all got worse.

"Carry on," the counsellor says, peeking over the top of his glasses.

"I agreed to take redundancy with gardening leave, so now I have six months to find a job before my money runs out. I'll never go back to OO-TO Travel."

"And how do you feel about that?"

Holly pauses. "I don't know." She's been asking herself that question since Tasha's visit. It's not like she loved working at OO-TO Travel – she'd never worked anywhere else. Sure, she took pride in her work, and the customers were usually nice, but she mainly worked there because she had no clue what else to do with her life.

"Remind me, how long did you work there?"

"Fifteen years."

"Always in the Liverpool branch?"

Holly nods.

"That's a long time to work for the same company."

"Yes." The room feels stuffy, and there's the slightest hint of body odour in the air. Please, let it not be her. Holly turns her head in a surreptitious and ultimately unsuccessful attempt to sniff her own armpit, just in case.

"We talked a while back about you getting another job, didn't we? I don't think you ever acted on that."

Holly purses her lips.

The counsellor taps his pen against his teeth. "Even though," he continues, raising an eyebrow, "your colleagues were never particularly nice to you."

"Nobody's ever particularly nice to me." She knows she sounds sulky.

"Nobody?" He raises his other eyebrow.

"You're different. I don't know how you'd be towards me if you weren't my counsellor, if you weren't paid to be nice to me." Holly pulls at the cuticle around her thumb.

He smiles at her. "What about your parents? Friends?"

"You know all there is to know about my parents, and I don't have any friends." Holly wonders if he ever bothers to refer back to those copious notes he scribbles down during their sessions.

"No friends at all?" He writes something in his notebook.

"Not really. Jen, I suppose. We lived near each other, growing up. Went to different schools though. We drifted apart after she had a baby, before the pandemic."

"I see." Scribble, scribble. "And why do you think that no one is ever nice to you?"

"I don't know. They haven't been for a long time. Not since – well, since Rose."

"This all stems back to your sister, then?"

"Everything always goes back to Rose." How many times do they need to go over the same old ground? Of course everything goes back to Rose. He's a nice man, but right now, Holly's thinking this time could be better spent.

The counsellor glances at his watch. "We're nearly out of time. We can pick up about Rose next month. Before you go, I wanted to ask if you have used that holiday that the company gave you after the attack yet?"

Him too? Why is everyone on at her to book this blooming holiday? "No. I don't like holidays."

"What do you think might be blocking you from taking them up on their offer?"

"I just said, I don't like holidays." A soft sigh escapes from the counsellor's throat. Holly is pretty sure he's not meant to show his own feelings. "I don't like flying. And if I did fly, there's nowhere I want to go."

"Have you considered that you don't need to fly? You can stay here, in the UK. There's plenty of lovely places to visit. And you don't have to do a family holiday. What about a walking holiday, or a fancy spa, or a yoga retreat?"

Holly shrugs noncommittally. This is too much. She doesn't want to go on a holiday – the thought of it makes her heart race. It feels like Tasha and her counsellor are in cahoots.

"We've talked about this kind of thing before, Holly. Think outside the box. What else could you do?"

"But – I don't . . ." Holly squeezes her eyes shut for a moment.

"OK, OK." The counsellor crosses his legs, rests his notebook precariously on his lap and crosses his arms. "What would your grandparents say about the free holiday?"

Oh, now *that's* not fair. Holly bites her top lip, not wanting to bring Nan and Grandad into this. "Don't look a gift horse in the mouth," she says quietly.

"They'd want you to use this gift?"

"Suppose so." Holly looks at the watch on her counsellor's wrist, willing it to tell him that their time is up. The whole idea of taking the holiday is making the butterflies in her stomach crash into each other.

"OK, then. That's good. And if they were here, would you listen to their advice?"

"Of course I would," she says in a near whisper.

"Good, good," he says, looking down at his notebook and smiling to himself, as if that's all sorted. "Let's spend the last couple of minutes talking about your future. How's your job search going?"

"It's not." This counselling session really isn't helping today. Holly closes her eyes again, in an attempt to shut him out. When she opens her eyes again, he's still there. She's not yet ready for a career as a magician.

"How about thinking of this as a liberating time for you? You're free to do whatever you want. What might that be? Is there anything you've always wanted to do?"

"I don't know." Holly glares at him, exhausted from the line of questioning. Whenever Holly has thought about the old what-do-you-want-to-be-when-you-grow-up question, her silent answer is always what she doesn't want to be: she doesn't want to be known as Holly Bush. For years she's wanted to change her name; become anonymous. But what does she want to do for a job? She has no idea.

"Over the next month, Holly," her counsellor continues, "I want you to think about your purpose in life. Use your journal, jot down random thoughts that come into your head. What are you on this planet to do? What is it that nobody else but Holly Bush can bring to the world? We've talked in the past about the 'act as if' game, and this month I want you to add to that and play the 'what if' game. *Act as if* you do know what you want to do, you simply need to remember what that is. And then keep asking yourself what if . . . *What if* I did this, *what if* I did that? See what comes up for you."

Holly stares at him. Has he any idea what he's talking about when it comes to her life? He's worked with her for long enough; he knows what she's lived through. Sure, she can play his 'what if' game. *What if* Rose hadn't died? *What if* her parents hadn't run off to France? *What if* her grandparents hadn't caught COVID in the care home? *What if* she hadn't been attacked? *What if* she'd not lost her job?

What if she went to sleep one night and didn't wake up?

Would anyone actually notice if she wasn't here any more?

Probably not.

"Your conscious mind is going to attempt to answer the questions immediately, and probably with a negative response." Holly's heart leaps into her throat, and she finds herself irrationally wondering if he'd read her mind. "But," he continues, "I'm asking you to sit with the *what if* questions for a little while and see what your subconscious mind comes up with." The counsellor glances at his watch again. "Our time's up for today. Your actions this week," he looks down at his notes, "are to keep journalling, look at booking that holiday, *act as if* you know what you want to do and are trying to remember your purpose, and play around with *what ifs*. What if I was a primary school teacher, or went to university, or wrote a novel? This is all to help you find your purpose in life, Holly, which in turn will help you find a job. I'm sure of it."

Ah, yes, keep journaling. Holly cringes internally. Her counsellor started her on the journal a couple of years ago, and she writes down her thoughts whenever she needs to empty her head – or when he reminds her to use it.

Holly nods, more to encourage the end of the session rather than in agreement with his reminders of her actions for the week.

* * *

The train journey home is unpleasant. The carriage is hot and airless, despite all of the narrow-slit windows being wedged open. After a cold, damp spring, the sunny day has taken everyone by surprise, including Holly; jackets are discarded, ties loosened, collars pulled, brows mopped. Holly looks up at the open window again, willing it to let in a waft of cooler air.

"Too bloody hot, isn't it, lovey?" says an elderly woman, who drops herself into the seat across the aisle from Holly. Holly nods her response and quickly picks up a copy of the *Metro*, in the hope that it sends the signal that she is not up for a commuter conversation.

The *Metro* news stories offer nothing new and Holly considers giving up on the pretence of being occupied by the paper. Glancing up, she catches the old woman's eye. She's staring.

"Nasty scar, that," the old woman says.

Holly blushes, her fingers instinctively moving towards the scar on her cheek. Her heart thuds. She reminds herself that she can't control this situation – so how can she control herself? Looking down the carriage, she sees there's an empty seat further along. Holly stands up and without looking at the woman, she walks down to the empty seat, burying her head again in the *Metro*.

Holly blinks away the tears that threaten to flop over her eyelashes, holding the newspaper up in front of her face. She turns to a full-page advertorial for a place called Pinewoods Retreat in Formby, just up the coast from Liverpool. It's the kind of thing that on any other day she would ignore, but right now she needs the distraction. There's a watercolour painting of a house surrounded by trees, and photographs of a yurt with a circle of yoga mats, delicious-looking food and a sunset on the beach. Holly has seen plenty of marketing for spas and retreats during her years at OO-TO Travel and they're all much of a muchness, with little to distinguish one spa from another – all aimed at the aspirational millennials, desperate to emulate the celebrity lifestyle. But this piece in the paper is different.

The write-up gives a little information about the ethos of the retreat and its owners, and then, at the bottom of the page, there's a poem.

PEACE AT PINEWOODS
Come, sit, rest your tired feet.
Let the trees wrap their arms around you.
Let go of your worries, your cares.
Let the sand warm your toes.
We've no interest in where you're from,
Where you thought life might take you,
Who your friends are, or what you do.

Your past, your job, your education:
None of that matters at Pinewoods Retreat.
We're here to feed your belly,
 your heart, your soul.
Open your mind to the freedom to be you.
At peace,
At Pinewoods Retreat.

An escapee tear plops over Holly's eyelashes and courses down her cheek, following the line of her scar. She brushes it aside.

A place where Holly can be herself, and never feel judged. Could such a place exist?

Pinewoods Retreat is close to home. She could leave if she wanted to – if she *needed* to. What if she does play that 'what if' game her counsellor wants her to? What if, maybe, she booked this as her holiday?

As the train pulls into her station, Holly rips the page for the retreat out of the *Metro*, folds it roughly and stuffs it into her bag – before looking around guiltily to see if anyone noticed what she'd done. As she steps off the train into a welcome breeze, the doors swish closed behind her. Nobody grabs her collar to pull her back for stealing. She marches off in the direction of home, clasping her bag tight to her body.

A little smile spreads across her face as she imagines stepping off the train in Formby instead of here, near home. What would it be like to actually go to the retreat? Could she do it? Or would it be like everything else she's tried to plan since Nan and Grandad died? She turns and looks back at the train as it pulls out of the station. A lovely idea – but not one that she's sure she can actually follow through on.

JOURNAL ENTRY
Friday 4th June

HOW I FEEL: 3/10

SLEEP: two hours

WEATHER: Grey and dull

WEARING: Baggy shorts, green T-shirt, once-white pumps

I suppose I should write something in my journal.
Not written in it for days.

Found somewhere the other day that I could maybe go to
for that holiday, and it's not far from home. Might book
it, might not. Probably need to find a job first.

It's hard to be bothered, though. I don't have motivation
to do anything.

That'll do for my journal. My counsellor will never know
I'm not really writing in it every day. And I've written in it
at the start of the day today just to get it out of the way.

3

BARISTAS, BAGGAGE HANDLERS & BRAVERY

AT precisely 11 a.m., Holly wonders if alcohol does in fact numb pain. Not the physical pain. That went months ago, mostly. No, it's the emotional pain Holly wants to dull. She'd had another sleepless night last night – the attacker hiding behind her eyelids, ready for her to close her eyes. Menacing. Growling. Gnashing his teeth, like an angry dog. The dream gets stuck in that same moment, every single night.

Is this what turns people to drink? The need to shut things out. Holly's had enough of the insomnia, the dreams, the night terrors. She needs something to make it stop – but she knows she can't turn to drink. The ghost of the attack is no reason to start now. Holly's seldom been drunk; never been much of a drinker, for that matter. Anyway, she's meant to be job hunting, not losing herself in melancholy.

With her laptop perched on her knee, she clicks on one of the online job websites and hovers her cursor over the search box. She types in 'travel agent'. After all, it's the only job she's ever had. But except for an 'exciting franchise opportunity', encouraging her to become her own boss as a 'travel consultant', nothing comes up.

No surprise there, with basically everyone booking their holidays online nowadays.

What else can she do? She types 'admin' into the search box – hundreds of jobs flash up on to the screen, all wanting experience of Microsoft Word, Excel and other software packages she's not familiar with. Sure, she can use computers, but OO-TO Travel had their own in-house system, which means Holly's never needed to do more than the basics in Word.

This is hopeless. She snaps her laptop shut and pushes down the rising panic. This feeling of despair is as bad as her anxiety. What on earth is she going to do?

Reluctantly opening her laptop again, Holly changes her search to 'all jobs in the local area'. Pages and pages of jobs come up. Lots of carers – no, she's not cut out for that. She cared for her grandparents before they went into the home – if you call it caring when it's people you love and live with – but doesn't that type of job require a particular kind of practised social skills? Holly's never felt particularly experienced in that respect. Loners don't get many opportunities to socialise.

An independent cafe wants an experienced barista, minimum wage. Goodness, what does an inexperienced barista get paid? Anyway, that's another job that needs that particular set of social skills. There's a pattern in Holly's lack of suitability for these jobs.

Baggage handlers at John Lennon Airport. No, she's not physically strong enough for that kind of job. Shelf stackers at the Asda. She could probably do that but the hours aren't ideal, starting at 10 p.m. She's usually tucked up in bed by then.

Finally, she comes across a job that looks perfect – a gardener. But they're looking for experience, and not any old experience, either; experience of organic vegetable gardening. Holly can hardly call the gardening she did with Grandad down at the allotment *experience* of organic gardening, even if he did tell her she had green fingers.

Holly loved helping Nan and Grandad on the allotment. She started doing little jobs with them from as young as she can remember, well before her life changed. She was always happy to spend hours on end down at the allotment, learning what were plants, what were weeds and how to plant seeds. Grandad bought her a set of tools that were all her own, and Nan sewed her a gardening apron with hedgehogs and rabbits on it. She still has that little apron somewhere upstairs, and her gardening tools are in a box under the stairs. But all that time spent at the allotment, learning about gardening, will never be classed as relevant experience by someone who's looking for an organic gardener. Not enough for her to apply for the job, anyway.

Holly sighs and, for the second time, slams her laptop shut in frustration. With her head leaning on the back of the sofa, she fights the rebellious tears threatening to run amok. Enough of that – no wallowing. Time for a hot chocolate and that packet of Jaffa Cakes that's calling to her from the kitchen cupboard. And it's not too soon to indulge in a third binge-watch of *Bridgerton*, right from the beginning.

* * *

Mid-afternoon, Holly closes down Netflix on her laptop, very aware that she's letting the day slip away from her. She wouldn't have watched TV all day if Nan and Grandad were here. She'd loved living with her grandparents and she knows if they were still here, they'd be nudging her to do something – anything – as long as it didn't involve basking in the glory of self-pity.

Holly looks out of the window. The small back garden needs attention. She's neglected it for too long. There's a light drizzle, but Grandad would simply say: 'Get on with it, queen. Damp ground releases its hold on weeds, dry soil tightens its grip.'

Grandad was full of sayings, quotes, proverbs and parables from his days in the navy, all about making the most of whatever situation you found yourself in. He protected her the best that he could during the bullying school years, filling her head with ways to cope with what she endured every day, giving her little mantras to say in her head to keep her going. Holly recites one of them now – he'd say she should repeat it three times a day to make sure it worked.

"Every day, in some small way, I'm getting better and better."

Goodness, how long is it since she used that mantra? Maybe now's a good time to start again. He was a wise man, was Grandad. If he was here now, he'd cajole her to get outside, fill her lungs with fresh air and get close to nature. Nan, on the other hand, would check that Holly was eating properly, suggest they baked together and get a hearty meal down her. Both of them would be right – she does need a good meal, better than the ready meals she's relied on for months, and she needs fresh air too.

Holly feels the familiar ache of missing them still, a little over two years since they died. How cruel that the care home they moved to became ravaged by COVID, having got through the worst of the pandemic unscathed.

Giving herself a shake, Holly makes a silent promise to Nan and Grandad. Every day, in some small way, she's going to get better and better. It's time to sort herself out. Although Nan would probably say to have tea and toasted crumpets first.

* * *

Holly licks the last of the butter from her fingers, and decides it's time to act on impulse. Most unlike her – and, in truth, others would undoubtedly argue about the validity of her claim that she's being impulsive, considering she's ruminated on the retreat in Formby since she read about it in the *Metro* earlier in the week. It's that poem. She keeps going back to it. This is the place she should try going to for her holiday – and it's close enough to Liverpool that she can come home if she hates it.

A quick call to Tasha confirms that Holly can book her holiday and get the invoice sent to OO-TO Travel. When Holly tells her what she's chosen, Tasha scoffs.

"You're kidding me, right? Formby? It's only up the road." Tasha's laugh is hollow.

"Sorry, I know, but – well – you said it's up to me where I go." Holly's mouth is dry at challenging her manager – ex-manager, she reminds herself. "That's where I want to go. Is that OK?" Why the heck is she asking? For goodness' sake, Holly.

"Fine by me. Have fun, I guess."

Hopefully, that's the last time she will ever need to hear Tasha's voice.

Next, Holly calls the number on the page she ripped out of the *Metro*, her heart thrumming.

"Thank you for calling Pinewoods, how may I help you?" The woman's voice is like honey.

"I-I . . ." Holly has no idea what to say now that she's called the number. The butterflies in her stomach are leaping about, like they're on trampolines. Maybe she should just put the phone down?

"Hello there. My name's Lorraine. What can I do to help you?" That honey voice again. Friendly, warm, comforting.

"The *Metro* – erm – retreat . . ." She sounds like a nutcase. *Weirdo*. That's what people called her in school, and she's proving them right. She always sounds odd when she's nervous.

"Oh, yes, our piece in the paper." Holly hears the smile in the woman's voice, even though she can't see her.

"Yes. No. I mean – well, yes, I saw it on the train and, well, the poem."

"I love that poem. One of our previous guests wrote it after she enjoyed a two-week break with us."

"I need to book a break, and the poem – I . . . I mean . . . it made Pinewoods Retreat sound like the kind of thing I need just now."

"Perfect. Pinewoods finds people at the right time for them. We have a range of options for you, from the Rest and Relax package which is bed, breakfast and an evening meal, leaving you to choose how you spend your days, all the way up to our Deluxe Package which includes massages and treatments, personal training on alternate days throughout your stay, as well as yoga sessions, trips out, meditations and so on. You're free to book on to activities when you're here if you choose the Rest and Relax package – it gives you freedom that way – and the Deluxe has everything organised for you. Would you like me to take you through our other packages, or is the Deluxe what you need right now?"

"Deluxe." A little giggle of excitement wriggles about in Holly's throat. Well, OO-TO Travel are paying, after all – she might as well book the best package.

"Perfect," the woman says again. "And when would you like to come?"

"Soon?" Is she asking this woman, Lorraine, or herself? Even Holly can't tell, but she has a feeling that it's best to act straight away before she changes her mind.

Holly's no longer sure if it's fear or excitement she can feel in her stomach. She checks her breathing. Everything's fine there. Her heart isn't pounding, chest isn't tightening and her hands aren't sweating. It's a flutter, this feeling in her stomach, like butterflies flying in formation instead of crashing into each other like they usually do. Yes, she's excited.

As soon as she's finalised the arrangements, booking in for three weeks in just one weeks' time, she writes a list, planning and packing for her trip.

Part Two

4

CINDER TRACKS & ROSE QUARTZ HEARTS

THE taxi pulls up in front of an imposing pair of black iron gates, closed tight shut and flanked on either side by two smaller pedestrian gates that are wedged open. Holly unfolds the piece of paper that she's gripped hold of since the taxi drove off from the station a few minutes earlier. Lorraine warned her that Lifeboat Lane is a private road.

"That's as far as we go, girl," the taxi driver says, putting his handbrake on. "That's," he looks at the meter, "three pound fifty."

"Oh, no, sorry. It's OK, I've got a number here that we're to call. They said they'll open the gates for you to drive through."

The taxi driver gets out and opens her door on his way round to the boot where he retrieves her suitcase.

Holly climbs out of the car. "Pinewoods is through the gates – it's apparently quite a way down the lane, and I was told to make sure you take me all the way." The taxi driver plonks her suitcase in front of the gates. Holly puts a hand to her mouth as she realises she is beaten, and will have to make her own way from here. She fumbles with her purse and pulls out a folded fiver. She hands it over to the taxi driver who pockets the money and climbs back into the driving seat, ignoring Holly's outstretched hand.

"It's just down there, girl," he says, nodding at the gate as he slams his car door shut.

"My change . . ." Holly says to the air. The driver backs his taxi away from the gates, does a careless two-point turn, and skids off, kicking up gravel and dust.

A lump in Holly's throat threatens to escape as a sob. She swallows it down and stares at the gloomy route ahead of her, trees overhanging the cinder track. Well, she's no other choice than to finish the journey on her own. She yanks her suitcase behind her, struggling with the tiny wheels on the rough surface of potholes and stones. She probably shouldn't be surprised that it's such a struggle – that's her whole life. Humungous scar on her cheek, no job, no friends to speak of any more, anxiety and panic attacks, parents living in France – mind you, that may be a blessing, that they live abroad. At least she gets to choose how to live her life for herself. Not that she actually allows herself the benefits of that freedom. It's like she's gone from the coercive control of her mother, aided and abetted by her father, to her own version of a tightly orchestrated life.

Somehow, they still have a hold over her, with their sighs of disappointment on their Sunday evening FaceTime calls, their rebukes that 'a Bush never gives up', that her job in a travel agency is no job for a Bush, asking her when she'll start her real career. She could start now – if she knew what to do. But in truth she's absolutely no idea what she's good at. The voices in her head tell her she's good for nothing, she should have gone to university, she's wasted her life – and, quite frankly, is wasting time coming to this blasted retreat.

Holly's arm aches as she pulls her case behind her and, as she notices this, it occurs to her that her heart aches too. She never stands up for herself, and situations like she's just had with the taxi driver make her feel useless – a hopeless case.

Really, this whole trip is a stupid idea. She should've stayed at home, watched *Emily in Paris* for the umpteenth time, eaten share bags of Haribo and hidden away from the world. Maybe she should have investigated that option of alcohol-before-lunch instead of gallivanting off on a three-week trip at a ridiculous retreat that's less than twenty miles from home. She could have had a coffee with Jen rather than get on the train to Formby – well, she could have if she'd been better at keeping in touch since her old friend had a baby. The baby must be two or three by now. Wait, no – the pandemic and lockdowns have distorted time. That baby is probably starting at school in September.

As the suitcase grows heavier, Holly feels the weight of her life on her shoulders. The list of things she feels she's useless at grows: no job, no degree, no good at keeping in touch with the handful of friends she's had, wasting her life, wasting time on a retreat. *Argh! These annoying voices. Enough. Breathe, Holly. Breathe.* But, like real people, the internal critics take no notice at all and continue to hound her as she wends her way to Pinewoods, the suitcase getting heavier and heavier with every pull, tug and drag along the rough track.

Long after Holly loses her nerve, knowing she must surely

have missed the turning for the retreat and maybe can now justify turning back to catch a train home, an imposing red-brick Victorian house emerges, surrounded by trees. Pine trees, obviously. There's no other houses nearby, and yet it's the kind of architecture you'd expect to see in a Victorian town thronged with the nineteenth-century version of cookie-cutter homes, standing to attention in lines.

This is it, Pinewoods Retreat.

Holly stands at a rose arch that frames the entrance to the front garden. She catches her breath for a moment, looking up at the house. The ominous, dark windows watch her, seeing deep into her soul – fully aware of her regrets about coming here.

A crazy-paving path, trimmed with lavender, leads to an open door. A selection of metal tables and chairs are placed either side of the path on the front lawn, and a couple of women in gym gear nurse hot drinks at the only occupied table. One of the women glances over at Holly, looks her up and down, and returns her attention to her friend.

In the distance, the cries of gulls and cawing of crows laugh at her. Somewhere, a man is shouting numbers out loud. "Down for eight, seven, six, five, four, three, two, one. Hold two, three, four. And up seven, six, five . . ."

Pots of red geraniums line up on the front steps, like soldiers in dress uniform ready to usher her inside. Next to the open door is an old-fashioned bell pull. Holly yanks on it. A bell jangles in response somewhere deep inside the house and moments later a young waitress with a short denim apron half-walks, half-skips, to the door. As she comes to a stop at the door, a broad smile covering her face, she rests her hands in the pocket of her apron.

"Do you want to take a seat?" she says. "I'll be out to take your order in a moment."

"Oh, right, no, I mean – I'm staying here."

"Sorry, of course! The suitcase. Silly me." The young woman laughs with ease. "You must be one of the journalists. Please, come on in."

Journalists? Holly's heart drops to her stomach with a thud. This can't be happening. Being on a retreat with nasty, loathsome, ruthless journalists, of all people, is one of Holly's worst nightmares. Now she is certain that coming to Pinewoods was a mistake.

"No, I'm not a journalist." Holly's breathless voice rises in pitch. "I've booked in to stay here for three weeks. For a holiday."

"Oh, my mistake." The young woman smiles. "It's with you being early, I thought you must be one of the journalists. Check-in's at 3 p.m., but it's not a problem, I'm sure. Welcome to Pinewoods Retreat. I'm Jess. Follow me, please." Jess leads the way into the hall which seems all the darker for coming in from the brightness outside. A heady mix of essential oils permeates around Holly as her eyes adjust to the gloom.

"Why are there journalists staying?" Holly asks.

"It's for marketing. They get to stay here for a week, with the agreement they do a write-up in their paper or magazine. One guy is coming from Ireland and will be writing about the natterjack toads for some nature magazine, but I think the rest are all doing travel stuff."

"They won't write about guests, though?"

"No, not at all. They're here to write about Pinewoods." Jess flashes another smile. "I'll let Lorraine know you're here. I don't know if your room is ready yet, with you arriving so early. Take a seat in here a moment." She gestures towards a large living room and half-skips off down the hall, vanishing through a door that swings back and forth on its hinges, as if tempting others to follow.

Ever the obedient one, Holly does as she's told and enters the living room. It's painted a pale grey with buddhas standing guard on either side of the fireplace, a vase of garden flowers sitting between them. Ambient music plays soothingly from a speaker in the corner by the window and a gentle mist rises from an air diffuser, filling the room with the scent of aromatherapy. A sense of calm washes over Holly, the likes of which she can't recall – from recent times at least. She takes in a deep breath and notices the for-ever-there-tightness in her chest release its grip, just a smidgen. She sinks into the sumptuous sofa in the bay window, which swallows her up and, closing her eyes, she lets the essential oils soak into her lungs.

"You look at peace." Lorraine's honeyed voice announces her arrival in the room.

"Sorry, sorry." Holly tries to jump to her feet but the sofa refuses to liberate her, leaving her to execute an ungainly exit. "The room, the music, the smell – it all just took over me." Lorraine offers a hand to help Holly up. She accepts the proffered hand, her cheeks burning, her scar throbbing.

"No apology needed." Lorraine is a few inches smaller than Holly expected, but then, how could a voice on a phone ever provide clues to a person's height? She's younger than Holly expected too – maybe late forties. She has smiling blue eyes, and blonde hair that is mainly held in place in a messy bun at the nape of her neck. "That's exactly what this room is designed to do, relax you. I have crystals planted around, hidden in corners and under cushions, all carefully chosen for their relaxing and healing properties, and for their own unique superpower. You were sitting on a piece of rose quartz, by the way. It's hiding behind the cushion." Lorraine only pauses for a second before answering Holly's unasked question. "The crystal for love, self-love, friendship and deep, inner healing. We all choose the right stone for us, for the moment we're in. It would seem you need some rose quartz in your life just now."

Lorraine opens a wooden box on the fireplace, fiddles around with the contents for a moment, and brings out a small crystal cut in the shape of a heart. "Here, my gift to you." She takes Holly's hand and places the heart in the centre of her palm, closing Holly's fingers over it. "Keep it with you. Put it under your pillow, carry it with you wherever you go. It will help you heal in whatever way you need." That honeyed voice that Holly heard on the phone, that lulled her into coming to Pinewoods Retreat, wraps itself around her – light, calm, warm. It reminds her why she decided to come.

Holly opens her fingers and stares at the rose quartz heart in her hand. "Thank you," she says, fighting the tear that's dangling on her eyelashes. Such kindness from a woman who doesn't even know her.

"Now, let me give you the full tour. It's a magical place. We fell in love with it well before it was on the market. We used to walk the dog around here and always knew we'd found our happy place, so it was natural for Dee and me to settle here when it came up for sale. Come on, let me introduce you to Pinewoods and all it has to offer." Lorraine's smile is as warm as her voice, and Holly follows her, mesmerised. "This is our dining room." Lorraine walks Holly into a large room with wood panelling and French windows opening out on to the front lawn where the cafe tables are set up. "We dine here each evening, and have breakfast here too. Lunch is up to each guest. You can have a picnic, or sit at the cafe tables, and occasionally we have guests join us at the kitchen table too. We create a relaxed community for our guests, encouraging kindness to each other. Let me show you the therapy room, and then we'll go into the kitchen garden. We grow as much of our own food here as we can."

Holly follows, as Lorraine shows her where she does the massages and Reiki, and then takes her through the kitchen, where a mix of coffee and cake aromas fill her nostrils. Lorraine says a quick hello to the chef, Dee, a small, curvy woman with rosy round cheeks that almost match the colour of her short, pink hair, and then they go on through to the kitchen garden. It's a beautiful, tranquil place, if a little overgrown and looking in need of some love. Does the garden need a little rose quartz too? Holly can see herself wanting to spend some of her time at Pinewoods in the garden. She spots a couple of benches scattered about, and wonders if she can take her lunch here.

They walk around to the yoga yurt at the side of the house. Finally, they walk to the front garden cafe and the trailer-turned-takeaway serving hot and cold drinks, cakes and cookies for ramblers, runners and dog-walkers – and not forgetting the dogs, too.

Lorraine takes Holly back through the open front door. "I'm proud of what we do here at Pinewoods. We make sure our guests can totally relax and switch off from whatever is going on in the real world. You can get involved with any of the activities that suit you, like meditation, yoga, dune running, beach marches, local trips and, of course, all of our treatments too. And then you have your personal training sessions every other day. Have you been on a retreat before, Holly?"

"Er – no, no." Holly stumbles over her words. She's not saying anything about the retreat her mother took her on when she was sixteen, shortly before her seventeenth birthday and a few weeks before her parents moved to France. It's the holiday she wishes she could forget, one of the worst experiences of her life – after losing Rose and having her face slashed, that is. It's one of those life events that has a nasty habit of creeping back into her consciousness, unexpectedly, like an uninvited guest who intends to stay for the weekend.

The trip was just for the two of them, her and Mags. It was marketed as a week to 'find your true self' and was aimed at peri-menopausal women, but the organiser said that of course she'd love for Mrs Bush to bring her daughter along, what with her own rite of passage: entering womanhood. It would be a special time for the two of them to share, mother-daughter bonding; it would be liberating.

It was traumatising. For Holly, that is. She still can't think about the nudity, and the workshops – 'Finding the Woman Within', 'Woman-to-Woman' and 'Wild Woman, Inner Goddess' – without blushing from her naval up. Can you imagine the what-did-you-get-up-to-in-the-holidays conversation on the first day back at school?

"Oh, you know, the usual – a day at the fairground, went to the cinema, bit of shopping. Oh yeah, and how could I forget? An orgasm circle with my mum and a whole gaggle of full-on nude, middle-aged, peri-menopausal women, all holding mirrors up to their fannies, finding their pleasure points and panting in unison with a soundtrack of whales and dolphins. What about you?" Holly still can't believe her mother thought it was OK to take her teenage daughter to something meant for grown women – Mags must have lied about Holly's age, surely.

"No," Holly shakes her head now, to Lorraine. "No, I've never been to a retreat. This is my first time."

"Great. We'll make sure it's the best experience for you. Here," Lorraine says, holding a canvas bag out to Holly. "This is for you. A little bag of goodies, my way of saying welcome to Pinewoods. I hope you enjoy your stay."

"Thank you, that's kind of you."

"And this is something I'll put in specifically for you." Lorraine reaches up to a shelf of products and picks out a small box. "Bio Oil. It's amazing for healing scars. Helps reduce the redness.

I used it on my scar, here." Lorraine points to a faint white line on her wrist. "Carpel tunnel. That scar was so angry after the op. Bio Oil was the only thing that helped." Holly's cheeks burn. Apart from her plastic surgeon, who she hasn't seen in a few months now since he gave her a clean bill of health, the only people who've mentioned her scar simply want to know how she got it. They inevitably ask *The Question* – what happened? Cue Holly falling over her words, going bright red and making excuses so that she doesn't have to relive the horror.

But Lorraine is different. She hasn't hinted at asking *The Question* – just offered to help. Holly is thrown by the act of kindness.

"I'm sorry, I don't mean to make you feel uncomfortable by bringing it up," Lorraine says. "But I promise you, the Bio Oil will do the job and you'll notice a difference in a matter of weeks. Maybe even before you leave us in three weeks' time." She passes the box to Holly.

"Thank you." Holly takes the bag and peeks inside. "Gosh, that's a lot of goodies."

"It all comes with our deluxe package," Lorraine says with a smile. "Oh, I nearly forgot! Your journal and pen."

"I already have a journal," Holly says, her cheeks reddening up again. She's never admitted to anyone before that she keeps a journal – well, *has* a journal. Can she say she keeps one when she only occasionally writes in it?

"Great. You'll be used to doing daily streams of consciousness, then. Here at Pinewoods, we give you a prompt each evening and ask you to simply leave that to float through your mind as you sleep." Sleep? Holly can't remember the last time she got some proper sleep. "No writing until the next day," Lorraine continues. "Then, throughout the day, add to your journal with streams of consciousness. Write anything that pops into your head – no thinking about it, simply go with the flow. Start with the prompt and see where it takes you. Questions you want answers to, random thoughts, memories."

"Oh, right." Memories. Some of hers are best kept locked away. It always feels better that way. Though they still manage to creep into her head whenever they get the chance – uninvited guests. "OK." She smiles at Lorraine and nods. Like her counsellor always says to her, it's not homework. Nobody will be checking what she writes – or, more to the point, what she doesn't write.

"The point of your journal is for you to work with the voices inside your head."

Crikey. The voices in Holly's head are far too loud – she does her best to quieten them, not listen to them. She doesn't need to *work* with them, not when they tell her how useless she is.

"It's that inner critic, isn't it? The voices," Lorraine says. "We all suffer from them having so many opinions. Now, if anything comes up for you that you want to work through with someone else, let me or Dee know. We're both trained in helping people deal with inner demons. You're not alone here at Pinewoods." Lorraine smiles at Holly, her face full of kindness. "Come on, follow me. Let's get you settled in your room, and then you can relax."

Holly pulls her suitcase behind her, following Lorraine to the stairs.

"You can leave that here, if you like. I'll ask Hunter to bring it up to your room for you."

"It's OK, I can manage." She dutifully follows Lorraine, struggling with her case up the stairs to a room in the attic on the top floor, wondering if she should have left it for this Hunter person to carry up for her. But she's never keen on being beholden to people; they soon use it against you, if you're not careful. As she puts her case down on her bed, Holly realises that there's something about Lorraine – a way about her that's calming. Against her better judgement, from a lifetime of dreadful experiences when she thought people were on her side, Holly finds Lorraine very easy to put her trust in.

Friday 11th June

HOW I FEEL: 5/10 - a little bit excited that I made the effort to come to the retreat

SLEEP: Three hours

WEATHER: Clouds and sunshine, warm

WEARING: New shorts that fit, bought online last week (consigned old baggy ones to charity shop bag), pink blouse with Peter Pan collar, barefoot

Arrived at Pinewoods Retreat an hour ago. I've promised myself I'm going to give it four days. If I hate the place after that, I'm going home.

Got an amazing goody bag, filled with essential oils, eye mask, tissues - they're going to come in useful. Sports towel. Water canister. A novel - not read this one. Nobody's Perfect. Sounds like it's written for me!

Love this rose quartz heart Lorraine gave me. Very tactile and such a beautiful colour of pink. It's just the right size to fit in my palm. Pocket-sized.

I'm expected to keep a journal during my stay. Stream of consciousness stuff. Whatever comes into my head, I've to write it down. Lorraine will give me a prompt every evening. She said last night's prompt was to write about a time you felt safe.

Maybe I'll add PROMPT to the top of each page of my journal, starting tomorrow. Yes, I'll do that. Gives me something to write, even if I don't actually do the stream of consciousness thing.

OK, let's give this a try.

PROMPT: When is a time when I felt safe?

Always felt safe with Nan and Grandad. They knew how to create a safe space for me. Nan pulling me in for one of her warm hugs. She smelt of baking or the garden – an earthy, homely kind of smell. Grandad crouching down next to me to teach me what to do on the allotment. He always let me have a go, never took over like Mags would do.

Yeah, I guess that's it.

Will I ever feel safe again, without them in my life?
Doesn't feel like it.

Is Lorraine expecting me to write that I feel safe here, at Pinewoods? It's hard to even imagine feeling safe anywhere but home.

This place is full of strangers. That makes me feel anxious. I definitely don't feel safe around strangers. Even thinking about it makes my heart beat a little faster.

Might go for a walk. That way I can avoid bumping into any other guests before I have to. Lorraine showed me some places to go on the map.

Lorraine said to keep writing and try to write three pages. How the heck does anyone write three pages? I've never written that much in all the time I've kept a journal for my counsellor.

That'll do for now. No need to write more. She'll never know, anyway.

Is this what stream of consciousness is?
Who knows.

5

SKYLARKS & SOUND BATHS

HOLLY listens as Lorraine directs her to the beach. It's simple and direct enough – follow the cinder path until it hits sand dunes, go over the top, and there's the sea.

"Well," Lorraine says, "only when it's high tide. Right now, it's low tide so you'll need binoculars to see the sea." She laughs, a light tinkle of a laugh. "It goes out a long way here, and people think it never comes in, but it does. Fast too."

"When we used to come to Southport as kids, we always said it was like the sea never came in."

"Many a person's been caught out on the sand banks when the tide turns. As long as you don't try to walk out to the sea today, you'll be fine. Anyway, you've a huge beach to walk, and the views across Liverpool Bay are fabulous. If the light's right, you might even see all the way to Snowdonia and Anglesey. Now," Lorraine rests a hand gently on Holly's shoulder, "be back in time for lunch. Dee will set something up for you in the kitchen, and later on there's a sound bath in the dining room. Oh, and did I tell you about Friday Fizz Night?" Holly shakes her head. "Before dinner, we have drinks on the house to welcome our new guests.

Kombucha fizz. A mix of health, fizz and a bit of fun."

Socialising. With strangers. Not Holly's idea of 'a bit of fun' at all.

She wanders off down the cinder path. A few walkers say hello as they trip past her, following their energetic dogs. There's a surplus of cockapoos, and Holly wonders what Nan would say the collective noun might be. A 'pack of cockapoos' is too obvious. What about 'a colony of cockapoos'? A 'clutch'? Watching the dogs bound eagerly after each other, she settles on an 'excitement of cockapoos'.

As Holly reaches the top of the dunes, she can see that Lorraine is right – the beach stretches as far as the eye can see. She fills her lungs with the fresh air and takes in the view. In the far distance, Snowdonia peeks up from the hazy horizon. Closer, there are rows of wind turbines, steadfast and tall, watching over the entrance to the Mersey and the Liverpool docks. Holly's struck by how different the view is from here, only a few miles along the coast from home and her view across the river at Otterspool Prom.

She walks along the beach in the general direction of Liverpool – home and familiarity ahead of her. A few dog-walkers and runners trot past, going in the opposite direction, with a nod or a mumbled hello, and soon she has the beach all to herself, with not even a distant figure ahead. Eventually, Holly turns inland, unsure how long she's been walking, and scrambles over soft, steep dunes.

Such exertion, after being inactive for too long, leaves her breathless. Sliding down a particularly steep dune, she finds herself in a quiet and secluded hollow, hidden from view. Holly sits down and leans back into the warm sand. Is that a skylark she can hear? Grandad would know. The repetitive pattern of the birdsong is high above, as if the bird is hovering right over her. She could get used to this feeling of – what is it exactly? It's like it's not a specific actual feeling, more the absence of a feeling that's haunted her for too long. The lack of anxiety, that background niggle of panic, the need to check her breathing every ten minutes – it's not here, and its absence feels strange, but welcome. The only time she ever feels close to this is when she's hiding in her living room, lost in reading *Pride and Prejudice* or *Sense and Sensibility* for the umpteenth time. Even then, something lurks in the back of her mind, recognising that romantic novel escapism isn't real life – which inevitably leads to anxiety at the thought of getting back to some kind of normality. But right now, there's none of that.

Holly's eyes get heavy. She soaks in the warmth of the sun, the songbirds, the smell of the sea and gradually, unexpectedly, she drifts off into a deep, sun-filled slumber.

Something wet nuzzles at Holly's cheek. Startled, she opens her eyes and discovers a huge, hairy dog staring down at her. In the distance, someone is shouting: "Alfie, Alfie! Get here now!" The dog sniffs Holly's hair, lifts his head to sniff the air, gives Holly one last wet nudge with his nose, and flolups off in the direction of his owner.

Holly's stomach growls. For goodness' sake, what was she thinking, dropping off to sleep like that? She checks her phone – it's gone two o'clock. She's missed lunch. Half-walking, half-running, Holly scrambles through the dunes as fast as she can.

In the distance, there's the sound of banging – gunfire? There it is again. Disorientated, she spins around, looking for a path to take her back to Pinewoods Retreat.

After ten minutes of walking, nature's peace intermittently ruptured by the rapid rattle of gunfire, and still not having found anything more than a narrow path, Holly takes a route off towards some trees. Surely that's where Pinewoods is – it's in the woods, after all. She marches on, her heart pounding, a hint of anxiety building. What if she can't find her way back? Her chest tightens. The trees ahead are just a clump, not part of the woods. This is all wrong.

She swivels round and round, looking for something, anything, that tells her where she is. Her skin prickles. Panic gathers in her chest. The butterflies in her stomach smash and crash into each other and she drops to her knees, her breath catching in her throat. The mantra her counsellor gave her plays out in her head – you can't calm the storm, so calm yourself. She must breathe slower. Breathe in . . . and out. In for two, three, four, five . . .

But it's too late. The panic attack takes over and Holly fights for breath.

"Are you OK?"

Holly lifts her head. Coming towards her is a tall, broad man with curly chestnut brown hair that bounces as he strides in her direction. "I'm . . ." she breathes out, struggling to slow her breathing, ". . . fine." She clambers to her feet and tries to walk on, lungs burning, heart thudding, head swimming. She stumbles.

"Stop." The man is right behind her and grabs her arm.

No! No! A surge of adrenaline blasts through Holly's veins. What's he doing? She tries to shout out, but her lungs are preoccupied with this blasted panic attack. Twisting her arm, she tries to loosen his grip. She needs to get away from him.

"It's OK," he says calmly, letting go of her arm. "You're having a panic attack. Breathe in through your nose. Come on, we'll do it together." He breathes with her. "Rub your palms together. It helps your breathing." He nods at her as he rubs his own palms together.

Holly copies the motion and feels a slight calming in her lungs.

"You're all right, you're going to be OK." Gunfire explodes in a crescendo, and he flinches. "Now breathe in slowly, and let's see if we can count to four. OK?" He nods at Holly, and she nods back. "One, two, three, four. Good, good. Well done. Keep rubbing your palms together." As he continues to count slowly with Holly, her breathing slows and her heart calms. They stand facing each other. His gold-flecked hazel eyes look straight into hers.

"You're Holly."

She nods, wanting to look away, but his eyes are kind, punctuated with laughter lines.

"I'm Hunter. Work for Lorraine. She sent me out to find you. And here you are, wandering off god-knows where." His calm of a few moments before is nowhere to be seen, with his shoulders tensing, his fists clenched by his side. More rapid gunfire. She sees him flinch again and look off towards the noise.

"What's happening?" Holly asks, her breath still feeling tight in her chest. "What is that?"

"Altcar." Hunter shakes his head. "Firing range." He lifts his chest and breathes in slowly. "Lorraine's worried. What the heck were you thinking?"

"I told her I was going for a walk," Holly says, irritated by his interrogation.

"And that you'd be back for lunch." He raises an eyebrow. "You got lost. What would've happened if I'd not come out to help you?"

"I don't need your help." Holly purses her lips.

"Oh, yes you do." Hunter laughs, softening again for a moment. "Aside from your panic attack, you were going in the wrong direction. Due east. Pinewoods is north-northwest." As a stuttering of gunfire sounds out in the distance, Hunter stuffs clenched fists into his pockets. "You're bloody lucky I only live at the caravan park, so I could come out to find you."

"I was fine," she says, rubbing her chest.

"Yeah, course you were." Hunter breathes heavily, glaring at Holly. Then he shakes his head. "Come on, let's get a move on."

Holly opens her mouth to speak. She can't think of anything to say that won't sound stupid. She lets out her go-to response whenever her brain freezes. "Sorry."

"Lorraine's worried you walked out to sea – got trapped by the turning tide. She seems to have really taken to you. Always collects the waifs and strays, that woman."

Holly spots the hint of a smile as she gives Hunter a sideways glance. He has the tan of someone who spends a lot of time outdoors, which suits his high cheekbones and clean-shaven jaw line. "I didn't mean to worry anyone. Sorry."

Hunter marches off, before glancing over one shoulder, then the other, like he's taking in the lay of the land. "Lorraine's going to want to know you're safely back before she does her bloody woo-woo stuff with the sound bath thing this afternoon."

"Of course, sorry," Holly says, following on behind.

"Shit, is that the only word you know?" He picks up his pace, and Holly has to break into a half-run, half-walk to keep up. "Stop saying sorry."

She cringes as she stops herself from saying it again. "But I am."

"Sure, you said it. You don't need to keep saying it." Hunter stops in his tracks, turns to Holly and stares at her for a moment. He must be taking in her scar, like that woman on the train. Is this her life from now on, people staring at her? She runs her fingers down the course of her scar. The Question will follow; he'll want to know how she got it. "Take it from me," he says, continuing in a gentler tone, "if you keep saying sorry all the time, you'll always be the victim."

Holly waits for Hunter to say more – something, anything, about her scar. *Go on, get it over with.*

"What happened?" And there it is, right on cue. "I mean," he carries on, before Holly can blink, "it's not exactly that big an area around here that you can walk for hours and get lost." Holly is surprised at the direction Hunter has taken the conversation, not even mentioning her scar. "The sea's to the west. Everyone knows that. All you needed to do was get on to the beach. You'd soon've found your way back."

"I-I . . ." Holly sighs, her lungs still sore from the panic attack.

"It was an accident. I fell asleep. I didn't mean to. And then the guns were going off."

"Yeah." Hunter nods slowly. "Lorraine said I'm to take you straight to the kitchen. Dee's saved you some lunch so you don't go hungry. Come on, keep up, it's not far."

He says nothing more. Perhaps he's saving up some cutting remark for later, the way her bullies at school used to hold on to stuff. She can imagine him now, telling the people at the retreat the tale of him having to save the stupid woman with an ugly great scar down her cheek.

* * *

Hunter leads Holly straight to the kitchen, and immediately takes his leave. After a great deal of fussing from Lorraine and Dee, and many apologies from Holly, a plate full of delicious food is put down in front of her. There's a salad, homemade sourdough bread, relish and pickles, delicious falafel and a platter of vegan cheese. Not a ready meal or noodle pot in sight.

"You make all this yourself?" Holly asks, loading a piece of sourdough with cheese and relish.

"Not the vegan cheese, but everything else, yes. And we grow everything ourselves – except the wheat for the bread, obviously." Dee smiles.

"Dee's been nurturing her own sourdough starter for over ten years, haven't you?"

"Uh-huh. She's called Martha."

"Who is?"

Dee laughs. "My sourdough starter. Every sourdough baker gives their starter a name, and mine's Martha. It's just water, bread flour and warmth to get the bacteria growing and bubbling away, along with lots of loving, and then you use it to make your own bread. You have to get your measurements right, but it's nature's own yeast. That's what I used to make the sourdough you're eating."

Holly bites a chunk out of the slice of bread. "Mmm, it's so good."

As she eats, there's laughter and chatter centred around how silly the retreat owners were, going into a spin when they suspected Holly was missing. A right old pair of mother hens – Holly's going to have to get used to their ballyhoo, they tell her. She laughs with them, relaxed enough to share how the dog nuzzled and sniffed at her, waking her up.

"You're bloody lucky he didn't cock his leg and mark his territory over you," Dee says, and they hoot with laughter.

Jess rushes into the kitchen with empty plates and an order for tea and cakes. "It sounds like a pack of hyenas in here," she says. "What's got into you lot?" The three of them look at one another, which sets them off again.

When has she ever laughed like this? Not since Nan and Grandad were alive and well, for sure. These two women have a lightness of spirit, a kind and caring attitude towards each other and everyone around them that she's only ever seen in her grandparents and their friends down the allotment. If only she could eat all of her meals here in the kitchen and spend her time at the retreat like this – but Holly knows it's only a concession for her having gone missing.

"You're looking brighter, Holly," Lorraine says.

"Yes, I was worried when you got back," adds Dee. "You were as white as a sheet."

"I . . . I had a panic attack." Holly is surprised to hear her own words. Where did that come from? She never talks about her panic attacks with others.

Lorraine gasps. She leans over and takes Holly's hand. "I'm so sorry. Are you OK now?"

Holly nods. "Yes," she says, her reply almost a whisper. She coughs. "I got a bit disorientated, lost my way, and then the gunfire – it threw me. I didn't know what was happening. Hunter helped me with my breathing."

"Ah, he's a good lad, that one. One of the best," Lorraine says, smiling at Dee. "I'm used to the noise from the firing range now," she continues, "so much so, I don't hear it any more. It doesn't happen every day but just your luck it was today. Sorry it scared you. And good to see you looking more yourself now. Anyway," she says with a sigh, gently stroking Holly's hand, "the day's running away with itself, and I've places to be, things to do." She pushes her chair back. "Can't spend all day having a laugh with you lot, however much fun it is." She smiles, laughter lines radiating from her eyes like rays of sunshine. "Are you joining us for the sound bath, Holly? I'm setting it up in the dining room."

"I don't know what a sound bath is," Holly admits.

"Come and join us, then. This whole experience can be a journey of discovery for you." Holly nods in agreement, encouraged by this lovely woman and her warm, honey voice. "Enjoy the deep relaxation that comes from letting the sounds float around you. It's just what you need after your little adventure." As she leaves the room, Lorraine gently strokes Holly's back with the familiarity of an old friend.

* * *

There's a hubbub in the dining room as Holly joins the rest of the guests. There are too many people here; too many strangers. They're busily moving the dining table and chairs up against the wall. A couple of young, attractive women, wearing all the 'right' yoga gear, turn their heads and smile at her. She nervously smiles back. Hopefully everything will get started soon and she won't need to talk to anyone.

Lorraine asks everyone to sit on the floor in some semblance of a semi-circle as she places a range of bowls, varying in size, in front of the fireplace. Holly can't tell what they are made from – glass? – but they are beautiful. Lorraine settles herself on the floor and invites everyone to close their eyes when they're ready, and to take a slow, deep breath and let the sound in. The warmth of her voice is calming and Holly watches as everyone gently closes their eyes. She's reluctant to follow suit straight away. Instead, she watches.

Lorraine picks up two wooden blocks and gently taps the side of a bowl. A warm, comforting note fills the room. She taps another bowl that resonates in a different, deeper note. Then another, and another. The sound washes over Holly, giving her goosebumps. Lorraine nods at her and smiles as she runs one of the blocks around the rim of a bowl, and then another. Holly's breathing slows; she lets herself close her eyes, and gives herself up to the reverberations coming from the bowls.

The butterflies in her stomach rest their wings, and she's flooded with relaxation.

6

FRIDAY FIZZ NIGHT

HOLLY is still enjoying the feelings of relaxation from the earlier sound bath as she looks down the stairs at the crowd of people gathered in the hallway. The butterflies scatter around her tummy as a sense of discomfort awakens inside her. Lorraine had mentioned after lunch that she does a special welcome session before dinner on a Friday night, but Holly had hoped it would be in full swing by now and she could creep quietly into the dining room without anyone noticing. Instead, she sees that all the guests are assembled, waiting.

"Come on into the living room, everyone!" Lorraine calls out over the hum of conversation. "Time for our special Pinewoods Friday Fizz Night."

Perhaps if she stands still, here, out of the way at the top of the stairs, for a moment or two longer . . .

"Ah, Holly, lovely to see you." A barefooted Lorraine, wearing loose yoga pants and a tie-dye T-shirt, waves to Holly. "Come and join the fun!" No chance of escape, then. One of the men in the group stands aside and waits for the rest of the guests to go ahead of him. As Holly passes him she feels slightly awkward, aware of his eyes on her.

"Drinks are on the house tonight, with it being the first night for most of you. We call this Friday Fizz Night, and this delicious kombucha cocktail is our way of saying thank you for joining us."

"Oh lovely, is this that fizzy pop again?" A small woman with short salt-and-pepper hair, who looks in her seventies, elbows her way to the table where rows of drinks are laid out.

"Evening, Ruth," Lorraine says, handing a drink to each of the guests as they go to the table. "Yes, it's the kombucha cocktail. Welcome, everyone!" Lorraine raises her voice, addressing the group. "Kombucha is nature's very own probiotic, full of health benefits. It's thought to be good for heart disease, type 2 diabetes and may even protect against some cancers. It's also thought to be good if you have a chronic illness. This is the perfect way to start your stay at Pinewoods Retreat. Bottoms up, everyone. Enjoy!"

Holly takes the glass that Lorraine hands to her. Yay, just what she needs – a healthy drink. This is going to be disgusting, for sure. Whenever Mags gave her so-called healthy foods when she was a child, they were always disgusting. Hesitantly, Holly takes a sip. She's pleasantly surprised – slightly sweet, but not in a sickly way.

Resting her glass against her nose, as if it might hide her, she lets her eyes dart around the room to take in the guests. She counts twelve people, including herself, plus Lorraine. Goodness, the house doesn't look big enough to sleep this many people. Maybe some guests came as a couple, or agreed to share a room.

Of course, some of the guests are journalists, she knows that from Jess mistaking her for being one when she arrived. A shiver runs down Holly's spine, even though the room is warm. Yes, some of these people definitely look like journalist types – or at least her image of what a journalist looks like. Over-confident, cocky, loud. She knows she won't be able to fit in here with this gaggle of journalists. Is that the collective noun for a group of people who work for the press? Nan would know what it is. Either way, all of the journalists she's ever come across – which was a lot when Mags was campaigning – definitely gaggle.

She hasn't always been like this, flustered and nervous around new people. Before Rose's death, she loved being part of a crowd and having fun – you could even call the group she was in back then a gaggle of teenagers. But with Mags's campaigning and all the attention that heaped upon her, Holly has found she prefers anonymity these days.

She spies an empty chair in the corner of the room, and moves to walk over to it. Her way is blocked. The man who stood back for her as she entered the room stands in her way. Holly steps to the side. So does he. Holly laughs nervously.

He's about the same height as her, with floppy fine hair that he pushes out of his eyes. He crosses his arms over his slight paunch and looks straight into Holly's eyes, a half-smile working its way to his cheeks.

"Evening," he says, his aftershave wafting around Holly. "Do I . . ." he tilts his head. "Do I know you?"

"No." Holly shakes her head and steps to her left, attempting to move away from him, but he moves with her, blocking her way again. "I-I don't think so."

"You sure?"

"No, I mean, yes, I mean – I don't know you," Holly whispers under her breath, desperate not to cause a scene in front of everyone.

"No? Right. Thought I recognised you." The man laughs. "My mistake."

Holly pushes through the group of people to her left, finally putting some space between them.

"OK, everybody!" Lorraine calls out over the slight hum of stilted conversations warming up across the room. "Can you all take two of these little squares of paper and a pen?"

A woman with bright red lipstick, a warm smile and a jet-black sharp bob passes a pen and piece of paper to Holly and two other women standing close by. "Hi," she says. Holly manages a weak smile in response, not trusting her voice after her encounter with the creepy man. "Come and sit here with me." She places a hand on Holly's arm and steers her towards one of the sofas.

"Now then," Lorraine continues, "we're going to have a little bit of fun. On one square, write down a question – any question you like – and on the other, write your first name. Fold them up separately. When you're done, put your questions into this," she holds a glass bowl aloft, "and hand me the square with your name on." Everyone follows the instructions like they're back in school, obeying rules set by the teacher. "And then, find a perch." She smiles and nods as people place their folded squares into the bowl. Holly scribbles down the first thing that comes into her head. It's not a particularly insightful question, but it will have to do.

As people settle themselves into their chosen seats, there's a mumble of hellos until Lorraine takes charge again.

"Here we go. The first person to answer a question is . . . Audrey."

"Oh, that's me," a woman says, throwing her arms dramatically up in the air, filling the room with a jangle of bangles that cover her arms.

"And your question, Audrey, is . . ." Lorraine's hand dives into the glass bowl and brings out a neatly folded square. "How far have you travelled to get here today?" It's Holly's question.

"Well, I'm originally from Bangor in North Wales, so I'm Welsh, in case the accent isn't a big enough giveaway." She grins around the room. "But today I've travelled from Didsbury in Manchester, where I now live with my three cats. Went to uni there, and never quite got around to leaving."

"Welcome, Audrey! And, as a follow-on question for all of you, let's see who's travelled the furthest."

"We're from over the water in Wallasey," Ruth says, looking at the younger woman next to her, whose likeness tells everyone that they're mother and daughter, "so it'll not be us who've come the furthest."

"We've also been here a week already, Mum, so I don't think we count."

"Of course we do, Rebecca. We're just as important as anyone else in this room."

"We've travelled from Chester," a young woman says, smiling at her friend, the two of them raising their phones as if they're glued to their hands.

"Then I think I might have come the furthest," a man with black hair and a Cupid's-bow lip says with a soft Irish accent. "I'm a naturalist from Killarney in Ireland. Flew in from Cork to see the natterjack toads on this coastline. One of the biggest populations in Europe is right here!"

"Can anyone beat that?" Lorraine asks.

Everyone looks around the group.

"You're our winner, then," Lorraine announces. "Tell us who you are?"

"Conor. I'm Conor. Nice to meet you all."

"Thank you, Conor. OK, so who's next for a question?" Lorraine picks out another name. "Ruth, it's your turn."

Ruth claps her hands. "Let's see what question I get this time," she says, leaning forwards in her seat.

"Your question is . . . why did you come to Pinewoods Retreat?"

"Oh, to get out of the way of the workmen that are all over our house doing repairs," she says. "We were flooded. What a mess the house is in." Ruth tuts and shakes her head. Her daughter shoots her a look and opens her mouth to speak, closing it again almost immediately.

"Thank you, Ruth," Lorraine says, "it's lovely to have you both with us for another week. And next we have San! Your question is, what makes you smile?"

"Hi everyone, I'm San." It's the woman with the red lipstick and black bob sitting next to Holly.

"Evening, Sandra," comes the voice of the man who blocked

Holly's way before they all sat down. His voice is jolly and he gives San a wide grin.

"Yeah, so my name's San, and woe-betide anyone who calls me Sandra." She smiles. A gentle laughter flows around the room. "Everyone I like knows to call me San. And you know that, Dylan, having worked with me." She raises an eyebrow at the man who used her full name and he winks back at her. San doesn't smile back. "So, what makes me smile? Hmmm, not a lot at the moment, cos I've just come out of a pretty toxic relationship. But I'm full of hope being here at Pinewoods. And meeting all of you puts a smile on my face. I like meeting new people, and I've wanted to come here for ages. Couldn't believe I was lucky enough to get sent to Pinewoods by the *Standard*. Oh yeah, I should've said. I work for the *Liverpool Standard News*."

"Welcome, San. We look forward to reading your write-up about us in the newspaper very soon." Lorraine smiles comfortably at San. "Bex is next, and your question – who's your ideal man?"

"You can't be choosy at your age, Rebecca," Ruth says, before Bex has a chance to answer.

"Mum!"

"The truth hurts," Ruth says, shrugging. Bex shakes her head – her full, freckled cheeks turning bright red – and Holly wonders how this young woman puts up with her mum. At least Holly only gets cutting remarks once a week down the phone from her own mother.

"I wouldn't mind," Bex clears her throat, "if he was a cross between Ryan Gosling and Idris Elba." She has the kind of face that suits her pixie haircut, and Holly notices that she's all golden, with her freckles, a golden tan and strawberry-blonde hair – all golden, like autumn.

"Ha! No chance," Ruth laughs. Bex juts her chin out and smiles to herself, as if she's proud of her mix-up of an ideal man.

"And next," Lorraine quickly pulls another name out, "we have Dylan. Your question – what was your favourite toy as a kid?"

"Ah, that was my own question," Dylan says, throwing his head back as he guffaws. "How about I ask all of you what your favourite toys are instead?"

Holly's heart thuds in her chest. Why would he put that question down?

"Hey, hey," Lorraine says, a tinkle of laughter in her voice. "It's my rules tonight." She smiles warmly at him. "You answer the question please, Dylan."

"OK, I hear ya." He puts his hands up in surrender. "Evening, everyone. Dylan." He points both thumbs at his chest. "Lovely to meet you all." He sends a smile filled with charm around the room, and Holly sees the other guests smile back. All except San and her. "Let me see – my favourite toy." He speaks slowly and deliberately, tapping a finger on his chin. "Well, I loved my skateboard, but what lad of the 80s didn't spend hours on one of those, huh? No, I guess I'd have to say that my favourite toy when I was a kid – it's . . . got . . . to . . . be . . . the Boffin Bop! Do you remember those?" There's a few nods and smiles around the group, and mumbles of "Oh yes, whatever happened to that?"

"The science toy that you could do experiments with," Dylan

continues. "I used to do this one thing . . ." Holly scrambles to her feet and rushes from the room, letting the door slam behind her as Dylan finishes talking and laughter fills the room. She collapses on to the bottom stair, leaning her head on her knees.

"Here." San is standing over Holly, holding a Kombucha Fizz out to her. "You look like you could do with another one of these."

Holly takes the drink from her, gratefully. "Thanks."

"You OK?"

"Uh-huh." Holly wipes beads of sweat from her forehead.

"Did he make you feel uncomfortable?"

"That man? Yes. I mean – I don't know him, but . . ." Holly doesn't know how to describe the feeling she has around him, and stalls.

"Yeah." San settles herself on the step next to Holly. "He's a charmer, that Dylan – at least that's what everyone thinks. But honestly, he's a tosser. My advice is to avoid him like the plague."

Holly quietly nods, not wanting to say anything more to someone she's only just met.

"I used to work with him when he was at the *Standard*. Stole my by-line. Bastard – and that's me being polite in company I don't yet know." San nudges her shoulder up against Holly's. "Come on. You go and get yourself settled in a chair at the end of the dining table. Save me the seat next to you, and I'll bring you through another Kombucha Fizz when we all come in for dinner." She helps Holly to her feet, opens the door to the dining room and gives Holly's arm a light rub before returning to the rest of the guests.

Holly selects the chair furthest away from the door, her scarred cheek turned away from where the rest of the guests will be sitting. The table is old – not polished mahogany like you'd expect to find in a house as grand as this; more like a refectory table from an old school dining room. It's surrounded by a mismatch of vintage chairs – some with arms, some with hard seats, others upholstered – and, if the one Holly is sitting on is anything to go by, probably all a bit creaky and on the wobbly side.

Mags would love this – the long communal dining table, where everyone is expected to be sociable. Anything Holly's mum can do to get attention works well for her. But it's not Holly's idea of a relaxing meal. She'd much prefer a quiet table in the corner, on her own, with a good book in front of her, ignoring the rest of the world. She hates communal dining – come to think of it, she hates communal anything. Thanks to Mags. That blasted campaign has a lot to answer for, with the impact it had on all of their lives.

Holly wishes herself away to somewhere else and is considering a retreat to Dee in the kitchen, when the rest of the guests start to join her in the dining room. Chair legs scrape across the floor and chatter builds as guests settle themselves around the table. Ruth and Bex position themselves opposite Holly. The Irish guy – Conor, the naturalist – sits down next to Bex. The chair next to Holly scrapes particularly noisily across the wooden floorboards and she looks up, ready to smile at San.

"All right." Dylan's tone is jolly and upbeat. "Didn't catch your name. Thought we could have a nice little catch-up over dinner." He winks.

"I . . . I'm . . . someone's . . ."

Dylan lowers himself into the seat.

"I'm sitting there." Suddenly, San is standing over him, her hand on the back of the chair.

"I'm fine right here, thanks Sandra."

"The name's San," she says in a friendly tone. "And I don't care if you're fine right here." She leans in close to his ear. "If you don't want me to create a scene about how you just grabbed my boobs, you'll get up and move off down the other end of the table."

"But I didn't do that," Dylan says, picking up his napkin.

"Who do you think people will believe?" The words clash with the warmth in San's calm voice.

Dylan slowly pushes himself up out of the chair, not taking his eyes off Holly. "You want to watch her," he says, only just audible over the chair scrapes and chatter. "She's a nut job, is our Sandra." He winks at Holly again and walks off down to the other end of the table.

San settles herself down next to Holly and beams at her. She puts two glasses of Kombucha Fizz on the table. "One for you, one for me. I reckon we both need it, with that sleazebag being here. Cheers." She raises her glass and Holly chinks hers against it, relief washing over her.

"Rebecca, my shawl?" Ruth's voice comes from the other side of the table.

"Where is it, Mum?"

"I don't know. The room across the hall? Or maybe I left it on my bed." She flicks her napkin and lays it across her lap.

Holly watches as Bex pushes her chair back, her lips pursed, and rushes out of the dining room at the same moment that silence descends around the table for food to be served.

"I'm San," San says to the people at their end of the table, "which I guess you already know. Please don't shoot me for being one of these bloody journos. I know, I know." She holds her hands up, laughing. "The pariah of society. But honestly, I'm here to write about the retreat, not about any of you." Warmth flows from the woman, her smile creating the most beautiful laughter lines around her eyes. She has a calm, friendly presence about her, and her voice is soothing and kind. Holly notices how like Lorraine San is – warm, welcoming, gentle.

"I'm Holly. Pleased to meet you, San," Holly says, realising she hasn't introduced herself yet. There's a bubbly warmth in her belly, and she feels relaxed and happy as she takes another sip from the drink that San brought her.

"Are you from one of the newspapers, or a travel magazine?" San asks.

"Oh, no, sorry. No, I'm not from either."

"No, no, my fault. I shouldn't assume. I thought most people here this week were journalists, and what with you being on your own . . . Sorry. It will be interesting to get your take on the place as a guest. That's if you don't mind."

"Oh! Right, yes, no, OK," Holly says. She hiccups and giggles, embarrassed.

Bex returns with her mother's shawl and starts wrapping it around Ruth's shoulders.

"What are you doing?" Ruth asks.

"Giving you your shawl," Bex says.

"I don't need it. I'm warm enough. Leave it on the back of the chair."

"But you said . . ." Bex stops. Holly watches her as she looks up at the ceiling and squeezes her eyes tight shut. Opening her eyes again, Bex slides back into her seat, picks up her drink and holds it in front of her face for a moment, before taking a large sip.

San turns her attention to the man sitting next to Bex. "So Conor, you're a naturalist, you said?"

"I am indeed."

"Help me out here. Which one is that? The naked guys?"

Bex spurts out some of her drink.

"Definitely not." Conor laughs. "The nature guys, that's us. I'm over from Ireland to look for natterjack toads. Writing about this place for my nature magazine, *Frog and Toad Fanatics*. We call it FaT Fans." He nods and shoves an overloaded fork into his mouth.

San stares at him. "So you're not part of a nudist colony then?"

"I get that all the time," he says. He brings his napkin up to his mouth as he talks through his food. "Absolutely not a nudist. Not that I have a problem with nudists but, well, that's not me."

Holly smiles, listening to the conversation. Like San, she's never been able to remember which of the two words is the one for nudists.

"And then we have Rebecca and Ruth," San says to the two women sitting opposite her and Holly.

"Bex, please. I hate being called Rebecca. Though Mum does

insist. Still. After all these years." Bex smiles weakly at San.

"It's a mother's prerogative," Ruth says, laughing. Then: "What have you done to your face?" She is staring at Holly.

Wallop. The Question, of course.

"Mother! Don't be rude," Bex says, her eyes widening in a look of horror. "I'm so sorry." She looks across the table at Holly. "Mum forgets her manners at times."

Holly bites her lip. She's not going to cry. Not here, not in front of all these people.

"She's got a ruddy great scar down her cheek. You can't exactly ignore the damned thing. I'm just being polite asking how she got it." Ruth picks up her napkin from her lap and dabs the corners of her mouth.

"It's none of your business how she got it. I'm really sorry. Please, don't indulge my mother by answering."

Holly's cheeks burn, her scar throbs, and the delicious food, that moments ago made her taste buds zing, has now formed a lump in her throat. She takes a gulp of the Kombucha cocktail to help the food go down, and hopes the glass will serve to hide her embarrassment. She puts the glass down and glances down at her plate of food.

It's no good. She can't swallow any more, not with the unanswered question hanging between them.

"I was attacked," Holly says. She looks up, straight into Ruth's eyes, blood pounding in her ears. "But I don't like talking about it."

"See?" Bex snaps at her mother. "Now, leave her alone."

Obviously people are going to notice the scar, but it doesn't make it any easier to deal with their questions. And Holly's obviously destined to become the talk of the retreat, if Ruth is anything to go by. She should never have come. And now she's stuck here in the middle of nowhere and there's loads of people she doesn't know, and a gaggle of journalists to boot, and really, truly, this holiday *isn't* going to work.

Coming to Pinewoods was a mistake.

* * *

Chairs scrape across the floor as dinner comes to an end, with some guests wandering into the living room and others retiring for the night. San opens the front door and stands on the step, looking up at the night sky.

"Holly, Bex," San calls behind her. "Have you seen this amazing sky?"

"Hang on," Bex says. "Let me get Mum safely deposited upstairs and I'll join you."

Holly follows San to the step, not sure what to say.

"You OK?" San asks. "You've been quiet."

"Yes. No. I don't know." Holly shrugs and looks up at the stars twinkling brightly in the clear night sky. "I'm not sure I'll fit in here."

"Yeah, new groups of people can be daunting, can't they?" Holly nods. "And it takes time to find your place in a group," San continues.

"Hmmm."

"You've got me, though. I could do with a friend right now."

Holly turns to look at San, surprised that someone like her, pretty and confident, needs a friend. "Oh. Me too."

"Let's make a pact to be friends over the next week. We can bring Bex in on our pact, too. I get the feeling she could do with a friend or two here."

Holly nods again, chuffed that San wants to be friends with her. "I'd like that."

"Here." San passes Holly a glass. "These were left on the console table in the hall."

"Thanks," Holly says. "I really like these drinks."

"Yeah, the kombucha makes you forget there's gin in there, doesn't it?" San laughs.

"Gin?" Holly puts her glass down on the porch step.

"Didn't you realise?"

"No. It didn't taste alcoholic."

"Well, you've not had many. Three? Or was it four?"

"I don't drink much. No wonder I feel a bit giddy." She looks up at the sky again. "Look at them all. More stars than you'd normally see because there's no light pollution." She points upwards at one of the constellations. "That's Orion's Belt."

"So it is. And what's that one?"

"The Plough, maybe? Grandad would have been able to say, but I can't remember."

"There's an app you can get on your phone that shows you all the stars, but I've not got it." San steps back into the house and grabs a key from a hook. She lifts it up to Holly. "Just in case we get locked out."

A few minutes later, Bex joins them and the three stand in the front garden with their heads craned back to the night sky.

"This would be amazing lying down in the dunes with the sounds of the sea," Bex says. "Come on, the moon's bright enough to light the path ahead of us. I've got about thirty minutes before Mum decides she needs me again."

"Do you think we should?" asks Holly, surprised at the small spark of excitement she feels.

"Why not?" San says. "I've picked up a key. We'll not get locked out."

As they clamber over the dunes, they're greeted by the sound of waves crashing on to the shore. Holly feels the sudden urge to run down the dune, her arms out wide. Ignoring the quiet little voice at the back of her head that tells her she's making a fool of herself, she gives her head a little shake to push the thoughts away and calls out to the other two behind her. "I'm going for a paddle!"

Laughter and squealing follow as San and Bex hop about after her, taking their shoes off.

"Holly, what are you doing?" San calls out over the waves. "You've still got your pumps on!"

Holly laughs. "I don't care." She splashes about in the water, jumping over the waves as they break on to the shore. What a wonderful feeling. She can't remember the last time that she felt this light and free. Not since that holiday on Anglesey, the last May when Rose was still alive, and they held hands, jumping the waves together. Now, San and Bex link arms with her and they count each wave in, skipping over them in unison.

"I best be getting back," Bex says, after a particularly big wave splashes up to their knees. "Mum's going to be needing a hand."

"What with, at this time of night?" San asks.

Bex shrugs. "I won't know until I get there." She pulls her shoes on over damp, sandy feet, stuffing socks into her pockets. "I'll see you both in the morning, right? Sunrise yoga." Bex starts walking off back up the beach in the direction of Pinewoods Retreat.

"Yoga in the morning," San agrees.

"Yoga in the morning!" Holly repeats.

7

SALUTE THE SUN

THERE'S a banging in Holly's head and it takes her a moment to realise that someone is actually knocking on her door. She lifts her head off the pillow and groans.

"Holly? It's San. Are you coming down for yoga?"

"I don't feel well," Holly says.

"Can I come in?"

Dragging herself to the door, Holly let's San into her room and throws herself back on her bed, immediately regretting the sudden movement. She holds her head, like she thinks it's in danger of falling off if left to its own devices.

"Oh dear. Someone had one too many Kombucha cocktails last night." Holly groans again. "Did you have a glass of water before you went to bed?"

"I meant to, but I was too tired."

"You'll be OK, you didn't have many drinks." San gives her a tender rub on the back. "I'll go and grab you my hangover cure kit, while you get into your yoga gear."

"Yoga." Holly remembers the night before, when they all agreed to start the day with sunrise yoga – but now all she wants to do is stay in bed and recover from this sore head. She's not keen on group activities anyway, and it's been a long time since she and her old friend Jen went to yoga classes. "You go on without me," she says. "I . . . I think I'll give yoga a miss." She smiles feebly at San. "It's not really my thing."

"Nonsense! You get yourself changed. It'll be fun. Besides, it's a chance for you, me and Bex to get to know each other better. We made a pact, remember?" San smiles as she leaves the room.

Reluctantly and gingerly, Holly changes her clothes. As she plays over last night's events, her thoughts go to Dylan. She immediately tenses up. Why does he think he knows her? And how come he brought up the Boffin Bop? She rubs her eyes with the heels of her hands. There's something about that man that makes her feel really uncomfortable – and clearly San feels it too. What if he's at yoga, too? Holly is considering locking her door and getting back into bed when San reappears with Bex in tow.

"San says you're a little worse for wear," Bex says, smiling sympathetically at Holly.

Holly nods her head, immediately regretting it as she feels the pain bounce from side to side like a ball battered around a pinball machine. "I'm dehydrated. I was out in the sun all afternoon, and then I got a bit tipsy with those Kombucha drinks. I should have drunk a pint of water before bed, like San said." She holds her head with one hand on the top, and takes a mouthful of whatever is in the glass that San presses into her hand. "Urgh. What is this? It's disgusting." Holly shudders, screwing up her nose to labour the point.

"Nobody likes my hangover cure, but in half an hour you'll be on the mend, I promise," says San.

"You could have told me there was gin in that fizz." Holly looks woefully at Bex. "Your mum called it 'fizzy pop'!"

Bex laughs and bends down to tie Holly's shoelaces as she downs the last of the concoction. "My mum calls anything with bubbles 'fizzy pop', including Pepsi, champers and Prosecco. Never believe a word that comes out of my mother's mouth when it comes to alcohol."

"For future reference, Holly," San says, "kombucha fizz is made with one measure of gin, about four measures of kombucha, and a twist of lemon or a circle of cucumber."

"Come on," Bex says. "We'll miss sunrise and the yoga if we don't get outside soon."

"Oh no," Holly gasps, as another realisation hits her.

"What?" San and Bex ask in unison.

"I've got personal training at ten. With that guy, Hunter."

"What joy," San says, mocking a swoon. "He's such a dish. Have you met him yet?"

"I have." Holly covers her face with her hands. What's this guy going to think of her? The first time he saw her she was lost. The second time he'll see her, she's nursing a sore head.

"Hopefully my hangover cure will help you. I'd hate to do a training session with a thick head. Come on, you two," San says. "Now I've got up early, I want my post-yoga smoothie."

Dee has promised fruit smoothies for everyone who is up in time for the sunrise yoga and morning meditation. Holly wonders if it's a worthy bribe for such an early start on a Saturday morning, particularly with a pounding head. Surely the idea of a retreat is to relax, and in her case this morning, rehydrate – not to get up with the crows to do yoga. Still, she made a pact last night with two women she barely knows who, for some unknown reason, want to be her friend, and she did promise herself that she'd get involved with as many of the activities as she could and make the most of her time away. It's likely to be the last thing she'll do for herself until she gets a job. *If* she gets a job.

In the yurt to the side of the house, Holly settles down on a yoga mat, with San on one side of her, Bex on the other. The bohemian woman, Audrey, whose wrists jangled with bangles the night before, is already sitting, cross-legged, on her mat. A couple Holly vaguely remembers from last night are chatting like there's no one else in the yurt. They're far too chipper for this hour of the morning.

Soraya, the yoga teacher, passes around lavender eye masks made out of a soft cotton lawn, telling them that they are theirs to keep. She gives them each a blanket in case they get cold when they go into the meditation, and starts the small group off with a few stretches. These, Soraya tells them, will prepare them for meditation – something about saluting the sun.

Holly struggles to get into the stretches at first, but soon finds the rhythm of the moves sooth her aching head. They finish with the full sun salutation and lay down on their mats, ready for the deep meditation.

"Take in a slow deep breath," Soraya says. "And breathe out, nice and relaxed. Welcome any thoughts that pop into your head . . ."

Holly follows Soraya's instructions. She breathes in. *Head's hurting a little less than it was.* She breathes out. *That doesn't change my job situation, though.* Breathes in. *Well, the crows seem to be wide awake. Can hardly hear myself think.* Breathes out. *Gosh, I really can't relax . . .*

"Notice any tension in your body, and let it go," Soraya says.

She breathes in. *Yup, lots of tension, just about everywhere.* She breathes out. *Like a tarmac road has been laid across my neck and shoulders . . .* Holly's thoughts are a full-on cacophony now, like an orchestra warming up for a performance inside her head.

"When you're ready," Soraya says, "bring your attention back to your mat, to the yoga yurt. Notice your fingers, your toes, the ground beneath you . . . and when you're ready, open your eyes."

"That was amazing," Bex says, as she leaps up from her mat at the end of the session. "I've not felt this good since, well, since Mum became the whole of my life."

"It's the perfect start to the day," San agrees, holding out a hand to help Holly back up to her feet.

They follow Soraya to the back of the house and into the kitchen garden that Lorraine walked Holly through the day before. A table is set out with a range of fresh fruit and smoothies with a bunch of garden flowers arranged in a chipped jug. Holly's stomach rumbles and San, standing next to her, laughs.

"Your stomach is speaking for the both of us. You must be feeling better."

"At least I don't feel like dying is the only option available to me."

"That yoga and meditation was perfectly relaxing," Bex says, as she plops a whole strawberry into her mouth. "The sun saluting thing was good, I enjoyed that."

"Salute to the sun, yes," San says. "I always love doing that sequence. It's energising and relaxing all in one. Sets you up well for the day."

Energising and relaxing – right now, Holly would settle for just one of those.

"I struggled at times with quietening my mind," Bex says. "Thoughts of Mum kept popping into my head. I never get a moment to myself these days and, on the odd occasion I do, I just end up thinking or talking about her." Bex laughs and shakes her head. "Like now. Here I am with you two wonderful women, and what am I doing? Talking about Mum again." She plops another strawberry into her mouth. "Mmmm, these are so good."

"They're from our own garden," Dee says, as she pours smoothies from a large jug. "This smoothie has our own strawbs in it. Bananas, strawberries, oats and plant milk with a spoon of peanut butter for good measure. Packed full of nutrients, and particularly delicious when you know it's got home grown strawberries in it." There's a universal murmur of approval as everyone takes a slurp of their smoothies.

"Rebecca! Rebecca!" The peaceful air is broken, and everyone's faces turn upwards to see Ruth's head leaning out of a first floor window.

Bex purses her lips and, without waiting to find out the purpose for Ruth shouting her name, she puts her half-drunk smoothie down on the table by the back door. "Coming, Mum," she says, as she vanishes through the back door and into the house.

"Christ, she's not joking when she says she's always at her mother's beck and call. Poor Bex." San turns her back to the house, and checks out the garden. "Isn't this lovely?"

"Beautiful," says Holly, looking around the kitchen garden. An old Victorian brick wall runs along one side and again at the back, with a modern fence down the other side. The trees are close enough to provide protection, and far enough away that they don't throw shade over the growing vegetables. "It looks like it's in need of a bit of attention, though. The poor veggies are being strangled by weeds. Those peas and beans over there need tying up on supports."

"Is gardening your thing?"

"Yes." Holly surprises herself, but it's true – gardening has always been her thing. "Yes, it is. Started when I was a kid. I used to help my grandparents with their allotment. I really shouldn't be judging the state of this garden, though. I've not touched my own much this year, until recently that is. I'm ashamed to say I let it go, and it's in a far worse state than this kitchen garden."

"You've obviously had a tough time. I'm glad you've been giving yourself time to recover. Hopefully Pinewoods will help with that."

Holly takes in a sharp breath and waits for San to ask The Question. It'll be on her lips; the woman's a journalist, for goodness' sake. Holly waits for the probing, intrusive question.

San points to the left of the garden. "Look at that gorgeous old greenhouse. The Victorians knew how to build them, didn't they?

Come on, let's go have a nosy." Shaking her head in slight surprise – and not to mention relief – Holly follows San through the kitchen garden towards the large, wood-framed greenhouse. San stops by a raised bed of strawberries and picks a couple, popping one into her mouth. "Mmmm, Bex is right, you should have one of these, Holly. They're so sweet. Oh look, they grow their own tomatoes too. It's no wonder the food here tastes so delicious, with all this fresh produce."

San chatters on, like the meditation cranked up her energy levels. Holly lets her natter, making 'uh huh' and 'mmm' sounds every now and again, but really she's losing herself in the comfort of the kitchen garden; its neatly laid out rows of raised beds, gravel paths and an original Victorian greenhouse. It's a corner of heaven. Such a shame it's not been looked after recently – like her own garden but on a bigger scale. Everywhere else at Pinewoods Retreat is neat and tidy, but here in the garden, something's not right.

Holly stoops down to the raised bed of strawberry plants, her temples throbbing with a telling reminder of her bad head. She pulls up some of the weeds that are threatening to take over. Why aren't the strawberries sitting on a bed of straw? She looks around, sure that she's seen some somewhere. There, under the bench in the greenhouse. She clears the weeds and fetches the straw, carefully laying it under the ripening berries.

"Goodness, Holly," says Bex, watching her work. "You know what you're doing, don't you?"

"You're back." Holly smiles at Bex.

"Mum couldn't find her glasses. They were hiding on the bed under her nightie. She's lucky she didn't sit on them." Bex lets out a light laugh. "Anyway, you seem at home in the garden."

"I am. Comes from years of helping Grandad."

"What's with the straw?"

"It stops the strawberries from going mushy, and protects them." Holly, happy at getting her hands dirty, wipes them on the back of her gym pants and smiles. "They could do with some protection to keep the birds off too, though, or Dee won't have any strawberries to put into her smoothies."

"Breakfast, everybody," Dee calls, on cue, from the kitchen door. "I've set up your full breakfast in the dining room."

Holly, Bex and San pause, looking over the raised beds. "We'll have to come back into this garden another time and give it a bit of love," San says.

"I'd like that." Holly takes in a deep breath, the kind she couldn't manage during sunrise yoga.

"But right now, lovey, I'm starving. Come on, let's go and eat. That yoga's worked up an appetite in me."

Holly picks a ripe strawberry. She smells it first, breathing in its sweetness, before biting into the juicy flesh as she follows San and Bex back to the house. Weaving her way along the gravel paths, Holly stops here and there to pull up a weed and right a couple of pots of herbs that have been knocked off their perch by the wind or some nocturnal creature.

At the kitchen door, Holly looks back and takes in the beauty of the kitchen garden. She'd happily spend all of her three weeks right here. It's much bigger than the allotment Nan and Grandad had – four times the size, probably more – but there's something about it that comforts her in the same way. That allotment was her sanctuary through the worst years. Perhaps this kitchen garden could be the same.

Fingers of sunlight cut their way through the clouds like golden daggers . . . like the knife that sliced through her cheek. And just like that, the hint of happiness, wrapping its warm, comforting arms around her, is cut to shreds.

8

A FLATTERING OF FEMALES

ACCORDING to the notes in her goodie bag, Holly is to meet her personal trainer on the lawn at the front of Pinewoods where the cafe tables are set up. She stands in the front doorway and looks around. The garden is buzzing with people. There's a crowd of women in gym gear, standing in a tight group, and most of the seats are taken. She notices Dylan sitting at one of the tables. Holly quickly snatches her head away from his gaze, but from the corner of her eye she sees him fold his newspaper in half and stand up, sensing his eyes fixed on her.

"Morning," Dylan says, as he gets close to Holly. "How are you this morning? Off to get fit, are we? Have to catch up when you get back. Be good to get a quote from you about why you came to Pinewoods." He's so close now that his breath tickles her ear.

A chill runs down Holly's spine and she steps back against the porch wall, her heel knocking one of the geranium pots on the step. She desperately wants to tell him to get lost, but her mouth won't open.

"See you later." He winks, taps his newspaper on her arm and wanders off into the house.

Holly shivers. What's that supposed to mean? She has nothing to 'catch up' on with him. She leans her head out from the porch and looks around again with a hollow hope that Hunter will be nowhere to be seen, so that she can slink off to her room, pack her bags and get the next train home.

No such luck. Hunter's right there, standing on the lawn in the centre of the gym-clad women, looking her way. Now she's got to spend a whole hour with someone who thinks she's crazy. Damn it, damn it, damn it.

Hunter is wearing a black T-shirt and commando pants, and even though it's a dull day his eyes are hidden behind dark sunglasses. He exudes the outdoor life – his light tan suggesting he spends much of his day outside, but not in a sun-worshipper kind of way. Tattoos bulge over his muscled arms that sit crossed over his chest, and he stands, legs astride, like he's guarding the exit from Pinewoods. *Only those who've completed their rigorous training session are ever allowed to leave.*

"Right," Hunter says, clapping his hands together. "Which of you lovely ladies is Holly?"

The group of women look around at each other.

"Can I be Holly?" one woman coos. Everyone laughs.

"I'll be Holly, if you like," says another, fluttering her eyelashes.

Others follow suit, and there's laughter all around the group of women. Holly doesn't recognise any of them from Pinewoods – they're not guests. Hunter must run fitness classes for the locals too. What would Nan give as the collective noun for a group of fawning women? A love-in of ladies? A gushing of girls? A flattering of females?

Hunter laughs. "I reckon Holly is hiding from me, trying to avoid her first training session."

"How could anyone dread being with you, Hunter darling?" the cooing woman asks.

Holly walks towards the group and raises her hand, a little confused. Hunter knows that she's Holly – he knew her name yesterday when he 'rescued' her. And she could have sworn those sunglasses were looking straight at her a second ago.

"That's me," she says in a squeak. Nobody hears her. She clears her throat. "Me," she says again, speaking louder and raising her hand again. "I'm Holly." Everyone's heads shoot round to face her.

"Great," Hunter says, rubbing his hands together. "Good morning, right on time. Well, lovely ladies, nice as it is to chat after bootcamp, I've got a job to do. See you all next week, bright-eyed and bushy-tailed." He walks through the group, a fluttering of eyelashes following him. Hunter holds out a hand to Holly. "Hi, I'm Hunter," he says, as if they've never met before. "Lorraine tells me you've booked in for PT with me – the deluxe package."

"PT?"

"Personal training."

"Oh, yes, sorry. Yes, I have." For goodness' sake, why is she so nervous all of a sudden?

"You've got a dozen sessions booked in with me."

Someone shouts 'lucky you' from the group of departing women and there's a ripple of laughter.

"We better get started then." Hunter guides Holly out of the front gate and on to a patch of land behind Pinewoods, where he tells her to sit down on a large log.

"Well, if this is personal training," Holly says, "I reckon I can cope with this." She tries a laugh, and Hunter gives her a weak smile.

"Let's talk. I need to know a bit about you."

Holly obediently answers Hunter's questions – no, she's not exercising regularly; yes, she used to until the start of the year; running is pretty much it for her; no, she's never had a gym membership; yes, she likes being outdoors, particularly in the garden; she'd like to get fit again so she can . . . but she doesn't actually know why she wants to get fit. It's just something she told herself would be a good thing.

"Maybe to look after yourself?" Hunter asks, taking off his sunglasses. His eyes rest on her scar. "Right, for starters," his voice softens, "we need to find out what you're made of. What your physical limits are."

Holly sees his eyes flicker to her scar again and she lowers her eyes. "'I suppose you're going to ask me how it happened," she says, deciding to bring it up first. She runs her finger along the length of the scar.

"Nope. None of my business. I'm your trainer." Hunter flashes her a smile. "My job's to get you physically fit. Now, time to get started. Water." He passes her a small water canister, like the one she received in her goodie bag. "I see you didn't bring any." Holly blushes. *Note to self: bring water canister next time.* "On your feet. Follow me."

Holly breaks into a half-walk, half-run to keep up with Hunter as he strides off. When he stops in front of a steep dune, Holly arrives in a pant of puffed-out breathlessness a few seconds behind him.

"Run to the top," Hunter says, pointing at the dune. "Then turn around and come straight back down to me. Three times."

Holly looks at the dune, and looks back at Hunter. "Up there?"

"Yes, up there." His eyes crinkle as he hints at a smile. "I still want to see what you're made of, even with a hangover."

"I've not got a hangover!"

Hunter laughs. "This is you on a good day, is it?"

"I . . . I've got a sore head from getting dehydrated yesterday."

"If you say so. Either way, I'm not going easy on you, Holly. Come on. Get up that dune." Holly glares back at Hunter, now seriously regretting getting out of bed. "Now," he barks.

"Oh, right. Sorry—"

"Woah, woah, woah. You can stop that, here and now."

"Stop what?"

"Saying sorry. You seem to say that word a lot. Maybe this will help." Hunter takes a step closer to Holly, resting his hands firmly on his hips. "Every time I hear you say sorry, you get to do an extra rep, of whatever exercise we're doing. That'll give you something to be sorry about." He breaks into a grin. "This is your one and only warning. OK?"

"Right, yes." She almost adds 'sir' on the end, and blushes.

"Good. Ready?" Hunter doesn't wait for Holly to answer before counting her in: "Three, two, one, go!"

89

Holly trudges up the dune, the soft sand giving way under her feet, making it all the harder to run uphill. Each step thumps inside her head. She turns around at the top, and slide-run-slides back down again.

"Come on. Pick your feet up this time. I'm timing you. Let's go."

"I'm paying for these sessions," Holly pants. "Aren't you supposed to be nice to me?" Well, technically, OO-TO Travel is paying, but Hunter doesn't need to know that.

Hunter smirks. "Nope. Not paid to be nice." His smile is playful, his eyes glinting in a way that belies his sergeant major tactics. "You've paid to get fit, not get a friend."

Ouch. That stung. But he's right.

Holly pushes herself up the dune, trying her hardest to run, but the sand sinks away beneath her. Her head throbs, right behind her eyes. San's hangover cure has well and truly worn off now, and the pain is like a metal band, tightening around her head.

"Come on Holly, put your back into it! I reckon you've got more in you than you're showing me. Nothing to be gained from being weak."

Weak? Ouch again. "I'm just not feeling great today," Holly says. Even she notices how sulky she sounds, but this is so hard. "I feel sick."

"No wonder. I'll hold your hair back for you when you actually are sick. Done it many a time for my sisters." Hunter holds out a canister of water. "But now, if you're dehydrated, you need to be taking in plenty of water. Drink about a third of this."

Holly guzzles the water before passing the canister back to Hunter gratefully.

"OK, here we go. Back up the dune. And put all you've got into it, or you can do another three reps."

"That's not fair!"

"That's life." Hunter shrugs. "I don't think you're the type to give up, Holly." His voice softens. "Stuff has happened to you, sure, but you're no quitter. So show me what you've got. Get your head in the game and your arse into gear and get up that dune. You can do this." Hunter claps his hands together three times and points to the top of the dune.

Who does he think he is, telling her to get her head in the game? Who's he to push her around? She's paying for this bullying. OK, so it's not bullying. But he's got no right to be hard on her, to get into her head and tell her she's weak. She shouldn't have to put up with this here – not like she did when she was at work, where everyone put her at the bottom of the pack and stepped all over her.

Except Hunter isn't being mean, and really, she knows that. He's nothing like her old colleagues. Hunter's helping her. And maybe it's time she put in the effort to help herself.

Holly clenches her hands into tight fists and a burst of anger at everything she's put up with for the last few years courses through her veins, powering her up to the top of the dune. As she gets to the top, her lungs stinging from the effort, she wants to turn around and vent her pent-up anger at Hunter. She showed him: she's not weak. She turns and looks down to where he is standing, ready to give him a piece of her mind, but the smile of pride on his face throws her. Instead, she powers back down the dune without saying anything.

When she reaches the bottom, Holly lets out a puff and flops down on to the soft sand. "Done."

"You don't think that's it, do you?" Hunter raises an eyebrow, the ghost of his smile still on his lips. "On your feet," he says. "Next exercise, we're doing lunges."

Holly groans. "We?"

"The royal 'we', obviously." The sides of his eyes crinkle as Hunter grins at her. "I tell you what to do," he says, " and you do it. That's how this 'we' works in my exercise classes." He winks at her. "Have you done lunges before?" Holly nods. "Right, over here where the ground's firmer. I reckon you can do ten lunges between me and that bush over there. Three, two, one, go." He's back to that army voice again, the one that Holly doesn't know how to react to beyond snapping into action – albeit reluctantly.

She follows his barked orders as she does lunges towards the bush. "Hands on your hips . . . lower that knee . . . keep going . . . chin up . . . widen that stride . . . get those hands back on your hips, Holly . . . doing well . . . just five more . . . you've got this."

She wobbles and topples, but manages to complete the three repetitions of ten lunges each way. Her glutes and thighs burn, screaming with the effort. And still her head pounds. Holly plonks herself on to the ground and rests her head on her knees.

"What do you think you're doing, Holly?"

"Resting," she says with a whimper. "I've done three reps."

"One minute, no more." Holly knows that if she had the energy to do it she'd be shooting Hunter a filthy look right now, but she's exhausted. Instead, she glugs more water.

"OK, next exercise."

"I don't feel well. I need a moment."

"You're fine, Holly. Come on, you wanted this . . . remember? You booked in for personal training sessions." Hunter crouches down, his face close to Holly's. "I'm being kinder to you today than you'll get other days."

This is his kinder side?

"You can use this as a turning point in your life, Holly. Or . . ." Hunter pauses.

Holly looks up at him, their faces mere inches apart. Her heart skips a beat. "Or what?"

"Or," he clears his throat, "well, you'll stay stuck where you are in life. Believe me, I know. Now, if that's what you want, there's no point working with me. But I think you want more." He pats Holly on the shoulder, and bounces back to standing in one smooth move. "Up you get. On your feet. Upper body now. We'll give your legs a rest. Take my hand, I'll pull you up." Holly takes his firm hand and locks eyes with his for a moment. They are deep hazel with specks of gold dust. And those laughter lines. Holly blushes. Thank goodness she's already sporting an exercise-induced scarlet flush across her face.

Hunter takes Holly through a boxing routine, quickly followed by another exercise, and another, and another, until he finally announces they're done. She doesn't even attempt the run-walk to keep up with him on their return to Pinewoods.

Back at the retreat, Holly hauls herself up the three flights of stairs to her attic bedroom where she throws herself on to her bed.

Hunter's right. She has been stuck in this horrid life. She needs to build herself up, instead of knocking herself down all the time. Nan and Grandad would want her to be happy, to be able to care for herself like they would have done. Heck, she wants that for herself too. Maybe if she'd been in a better place, mentally and physically, when she was attacked, and hadn't been rooted to the spot, she wouldn't have this ugly great scar down her cheek; maybe she wouldn't be suffering from PTSD; maybe she'd still have her job. Maybe, maybe, maybe . . .

She closes her eyes in exhaustion, and falls into a deep, dream-filled sleep. The same recurring dream she's had since the day of the attack at OO-TO Travel.

HOW I FEEL: 4/10 - might have given today a higher score if I didn't have a sore head

SLEEP: No idea - more than usual. And I had an afternoon doze

WEATHER: Cloudy and dull, no breeze, warm

WEARING: Pyjama shorts, thin T-shirt, barefoot

PROMPT: What memory do I keep playing over in my mind?

There are too many memories that I can't forget. The memory of this bad head will be one of them. How to make a good impression with a group of strangers, Holly - not drink enough water after getting lost in the dunes and get tipsy on the first night. Idiot.

That horrid exercise session that Hunter put me through will probably become another memory that lives to haunt me. He has this way of barking out orders with a hint of humour. I've got a feeling he's not going to take it easy on me in these training sessions. San was right, though. He is nice to look at. But I won't be seduced by his toned muscles, hazel eyes and cheeky grin, like his flattering of female followers.

Hang on, I've gone off the prompt. Lorraine means for me to write about a memory from my past that haunts me.

Do I really have to go there?

The attack. It haunts me every night. His face.
The knife. Blood.

Rose's death is still with me too. Not as bad as it once was. Time doesn't heal, exactly. The memories just fade like an old pair of jeans. It doesn't get less painful – you just get used to the pain.

Her death doesn't haunt me half so much since the attack, though. That's taken over. It doesn't help that I've a blooming great big, ugly scar smack bang across my face, for everyone to see. I hate looking in the mirror. It's all I can see.

Yeah, that's a memory I play over and over in my head.

Not having a job – there's another memory. The way Tasha told me, going round the houses and making out it was tough for her, because she was the one who had to tell me. It was me it was tough on, not her.

God, no, why did I have to think about OO-TO Travel?
I didn't even enjoy working at the travel agency, not since
Tasha took over as branch manager. When was that - six
years ago? It only took a couple of months for all the old
crowd to leave. I was the only one left. Why did I even
work there for so long after Tasha and the others arrived?
Convenience? Habit? It certainly wasn't for the money!

And now I have to find another job after this holiday. It'll
have to be one that's close to home, so I don't have to move.
I love living in Nan and Grandad's old house. I'm so lucky
they left it to me in their will - if it'd been down to Mags,
she'd have sold the house the moment the funeral was over.
Anyway, I don't like change. Right now, the blasted job
situation is as big a change as I can cope with.

It all feels so hard, having to cope with these things while
not having Nan and Grandad around. I know I'm going
to have to find a way to face all these blasted challenges
life throws my way. The thing is, I've always run away
from things or given in to the bullies - since I was a
teenager, anyway. A strong person doesn't do that. They
stand up for themselves. But I don't know if I'll ever
be strong enough for that.

9

DIVE BOMBING &
BRAIN FROGS

HOLLY stands on the edge of the chatty bunch of guests and journalists on the front path, her legs screaming with pain from yesterday's training session. There's a sense of excitement in the air, like when her class used to go on school trips. And just like on those days out, Holly feels alone. It never ceases to amaze her how lonely she can feel in a crowd. She often feels far less lonely when she's actually on her own, and can lose herself in her own thoughts.

Conor glances over in Holly's direction as she edges closer to the group, quickly followed by Audrey, who smiles at her. Holly returns a hesitant smile. As she looks around at the people gathered on the path, she can't ignore a nagging worry that some of them are talking about her.

"Morning. Holly, isn't it?" It's Dylan. Loneliness in the crowd was preferable to this journalist popping up out of nowhere. He nudges up against her, and she takes a step to her left, but he rests his hand on her arm, gentle yet firm enough to root her to the spot. "How are you today?" His smile sends shivers down her spine. He leans in close to her face. "Still need to get that quote from you. Would love to hear what brought you to this ramshackle place." He jerks his head at the house.

Something about him makes her want to run – and she probably would if her leg muscles didn't hurt so much from the excesses of exercise Hunter put her through yesterday. And, right on cue, as if thinking of him makes him materialise like the genie in the lamp, Hunter walks through the gate. His eye catches hers.

"Morning, Holly. How are the legs today?"

"Sore," she says, welcoming the opportunity to turn and face him. Dylan's hand falls away from her arm. "And not just my legs."

"Rest day today. Make sure you still move your legs, however much they hurt. Stretches tomorrow before we start. Get your muscles ready for more hard work." Holly nods. "Anyway, enjoy your day trip." Hunter glances at Dylan and back at Holly, and walks off into the house. Holly looks down at the ground.

"Hello, everyone," Lorraine says, standing in the open doorway to Pinewoods. "The minibus is just coming down the lane so you can all go and wait at the end of the track." She smiles at them as she ushers them out of the garden, one by one. "Enjoy yourselves, have fun, see you all later."

"It's not like I've never been to Another Place before. I only live in town," San says, as she walks down the track alongside Holly. "But I love it."

"I'm ashamed to say I've never been, and I'm local too," Holly says.

"What is it, then, this other place?" Conor, the Irish naturalist, stops and waits for San, Bex and Holly to catch up with him.

"It's called Another Place," San says. "An art installation on the beach. There's something like a hundred or so iron figures fixed into the sand, looking out to sea. I suppose they're contemplating life. Or maybe it's a metaphor for all the people who left Liverpool looking for hope across the Atlantic. They're all exactly the same, the figures. Full-sized casts of Anthony Gormley's own body. He's the sculptor."

"Sounds thrilling," says Conor, rolling his eyes.

"It's very popular," Bex says. "Me and Mum brought some visitors to see the statues a few years ago, cos it's not that far from where we live. We're only half an hour away. They're quite soothing, actually."

"I agree," says Dee, who is handing out packed lunches to everyone as they file past. "There's something truly tranquil about the place. I suppose you can't help but enter the contemplative state of the Gormley men, all of them gazing out at the horizon."

Conor laughs as he boards the minibus, taking his lunch from Dee and nodding his thanks. "I'll report back later."

Bex glances behind her, looking back at Pinewoods.

"Everything OK, Bex?" Dee asks.

"Yes, yes I think so. I was expecting Mum to be standing on the step. Thought she might need a hand with something before I left."

"She'll be fine, I promise you. I'll keep an eye on her, keep her company. Now you go and enjoy yourself." Dee gives Bex a big smile.

Holly is the last to take her packed lunch from Dee. "Thank you. That's very kind of you, to do us all a packed lunch," she says.

"My pleasure," Dee says. "You all right, lovey? You look a bit overwhelmed."

"Fine, yes. I'm OK." Holly puts the packed lunch into her bag. "Thank you." If Dee wasn't standing there, she might have turned around and not got on the minibus. But she doesn't want to appear rude to Dee, so follows everyone on board.

Bex is sitting next to Conor and, thank goodness, San is settling herself in next to Dylan. What a relief – though she knows that San doesn't like the man either. Holly smiles weakly at San, who nods back. With that, Holly gingerly lowers herself into one of the two empty seats, a single seat right behind the driver, her legs complaining at the expectation that they have any ability to function the ways legs ought to.

* * *

Standing on the promenade above Crosby beach, Holly looks down at the iron men all gazing out to sea. Some are up to their knees in the sand, and others are so far out that they're waist deep in the water. There's something eerie about the figures from Holly's viewpoint.

As she looks along the beach, Holly sees San taking photographs. They must be for her article for the newspaper. Holly climbs down the steps on to the sand and walks over to one of the figures. She stands next to it, following its gaze out to sea.

Dee's right: there's a sense of calm about the sculptures. It's soothing being next to an iron man – still, quiet, asking for nothing, giving nothing, taking nothing away. Holly's breathing slows, and she soaks in the sense of calm. She takes a step nearer to the iron man, and stands up close to him – like she's there on the beach with a friend next to her, staring out to sea. Without even having to focus on her breathing, like her counsellor tells her to, it regulates itself. Yes, Dee is right. This is a tranquil place.

That is, until a huge black Labrador bounds along the beach in a straight line from the sea, aiming right at her. She stays still, in the hope that the dog will run around her. Instead, it runs straight at her and leaps up. Holly topples backwards and lands hard on the wet sand. The dog leans over her face and licks her forehead. What is it with dogs and their need to lick her?

"Sorry, sorry! He thinks you've got treats," Holly hears someone shout. "You've got your hands in your pockets, so he thinks you're giving him a treat."

"Get him off me," Holly shouts, struggling to get her hands out of her pockets.

"Buster, here!" The owner grabs hold of Buster's collar and pulls him away from Holly. "Sorry about that. He's a friendly old fella, doesn't mean any harm."

"What the hell are you doing," Bex shouts from a little distance away, "letting your dog off the lead if you can't control him?" She rushes over to Holly. "Are you all right?"

"I said I was sorry, didn't I? Buster's just being friendly, aren't you, old boy? No harm done."

"Well, he just dive-bombed my friend. I'd call that harm," Bex shouts, like she's angry on Holly's behalf. "You need to keep your dog under control. Get him on a lead and get him away from here." She turns back to Holly and holds out a hand to help her get up from the wet sand. As Bex pulls her up, Holly shouts out in pain. "What's wrong? Has the dog hurt you?"

"No, no, I'm OK. It's just that – well, I can't move."

"Oh my god, Holly. See!" Bex snaps after the dog owner, who's already some distance off, holding Buster by his collar.

"Honestly, I'm OK," Holly says, grimacing. "It's not the dog, it's yesterday's personal training session. I'm in pain everywhere. It hurts to stand up." Holly finds herself somewhere between laughter and groans from the pain in her muscles. She wipes down the back of her jeans and smiles at Bex.

She just called Holly 'my friend'. Nobody has called Holly their friend in a long time.

"Are you sure you're OK?"

"I'm sure. Thank you. I'd say it's only my pride that's dented, but I can't see what my bottom looks like." Holly tries to twist around and see what damage there is, pulling on her jeans.

"Let's have a look." Holly turns to show Bex the damp patch on her bottom. "Oh dear, you're in a right old mess. I'd offer to pat you down, but we're a bit too early on in our friendship for me to do that. Can't see the minibus driver wanting you to sit on his seats with that muck on your backside. It looks more like mud than sand."

Bex puts her arm through Holly's, and Holly automatically flinches slightly, unused to the ease with which Bex is befriending her.

"I hope someone has a plastic bag I can sit on when we get back to the minibus," Holly says. "Ouch!"

"God, you are hurt. Poor Holly."

"I've been standing still too long, that's all. My muscles are seizing up."

"That personal trainer worked you too hard."

"He's a master in torture. But it was me who booked in to have twelve sessions with him." Holly shakes her head. "I'm giving him permission to torture me. What was I thinking?" She laughs.

The pair weave their way across the beach, avoiding puddles, aiming for the promenade. "You're at Pinewoods with your mum then?" Holly says, embarrassed that she's asking the obvious question because that's all she can think of. She's not used to making small talk.

"Yeah, I'm her carer. Though there's many a time I *don't* actually care about her, not these days. Sorry, that sounds mean, doesn't it? It wasn't supposed to go on for this long, and it's really hard caring for someone who presses all of your buttons with her rudeness and lack of appreciation. All my friends have given up on me, my brothers all live away – a long way away. It's just me and Mum now. The whole thing is really tough."

Holly is quiet for a moment, taken aback by Bex's openness. "I'm sorry. Anyone would find it hard in your shoes. My mum bosses me about, even from the comfortable distance of France."

"Why are you here? At the retreat, I mean."

Holly pauses. She's not used to sharing personal details with others, in case they get used against her. "I'm having a holiday before I start looking for a new job. I was made redundant from a travel agency."

"Oh, that's a shame. I suppose everyone is booking online now."

"Exactly. This trip is – well – kind of a treat, I guess. I'll look for a job when I get back home."

"Don't fancy being a carer, do you?" Bex asks. Holly laughs. "I was being serious." Bex smiles at her.

"Coo-ee. Coo-ee." San is standing on the prom, waving both arms in the air, her camera hanging around her neck. Holly and Bex wave back and make their way over to her.

"Follow me," San says. "I want to show you something."

Holly and Bex walk along the coastline with San, until they reach a section that looks like piles of rubble, stretched out as far as the eye can see. San gingerly picks her way over bricks and stones. "Come on, you pair. You've got to see this."

"What is it?" Bex asks.

"People's homes, shops, hotels, banks. All of this," San says, pointing along the coast, "is from the war. People don't talk enough about the Liverpool Blitz, but in 1941 parts of the city were destroyed. Flattened. There was so much rubble from the bombings – all the houses that were razed to the ground or had to be demolished – and they had to get rid of it. This is where they brought it."

"Here?" asks Holly. "To the beach?"

"Yes. It's helped to stop erosion of the coast, so it's a good thing. Look at this." San bends down and picks up part of a red brick. "I love how the sea has smoothed the edges of these bricks. Rounded by decades of pummelling, brick against brick, as the waves crash up on the piles of rubble."

"Is this a front step?" Bex is resting one of her feet on a large sandstone slab.

"Probably, yes. You can see the dip in the centre from decades of people's feet walking on it."

Holly picks up a small worn brick with soft, rounded edges.

"It looks like a candleholder," she says.

"We should take a couple back for the dinner table tonight," Bex says. "A memento of our day out."

After collecting a small selection of bricks, the three women find some larger pieces of stone to sit down on. They look out to sea, contemplating the horizon in comfortable silence.

"This is lovely," Bex says. "My days are always taken up with looking after Mum, to the point where I feel like screaming by lunchtime. I know Mum doesn't mean to be hard work. It's tough on her. She went from being spritely before COVID, to now struggling to even walk around the block. That leaves me having to do everything. And god forgive me, but she can be so demanding. To have a few hours all to myself, to not even have to think about her, let alone worry about her . . . it's bliss."

"You got flooded out of your home, didn't you?" San asks.

"We weren't flooded. Not exactly."

"Your mum said you were?"

"What Mum meant," Bex says with a sigh, "is that *she* flooded the place. Left the bath water running for at least two hours when I was out at the shops. I shouldn't have left her for so long, so it's my own fault, I guess. I came back home to water running down the stairs and through the kitchen ceiling. She's been forgetting things, you see. She's got that Long COVID thing going on. Brain fog. Or brain *frog*, as she calls it."

"I don't know how you do it, Bex," San says, shaking her head. "My mum had cancer and died years ago. Dad remarried and moved to Wales with his new – and much younger – wife, so I'll never have to do what you're doing. You're a saint in my eyes."

"Believe me, I'm no saint."

"It can't be easy for you, though."

"It's not, but let's face it, it's Mum that has it the worst. Long COVID hasn't been kind to her."

"What exactly is Long COVID?" Holly asks. "I mean, I've heard about it, but what's it actually like?"

"Seems different people have different symptoms. Taste and smell go for some, but Mum has been fine with that. She struggles more with the fatigue and insomnia. And there's some days she has difficulty breathing, which then seems to make her a bit dizzy. It's been a year now, and I'm only just starting to see her improve."

"That's a lot for you to take on, Bex," San says. "Like I said, a saint."

"Honestly, I'm not. Surely you've heard the way I speak to Mum? I embarrass myself sometimes. I used to think older women I'd hear talking sharply to their mums were unkind. How little did I know what they were living through. I hear the two of us talking to each other, and I'm appalled at how horrible we sound. We're no longer mother and daughter, we're duelling enemies, always making jibes at each other. I'm exhausted. And I'm fed up that I've given up my life for my mum."

"Have you spoken to her about how you feel?" San asks.

Bex picks up a stone and passes it from hand to hand. "No, she wouldn't understand. I tried to tell my brothers, but they wouldn't listen. And here I am, not yet forty, given up work so my brothers don't damage their careers. I can't see an end to it." She shakes her head and stares off into the distance. "They won't even take her for the odd weekend to give me some peace. Their wives – there's four of them – have *suggested* it'd be *too disruptive* for Mum. That's what they say. Yeah, great – for them."

Holly listens in silence, shocked to hear what Bex is living with. What does she say to someone going through this kind of stuff? She's spent so many years focused on her own situation with Mags, she's never thought about what other people may be going through. At least for Holly, most of her pain is in the past. Bex is living through her own agony right here, now.

"I mean," Bex goes on, "I didn't mind at first. Looking after her, that is. We thought she'd only need my help for a few weeks, and work was OK about it. They let me work from home. It's got harder since the weeks turned into months – and now, here we are, a year on." Bex sighs. "I ended up having to give up my job as a graphic designer. I loved that job – and I was good at it. And my brothers just shrugged it off, saying 'someone has to look after Mum'." She throws the stone with some force ahead of her, as if it might carry all of her irritations away. It lands with a thud in the sand.

"Stand firm, Bex," San says. "You need to *tell* them what they're *going* to do – don't ask them. When you get home, email or WhatsApp your brothers and tell them that every week until

Ruth can look after herself again, you expect one of them to either come and stay with their mother for a night, or have her to stay with them, to give you a break. And don't take no for an answer."

"You know, I should." Bex nods. "I will." She straightens her back and puffs out her chest, as if to bolster her determination. Within seconds she slouches again. "Trouble is, I'm useless at that kind of thing. No good at confrontation."

Holly knows what Bex means. Confrontation is tough. She knows that's why she stays quiet so much, why she avoids close relationships these days: because there's always a chance it will lead to confrontation. But that just means she avoids doing anything much. Look at this holiday – she almost didn't come, and already she's making new friends. Is this the kind of thing that Hunter means when he says she'll stay stuck in life? That if she avoids stuff, she won't move on?

"I'll help, Bex," San says, bringing Holly back to the conversation. "I'm good with words. We'll get an email written and sent this week, if you like."

* * *

Back at the minibus, Dylan is laughing and joking with the rest of the guests as he regales them with stories of life as a journalist. He rests a hand on Conor's arm, gesticulating with the other, as if he's in the middle of a Shakespearian monologue, the audience around him hanging on his every word. Holly's stomach tightens. She can see right through his act – he's a creep who switches on the charm when he needs to. How can the rest of the party not see him for what he is?

A plastic bag is found languishing at the bottom of someone's rucksack for Holly to sit on, and everyone climbs on board the bus. As Bex manoeuvres to slide in next to Holly, Dylan gets hold of her shoulders and moves her out of the way.

"Come on, Rebecca, let's mix it up a bit, huh? You go and sit with someone else." He deftly lands himself in the seat and butts his shoulder up against Holly's. "Hiya, Holly."

"Bex is sitting there." Holly looks at Dylan and then quickly looks away again.

"Erm – nope." Dylan over-exaggerates a search, looking around the seat. "No, she's not. It's definitely me sitting here." He guffaws and gives Holly one of his smiles. Like Tasha at OO-TO Travel, Dylan's eyes don't bother joining in with his grins. "We've not had a chance to have a chat yet, you and me."

"Please, move out of the way. I want to change seats." Holly keeps her voice low and quiet, not wanting to appear a nuisance to the other guests.

"I'm cool here."

"I want to get out." Holly's heart pounds, her skin prickling.

"You've caused more than enough fuss for this trip, what with your mucky backside." He laughs, comfortable and relaxed. Then he wraps his arms around his messenger bag on his knee, and looks past her, staring out of the window. There's nothing she can do, beyond making a scene, and the thought of that makes Holly's cheeks burn with embarrassment.

As the bus drives away from the car park, Holly waits for Dylan to say something. She counts down from ten, back up to ten, and back to zero again. But Dylan sits in silence. What's going on in his head? She has no intention of being the one any of the journalists writes about. She's been the story too many times before. No, not this time. Please, not this time.

"Isn't the internet amazing?" Dylan asks, his voice low and quiet amongst the hubbub of conversation in the minibus. "You can find out almost anything about almost anybody. A few clicks of a button, and a whole world opens up in front of your eyes. Like you and that scar."

Holly's heart misses a beat. The minibus suddenly feels claustrophobic and she has to fight the urge to clamber over Dylan and get off. "I don't talk about it," she snaps, staring out of the window at the passing traffic as she works on controlling her breathing. That response worked with Ruth – hopefully, Dylan will get the message too.

"Fair enough," he says, pulling his phone out of his pocket. He scrolls, pauses as he reads something, makes a few 'hmmm' sounds, scrolls some more.

For the rest of the journey, Holly looks out of the window, slowing her breathing down, trying desperately to ignore Dylan beside her.

And she has never felt weaker.

10
SHARE BAGS
FOR ONE

As they all pile off the minibus back at Pinewoods, Bex waits for Holly and San.

"Catch you later," Conor says to Bex, lifting his hand in a little wave. Bex nods eagerly, and waves back.

"Would you two come in and say hello to Mum?" Bex asks, catching hold of Holly and San's hands. "She said she'll be waiting in the living room when we get back. Please come with me. We'll be less likely to snap at each other. After the lovely day we've had together, I don't want anything to spoil it."

"Of course we'll come, won't we, Holly?" San says. "We're here for you whenever you need us."

Holly nods. She's not sure what support she can offer, but if going with Bex helps her, she's more than happy to do it, especially after the kindness that Bex has shown her.

"Thank you. I know we'll be kinder to each other with both of you there."

They find Ruth asleep in the living room, despite the noise everyone is making in the hall, her rumbling snores almost drowning out the ambient music coming from the speakers.

Bex gently rocks her mother awake. "We're back, Mum."

"Hmm, what? Is that you, Rebecca?"

"Yes Mum, it's me." Bex sighs audibly through a probably-too-jolly smile, hands on hips, as she stands in front of Ruth.

"No need to bark at me," Ruth says, her voice thick with sleep. She purses her lips and furrows her brow before she notices Holly and San. In a blink, she is smiling. "Oh, hello San, Holly. Did you have a lovely time on your little day trip? I just had forty winks, I wasn't asleep – I get a bit tired in the afternoons, can't keep my eyes open sometimes. Anyway. The weather stayed nice for you! Thank you for looking after Rebecca for me. She's not too good at looking after herself."

Bex sighs again, and Ruth shoots her a look that is full of history.

Ruth pushes herself forwards to a more upright seating position, and grunts as she gradually nudges herself to the front of the wingback chair that has served as a daybed. "It's not my fault I'm old and still suffering from this Long COVID malarkey." She clutches tight hold of a half-finished, half-squashed packet of Jaffa Cakes that she rescues from the side of the chair. As she pushes herself to standing, she reveals a Mars Bar wrapper and two empty share bags of Walkers Crisps partially stuffed down the side of the seat cushion.

"Mother! Where did you get all of this food from?"

"I was peckish, and there was nobody about so I had no choice but to pull together what morsels I could find."

"You didn't find this lot in the kitchen!"

"Did I say I found it in the kitchen? No, well, it was all in my bag. So, that's that then."

Ruth shuffles past the three women towards the hall, patting Bex on the arm. There's no warmth in the act; it's more like Ruth's way of shutting Bex down.

"How was your day?" Bex asks after her.

"Oh, you know, mustn't grumble."

"Well, then," San says, taking Ruth's elbow, "let's not grumble about our days either. If we were to grumble, Holly could start us off with her wet and muddy backside from being knocked over by a huge beast of a dog on the beach. If I'm honest with you, Ruth, it was hilarious to watch, but I don't think Holly found it that funny." San laughs and winks at Holly. "But you're right: let's look instead for sunshine in the rain, as my dad used to say." She beams a beautiful, relaxed smile, and as she holds Ruth's arm, she deftly relieves her of the pack of Jaffas, passing it to Bex.

With Ruth's back turned, Bex tosses the Jaffa Cakes into the bin by the console table in the hall.

"And how was your day, San?" Ruth asks.

"Lovely. Thank you so much for letting Bex come with us. It's such a joy to spend time with her. She did my soul good, I can tell you. The three of us needed some girly time together, getting to know each other."

Ruth stops at the bottom of the stairs and puts a hand to her head. "Oh dear, I'm coming over all funny. Let me sit down." San steers Ruth towards a chair by the console table. "I'll be all right in a moment. When I get one of my funny turns like this, I have to sit down. It's the dizziness, you see." Ruth looks at San. "When I get like this, I can't risk the stairs."

Bex sighs and turns to San and Holly. "You two go and get on. Thank you for today. I'll see to Mum now."

"Are you sure?" San asks. Bex nods, her lips pursed together. "As long as you're sure. It was fun today."

"Yes, thanks for a lovely day, Bex," Holly says. "See you later, Ruth." Ruth is busy reaching into the bin that is now within reach, due to her sitting down on the chair. She retrieves the Jaffas, cannily stuffing a whole one into her mouth.

"Lovely to see you, ladies," Ruth says, her words muffled by the food she's chewing. As San walks into her bedroom at the top of the first flight of stairs, Holly turns to see Bex snatching what's left of the packet out of Ruth's hand. Ruth lets out a little sob. "Humph. I hope you enjoyed yourself, leaving me here on my own all day."

"You told me to go, Mum. And besides, you were not on your own all day. I know the staff will have been in and out to check on you. And I noticed there were two cups on that tea tray in the living room, so you had a cuppa with someone."

"Spying on me now, huh? You left me alone while you went off galivanting with your friends, not a care in the world for your elderly mother and what she might need. You want to try living with Long COVID. Humph."

"You said I was to go!" Bex argues. "'That I should have some fun.'"

Holly wonders if there are as many versions of mother-daughter relationships as there are mothers and daughters. For her and her own mother, there's not only physical distance between them nowadays – if Holly's honest with herself, she doesn't really know her parents any more. A weekly call, mainly involving Mags talking at Holly, plus brief glances at her mother's timeline on Facebook, filled with narcissistic posts, is hardly a way of truly knowing your parents.

As she peels her soiled jeans off in her bedroom, retrieving the rose quartz heart she's taken to carrying around with her in her pocket, Holly thinks about how many years it is since Mags and Dom moved to France. She was almost seventeen – so it was half of her life ago that her parents went away. It was her first year of studying for A Levels, and she galvanised support from her grandparents to persuade her parents not to take her out of college and let her stay with them. Grandad took control and made strong arguments for Holly finishing her education in a system she knew, expertly explaining how unsettling it would be for Holly, on top of Rose's death, to move her from the place in which she grew up.

The butter on top of the toasted crumpet was when Nan joined in. She told Mags that she'd hardly been there for Holly during all of her years of campaigning. She had been an absent mother, consumed by her mission, and it had fallen to her, Nan, to pick up the pieces and take on the role of mother to Holly. Mags cried – noisy, snot-filled sobs – called her mum an evil witch, and accused her of turning Holly against her, of stealing Holly's heart from her, of replacing her as Holly's mother at the first opportunity.

Dom had put his arms around Mags, in the customary way he'd been doing since Rose died. Then Grandad took Holly out into the garden, gave her a big bear hug, leant up to kiss her on the top of her head – as she'd grown in height, he'd shrunk in stature – and assured her she was going nowhere.

Mags and Dom didn't come out to the garden to say their goodbyes. The next day they dropped a few boxes of Holly's belongings at the front door and left on their drive to France. They've only been back to Liverpool three times. Emotional blackmail over the phone about how empty their lives are without their only living daughter continued for a couple of years, but suggestions that Holly join them in France stopped as soon as she got her job at OO-TO Travel.

Stepping into the shower, Holly muses that maybe her parents' move to France has been a blessing. At least she's had a freedom she might not otherwise have had. And she knows she was fortunate to have her grandparents looking out for her.

Massaging the shampoo into her hair, she finds herself nodding – yes, there really are some positives in how her life turned out.

JOURNAL ENTRY
Sunday 13th June

HOW I FEEL: 6/10

SLEEP: Three hours and another two hours later

WEATHER: Blue sky with wispy clouds, no breeze, warm

WEARING: Clean jeans, 'Bookworm' T-shirt I got from the
Asda, barefoot. I had my flowery wellies on earlier but they
got a bit muddy from our trip to Another Place

PROMPT: How do I feel around the key people in my life?

Lorraine said to think of people you work with for the
prompt, as well as friends and family.

I can't really say I've got any key people in my life. Not
any more. Mags and Dom are in France. Nan and Grandad
are dead. Rose is dead.

Let's start with Mags and Dom. Hmmm . . . inconvenient.
That's how I feel around them. I've always been in the way,
and still am now. I remind them that they'll never see Rose
at my age.

Nan and Grandad. If they were still here, I'd feel safe, wanted, cared for, loved. But they aren't here. I miss you, Nan. I miss you, Grandad.

Who else is there?

I've got no real friends to speak of. There was Jen, but our lives have gone in different ways since she had her baby. We were such good friends for years – we told each other everything. She was the one person I could truly open up to. With her, it felt like I belonged – like we were two halves of the same penny. We could finish each other's sentences and always knew what the other one was about to do. But I guess that's what comes from growing up with someone.

Maybe I should get back in touch with her, when I get home from Pinewoods. I've been waiting for her to call me, but I suppose she could be waiting for me to do the same.

I guess if I call San and Bex friends then I can write about how I feel around them. And they both called me their friend, didn't they? San and Bex make me feel happy. And relaxed. They're interested in me, but not in a nosy way. They don't care about my past. It's the me now that they want to know. And that makes me feel . . . warm and happy.

Lorraine and Dee make me feel warm and happy too.

What about work? Tasha and everyone at OO-TO Travel.
Not that I actually work with them any more. Around them
I felt . . . what's the right word? Insignificant. Worthless.
Nobody.

Good grief. When I write it out like that, I can hardly
believe I worked there for so long.

Hunter makes me feel very sore. LOL. And a bit uncomfortable. It's like he sees inside my head to my inner
thoughts. But he seems like a nice guy. In fact, everyone
at Pinewoods seems kind – except for that man, Dylan.
What a shame they won't be in my life for long. I could
enjoy being around kind and caring people, like the
people I've met at Pinewoods.

11

SHIFTING SANDS

MID-MORNING on Monday, Holly stands at the back of the group gathered in the hallway. San is sitting on the bottom step of the stairs, tying her laces. Glancing up the stairs, Holly hopes that Bex will join them. It's been nice doing things as the three of them. It's starting to feel like they're a little friendship group, and she admits to herself that she enjoys San and Bex's company. It's a good feeling – one she could get used to.

"Have you done anything like this before?" San looks up at Holly from the bottom stair.

"Dune running? No, I don't think so."

"Me neither. And I've no idea what to expect. Except that dune running sounds like it's going to involve two things – dunes and running." San laughs. "At least I run a bit. You?"

"No, not recently. I've done Parkrun, before . . . you know." Holly waves her hand in the general direction of her face and immediately blushes at her clumsy attempt to be casual about her scar. "And I'm booked in with Hunter for these personal training sessions."

"Lucky you," San says, smiling at Holly. "I'd be happy to have a good-looking fella like him as my personal trainer." She laughs.

"This dune running, it can't be that bad – can it?" Holly doesn't have the chance to answer.

"Listen up!" Hunter's voice booms around the hallway, and the space suddenly feels small in his presence. "Have I got a treat for you all." He grins.

A nervous silence descends on the group as everyone follows Hunter out into the front garden.

"I'm Hunter, and I mean business. Follow me, crew. I want you all lined up on the cinder path, two rows. Step on it!"

Everyone lines up on the path, making two lines. Holly looks back over her shoulder with one last hope that Bex will tag along, but clearly Ruth is not releasing her from caring duties this time.

Hunter marches the group off at a fast pace, down the cinder path and towards the sea. As he gets closer to the dunes, he veers off to the left on a narrow path that is barely visible. The group follows in single file and when they reach a high dune, Hunter stops. It's the dune he had Holly running up the other day. So that must have been dune running, then. Great. "This is it, guys. Listen up. A few tips first, so that you get the most out of the dune running."

Hunter tells the group this is lower impact than running on hard surfaces; they'll be tired afterwards because it can take over fifty per cent more energy; there's a technique, pushing off with the back foot when going up hill; and for coming down, digging heels into the sand which means the body weight creates a semi-slide down the dune. A technique? And he never thought to tell Holly all of this in her personal training session? She makes a mental note to remember these tips in her next session with Hunter – and give him a piece of her mind for not telling her sooner. If she can pluck up the courage, that is.

"Off you go," he barks at the group. Some of the men push hard, like they've something to prove. Dylan is off like a dog chasing a rabbit, and gives a loud *whoop!* as he reaches the top. A couple more people reach the top of the dune and Hunter shouts at them to come straight back down and repeat the exercise. Holly and San bring up the rear, both of them going at a far more leisurely pace than the others, just about reaching the top on their first round as Dylan turns and half-runs, half-slides his way back down again on his second.

"Come on you two lazy buggers, dig in and get yourselves down to the bottom!" Dylan flies past them, sweat already dripping down his face.

"Keep going, everyone," Hunter calls out. "I expect at least five repetitions. Go, go, go!" He claps his hands, as if it's an encouragement.

"Yeah, yeah, we got it," says San, not altering her pace. Holly digs her heels into the moving sand, but the backs of her calves burn. As soon as she gets to the bottom, she does as they've been told and turns around to start again. This time it's slightly easier, with footprints carved into the sand. She plants her feet in, but soon finds that whoever made the depressions in the sand had a much wider stride than hers, and she can't quite stretch far enough. She's back to pushing her way up, and turns around at the top for the rapid descent.

On her third repetition, Holly's had enough. She plonks herself down in the sand, her legs stretched out in front of her. San drops to the ground alongside her, lays flat on her back and starts flapping her arms about.

"Look, Holly. Sand angels!" San laughs, and Holly joins in.

A shadow falls over them, blocking out the sun. "Up, now," Hunter says, hands firmly planted on his hips. He really does enjoy being in charge. "You've only done three reps, so back on your feet and get those arses up that dune."

"Want to carry me, Hunter?" San sits up, grinning at him wickedly.

Hunter sticks his face right up to San's, so that their noses are almost touching. "Get off that lazy arse and push it up that dune."

"Aye, aye, captain," San says, blowing him a kiss.

Holly is back on her feet, brushing sand off the backs of her legs. San holds out her hand for Hunter to haul her up, which he does, before giving her a gentle kick on the bum.

San comes alongside Holly and the two of them climb the dune for a fourth time. As they get close to the top, Dylan can be heard shouting "finished!" back down at the bottom. San and Holly look at each other and burst out laughing.

"God, he's such a wanker. Dylan the Villain, we used to call him, at the *Standard*. Since he went to work for *City Magazine*, you'd think he's god's gift to women, men and the Liver Birds. Totally up himself," she pants. "He can't stand that I got a journalism award for my piece on the lasting impact of slavery on Liverpool. Probably hates that he couldn't steal that story from under me, like he's done before." At the top of the dune, San grabs hold of Holly's hand and gives it a squeeze. "Come on girl, we're in this together. Down we go. One, two, three – weeee!" They fly down the dune, screeching with laughter, and come to a halt in front of Hunter.

"We're done," San says.

Hunter stands with his legs astride, arms crossed in front of him, accentuating the muscles across his body. "One more. Now."

"I can't," Holly says, totally exhausted. "My legs are burning."

Hunter puts his face into Holly's, so close that she can taste his breath. A blush scoots up her face, despite her cheeks already being red from the exertion of the dune run. "Ask me if I care," Hunter whispers, deathly quiet. "Go on, ask me. You said you wanted to come on this dune run. Now turn around, last rep."

For a moment, Holly stares into Hunter's hazel eyes. He holds her gaze. Holly's breathing catches. The side of his mouth twitches. Hunter blinks, and pulls back from her. "Now!" he barks.

What just happened? Holly's heart thuds, the butterflies in her stomach crashing into each other – but not in a totally bad way. She gives her head a little shake and, to save any more embarrassment, turns on her heels and pushes herself back up the dune. San follows behind.

"Woah," San says at the top of the dune, fighting for breath. "What was all that about?"

"He's still annoyed with me because he had to come out and find me on Friday. I got a bit lost and wasn't back in time for lunch."

"Oh sweet, naïve, Holly." San laughs and rubs a hand over Holly's back. "That wasn't anger, girl. That was pure, unadulterated, animal attraction."

Holly's eyes widen. Attracted to her? He couldn't be. Anyway, San is far prettier than she is. It would be ridiculous for Hunter to be attracted to her over the other women at the retreat, not to mention the flattering of females from his bootcamp.

Holly shakes her head and starts the descent, digging her heels into the sand to make it easier. Without meaning to, her eyes find Hunter standing in the middle of the group. He's looking straight up at her, but when he sees she's looking at him, he looks away and starts handing out water.

After more dune exercises, the group walks back to Pinewoods, with moans and groans about how exhausted they all are. Holly finds herself walking behind Hunter and Dylan, most of the other guests dragging behind.

"All for the write up for *City Magazine*, mate," she hears Dylan say. "Be good to put something in about you and your credentials for doing this kind of stuff."

"Army."

"Yeah, right, thought so. Afghanistan?"

"Yup."

"What regiment, mate?"

"None of your business."

"Go on, our readers like this kind of stuff."

"Really?" Hunter stops and glares at Dylan. "You need that kind of information for your story? Bugger off, *mate*." Hunter's upper lip curls in obvious disgust.

There's a beat of silence as Holly draws close.

"Yeah, well, sorry mate. Didn't mean to offend," Dylan says, raising his hands in the air as if in surrender, at the moment Holly passes the two men. "Just makes the story more human, you know? People like to read a little about the human side of a business. How d'you come to go in the army, then?"

"Like I said, bugger off."

Despite the situation having nothing to do with her, the tension between Hunter and Dylan unnerves her and Holly feels a tingle of alarm run down her spine. She walks on, and suddenly senses someone walking up behind her. She glances over her shoulder. Dylan falls into step alongside her and puts his hand in the small of her back. She flinches. He looks behind them before coming even closer to her.

"Hiya, Holly," he says, his warm breath tickling her ear. She's seen the look on his face a million times before: the look of a predator; a bully intent on coming out on top. A journalist desperate to extract information.

"Your scar looks a bit angry after that exercise," he says. "How about a chat, Holly? The personal interest stuff. You know, that scar on your face, the traumatic stuff from your past, what brought you here. It'd be good to pull it all together for this story I'm writing." Dylan has eyed his target, and he's not letting go. Holly picks up her speed. Dylan matches her pace.

"Hey, Holly, wait for me!" She turns her head to see San catching up. "Crikey, lovey, where did you find that extra spurt of energy? Hard to keep up with you." San brushes Dylan's hand from Holly's back and nestles herself in between them, linking her arm through Holly's. "Hiya, Dylan. Collecting stories for your piece on the retreat, are you?"

"Yeah, yeah, you know me, Sandra. Got a nose for a good story." He taps the side of his nose and winks.

"San. The name's San, Dylan. But after five years of working with me, you know that."

Dylan laughs. "Shit, you're as uptight as ever, you are, Sandra."

"Get lost, Dylan. Come on Holly, I promised Bex we'd have a coffee with her and Ruth when we get back. She'll be wondering what's happened to us."

Holly looks back at Dylan as she and San pick up their pace and leave him behind.

"Don't ever let yourself be alone with that man. He'll do anything for a story."

"I try to avoid him, but he keeps appearing out of nowhere. Thanks for coming to my rescue, San. Again." Holly's hand instinctively goes to her cheek, but it's Hunter's reaction to Dylan that her thoughts return to. She knows all too well what it is to have a past you don't want digging up – and watching Hunter when Dylan quizzed him, she's pretty sure that Hunter has things he'd rather leave in the past, too.

Monday 14th June

HOW I FEEL: 6/10

SLEEP: Four hours undisturbed sleep

WEATHER: Blue sky, feathery clouds, light breeze, warm

WEARING: Jeans and 'Bookworm' T-shirt, again. Red pumps

PROMPT: What is a habit I want to build on?

That's hard. I don't know what habits I have.

Oh, apparently saying sorry is a habit of mine – according
to Hunter, anyway.

I guess I hide away from people, too. I know I've been doing
that for years now, even at times when I've wanted to join
in. I've probably missed out on all kinds of things in my
life because of hiding. There was school stuff that I avoided,
obviously – trips and holidays. I couldn't face those, not
after Rose died. Then, when Jen went to university she'd
invite me to go and stay with her. But after the first time,
when a drunken student recognised me from the newspapers
and made a big scene, I never went again.

Now I think about it, I've pretty much hidden away since Jen had a baby. Then we went into lockdown, which made it easy to hide away. I suppose I never fully came out of lockdown, or my own version of it, anyway.

Saying sorry and hiding away from people - is that pretty much it for my habits, then? Doesn't answer today's prompt because I don't want to build on them. It'll have to do.

12
SUNSET YOGA

TUESDAY'S yoga at sunset is something new for Holly – but then, many things about Pinewoods are new to her. Based on the hype that Lorraine has given this session, Holly has high hopes for a great night's sleep ahead. Her only disappointment is that San is chilling in her room this evening, and Bex is helping Ruth, so she is all on her own.

Soraya claps her hands as she stands by the open front door. "Namaste, namaste."

There's a muttering of "namaste" responses around the group.

"Are we ready, everyone?" Her voice is gentle and measured. "We need to wait on the cinder path. There are a few of my regulars joining us from the village, and I don't want to leave them behind. Everyone, pick up a yoga mat on your way out of the porch." She puts a careful hand on each person's back as they walk past her, tilts her head forwards, and says "namaste" again.

Soraya's presence and touch brings a sense of calm to Holly – even if she did struggle doing the sunrise meditation with her.

"Room for one more?" Bex is stomping down the stairs in a hurry. "I thought I'd missed you all."

"Of course. Namaste Bex, you're very welcome. Does Ruth want to join us?"

"Oh no, thank you. She's got the telly on in the room. She's happy catching up on a rerun of *Downton*." Bex sighs, something Holly's seen her do a lot in the last few days. "Gives me some time on my own."

Holly smiles at Bex. "I'm glad you can come."

"Me too," says Conor, giving Bex a little wave.

Bex smiles at Conor and waves back. She links her arm through Holly's. "I wanted to do the dune running yesterday, but Mum was struggling. Was it fun?"

"It was OK. Some of these people," Holly nods ahead at the group of journalists, "seemed to love it. Or they loved Hunter. I couldn't quite tell which."

Bex laughs. "Probably Hunter. He's a bit of all right."

"He's not my type." Holly clears her throat and hopes that Bex doesn't turn to look at her. There's a tell-tale blush rising up her cheeks. Even though the man irritates her with his abruptness, she has to admit that he *is* good looking. And she can't ignore how the butterflies in her stomach flutter when he looks at her with his gorgeous eyes.

"Nor mine." Bex lowers her voice to a whisper. "Conor's more my type." Two red spots spread across her cheeks. "Blue eyes, Cupid's-bow lip, dark hair with the merest hint of salt and pepper at his temples. And that twinkle in his eye. Plus, his adorable Irish accent, too. Sexy." Bex giggles. "Go on then, Holly, what is your type?"

"Erm – I don't really know."

"You must know! What were your exes like?" Bex squeezes Holly's arm close to her as they walk down the cinder path behind

Soraya and the rest of the beach yoga crowd, a yoga mat under their free arms.

"I – well . . ." Holly hesitates. It's been a while since she's talked about her ex-boyfriend.

"You're not telling me you've never been in a relationship?"

"No, I mean yes, I mean, I have had a boyfriend. But it was a while ago."

"What was he like?"

"Oh, you know, he was OK. For someone like me." She speaks without meeting Bex's eye.

"What's that supposed to mean? Someone like you?"

"Well, you know. Plain."

"You're anything but plain, Holly. With that gorgeous auburn hair, your striking green eyes, high cheek bones and that beautiful complexion, like porcelain. Honestly, you're anything but plain. You're like a pre-Raphaelite painting. Guys must fall over themselves to ask you out."

Holly blushes. "I – well – I mean, yes, I've been asked out, and I've been on one or two dates since me and my boyfriend split up, but there's some real oddballs out there and I didn't feel the vibe and I was helping Nan and Grandad, and I just started to find it easier to say 'no, thank you very much', so I've not had a boyfriend since before the pandemic." Holly pauses to catch her breath. "Thank you."

"What for?"

"Saying I'm pretty."

"You are, Holly. Very pretty." Bex beams at Holly, but it quickly turns to a frown. "My ex lost all interest in me when my mum needed looking after. He wasn't keen on playing second fiddle to Mum. Upped and left. We'd been together since school, too. Maybe Mum was just an excuse for him. Anyway," she gives Holly's arm a squeeze, "us singletons need to stick together. We'll have to stay in touch after we get home from Pinewoods. It's like destiny brought us together."

Holly glances across at Bex to check if she is teasing her, but sees the woman attached to her arm smiling back at her with kind eyes. Holly returns the smile and nods, not trusting herself to speak. Bex really wants to stay in touch with her?

The group marches in a line down to the beach. Soraya takes them to an area of sand that is firm under foot and slowly claps her hands.

"Everybody, lay out your yoga mats in a semi-circle, leaving a small gap in the circle at the back near the dunes for me, please."

"Shit." Dylan turns around and starts to stomp back across the sand in the direction of Pinewoods.

"Did somebody forget to pick up a yoga mat?" Soraya calls after him. "Come back, come back, I have a spare." She holds out a yoga mat and Dylan winks at her.

"Thanks, sweetheart," he says, and rolls out his mat.

Everyone sits down in a semi-circle, facing the sea where the sun will set, feet pointing in towards Soraya in the centre.

"This evening we are doing the moon salutation, Chandra Namaskar. This helps us to prepare ourselves for rest. I'll take you slowly through each asana – each pose – and then we will put it all together as Chandra Namaskar just as the sun is setting."

One by one, Soraya takes them through the poses. Holly wobbles time after time. Bex sniggers, and although Holly tries hard not to look at her, she can't help herself, and the two wobble in unison, fighting their giggles. As they move into goddess pose for the second time, they lose their balance and collapse in a heap on the yoga mat, laughing.

"You're trying too hard, Holly, Bex." Soraya's voice is gentle and kind. "Let go of perfection, and breathe into the pose." She strings out the word *breathe* as if that will encourage slower and deeper breathing in everyone. "Anyone who is struggling to hold these poses, simply focus on your breathing and notice the rise and fall of your breath. The in-breath and the out-breath."

Holly wobbles again. The breath work is nothing new to her; it's the same as the intentional breathing she does when a panic attack is coming on. But the balance is another thing altogether. Not to mention the stretches – is her body really supposed to be able to get into these positions?

As the sun sets, the yoga comes to an end and everyone shakes sand off their mats before rolling up them up. The earlier chatter that accompanied everyone to the beach is replaced with smiles and a sense of calm, the yoga having put everyone into a relaxed and peaceful state. They all stand for a moment, looking out to sea like the iron men, and take in the sunset.

"Beautiful," Holly says.

Bex sticks her arm through Holly's. "Thank you."

"For what?"

"Making this holiday for me."

"Me?"

"Yes, you. It's so lonely when it's just Mum and me. I'd be going crazy if you'd not come along."

Holly smiles. She knows that feeling. There's been many a time since Nan and Grandad died that she felt she was going crazy, with nobody to talk to.

They turn their backs on the horizon and start walking across the beach, back to the retreat, in the fading light. Conor falls into step alongside Bex, and as the path narrows going over the dunes, Holly lets the two of them go ahead of her.

"Crikey, that takes a bit of effort, doesn't it?" Dylan is breathing heavily, like he's run to catch up with Holly.

She steps aside for him to go past, but he stops next to her. "Please, after you," Holly says, giving him one of her best smiles.

"It's OK," Dylan says, resting his hand on her back between her shoulder blades. "I wanted to bring you up to speed with my research." His grin is a mix of charm and something else that feels like he's trying too hard.

"What?"

"OO-TO Travel," he says. "Didn't take me long to find an article about the incident online on the *Standard*'s website."

Holly is shocked by Dylan's revelation. She squeezes her eyes shut for a moment in the hope this nightmare of a man will have vanished by the time she opens them again. Nope, it doesn't work. What else is he going to find? As worried thoughts crash around her head, she purses her lips and walks on.

"You worked at OO-TO Travel when that bloke attacked his ex – and he slashed your face too. The travel agent slasher and our Holly."

Holly says nothing, picking up her pace. All traces of relaxation from the yoga have disappeared with the setting sun.

"Seems you were quite the little hero, trying to get rid of the fella. And look what you got for it."

Still, Holly says nothing.

"I rang OO-TO Travel for an update on how things are now. Apparently, you don't work there any more. What happened, Holly?"

She picks up her pace. *Breathe, Holly, breathe.* She has to get away from him. She has no intention of talking to him about the incident at work, or losing her job. He'll twist it and make her out to be the fool.

"Leave me alone," she says, over her shoulder.

"Is your mum going to start a knife ban now, to go alongside her Ban the Boffin Bop campaign?"

"What?" Beads of sweat cover Holly's hairline as a prickling heat spreads across her body. Of course he knows about the campaign. That's why he mentioned the Boffin Bop on their first night. Holly's cheeks burn and bile builds in her throat.

"Oh yeah, did I not say? I'd recognise you anywhere, despite that scar down your cheek. Spit of your mum, you are, Holly Bush."

"Leave me alone," Holly snaps under her breath.

"How is old Mags now, then? Got my first scoop with your mum's story, straight out of uni. You'll have to pass on my thanks to her." His laugh is cold. "She was the making of my career with that campaign of hers."

Surely, after all these years, she should be able to leave her past behind. Surely she has endured enough. But here it is again, with its nasty habit of knocking her down.

"Come on, Holly. You know I'm going to write the story anyway. Slashed lass is Boffin Bop Kid. It's too good! You might as well give me a quote I can use."

Holly breaks into a run, and passes Bex and Conor.

"Holly!" Bex calls after her.

But Holly ignores her, picking up speed. She must get away. She's got to get back. Lock the door. Hide away.

* * *

Holly can see Pinewoods ahead. Her vision blurred by tears, she almost trips over a tree root as she veers off the path to pass a group of three women she doesn't recognise.

"Ooh, careful girl," one of them says, putting a hand out to steady Holly. She doesn't even stop to acknowledge the help.

She rushes into Pinewoods, drops her yoga mat in the porch and dashes upstairs, locking her bedroom door behind her.

This whole trip was a dreadful mistake. She should never have come.

She desperately wants to leave her past behind her but the media coverage from her mum's campaigning means there's plenty of stuff for journalists to dredge up about Holly. Mags might have needed the campaign to handle her grief, but all she's done for Holly is give her years of hell that she's handled on her own since the day her parents ran away to France. And now, here she is, and Dylan's going to tell everyone who she is, she's sure of it, and then she'll be the talk of the retreat.

Damn it!

But it's more than that. Holly wants friendship – and the way she's been getting on with San and Bex, it felt like that might be a possibility. She's been lonely since her and Jen drifted apart, even though she realises now that's as much her fault as is it Jen's. It would be so good to have friends again – people like Bex and San. But Dylan is going to ruin it all.

They won't want to know her once they know she's the Boffin Bop Kid. They'll laugh at her. It happened at school, it happened at work. Heck, it even happened when her boyfriend introduced her to his family at a summer barbecue a few years back. That uncle of his told everyone who she was, and yes, sure, Will's mum tried to make light of it, but the damage was done. A group gathered around the drinks table, whispering, looking over in her direction, laughing.

And now it's going to happen again, here at Pinewoods. Just as she was starting to enjoy herself.

Holly throws herself on to her bed, and sobs into her pillow.

HOW I FEEL: 2/10. Maybe 1/10

SLEEP: Four hours

WEATHER: Blue sky, no clouds, light breeze, pleasantly warm

WEARING: New shorts, yellow blouse with dots on it, barefoot

PROMPT: What are my ten favourite things?

I wish the prompt was ten things I hate. I'm writing that list.

1. That horrid man, Dylan
2. Having a past that journalists get a kick from
prying into it
3. Mags and Dom. They should never have abandoned me –
parents shouldn't do that to their child
4. The Boffin Bop, obviously. If that'd never been invented,
Rose would still be here
5. Everyone at OO-TO Travel
6. Losing my job
7. Meeting new people. Though I'm glad I met San and Bex.
And some of the others at Pinewoods, too. OK, meeting some
new people

8. Oh god – sore heads from dehydration and gin!
9. Dune running
10. ~~Hunter, because he shouts at me in my personal training sessions.~~ No, that's not fair. I don't hate him

Are there ten things I love? It's difficult to think about anything I love at the moment. But I've said I'll do this journal stuff, so I'll give it a go.

1. Nan and Grandad's house. Well, my house now
2. Romcoms – I love some of those old 90s ones like Sleepless in Seattle and You've Got Mail
3. Bridgerton
4. Bex and San. Is it too soon in our friendship to put them on the list? Heck, I'll never get to ten, so I'll leave them on. I wonder if I'm on their lists?
5. My wellies with the flowers on them
6. The green dress I made with the book fabric and the pockets – pockets are always a favourite thing, surely? Every dress should have pockets
7. Reading and all my books – particularly Rose's books that I rescued from her bedroom before Mags emptied it out when they moved to France
8. Nan and Grandad. They should have been first on my list.
9. Oh, and gardening. Should have put that right up at the top of the list with Nan and Grandad

That's nine things. Never expected that. I wonder what Nan would say the collective noun is for a list of favourite things? A fan of favourites? Maybe a field of favourites?

The first list was much easier to write. And I know the collective noun for that one straight off: a horror of hates.

I don't think I can face breakfast in the morning. I don't want to see Dylan – and who knows what he's told everyone else by now. No, the best thing to do is get up early and leave before I have to see anyone. I've given Pinewoods Retreat five days, and I promised myself I'd stay for four.

I'm going home in the morning.

13

SIMPATICO

AT a couple of minutes to six, Holly puts her case and bags down in the hall and goes into the kitchen.

"Morning, Holly," Dee says, looking very awake considering how early it is. "Can't sleep?"

"I'm leaving, Dee."

"Aren't you booked in for three weeks?"

"I'm leaving early. I don't fit in here. It's the best thing for me."

"How can going home be the best thing for you?"

"Everyone is gossiping about me," Holly says in a near whisper. "Me and my past. It's time to go home."

Dee looks concerned. "I've not heard anything."

"You're here, in the kitchen, all day long. But out there," Holly speaks quietly as if she might be heard, and nods towards the main part of the house, "I bet they're all talking about me. About this!" She points at her scar, the familiar tears threatening to spill over.

"How do you know they're talking about you?"

Holly shrugs and rubs a finger over the bridge of her nose. "Well, OK, I don't know for sure. But that's how it feels."

"I don't actually live in the kitchen, you know," Dee says, smiling. "And I haven't heard anything. Believe me, Lorraine and the girls keep me up on any gossip going around, and I've heard nothing about you."

"Well, I bet they're talking about me now. One of the journalists, Dylan, he's . . . he's . . . ." Holly shakes her head and plonks herself down at the kitchen table.

"Go on. What about him?"

"It's nothing; forget it." She traces a crack in the old pine table with her finger.

"If it was nothing, you wouldn't have mentioned him. More to the point, if it was nothing, there'd be no talk of going home." Dee sits down opposite Holly. "Please, tell me." She reaches across the table and takes one of Holly's hands in her own.

"He's been pestering me," Holly says in a quiet voice, avoiding Dee's eyes.

"Pestering how? Is he harassing you? I mean, sexually harassing you?"

Holly shakes her head. "No, goodness. Nothing like that." She blinks, fighting tears. "Last night he told me what he's going to write about me. He found out some things . . ." Holly trails off.

"And you told him to mind his own business, I hope," Dee says, raising an eyebrow.

A lifetime of experience with the press has left Holly resigned to how journalists act around her. They tell her what they know, ask questions, dig about in the dirt, and then tell their readers, with whatever twist they can dream up, what they've uncovered. Holly sighs. "There's no point."

"I'd give him a piece of my mind for you, but it's not my place to do that. Stand up for yourself, Holly." She gives Holly's hand a light squeeze.

Holly shakes her head. She doesn't stand up for herself. It's not what she does. Mainly because she doesn't know how to. On the few occasions when she's tried, she's made a mess of it with burning cheeks and a stammer that comes from nowhere. Other people, like San, are so much better at it – like they've been to finishing school for feisty retorts. Holly missed that opportunity, for sure. She's not got it in her to stand up to anyone – and certainly not Dylan. Journalists are the very people who turned her family into the laughingstock of the nation.

"Lorraine believes that Pinewoods finds people when they need it most," Dee says. "And my old mum always says that everything happens for a reason. Are you sure going home now is the right thing to do?"

Holly nods, not trusting herself to speak. She hates that saying, that things happen for a reason. If that's true, what was the reason for Rose's death?

"Look," Dee says, "it's not for me to persuade you to stay, if you really want to leave. I just don't want you to do anything hasty. Let me make you breakfast first, you can think about it whilst you eat. And, if you still feel the same, well, then I'll phone for a taxi for you. I can't call yet, anyway. Six in the morning is a little early for taxis around these parts."

Holly nods again. Dee quietly busies herself around the kitchen, preparing breakfast, and Holly welcomes the silence.

* * *

With a hot mug of coffee warming her hands, Holly steps out on to the back step and looks across the kitchen garden. Lines of early morning sunlight cut through the pine trees, falling in strips across the raised beds like Venetian blinds. There are five straight rows of six raised beds, with gravel paths cutting their way through, creating a chess board pattern of planting. Many of the beds are planted with vegetables that fight with weeds for space to spread out, and Holly can't help but make a mental list of the tasks that need doing, just the way Grandad did whenever they arrived at the allotment. She adds the Victorian greenhouse to the list. It takes up much of the wall to the left of the garden and the glass is in desperate need of a wash. Towards the back of the greenhouse is a shed and a compost heap, and on the opposite side Holly can make out a low building, partially hidden by an overgrown trellis. That climbing rose needs pruning. Another task for the list she's making in her head for nobody.

Holly yawns. She barely slept last night. Thinking about Dylan and his digging into what happened to her got her thinking about all the mistakes she's made in her life. So many – too many. It was a mistake that she took so long off work. She'd never have lost her job if she'd gone back to work sooner. Throwing that tray of drinks at the mad man in OO-TO Travel, that was a mistake. He'd never have attacked her if she'd stayed still and minded her own business. Add to that, her agreeing to swap days off with Donna. She'd never even have been in work if Donna had done her normal days. Another mistake: coming to Pinewoods Retreat.

Holly sighs and steps out into the garden, rubbing the rose

quartz heart in her pocket. What did she expect to get from Pinewoods? Some kind of miracle? Fool. It's not like the place was going to find her a job or turn her life around for her. She only came because Tasha and her counsellor were on at her to book a holiday. The retreat is never going to put her life back on course for her – that's too big a job. And look at everything that's gone wrong already. She got knocked over by that dog at the beach, fell on her face at the dune running, wobbled all over the place doing the beach yoga. Not to mention running past everyone crying after that conversation with Dylan last night. And now, everyone at the retreat is bound to be talking about her. The story of her past never takes long to become gossip when someone finds out about it.

"For today's soup!" Dee's voice makes Holly jump. She was so lost in her own thoughts, she hadn't noticed Dee come into the kitchen garden. She holds up a bunch of freshly cut thyme. "Mushroom and thyme. One of my favourites." Holly nods and looks back out at the garden. "Do you have a garden, Holly?"

"A small one, yes. A bit bigger than a postage stamp."

"And you like gardening?"

"I used to garden a lot. My nan and grandad had an allotment as well as the garden. I helped them. Especially when I moved in with them when I was sixteen. Grandad had a saying." Holly smiles. "Grandad had lots of saying. He used to say that we grow veg with love so Nan could cook meals with love, and we could all eat with gratitude." She stops and blinks. What's she doing? She never talks about Grandad, but Dee has this effect on her, same as

Lorraine. They're kind people and she feels comfortable talking more openly with them than she usually would with others.

"Wise man, your grandad," Dee says. "Grow with love, cook with love, eat with gratitude. I might pinch that."

"I doubt Grandad made it up himself. It would be a good little saying for Pinewoods." Holly smiles at Dee.

"I've got the cooking with love bit sorted," Dee says. "The problem is, this kitchen garden is missing the growing with love bit. Just look at it. It's getting out of hand." They both look out at the weeds. "Simas, our gardener, loved working here, but he had to go back to Lithuania. We've had nobody looking after the kitchen garden for over a month now. Lorraine and I do what we can, but we can't keep on top of it. There's just not enough hours in the day."

"Do you use all your own produce in your cooking?"

"Mostly. And we're totally organic, as well. We're far enough away from the larger farms which means the soil isn't contaminated, and Simas grew everything using organic techniques. He was sad to leave, he loved it here. He even lived in that little Shepherd's Hut at the bottom of the garden. See it?" Dee points down the garden with the scissors she used to cut the thyme. Holly had assumed the little building at the back of the garden was an outhouse or brick shed.

"Why did he leave if he loved it so much?"

"Some ill health in his family – he had to go home to help with the family business."

"That must have been difficult for him. I can tell he worked hard here. There's the bones of a really good kitchen garden."

Dee nods. "He did. And now we're in danger of letting it go to waste. We advertised, but the only applicants we got knew little or nothing about growing organically and they were – how's the best way to describe them? – non simpatico, that's what Lorraine says."

"Non simpatico?"

Dee laughs. "In the language of millennials, they didn't get it." Holly nods. Gardens need people who get them, and connect with them. "Well," Dee says, "I'd best get on. This soup isn't going to make itself." She holds up the bunch of thyme again, and vanishes into the kitchen.

Holly wanders around the garden, stooping down every now and again to pull up a weed that is flourishing under the neglect. Simpatico – that's her when it comes to gardening. She gets it. Thanks to Grandad. This garden is crying out for love, and she's very simpatico to that. Before long she's perched on the end of one of the raised beds, engrossed in clearing the weeds to give spinach and kale the space they need to breathe and grow.

Before she knows it, an hour has passed. Holly stands, stretches her back, and admires her work.

Taking in a full, deep breath, her lungs relishing the fresh air, Holly realises that this is what she's needed. She feels much calmer than she did earlier on this morning, more at peace.

"Time for a break?" Lorraine is a few feet behind Holly with two cups in her hands.

"Oh, yes please." Holly puts the trowel she's holding down on the edge of the raised bed.

"This place does something to you. I've not seen you look this relaxed since you arrived. And it looks like you're doing something to it, too. You've been busy." Lorraine passes one of the cups to Holly. "Coffee. I'll ask Dee to make you some toast. You must be hungry."

"Dee sorted me out with breakfast. I hope it's OK that I've been gardening."

"Yes, it's more than OK that you're weeding my overgrown, rather sad, kitchen garden," Lorraine says with a grin. "You've been a great help."

A great help. Holly smiles. "Dee told me about your gardener. Would it be OK with you if I did a bit more work here? It saddens me to see it like this."

"I can't ask you to do that."

"I'm enjoying myself. If you'll let me, I'd love to spend a bit more time in the garden today."

"Are you sure? Dee said you're all packed and ready to go home."

"Yes. It's time for me to go home. I don't fit in here. I'll catch a later train. I'll do a bit more on the garden first though."

"Just think of all the other things you could be doing instead. There's activities planned for later today. Wouldn't you feel more at home doing one of those?"

"You know, it almost feels like I'm at home here, in your garden." She smiles at Lorraine and holds her mug up. "Cheers."

"Then I'd love you to lose yourself amongst our weeds." Lorraine holds her mug up to mirror Holly's.

* * *

By lunchtime, Holly has removed the worst of the weeds from half of the raised beds. Some of the beds show emerging evidence that Simas used companion planting, each plant providing support to the others around it. Onions planted alongside carrots and beetroots, lettuces grown with chives and garlic, and potatoes next to corn, squash and pumpkins. Grandad would be impressed – heck, she certainly is. Simas definitely knew what he was doing.

Dee calls her in for lunch and Holly settles herself at the kitchen table, devouring a big bowl of the mushroom and thyme soup with a slab of fresh sourdough bread. She hasn't felt this kind of hungry for months – years, maybe. The hunger that comes from doing physical labour.

Holly glances up at the clock. How is it already one o'clock? She completely lost herself in the garden, forgot all about getting a taxi. Like Grandad used to say, 'cares melt away when you kneel in the garden'. She realises that she hasn't felt this content in months, despite her sore knees and aching back. She stretches, and bends her back from side to side.

"You need a bath with Epsom salts to ease those aching bones," Dee says, picking up the dirty plates and bowls, and stacking them in the dishwasher.

"I do, yes." Holly smiles. "Oh, my bags . . ."

"They're already back in your room, lovey. I took them back up a couple of hours ago."

"You did?"

"I've got a feeling that my kitchen garden is going to see a lot of you over the next day or two."

Holly nods. It's hard to believe how low she felt in the early morning, before she started pulling up a few weeds. A feeling of calm has comforted her today as she spent time in the garden, and she can see already that she's made a difference – much like the old days with Grandad. "Yes, you're right. I'll stay. For now. The garden needs me."

Holly looks out through the open door. Yes, the garden needs her – and she may well need it, too.

14

BANANAS, PEANUT BUTTER & DATES

AT the end of her training session a little later that afternoon, Holly finds herself walking in step with Hunter feeling surprisingly good. She only agreed to do the session on Lorraine's insistence. Now, she's tired from how hard he pushed her with lunges, star jumps, press-ups, a bit of sparring and the inevitable dune running, but she also feels energised and lighter somehow.

"That was great," Holly says with a smile.

"I'm glad. It's always a good place to reach, when the exercise becomes enjoyable. It's not much fun at the start when you feel like crap." Hunter laughs. "That's one of the reasons I always keep myself fit. Can't stand the thought of having to start again with all the pain."

"Believe me, I'm still in pain." Holly laughs, and surprises herself with how light her laughter is.

"You enjoying Pinewoods, then?" Hunter turns his face towards Holly as they walk. She's taken aback by the warmth in his tone.

"Erm . . ."

"Oh dear." He raises an eyebrow. "Dee said something about you possibly going home."

"Yeah. I'm thinking about it. But I'm staying tonight, and maybe tomorrow. We'll see."

"What's not working for you? And what're the good bits?"

"I don't know. I'm enjoying some things. Others less so."

"Like what?"

Holly looks ahead, not sure she can meet Hunter's eye. She shrugs. Hunter stops walking.

"When I was in the army we would ask ourselves 'are you running to something or away from something?'. Our actions will be different depending on what the outcome is, but even running away needs to have a purpose. There's got to be a reason for it. And I'm wondering if you going home would be you running away, but without a good purpose."

Holly takes in what he is saying. "What makes you say that?"

Hunter takes a step towards Holly and puts his hands on her shoulders, turning her towards him. "Let's just say I recognise the signs. What's going on, Holly?" His tone is soft, tender, and Holly feels a kaleidoscope of butterflies rise up in her stomach – she's always loved Nan's collective noun for butterflies, and the feeling of their wings fluttering inside her is exciting. She can't hold his gaze any longer, noticing a blush rising up her neck. As she lifts her eyes back to his, she considers, just for a moment, telling him that these training sessions with him, the way he teases her, challenges her to make herself better, this is what she's enjoying. He is one of the good bits of being at Pinewoods Retreat.

"Nothing, it's nothing." Holly shrugs, turning away from Hunter and dislodging his hands from her shoulders. "It's just one of the journalists getting under my skin." She starts to walk off. "It's OK. I know I shouldn't let it get to me."

"Not always as easy as it sounds, though," Hunter says, falling into step beside her once again. "I'm guessing it's that Dylan guy?"

Holly nods.

"Does it make you feel any better if I tell you I get a bad vibe from him too?"

"It's that vibe that's getting to me. I don't trust him."

"Trust your instincts. In the army, we always said that we had a kind of sixth sense. We knew there was danger up ahead, even when there was no actual evidence of it. It was like there was a change in the air. And we could tell if someone was trouble when they walked into a bar – before they even said anything. So, my advice is trust those gut feelings, Holly. You're probably right not to trust Dylan."

They round the corner and start walking up the last part of the cinder path to Pinewoods. "You're not letting that one thing spoil your time here, are you?" Hunter asks.

"It might be only one thing, but it's a big thing."

"Let's get coffee."

"What?" Holly is sure she must have misheard him.

"Coffee." Hunter bends his head to go through the arch that leads into the front garden cafe. "My treat." He sits himself at a table in the shade and nods to Holly to join him. "Take a seat. I've not got another client until the end of the afternoon."

"No, honestly, it's OK. I'll be all right."

"Great. I'm glad you'll be all right. And I'd still like a coffee. Or would you prefer a smoothie? Join me. Please."

"Oh." Holly feels her scar pulse as her face reddens again. She thinks back to a few minutes earlier when Hunter told her to trust her instincts, but she's really not sure what they're telling her right now. That he's kind, even if he does push her hard on her training sessions. That he's incredibly good-looking. That it feels great to be asked to join him for a coffee. "A smoothie for me, please. One of those Energisers."

"Good choice with the bananas, peanut butter and dates. It will help to keep your energy levels up. I'll join you." Hunter calls over to Jess with their order. "You're not doing any more work on the garden today, are you?" he asks Holly.

"I might." Holly settles herself into the chair next to Hunter.

"That wasn't really a question." Hunter smiles. "You've done enough exercise for today."

"There's a lot to do. Too much to do in a day or two."

"And what needs doing at home? Is there a cat to feed? Stale milk in the fridge? Bins to put out?"

Holly laughs. "None of that, no. I've a neighbour who'll put the bins out, no milk in the fridge, and there's no cat, as far as I remember."

Hunter beams back at her. "Right. So if you did go home, you'd just be running away from this journalist who's got under your skin."

"I guess. Yes." Holly knows she's running away; it's the easiest way she's found over the years to deal with difficult situations. But this is the first time someone else has commented on it. Even Grandad seemed to avoid actually naming her behaviour, tending more towards protecting her.

"Is that your go-to behaviour? Running away?"

"What's this, Doctor Hunter? Turning into my therapist as well as my trainer, now?"

Hunter smiles at Holly, and waits to respond as their smoothies arrive. He wraps his hands around his glass. "Sorry. You're right. I'm digging where I'm not invited. One of my mates in the army used to say that there's three things to ask yourself before you give advice. Is this about me? Did the person ask for advice? Does my advice help or hinder? So, answering those for myself, no it's not about me, no you didn't ask for advice, and hell, I've no idea if my advice would help or hinder."

"It's OK." Holly smiles. "I appreciate you caring enough to ask."

"Just remember, Holly. You are not the problem." He leans back in his chair and folds his arms across his chest. Holly bites her top lip, surprised at Hunter's assertion.

"OK," Hunter says, "let's change the subject, huh? How are you enjoying your smoothie?"

Holly takes a long suck on her straw before answering. "Well, that's a weak attempt at changing the subject. But yes, it's yummy."

"Fair cop." Hunter stirs his smoothie with his straw, and Holly is very aware of how long his eyes stay fixed on hers.

"How did you get into personal training?" she asks.

"That's a better question." Hunter's leg brushes against Holly's and she holds her breath until he moves it away. "Seemed like a good idea after being in the army. I was one of the fittest guys, helped others keep up their fitness levels, and it was like I had this knack for getting people to push themselves further than they thought possible. After I left the army I didn't really know what else to do. Lorraine was teaching yoga at a gym I used to go to, I got to know her a bit, and when her and Dee bought this place she offered me the job. Personal trainer and general dogsbody."

"Do you enjoy it?"

"Now who's turning into the counsellor?"

Holly holds up her hands, resisting the temptation to say "sorry", in case Hunter tells her to do press-ups on the cafe lawn.

"I love it," Hunter says. "Love being outdoors, meeting people, helping people." He looks into her eyes again. "People like you." His knee brushes against Holly's again, this time staying in place a moment longer.

"Hello, you two." Holly jumps as Ruth and Bex appear next to them. "Can we join you?" Without waiting for an answer, Ruth sits in the only other chair at their table, leaving Bex to pull one around from another table.

"You two look cosy," Ruth says. Holly can feel Hunter's eyes on her, and she blushes. "Hope I wasn't interrupting something."

"Not at all, Ruth," Hunter says. Then he flashes her a grin. "Had any more thoughts about getting fit and fabulous for your bikini this summer?"

"Oh, you are silly. You'll not get me in a bikini for love nor money."

The conversation turns to what Ruth and Bex have been up to today, and before long Hunter makes his apologies. As he gets up to leave, he rests his hand on Holly's shoulder for a moment.

"Promise me you'll rest up for the rest of the day? And, I'm glad you're staying. For now." He winks at Holly and walks off, ducking his head to go under the arch back out on to the cinder path.

Wednesday 16th June

HOW I FEEL: 6/10. Maybe even 7/10

SLEEP: Was exhausted, and still barely slept at all

WEATHER: Overcast and quite grey, moderate breeze that makes it feel cooler than it is

WEARING: Pyjama shorts, thin T-shirt, barefoot, under the duvet

PROMPT: What is something I am ready to welcome more of into my life?

Lost myself in the garden this morning, and before I knew it, I'd spent hours there. It was just like when me and Grandad were in his garden, and then Nan would bring us back to the real world with a cup of tea and some toasted crumpets.

I've barely touched the surface of all the tasks that need catching up on - it would take weeks to get the kitchen garden functioning as it should again. But at least I can make a start for Lorraine and Dee.

I'll go home in a couple of days. I know it might seem a bit like I'm hiding in the garden, but at least there I'm less likely to bump into Dylan. I'll do my personal training sessions, but I might avoid the group sessions for now - or, I suppose I could check in first with Dee to see if Dylan is on the list. Yeah, I'll stay for now, but I'm still allowing myself to go home any time I want to.

Good training session with Hunter today - definitely my best one yet. Hunter was especially gentle with me today. Said he'd seen me gardening and didn't want me doing too much. Made me drink loads of water as well, so I wouldn't get dehydrated again. He even took me for a coffee date in the cafe. Well, not a date exactly. It was a coffee date like you have with friends. So not like a date-date. And it wasn't a coffee, either. I had a smoothie. Anyway, he took me for a drink, and we had a chat. It was lovely.

Right, today's prompt. What I want to welcome more of into my life. How on earth do I answer that? I suppose I know what I don't want more of in my life. No more gaggles of journalists. No more bullies.

I used to want more loving parents, at least, after Rose died, that is. But Mags and Dom were too busy, wrapped up in themselves, and I'm glad they're not part of my life any more. As far as I'm concerned, they can stay in France and never come back. It's not like they bothered to come back when I was in hospital after the attack. Two phone calls. That's all I got. Of course, Mags was all over Facebook, telling her friends that she was beside herself with worry. It was her garden party that weekend, and she couldn't leave the final arrangements to Dom. And now she's making some excuse about Brexit and them having been in France too long. She reckons they won't let her back in because she's done the six months we're allowed now in Europe. Whatever. I don't care any more.

Hang on, I'm not following the prompt. Funny – I seem to do that a lot when I'm answering these.

Something I'm ready to welcome more of into my life.

Hmmm.

Well, I miss Nan and Grandad and all the love we had for each other. I can't have more of them, but I suppose more of that kind of love would be nice. It was good to come home to people who cared about me and wanted to hear about my day, and I miss that. Maybe a husband one day, that could be something I'd welcome into my life. That's probably a silly thing to hope for, though. Who's going to love me with my scar? I don't even love myself. Anyway, I know I don't want children. My own childhood's hardly a good advert for parenting – based on how Mags has been as a mum, it seems like motherhood is a recipe for disaster in the Bush family.

More Bex and San, and their friendship. It's nice having friends. People to laugh with, natter with, feel comfortable and safe with. If this is true friendship, a friendship that can last beyond a short holiday, then I definitely welcome more of them both in my life.

Work. ~~I want a job.~~ Nope, I need a job. I suppose I welcome getting a new one into my life.

More time to garden. Can I square that one off with needing a job? I've loved working in the kitchen garden today. It reminded me where my happy place is. I always feel safe in the garden. When I get home, I'll get Nan and Grandad's garden knocked back into shape. I've neglected it too much. Just as well I no longer have the allotment as well. Grandad gave that up a little before the pandemic. He said they were too old for it and someone younger than them deserved a chance to enjoy having the space.

What else? I hate to admit it, but Hunter's exercise regime is becoming enjoyable. I welcome more of that in my life, and the way it made me feel afterwards. It wasn't just a physical feeling. I actually felt better in myself – more confident, happier.

Anonymity. I'd love to welcome that into my life, more than anything right now. For my past not to exist. For nobody to know who I am. To be able to start afresh. Which reminds me, I did say once, a few years ago, that I'd change my surname. Not to be Holly Bush any more. If I did change my name, people wouldn't be able to go off and pry into my past like Dylan did. I thought of using Nan and Grandad's name but that still ties me to Mags, with them being her parents. People could still find me, and ask me about Rose's death, about the campaign.

Names are a strange thing, aren't they? Mags insists on calling me Hols or Hollybobs. I told her when I was twenty-one that I wanted her to call me Holly, but she said it's a mother's privilege to call her child by a cutesy name. She also demands that I call her Mags — has done since about a month after Rose's death. Not sure she sees the irony there — that she insists on what I call her, but doesn't give me the same choice. I feel like I basically never had parents that I got to call Mum and Dad, and that feels . . . I don't know. Odd, yes. But also something more than that. Distant. Far away from my parents. Which I guess I was, particularly after I moved in with Nan and Grandad.

Why wouldn't you want to be called Mum by your child? Mags says: "My name is my identity, darling". Well, what about my identity? My identity as a child, as Holly, as the fourteen-year-old whose sister died. And another thing – Mags says that calling someone Mum is anti-feminist propaganda because it's all about possession, and nobody deserves to be possessed by another. But I want a mum, not a Mags. I miss having a mum – and dad, too. Dom does what Mags tells him to do. I reckon if it was just the two of us left, he would be happy for me to call him Dad.

There I go again. I'm meant to be talking about my life now, but instead I'm talking about things to do with my past. My counsellor says I often do this. He says I need to look to my future, that it'll help me. He asked me recently what I could do to make myself a good future. He said it's difficult, if I'm always looking back. How do you answer that? I didn't know what to say, but it's gone around my head since then. What might it be like to shape my future and create a new me? Let the real Holly out of the cage that I've locked her in for too many years.

Dee's Mushroom and Thyme Soup
(she gave me the recipe so I can make it when I get home)

1 onion, roughly chopped
1 clove garlic
250g mushrooms, roughly chopped
250ml almond milk
350ml vegetable stock

2tsp fresh thyme (or 3tsp of dried thyme)
1tsp herbes de Provence
1tbsp tamari
1tbsp nutritional yeast
Pinch of salt
Pepper
1tsp coconut oil, to fry onions and mushrooms

Fry onions and garlic with pinch of salt to bring out
flavours. Deglaze pan with a splash of water, if needed.
After about five minutes add mushrooms and fry for a
further five minutes. Add tamari and mix well, then add
all remaining ingredients, except the stock and pepper.
Bring to boil, and then reduce to a simmer for 5 minutes.
Add stock and simmer for 15 minutes. Blend with a hand
blender. Add pepper to taste.

In the winter, add a tin of green lentils, drained and
washed, before adding stock, to make a heartier soup.

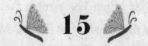

15

THE OLD WERE
YOUNG ONCE, TOO

THE early morning air is clean and pure, and the sky is perfectly blue. It reminds Holly of her favourite saying of Grandad's, which he said every time he looked up into the sky on a dull day and spotted a hint of blue breaking through the clouds. "There's blue in that there sky, queen, but not enough to make a sailor a pair of trousers". Thinking of him now, Holly looks up and decides that, today, there's enough blue to make trousers for a whole fleet of ships of sailors.

Her legs ache from yesterday's combination of gardening and personal training with Hunter. As she looks over the kitchen garden, she feels the urge to stretch, to do what she can remember of the yoga sequence that Soraya had them doing in the sunrise yoga and meditation. Salute the sun. Seems like a good way to ease her muscles and to say good morning to the plants before working with them.

Holly checks around. Nobody's watching. Breathe in, flop down so that her fingers reach for her toes – there's no chance of actually touching them – rise up slowly, one vertebra at a time, and reach for the sky. She lets the clean, pure air coarse through her lungs and into her veins. The stretch feels good, and Holly repeats it a few more times before walking down the garden path to the shed.

All the tools she needs are neatly stacked away. Holly admires Simas, the previous gardener, for the order he brought to both the garden and storage of his tools. Grandad would approve. She can hear him now: "a place for everything, queen, and everything in its place".

Across the garden, there are six rows of raised beds. One row is empty of veg, though there are plenty of weeds thriving after the recent spell of warm weather. Was Simas planning to plant some late-summer seeding varieties of vegetables there? It's a shame he didn't leave notes or some kind of plan. She remembers Grandad talking about setting a patch of ground aside to allow it to rest for a year, and wonders if this is what Simas was doing. The other five rows are full of vegetables, planted up at different stages of growth. Holly has so far completely cleared the first row, giving spinach, kale, lettuce and potatoes the space to breathe, and she's pulled out the easy, surface weeds in some of the other rows. Today's job is to get started on clearing the raised beds of troublesome dandelions.

Before she starts, she opens the windows in the greenhouse to let in some air, and waters the tomatoes, cucumbers and peppers. It's going to be a warm day, and some of these tomatoes will be ready to pick in a day or two.

Tap, tap, tap. Holly jumps. Ruth is standing outside the greenhouse, her walking stick touching the glass. Holly hadn't noticed her come into the garden. She gives Ruth a small smile, half-hoping the woman will go away and let Holly go back to enjoying the early morning tranquillity. Ruth comes into the greenhouse and leans her back into a shelf of seedlings.

"Hello, love," Ruth says. "I saw you from my bedroom window." She points her stick skywards, like she's been spying on Holly, god-like. "What are you doing?"

"Gardening," Holly says. She's not relishing a conversation with Ruth, not after seeing her being so mean to Bex – Holly feels a protective allegiance to her new-found friend.

"I used to enjoy gardening with my Neville, we had a lovely garden, you know, but I can't look after it any more. It's this Long COVID, you see, and my old bones are creaking, too, you know." Holly smiles and nods. People like Ruth were always coming into OO-TO Travel with no intention of booking a holiday, simply looking for someone to talk to. They'd list off their medical ailments as reasons why they couldn't fly any more, and talk of trips from years gone by. Holly knew they were probably lonely. "I'll have to get Rebecca to take me to the doctor again when we're back home in Wallasey. Can't keep going on with this fatigue, it's too much, you know." Ruth sighs. "I had a greenhouse," she continues, barely stopping for breath as she swerves into a new topic. "Nothing as grand as this old thing – it's lovely, isn't it? – mine was tiny, but big enough for me to grow all my own annuals from seeds, and Rebecca's father grew tomatoes, usually about five varieties each year, lovely they were. I've never tasted tomatoes like the ones my Neville grew, sweet as anything, they were. I used to make a delicious rich tomato sauce when we had a glut."

"I didn't realise you liked to garden, Ruth."

"No, well, that's the trouble with you young ones, you think our only life is this old one we live now – you never think that the old were young once, too. All you young people see is some wrinkly, old busybody to be pushed into the corner and ignored."

Holly wipes a small patch of soil off a shelf holding tomato plants. Ruth is right. Holly's not really spent any time alone with her, and realises that she's so far only seen Ruth as Bex's mother – not a person in her own right. "I'm sorry," Holly says.

"Sorry doesn't butter any parsnips." Ruth taps the crook of her walking stick on Holly's arm. It's not that the touch hurts particularly, but Holly strokes her arm instinctively.

"Why don't I fetch you a chair, Ruth? You can sit and chat to me as I work, if you like?" Holly gives Ruth a weak smile, accepting that she's unlikely to get as much done on the garden. But Ruth is lonely, and spending a bit of time chatting to her is the least she can do. If nothing else, it gives Bex a bit of time to herself.

"I'm amazed you have time for an old woman like me." Ruth purses her lips. "No, no, no, I don't want to be any bother, love, best leave you to it . . ." she says, waving her stick in the air. "Well, actually, if it's no bother, I suppose, that would be lovely, if you don't mind . . . though . . ." Holly walks back towards the house to find a chair, ". . . not one of those hard chairs, they're dreadfully uncomfortable, I don't know how anyone sits on them without a cushion . . . one with arms would be good." Holly smiles to herself.

There's something about Ruth that reminds her a little of Nan, the way she flits from topic to topic and yet still manages to keep tabs on every bit of conversation she's having.

Filling any hint of silence as Holly works on a raised bed, Ruth regales her with tales of Neville and how she met him. Dandelions have taken hold, and Holly digs down deep to get the whole of the root out as she listens.

"He looked ever so handsome in his uniform, did my Neville, they should bring back National Service, made men out of boys, and there was a lot less trouble from the youth of my time, none of these knife stabbings you hear of now." Holly momentarily pauses, mid-dig. "I wasn't talking about you, Holly . . . not your stabbing, I mean, you don't like talking about it, do you? Your stabbing."

"It's OK. I wasn't stabbed,' Holly says, slowly. "Slashed. Not a huge lot of difference, I suppose."

Ruth leans forwards and rests her hands on the top of her walking stick.

"Someone came into work brandishing a knife," Holly continues. "I threw a tray of hot drinks at him. He attacked me. And now I'm left with this." Holly points at her cheek.

"That's horrible, love."

"I didn't feel anything. Not when it happened."

"Very brave of you, to do that. Did you get a bravery medal, like you see on the telly?"

"No," Holly laughs. "I got made redundant."

Ruth pushes herself up from the chair she's sitting on. "Well," she says, indignantly, "that's not right. You should write to your MP."

"It's OK, Ruth. I didn't like the people I worked with anyway." Holly stabs at the dry earth with her trowel. "After this holiday, I'll start looking for a new job and I'll get on with my life."

"Well, I hope you feel proud of yourself, Holly, love. You deserve to. Now then, if it's OK with you, I need to go inside for my pre-breakfast doze. It's the insomnia, you see, from my Long COVID. Goodness me, but I'm fed up of it. I'm ready to be done and get back on with my life." She coughs, as if her body is reminding her of what she is living with. "Are you joining us for breakfast this morning? Dee said there'll be pancakes today."

Holly smiles to herself at the speed with which Ruth changes topics of conversation. She nods. "Thank you, Ruth," Holly says. "It's been lovely talking with you." Watching Ruth wander back towards the house, leaning on her stick, Holly realises how much she's enjoyed chatting to Ruth. She shakes her head – how judgemental she's been of Ruth, without even taking the time to get to know her.

She won't be going anywhere near the dining room, though, not as long as Dylan's around. Or the rest of the guests, for that matter. By now, Dylan is bound to have told everyone everything about her past, and Holly can't face the whispers and glances as people talk about her around the dining table. Just thinking about it, she is filled with a heady mixture of nerves and anger.

"Anytime, love." Ruth disappears back into the house, waving her walking stick in the air – suggesting, Holly thinks, that she might not need it quite so much as she pretends. Holly turns back to the patch of garden she's weeding, and works on, determined to make some kind of impact on the tougher weeds.

16

COURAGE AMONGST
THE DANDELIONS

HOLLY realises she's been busy gardening for almost two hours when San comes out with a mug of coffee and some toast.

"I thought you might need some sustenance," San says as she holds out the chipped mug. "Dee said you won't mind having a gardener's mug – by which I assume she means, you'll be OK with the chips around the rim."

"Thank you," Holly says, pushing herself up from the raised bed she's been working on, giving her back a stretch.

"You've been busy," San says. "I wondered why you weren't on any of the group activities yesterday. You missed a treat. Hunter took us off on a walk – dune safari, he called it. Showed us animal and reptile tracks, which was fascinating, and explained some of the history of the dunes. Did you know that during the war, in the Liverpool Blitz, bombs were dropped into the dunes by the Germans?"

"I had no idea. I thought all the bombing was in Liverpool. Why did they need to bomb the dunes?"

"Hunter said there are two stories. One is that there was an observation point that the Germans were maybe trying to knock out. The second theory is probably more likely. If the planes were still carrying any bombs at the end of their raids, they dropped them as they were turning for home, and Formby is likely to have been the place where they did that."

"Interesting. But how can you tell that happened in the sand dunes?"

San smiles at Holly. "That's what I thought, but Hunter showed us something called a blowout. It's like a huge crater in the dunes, and there's a path around the rim. You could really believe it's where a bomb was dropped." San pauses. "Anyway," she says, bending down to pull up a weed, "that's not what I came to talk to you about. Do you mind me asking you something?"

Holly's heart sinks. Here we go. Of course, Dylan will have spoken to San about her, and now her new friend will revert to being the journalistic type, too. She won't be able to help herself. "What?" Holly doesn't mean to snap, but she's had enough of her past being dug up.

"It's Dylan, the guy who works for the *City Magazine*."

Of course it is. "What about him?"

"Has he been bothering you?"

Holly sighs. She could just say "yes, he has. He's threatened to expose my past". But Holly wants to know exactly what Dylan has revealed to San first. "What's he been saying about me?" she asks.

"He told me he's been digging and has made a link between two stories. The scar on your face, and something about your mum after your sister died. Says he's managed to find himself a great story out of this boring and tedious place." San holds her hands up. "His words, not mine. To be honest, Holly, I'm not interested in your past. Really, I'm not. Nor what happened to give you that scar. But I am concerned that he's hounding you."

"Oh – I . . . oh." Holly looks San straight in the eyes. She looks sincere – the kindness around her eyes is still there, and there's no tension in her face. "Yes."

"Yes what?"

"He's hounding me. He's been hassling me for a quote."

"I'm sorry."

"It's not your fault, though, is it? Unless you're feeding him a story about me."

San's eyes widen and her jaw drops. "I wouldn't do that to you. I couldn't."

Holly sighs. "Sorry, no, I shouldn't have said that. It's just – well, journalists . . ." Holly kicks the raised bed with her flowery welly.

"I know, some are complete bastards. We're not all like that, I promise you."

"Did he say anything else?" Holly thrusts her hands into her pockets.

"No. He's showing off that he has a story that's more than Pinewoods, which is what we're all here to write about. The retreat, that is." San sits down on the edge of the raised bed, and Holly joins her. "Anyway, I've told him to leave your story where it belongs. In the past."

Holly rubs the back of her neck. At least San is on her side.

"He's bored," San says, "that's why he's going after you. Pinewoods isn't his thing." She pauses and looks back at the house. "Actually, this place is so much not his thing, what is he even doing here?" She turns back to Holly. "You know, I bet he's done something to piss off his editor at *City Magazine*, and this is his punishment."

"Well, he pisses me off." Holly lets out a weak laugh.

"Good. Use that against him. Like I said, however charming he can appear, he's a nasty piece of work. I'd happily help you to bring him down, just to get him back, but this is your fight. It's something you have to do for yourself."

Holly would happily bring him down – if only she could find some courage amongst the dandelions. She knows she needs to start standing up for herself, and stop being so pathetically apologetic all of the time, like Hunter says. But can she actually do it?

San starts plucking out a few weeds from the raised bed next to her. "What was your sister like?"

The question takes Holly by surprise. She can't remember the last time anyone asked her that. Holly searches for the answer, remembering Rose as she was when she was alive. "Funny. Bossy."

"Ohhh, she's your older sister. My sister's like that too. Always taking charge."

Holly smiles. "Actually, no. She was younger, but she got away with anything, so she always decided what game we'd play, and make up her own rules. But you know, even though she was younger than me, she looked out for me too. When we were in primary school together, if someone picked on me, she was always there by my side, standing up for me." Holly wonders if perhaps that's why she doesn't stand up for herself now: she's still waiting for Rose to appear and fight her battles for her. Holly takes a deep breath and lets it out slowly.

"My sister's six years older than me," says San, "so she never did that. Even now, with Ryan – he's my ex – she just told me to get a grip."

"Is he the toxic relationship you mentioned?" Holly throws some weeds into the bucket next to her.

"The one and only. I was with him for ten years, but in the end I accepted he's never going to leave his wife." San shakes her head. "I was a fool, Holly. Believed every promise he ever made to me. Every lie. Forgave him for all the missed dates because he couldn't get away." She closes her eyes and puts her head back, like she's forcing tears to stay put. "He kept me dangling for ten whole, stupid, wasted years. And I let him."

"You must have loved him."

"I did. Still do. I'm so embarrassed, Holly. I'm an intelligent woman. How did I let myself get taken in by him?" San wipes her eyes with the back of her hand.

"What changed?" Holly wonders if it would be OK to reach over and comfort San, but being unsure of where their friendship is at, she hesitates.

"I saw him with his wife a few times. She's beautiful. And then, one night they were at a posh charity do that I was reporting on at Knowsley Hall. She followed me into the ladies and, well . . ." San clears her throat and leans forwards, resting her head in her hands. "She told me she knew. She'd known for years. But it didn't bother her, because if he ever intended to leave her, he'd have done it a long time ago. And I knew she was right." San lifts her head and looks at Holly, her eyes damp. "Do you know what the worst thing about it was?" San shakes her head and wipes a tear from her cheek, leaving a streak of dirt. "She told me she forgave me. Pitied me. I couldn't handle it. If she'd shouted at me, been nasty to me, told me I was a bitch – anything like that – then I could have come out on top. I would have been able see her as the bitter wife who didn't deserve to be married to Ryan. But," her voice is almost a whisper, "she told me it was OK, that she didn't blame me. She told me she felt sorry for me, for how much of my life I've wasted on a man who'll never be mine. That's when I finally saw sense. After ten bloody years."

San sobs. Loud, ugly tears. Holly passes her a neatly folded tissue, and lays a hand on her back. She sits with San in silence as she cries.

"Sorry," San says, her voice thick with tears. "I think I needed that."

"Anytime," Holly says. "I mean, not that I want you to cry anytime, but I'm here for you when you need to talk. Or cry. Here get digging the dandelions up." She passes San a hand fork. "Make sure you get down deep to pull all of the root out. If you leave any of it in the ground, the dandelion will be back in full vigour in a few days."

"Thank you." San smiles weakly at Holly and takes the fork from her.

"For what?"

"Not giving me sympathy."

Holly nods. She knows what it's like to not always want sympathy. She smiles. "Here. You'll need this kneel pad. Grandad always told me to look after my knees so I didn't end up like him in old age."

San gives Holly a hug, puts the kneel pad on the ground and sticks the fork into the soil, gently rocking the dandelion root free. The two of them work on in companionable silence for an hour, when San stands up.

"Shit!" San says. "Have you seen the time? I've got a back massage booked in with Lorraine. Thought it would be good therapy for me, but being out here with you feels like it's been all the therapy I need. Thanks for letting me cry like that. I've not been able to, not since I told Ryan to take his things out of my flat and never come back. You've done me some good."

Holly nods, not trusting herself to speak. Suddenly, she feels in danger of crying herself. As San returns to the house with the dirty coffee mugs, Holly clears the tools away into the shed. Hidden from view, she lets out a confusion of tears – realisation that she did something to help someone else, mixed with relief that San didn't ask about the day she was attacked, or about Rose's death. San didn't pry into her traumatic past. She let her talk about Rose as a person: about her life, not her death.

And Holly was helpful too. San needed her. She needed space to let her own grief out. And Holly was able to give her that.

As she looks out over the garden, Holly is glad that she's not gone home yet. Maybe she'll stay another night. She can always catch the train home tomorrow, or the day after. If she still wants to.

* * *

With a weary body, Holly drags her aching limbs up the stairs. Her back is complaining, but in a good way. The tiredness of a long morning well spent in the garden, as Nan would say.

She's on the fifth step when she hears a cough behind her. Holly turns around. Dylan is standing at the bottom of the stairs, staring up at her, hands stuffed deep into the front pockets of his jeans. His flies are open.

"Holly Bush," Dylan says her name slowly. "Where have you been hiding?"

Holly looks down at him, enjoying the feeling of power she gets from her higher position. She says nothing, but holds his stare.

"Still waiting for that quote from you." Dylan grins, and Holly's blood turns cold. Still, she holds his stare, despite the desperate urge to blink and look away.

What would San tell her to say? "You . . . you'll have a long wait." Holly feels the words shake as they clamber out of her mouth. She stuffs a hand into one of the pockets of her shorts and her fingers rest on the rose quartz heart she's carried with her since Lorraine gave it to her on her first day. Closing her hand around it, she knows she can do this. She can speak up for herself.

Dylan shrugs. "It doesn't matter. I'm running the story anyway, you know."

"Why? I mean – well – it's just – it's a very old story." A trickle of sweat runs down her spine.

"Ah, but I have a new angle."

"When a story's as old as stale bread, the angle doesn't matter." Holly coughs nervously, her heart thudding so hard it feels like her whole body vibrates to the beat.

Dylan raises a surprised eyebrow. "Ooo, when did Holly Bush get all hoity-toity?"

"And," she swallows hard, "that *City Magazine* you work for is a glossy magazine – it goes in all the posh hotels. It doesn't even cover stories like mine. Your editor won't be interested in what happened to me."

"He will be when he sees how I tell the story."

"I-I think you're fooling yourself." Her mouth is dry now, the skin across her cheeks tingling under the heat of a red-hot blush.

Dylan puts a foot on the bottom step, and slowly climbs the stairs towards her. Holly's lungs tighten, and she clenches her fists tight. What has she started?

"Has that cow, Sandra Sartori, been coaching you in how to be a bitch?" He stops right in front of Holly, inches between them.

"This isn't about San." Instinctively, one of her feet moves to the step behind her. "I . . . all I want . . ." She shakes her head, bracing herself. "I simply want to live my life without people digging up my family's past and plastering it all over the front pages – again." Holly takes in a deep breath. Her ears ring, and she feels lightheaded. But she knows she has to finish what she's started. "I've had enough. Enough of . . . of . . . scum like you." Holly wills herself to stay calm. She slows her breathing, like when she's having a panic attack, before taking a step down, filling the gap between them. Her eyes focus on his. This time it's Dylan's turn to step back. "It's . . . it's . . . people like you, who . . . who made me what I am today. If you don't like the bitch, then stop digging her up." Holly's head swirls, dizzy with adrenaline.

Dylan's mouth drops open, looking surprised at the strength of Holly's words. "People like me? It's my job, you stupid bloody cow." He sneers at her, as if attempting to reassert himself.

"Dylan Brown!" San's booming voice makes both Holly and Dylan jump. She's standing in the doorway to the therapy room, looking furious.

"It's OK, San," Holly says, looking at her friend. "I've got this." San leans her shoulder into the door jam, crossing her arms, and gives Holly a slight nod of encouragement.

"She's the Boffin Bop Kid, Sandra." Dylan's laugh is cold and empty.

"Was," Holly says, jutting her chin out.

"What?" Dylan looks back to Holly, his eyes screwed up in confusion.

"I *was* the Boffin Bop Kid. I'm not a kid any more." She takes another step towards Dylan, who backs away again. "The Boffin Bop campaign ended over sixteen years ago."

Dylan crosses his arms and stands with his legs astride. "Do you really think I won't publish just because you've gone and got yourself a steel vagina?"

What was it San said earlier? There has to be some reason why

Dylan's been sent to Pinewoods. She's right. He's not the kind of journalist who writes about retreats like this. With her heart thumping in her chest, Holly takes in a deep breath. "I don't think you will publish. Does your editor know how you hound people like me?"

Dylan blinks. "Come on, there's no need to be like that. It's just a bit of fun, that's all."

"Oh well, that's OK then," Holly says, shrugging. "Maybe it's my turn to have some fun." She turns her back to him, gripping tight hold of the banister, and starts to climb back up the stairs.

Dylan claps, slowly. "Is that it? Is that all you've got? Well done, Holly Bush. You think you're so big, don't you?"

"No, actually, I don't." Holly stops, keeping her back to Dylan. "I'm simply standing here on the stairs, with aching limbs, trying to get on with my life, minding my own business. And right now, I'm going to have a bath." She carries on up the stairs, and as she turns the corner she calls back down to him. "You're flying low, by the way." Just before she loses sight of the hallway, she catches a glimpse of Dylan as he looks down and fiddles with his flies.

17

FRECKLED FACED, FOURTEEN & UNFORGETTABLE

LIFE started out well enough for Holly, in an averagely happy, average-family kind of way. The Bush family consisted of Dom and Mags, their two green-eyed, auburn-haired, freckle-faced girls, Rose and Holly, and a tabby cat. Yes, the Bush parents seriously had a thing about naming their daughters after plants – even the cat was called Lavender. People always remembered the Bush family, and not always for the right reasons; they found them odd, and invariably laughed at the name choices for the girls. Rose and Holly were probably the only two people who didn't laugh. No one ever knew Lavender's thoughts on the matter.

They lived a relatively happy life in a leafy suburb of South Liverpool, close to Sefton Park, where they all took their bikes on Sunday afternoons. Both Mags and Dom worked as academics at one of the city's universities where Dom studied system leadership and Mags delved into community engagement in reducing health inequalities.

But when Holly was fourteen, that averagely happy, average

life came to an abrupt end. It was a wet and miserable day in the school holidays, a bit cold for the time of year, and plans to go for a picnic in the park with friends were ruined. The forecast suggested there may be a light shower. The forecast was wrong. It poured down all day.

Instead of being in the park, the day was spent indoors, with twelve-year-old Rose making up games like they used to play when they were younger, and that had the two girls in fits of giggles; playing Uno (Rose won, as usual, due to adding in her own rules); and watching Disney films that Rose chose, in their very own cinema made out of sofa cushions. Mags left the two of them to it as she wrote up some research she'd been working on. The girls got on really well, in the main, and Mags left them to their own devices for hours at a time.

By early afternoon, Mags was in the kitchen, alternating between baking and marking student assignments. Holly was on the floor, painting her toenails – a towel under her foot to protect the carpet, just as Mags had told her to. Rose was reading. Eventually, she threw her book aside and sighed.

"Get out the way, Holly. You're in my way."

"No, I'm not. You're reading."

"Well, I'm not reading any more. Move."

"You're so bossy. I'm not moving. I'm in the middle of painting my toenails. I can't move until the nail varnish is dry."

Rose threw a cushion at Holly, and laughed. "God, you're such a baby at times."

"What did you do that for? Mum! Rose is being a pain."

"No, I'm not. Cry baby."

"Yes, you are. Mum, tell her to leave me alone!"

Mags stood in the doorway, barefoot, a wooden spoon held up to her mouth as she licked cake mix off it. "Be nice to each other, girls."

"She's in my way, Mum. She's taking up the whole room with the stupid towel on the floor, and she's stinking the place out."

"Am not!"

"Are too!"

"OK, girls, that's enough. I know it's no fun being stuck inside all day, but it's also no fun listening to you two bicker. Rose, come and help me in the kitchen."

"Can I get my Boffin Bop out? Please?"

"'May I', not 'can I'. And yes, you may." Mags and Rose vanished into the kitchen. Holly finished doing her nails, and took out her notebook and pen and started to write a short story. Since Rose went up to high school she'd become moody and took charge of everything, so Holly's make-believe story world was easy to get lost in. She could forget about this change in her sister, who hung around Holly way too much, pretending she was far more grown up than she actually was, always pushing to get her own way. A mean streak had started to emerge in Rose and she was a lot less fun than she used to be. Holly blew another raspberry in the direction of the kitchen and lost herself in her own little world.

The sounds of Mags and Rose chatting floated through from the kitchen, as they discussed experiments that Rose could do with the Boffin Bop. It was a new kit that she got for her birthday

– that year's big thing – and Rose loved it. She was much more interested in science than Holly was, who, in truth, only had three real interests: writing stories, reading and helping her grandad in his garden. If she had to add one more thing she liked doing, it was baking with her nan, but that was more about spending time with Nan than it was about the baking.

Holly had watched as Rose did her first few experiments with the Boffin Bop on her birthday. All you needed to add to the brightly coloured, hard plastic machine was household items like bicarbonate of soda, lemon juice, water, vinegar, things like that – and you could create mini explosions, erupting volcanos and foaming-at-the-mouth monsters. One experiment used eggs, which Rose loved, but Mags had only let her do that one once because of the mess it made. And the Boffin Bop instructions gave other ideas of experiments that could be tried, too.

There were rules, of course: she could only use the Boffin Bop in the kitchen; and she had to make sure an adult was around at all times. Rose, a goody-two-shoes in front of Mags and Dom, agreed, though Holly knew there were times when Rose took no notice of the rules.

Later that rainy day, when Rose was still in the kitchen playing with the toy, the phone rang in the hall. Holly heard Mags answer the phone and laugh.

"How lovely to hear from you. Hang on a moment – Rose, be careful in there, wait until I'm back before you finish that Boffin Bop-Experiment!" There's a moment's pause. "Oh yes, she loves it, we got it for her birthday, along with the new bike, of course.

I know, I know, where do the years go? She'll be a teenager next year. If ever I needed to know I'm getting old!" More laughter.

Mags carried on chatting on the phone for some time. And then there was the bang.

Mags stopped talking. Accident-prone Rose wasn't shouting her usual "sorries", like she did when she dropped something or knocked things over. It was incredibly, uncomfortably quiet.

Until Mags screamed.

The paramedics said that Rose died pretty much instantly. A big part of the hard plastic that flew off the Boffin Bop in the explosion landed right in her throat, and there were lots of smaller bits in other parts of her chest, neck and face. She'd have been dead within moments, they said.

Within hours of the funeral, Mags started a rant about the Boffin Bop. A dangerous kit, should never have been put on sale; must be removed from every shop, a national recall; people shouldn't be allowed to invent such things, let alone sell them. The tirade went on for hours. Holly covered her ears with the heels of hands to block out what Mags was saying. It didn't work.

Dom tucked his daughter into bed that evening. Mags locked herself away in their bedroom and refused to come out for days, that soon turned into weeks.

* * *

The panic attacks didn't start immediately after Rose's death. Holly's first reaction was more one of hiding, staying out of the way. She boxed away the PlayStation, the Wii, Uno and all their favourite Disney films, and told Dom to put them up in the loft, out of sight. Friends had no idea what to say to her after the initial words of comfort, and Holly herself no longer knew how to start any conversation that didn't concern Rose and her death in some way.

Who was she supposed to be, without her sister there – teasing her, helping her, hugging her, laughing with her? Who was she on her own? Still Holly Bush, but that was it. Just Holly. Nobody put an 'and' before or after her name any more. She was Holly, on her own.

Her parents didn't help, either. Mags was too distraught to leave her bedroom, and when, reluctantly, she did venture downstairs for breakfast, she looked at Holly and burst into tears, unable to face the reminder that Rose was absent. Dom was little better. He did the obvious caring duties for Holly – cooking meals for her, making sure her clothes were washed and ironed, getting her to school on time – just. But he worried about Mags, and put most of his time and energy into looking after her.

Holly found comfort in Rose's bedroom. It helped her feel close to her sister. She curled up on the rug next to the bed, and pretended that Rose was lying on her front on top of the duvet, kicking her feet in the air, humming to herself. Holly's eyes fell on the bookcase, and soon she was holding books that Rose had chosen, The *Princess Diaries*, *Sisterhood of the Traveling Pants*, The *Twilight Saga*, turning the pages that Rose's fingers had touched, reading the words that her eyes had taken in.

One day, Mags found Holly in Rose's bedroom. She shrieked and screeched and screamed at Holly for daring to mess with what remained of Rose. Dom intervened and held Mags tightly until she calmed down, telling Holly to take her book and read it elsewhere, to get out of her mum's way until she calmed down.

Holly hid in the shed at the bottom of the garden with Rose's copy of *Sense and Sensibility* that she'd bought her for her birthday. At lunch, when she gingerly came out of hiding, Holly sat across from her mum's glaring eyes. In that moment, she understood, in a way that made food stick in her throat, that Rose's death meant that she'd never again be enough for her mother. Holly couldn't make up for Rose dying, couldn't help that she was a constant reminder for Mags of Rose not being there. She'd never be enough, because she couldn't fill her sister's shoes as well as her own. Simply by not being Rose, Holly could only fail her mum.

As she struggled to swallow the food lodged in her throat, Holly's breathing laboured, her skin prickled and her heart thumped so hard that she looked down at her chest expecting to see it bouncing through her skin. Heat welled up from her belly button, and within moments Holly was struggling to breathe, feeling faint and lightheaded. She didn't know it at the time, but she was experiencing her first panic attack.

Mags shouted at her to pull herself together, as Dom scurried off to get her a glass of water. The panic attack grabbed hold of her, took over her whole body, and still Mags shouted hysterically: "Pull yourself together. You're making a fuss over nothing. Stop making it all about you."

Holly didn't feel much like finishing her lunch when the panic attack subsided. Later in the afternoon, she slunk back off down to the shed and carried on reading *Sense and Sensibility*.

The next day, Mags started her campaign against the Boffin Bop. She put all of her energy into that, like it somehow replaced Rose. She set up a blog, Ban the Boffin Bop, and wrote her first post: 'The Stark Truth Behind the Boffin Bop'.

Holly moved on to reading another Jane Austen book from Rose's collection.

* * *

Holly's mum was doing that thing she did. That thing with the sink, buffing it up with an old rag until it shone. She always did it when she was stressed – which was a daily occurrence since Rose died. But the response from the Boffin Bop company, refusing to acknowledge any fault in Rose's death, angered and stressed Mags more than usual. Dom made copious cups of tea, all of which were left on the side as Mags cleaned the kitchen within an inch of its life.

"Get the press involved," Dom said, as Mags rubbed at the same spot on the draining board for at least five minutes.

"What's the point? I might as well give up."

"If you don't take a risk with this, yes, you might as well give up. We might as well all give up. What's the point in any of this if we don't take a chance, Mags? Send out a press release, see what happens."

Mags stopped sink-polishing and stared out at the garden. She stood like that for a few minutes, staring at nothing in particular. "Yes."

"Yes, what?" Dom asked.

"Yes, let's write a press release. Let's get everybody talking about this."

The idea of "getting everybody talking about this" filled Holly with dread. Her stomach tied up in knots and she wished with all of her being that Mags would drop all talk of the Boffin Bop and give her a hug. All she wanted was a bit of her mum to herself – a few tender words, a sit down together to read a book, a bedtime kiss. She knew that if everybody did start talking about the Boffin Bop and Rose's death, all of this would have to wait even longer.

"I'm hungry," Holly said, as Mags and Dom chatted excitedly. Dom searched for a pen and paper, and they engaged in bouncing quick-fire suggestions between them. Holly made herself a jam sandwich, making sure she tidied everything away after herself, not even leaving a crumb behind on the worktop. She didn't want to set Mags off on another rant or manic clean.

And so the Ban the Boffin Bop campaign took off in earnest, right there, on the bug-free, squeaky clean kitchen table.

* * *

Ban the Boffin Bop took over the Bush family life. Mags wrote blog posts, sent out press release after press release, became an early adopter of Facebook and Twitter with regular updates, and it wasn't long before the local press picked up on the story. The national newspapers soon got in touch for a quote, and then Eamonn Holmes and Ruth Langsford had her on *This Morning*, talking to the nation.

They unleashed a monster. Mags took to the campaign trail and the TV attention like a seagull takes to flight. Being an academic, she was good at researching her facts and putting them together in an orderly manner, and she came across well on TV. Before long, Mags was on every talk show and in all the papers. She became a mini celebratory, appearing on a Christmas special of *The Weakest Link*, and the attention took over from all the grieving that you'd expect a mother to go through after losing her daughter.

Sure, there was the occasional tear that dribbled down her cheek for the cameras. But at home, there was no talk of Rose. It was like she had never existed. Holly wanted to talk about her, about how she missed her laughter, the silly games they used to play. Heck, she even missed their stupid bickering that started not long after Rose went to high school. But Mags made sure that all their energies were focused on protecting other little girls, and making sure that nobody could buy the Boffin Bop ever again.

Holly toed the family line and joined in the conversation about the Ban the Boffin Bop campaign. She sat on the arm of the sofa for a family photo shoot for the paper, with them all looking extremely glum, and she let Mags parade her in front of journalists as she waxed lyrical on the dangers of a science kit for kids. There was even a time when she gave a speech that Mags wrote for her to an audience of bereaved parents. She was ridiculously nervous, and hated all the attention she got from everyone at the event afterwards – everyone hugging her and telling her how brave she was, how incredibly well she was handling her grief.

But the truth was, Mags wouldn't talk about Rose, and implied that Holly needed to pack up her grief for the loss of her sister, and throw away the key. Or at least, that was how Holly interpreted her mother's behaviour towards her. Desperate to please her mum, hopeful for some attention from her, Holly did as she was told and took on the role of poster girl for the campaign, quickly becoming known as the Boffin Bop Kid. She also didn't want to annoy Mags – since Rose's death, her mum turned to anger very quickly. It scared Holly. On the odd occasion when she tried to talk about Rose, Mags barked at her: "We don't talk about Rose, only what happened to her. If we lose our focus, anything could happen."

As the campaign ramped up, Holly learnt how to fade into the background, and spent more and more of her week staying with her grandparents. Their house was only a little out of the way on her walk home from school, and going to see them was the only way she could find to reduce the anxiety and panic attacks that were now more regular than her periods.

And then Mags lost control. On *The One Show*, of all things. The most public place she could lose her cool.

The original plan, when the producer first got in touch, had been to film ahead of time and play the filmed piece during the programme, meaning that Mags didn't need to be live on the show. But then someone said that Mags was a natural in front of the cameras, and it was decided to do a mix of the filmed piece and a live segment. Mags had been through a particularly stressful few days that week, screaming and shouting at Holly and Dom that it shouldn't take two blasted, flaming, awful years to get a toy as dangerous as the Boffin Bop banned from shops. She even went on hunger strike to draw extra attention to the Ban the Boffin Bop campaign, and by the time she went on air on the Wednesday evening, Mags hadn't eaten for nearly 48 hours.

She started off OK with the first few questions that Adrian Chiles threw her way. And then, at 7:23 p.m. precisely, Mags lost it on national TV. She effed and jeffed, called Adrian Chiles "a little squirt of man with no balls and very little brain", threw her arms all over the place, hitting one of the other guests on the sofa next to her, and screeched when a production assistant attempted to calm her down and take her off set. Seconds later, a filmed piece about the recent decline in butterfly numbers replaced the scenes in the live studio – but by then the damage was done.

At school the next day, Holly was bullied mercilessly for Mags's TV meltdown. Kids flung their arms about, the way that Mags had done on *The One Show*, and Holly was called "a little squirt of a girl with no fanny and very little brain". Recently, the teasing had finally reduced, as things had quietened down on the campaign front over the past few months or so – but thanks to Mags, and what became her final TV appearance, Holly discovered that wasn't to last. The full nastiness and bitchiness of an all-girls' school was unleashed on to Holly, and her life went from a six or seven on the anxiety scale to a full-on ten out of ten.

After the disastrous TV appearance, there was one positive that came out it for Holly. There was no more Ban the Boffin Bop campaign. Nobody in the media would touch Mags – except, of course, to report on her epic TV rage, with some hinting that Mags's erratic behaviour suggested she'd fallen victim to Mother's Ruin, something that set Mags off into a private fury behind the closed doors of their South Liverpool home. She gained the name Mad Mags, and was suspended from work, pending an investigation into her behaviour and the reputational damage it could do to the university. During that time, Mags and Dom decided to move to France, and Holly moved in with her grandparents.

Holly was relieved, expecting that the past would cross the channel with her parents, and leave her alone to get on with her life. But being called Holly Bush kept her in people's minds for a long time to come. And when the journalists couldn't find Mags, they came after Holly, knocking on her grandparents' door – they wanted their story and they didn't care how they got it. Gradually, things tapered off, though there were new incidents with new toys impacting on a new generation of children, and Rose's name would get linked, which inevitably led to a journalist or two hunting Holly down for a comment, or bringing her name up as the Boffin Bop Kid.

Every time her past was dredged up, it felt to Holly like she would never escape her past.

HOW I FEEL: 6/10

SLEEP: Five hours. I was exhausted

WEATHER: Beautiful blue sky, not a cloud in sight, light breeze, getting warmer but not too hot

WEARING: Earlier gardening clothes, now a sage green skirt (with pockets, obviously), white seersucker top with puffed sleeves, white socks, flowery pumps with the yellow laces

PROMPT: What are the most important life lessons I've learnt?

OK, life lessons. I'll write a list.

· Life isn't fair and I'm best never to expect anything, because when I do, things only go wrong for me anyway.

· People are cruel and selfish and mean.

Hang on, I'm being all negative again. That seems to be a habit of mine, always look for the bad things first.

So, what positive lessons have I learnt?

· I'm happiest in the garden.

· When you meet the right people, you can make friends –
San and Bex are becoming good friends. And San seems to be
a journalist I can trust, which is something new in my life.

· I can stand up for myself and not have a panic attack.
I only went and stood up to Dylan! I didn't run away.
I didn't have a panic attack. I didn't even blush. And I
didn't say sorry. Not once. And, you know what, I'm brave.
I stood up to that attacker. Me. I did that. Yes, OK, I've got
this ugly, angry scar on my face now, but I was brave to
stand up to him.

See, good things have happened. It's not all been bad –
even though it does feel like it at times.

Nan used to say that even though bad things had happened
to me, I wasn't to forget the garden of my heart. I never
really understood that before, but now I think I do. It's
about looking after ourselves: weeding out the bad things,
concentrating on and nurturing the good things that happen.
In the past, I've let all the plants in the garden of my heart
wilt and die, particularly since my grandparents died.

Maybe my biggest life lesson has to be to remember the things Nan and Grandad taught me. It's time to look after the garden of my heart.

I've definitely decided to stay at Pinewoods for the whole time I'm booked in here. As long as I'm in the garden, or with my friends, it feels like this place is good for me. I'm enjoying being with San and Bex. It's good having friends to talk to and have a laugh with. I've missed that since Jen and me drifted apart. And I'm enjoying working in the garden so much – it's like we need each other. I'm even loving my PT sessions with Hunter. Have to admit, he's fit. Can't believe I just wrote that in my journal.

Ruth's Rich Tomato Sauce:
(Note to self: Share with Dee)

1 onion with 1tsp coconut oil for frying
1 clove garlic
300g fresh tomatoes chopped up, or a tin
of chopped tomatoes
1tsp herbs – Italian herbs are best,
but any mix of herbs works well
1-2tsp balsamic vinegar
1 stock cube
Pinch of salt

Fry onions and garlic with a pinch of salt. Add tomatoes
- if using fresh tomatoes, mash them up in the pan as they
cook. Add herbs, stock cube and balsamic vinegar. Bring to
boil, and then lower heat to a simmer. Leave on heat for
40 minutes to an hour, stirring occasionally.

If the sauce tastes bitter (which it sometimes can with tinned
tomatoes), add a little sugar or 1 tsp of tamarind paste.
Serve on pasta, or reduce down and use as pizza sauce.

BUTTERFLIES & BELONGING

HOLLY, San and Bex sit in the kitchen garden, admiring their work from the afternoon. Dee has given them each a Kombucha fizz, though this time Holly is sipping hers slowly. This is not a harmless drink, whatever the health benefits.

"I never knew gardening could be this relaxing," Bex says.

"You two've been fabulous support today," Holly says. "Thank you."

"All part of our mutual healing journey," San smiles.

"Mutual? Including you?" Bex says. "You've got it all together, San."

"I've definitely not got my shit together, Bex." San laughs. "Not since the end of my long-term, toxic relationship. Dating a well-known-in-Liverpool married man for ten years, and then dumping him after encountering his wife, puts you in a strange and lonely place. That's not a recipe for getting your shit together." She rubs her eyes.

"Sorry, I didn't know. That's tough."

"Nothing for you to apologise for, Bex. I told Holly about it all when you were busy doing something else." San puts her arm around Bex, and their heads lean in towards each other in a moment of support.

"But you at least have friends around you to support you," Bex says.

"Friends? Nah. Lost those years ago, lovey. With the hours I was working, and the man I was dating . . . I was totally unavailable. There's only so many times that you can bail on a night out, turn up later-than-late, or forget you were even due to catch up with everyone, for them to stop inviting you. Before you know it, you're seeing updates on Facebook, Instagram or whatever else with photos of *a fab night out, girls,* celebrating the drinks and the meals that you were never invited to. So no work friends, no long-term friends. Nobody wants to know Sandra Sartori any more.'

"You're so relaxed and friendly with people," Bex says. "I'd never have guessed that you're just as lonely as me. I'm sorry."

San nudges in close to Bex for a moment, and rests her head on her shoulder. "Thank you." San says.

"You're right on the mutual healing side of things." Bex sniffs. "I've certainly got a bit of healing to do, too. Lost my boyfriend and my job, gained a bad mood and a muffin top. And I've become a victim, always asking myself 'why me?'. I don't like that this is the person I've become."

Holly wonders how she became so self-centred that she is oblivious to the difficulties that others live with. Bex has a lot going on for her, and some of it really resonates, even though their experiences are so very different. "I'm always asking myself the same question," Holly says with a sigh. "But then I know 'why me' when it comes to this scar." She hesitates, realising she's about to share something she hasn't said out loud to San and Bex yet. "I threw a tray of hot drinks at the attacker, so he went for me. I came out worse than Cat at work – his ex. She's the one he came into the shop to attack, not me." Holly points at her scar and smiles, wryly.

San and Bex gasp in unison. Holly's heart thuds, though she is shocked at the ease with which she said this to her friends. Maybe opening up to Ruth a little helped her feel OK about telling her story, or maybe it's the desire to unite with her friends after they have shared their own personal needs to heal.

"I didn't even join the dots," San says. "I heard about what happened, you know, when it actually happened, but it wasn't my story at the paper, so I'd forgotten about it."

"That's big," Bex says, a look of awe on her face. "You're such a brave woman, Holly. I don't think I could do what you did if I'd been in your situation. Group hug?" The three women pull in close and hug each other.

"What would you like to do, Bex?" Holly asks as they pull away. "Instead of looking after your mum."

Bex shrugs. "I was a graphic designer. Thought I could do it from home, but Mum needed too much support in the beginning for me to get any work done." She pauses. "I think I'd like to travel, if I got the chance. I've only ever been on package holidays, but there's a whole world outside of Liverpool and Costa del Brits. What about you, Holly?"

Holly laughs. "Basically, the opposite. I would stay right here, in this garden. I feel like I belong here." The butterflies in her stomach take flight, like a murmuration, and settle gently back down again, as she feels an ephemeral excitement at the idea of belonging in the garden. Knowing that she will get to work there for the duration of her stay makes her happy. Yet a few days ago, she almost left Pinewoods.

"Keep working like this," San says, "and Dee will be begging you stay and work on the garden."

"There's so much to do, though. More than one person can manage – and certainly in two weeks." Holly surveys the garden again. It's a mammoth task.

"I don't mind helping."

"Same," Bex says.

Holly laughs. "Thank you, but it's more like an army of people we would need to do everything that's got to be done here. If it was just gardening, keeping on top of it all, I could do that on my own. But it needs knocking back into shape first. I can only do so much. Even with you two helping out."

"Well, we better get a move on then," San says, picking up her trowel.

Holly brushes dust from the back of her shorts. "I need to be done here in an hour. I've got another training session with Hunter." She picks up a ball of string and a pair of scissors, and smiles to herself as she returns to the job she was doing before their break, tying in the peas to train them up the trellis she put in place earlier.

* * *

Hunter is waiting in the front garden when Holly rushes outside, a few minutes late. He makes a point of looking at his watch.

"Ready?"

'Yes. Sorry to keep you waiting."

"Now that's how you use the word. Good to see you're learning." He grins at her, and Holly feels a blush rise up her neck. "We'll get down on to the beach today. Do some interval training and speed work."

They fall into an easy brisk walk, Holly matching Hunter's pace as he marches off.

"How's it going?" Hunter asks.

"OK. I've been helping in the garden."

"That's not what I heard."

"Oh?" Holly's stride falters as her stomach drops. Has Dee said something to him?

Hunter beams. "You're *doing* the garden. You're bringing it back to life, the way Simas had it. I never thought they'd find anyone who'd love that place as much as he did. But you do. And you seem to be doing a good job."

Relief floods through her veins, and Holly smiles. "I like being in the garden. I know what needs doing there."

"It's good for you. You look more . . ." Hunter looks at her. "More at ease." His voice is low and husky. His elbow touches hers and it's like a bolt of electricity runs between them. "Right, better pick up that pace!"

She matches his sudden speed, her lungs expanding to take in the fresh sea air, as they run on to the beach. The hour is spent in bellowed orders from Hunter. *Run. Thirty seconds fast, twenty seconds faster, ten seconds top speed. Pick it up, Holly. Repeat. Sixty seconds rest. I know you can do this. Start again. You're flying.*

* * *

Jogging back along the beach to the boardwalk at the end of the workout, Holly and Hunter see two young women in skimpy white bikinis sitting on a pale blue blanket. Holly stops and takes in the scene. There's a wicker basket, some books and a bottle of something.

"I know it's warm," Holly says, touching Hunter's arm lightly with her fingertips, in a conspiratorial way, "but this is not the kind of beach where you expect to see bikinis."

"The Irish Sea doesn't have the same appeal as the blue Med, does it?" Hunter laughs. He touches his skin where Holly's fingers brushed his arm.

The young women jump up, and with one of them holding a phone out as far as her arm will stretch, the two pout for the camera. They wave at Holly and Hunter before returning to their phones. One starts running towards the sea, looking back over her shoulder, as the other films her.

"Creating content for Insta," Hunter says, laughing. "Enterprising, I guess."

"Come on. I'll race you," Holly says, taking her chance to get a head start. She sprints off as fast as she can, knowing she'll soon be watching Hunter's toned body pass her and vanish off into the distance ahead of her. As she runs, she can hear him catching up with her. Holly slows to step on to the boardwalk, and Hunter grabs her around the waist.

"Gotcha!"

Holly gasps, shocked and unsure how to respond to Hunter's physical contact. Wide-eyed, she tucks a stray hair behind her ear, buying herself a second or two.

Hunter lets his warm arm drop from her waist. "God, sorry," he says. "Don't know what I was thinking."

She smiles at him, nervously, and lets out a half-hearted giggle. Damn! She should have laughed sooner, the same time he did, given him a sign that she's OK with his physical contact – more than OK. Why hadn't she done that? And now it's too late. The moment's passed.

"Come on," he says, "you still need to do a cool down. Five minute jog, two minute brisk walk, and that should leave us with about two minutes to slow it right down." Hunter steps straight back into a jog, leaving Holly to follow him.

Friday 18th June

HOW I FEEL: 7/10

SLEEP: Six hours. When did I last sleep like a log
for six whole hours?

WEATHER: Another gorgeous day.
Blue sky, light breeze, hot

WEARING: Denim shorts, grey T-shirt, once-white
plimsolls. (Nan always called them 'plimpsolls'.)

PROMPT: Who has had the most influence over my life?
Do they deserve to have that influence over me?

Goodness. Am I ready to deal with this prompt?
I'm honestly not sure.

The person who's had the most influence over my life
is my mother. Obviously.

Mags was in control of everything. Well, not quite
everything. She wasn't in control of what happened to
Rose, or how she reacted once Rose died. And I suppose
she wasn't in control that day she was on The One Show.

Something must have cracked in her that day. Everything else though, she was in control of.

Including me. Even now, with them living in France and me in Liverpool, she's still trying to control my life. I always kick myself when I answer honestly when she asks me what I'm up to these days. I basically always get her disapproval, and a response of "the Bush family doesn't do that". I need to learn how to say something without telling her anything at all.

I did resist Mags's contol once, though. She tried to take over Nan and Grandad's funeral. Playing the only-daughter card, she said that she had a responsibility to make the arrangements for her parents' funeral. She wanted to make a huge fuss at the big church on Ullett Road – that Nan and Grandad never even went to – with a slap-up meal afterwards at one of the big hotels in town. But before Nan and Grandad went into the care home they had made it clear to me exactly what they wanted. A cremation, not a burial, and drinks afterwards down the allotment, with their close group of friends.

I channelled my inner Nan and told Mags we were fulfilling my grandparents' wishes. I had it all arranged with two of the lovely old fellas who knew Grandad well. One organised a few big flasks of hot milk and hot water so that we could make hot chocolates - with additional brandy for those who wanted it, just like Grandad would have done - and another had his wife bake cakes. Mags kept saying that it wasn't a suitable wake, but it was what Nan and Grandad wanted.

All I've ever known is Mags's coercive control. I got so used to it. Perhaps the normality of it even began to make me feel safe - giving me familiar boundaries. Is that why I now control my life so much myself? Does it make me feel safe, keeping my world so small around me? I've not really thought of it like that before.

Back to the prompt. Who else has influenced my life? Rose, of course. She didn't mean to influence my life in the way she did, I know that. But her death affected me in so many ways. I envy sisters when I see them, as adults, chatting conspiratorially. I don't have anyone to do that with; nobody to reminisce about the past with, to moan to about our parents and all of their annoying little ways. It's more than that, though. Rose's death changed everything. It's not her fault, of course it's not. But the very fact that she died, and so cruelly as well, meant that Mags and Dom changed as parents. They did a weird mix of ignoring me and never letting me out of their sight. I saw the freedom my peers had in their teens, but I never really got that. Not that anyone wanted to hang out with the Boffin Bop Kid, apart from

Jen. Over time, I found myself alone more often, and so I'd walk to Nan and Grandad's house. Of course, they became two of the biggest influences on my life because of that. They were probably the best, too.

Tasha and her crowd at OO-TO Travel – they've all influenced me. I was quite chatty when my last manager was there, but Tasha soon knocked that out of me. And as all the others arrived, one by one, I found the best solution to working with people who clearly didn't like me was to keep my mouth tightly shut, and do whatever they said. It wasn't a nice way to be, but at the time I thought it made for an easier life. Look where that got me. An angry red scar down my left cheek, and no job.

Most of the journalists are going home tomorrow. San is staying on for another week, though. It would be great if she stayed the whole of the next two weeks, but I know she can't do that. At least I have another week to get to know her better. I already know it's going to feel strange for me and Bex not having her around in my last week here.

19

ALL HANDS ON HOES

AS Holly comes down the stairs, she sees Dylan standing in the hall, his suitcase next to him. She stops instinctively, wondering if she should try and avoid him.

As if sensing that she's there, Dylan turns around and looks straight at her, his pungent aftershave wafting Holly's way. She meets his gaze.

"I'm off," Dylan says. He flashes an insincere smile, then winks and taps the side of his nose. "Got stories to write up."

Holly walks slowly down the stairs without taking her eyes from his. Nervously, she stands for a moment on the bottom step, looking Dylan up and down. A familiar sense of dread starts to seep into her bones. Then, she sees him fiddle with the zip on his jeans – not quite his usual confident self. She takes in a slow, deep breath, then turns away from him and walks down the hall, towards the kitchen.

"My story about you will be filed by the end of Monday, right on time for next month's issue of *City Magazine*." Dylan's footsteps echo in the hall behind her. Holly keeps walking, through the kitchen and out the back door into the garden. Dylan's feet crunch on the gravel path.

Holly closes her eyes and holds her breath for a second, maybe two. She turns and faces Dylan.

"I might even sell your story to one of the dailies."

Holly says nothing.

"The public," Dylan continues, "deserves to know what happened to the Boffin Bop Kid. They have a *right* to know."

Anger bubbles away inside Holly. How dare he turn this all around to make out he's writing a story, *her* story, for the good of the public. Hoping that Dylan won't notice that he's riling her, Holly shrugs, keeping her face as deadpan as she can, despite the tension in her jaw.

"You're a public interest story, you and your family. People want to know what happened next."

Holly turns her head and looks out across the garden. She could walk away from him, along the garden path, ignore him. He's going anyway. She doesn't need to confront him.

"I'm letting the public down if I don't remind them about the Boffin Bop Kid," Dylan carries on. "Tell them what she's doing now. That she's living a loveless, lonely life, with a disfigured face: the legacy of the Ban the Boffin Bop campaign. Christ, your parents messed you up big style, didn't they? Do you think they realised when they started the campaign, what they'd do to your life?"

Holly turns to face him, her heart pounding against her rib cage. "Maybe that's the fault of people like you. It was you and your sort, writing stories without a thought for what you were doing to our lives . . . to me."

Dylan shrugs. "It's my duty as a journalist."

"Aren't you supposed to be regulated? I thought you were all meant to have ethics now."

Dylan's laugh is chilling. "Do you really think anything has changed? The public hasn't changed. They still want us to dish the dirt, and they don't care how we get it. They want to know how your sister's death changed your life, how your mum's obsession with her campaign destroyed you. They love looking into other people's lives – saves them from looking too closely into their own sad and pointless ones. I've already got my headline sorted." Dylan holds a finger and thumb in the air, moving them along as if following a newspaper headline. "*Who pruned Holly Bush? The Sad and Lonely Life of the Boffin Bop Kid*. Great, isn't it? Catchy." Dylan laughs. "I even captured a few photos of you when you weren't looking."

Holly closes her eyes. There's nothing she can say or do that's going to stop Dylan. Fighting him will probably lead to him having even more to print about her, if anything. Nan used to say something about changing the things she can, and accepting the things she can't change. Well, this is one thing she cannot change. So she guesses it's time for acceptance.

Opening her eyes again, Holly sighs. "Go on then. Do it." Her heart thuds, and despite the cool morning air, she can feel beads of sweat gathering in the hollow of her back. "I really don't care any more, Dylan." Deep down, she knows she does still care – but it's time for her to find a way not to.

A horn toots three times in the near distance.

"That, my dear, will be my taxi." Dylan steps back into the house and stops, turning back to Holly. "Thanks for making this a great trip. Pinewoods is ball-ache-boring. I'd have gone home after the first night if it hadn't been for you. Made my week, you did." He clicks his tongue against his teeth and flashes one last smile. "I'll send you a copy of my piece when it's published."

Holly waits for Dylan to leave before walking off towards the shed, her hands shaking slightly. She takes in a slow, deep breath. Her mouth is dry, and her heart pounds. But as she rests a hand on her chest, she's pretty sure there's no threat of a panic attack.

* * *

Later, after eating lunch with Dee in the kitchen, Holly walks back out to the kitchen garden and finds most of the guests standing in a group, looking at the door, like they're waiting for someone.

"Afternoon, everybody," Holly says, reaching for the spade that she left by the back door.

"We've come to help, love," Ruth says. She pats Holly's arm, her smile filled with pride.

"Help what?" Holly asks.

"You, lovey," San says, leaning on a garden fork. "It was Bex who came up with the idea." Bex beams at Holly, and Conor, standing next to her, gives her elbow a little nudge with his own. "Remember what you said about needing an army to get through all the work that needs doing?"

"Well," Bex adds, "here we are. Your very own garden army!"

Holly puts a hand to her heart. She can't believe that everyone has come together to help her. She looks around the group –

at San, Bex, Ruth, Audrey with the bangles, and more and more people.

"Should we all just get on with it, then?" says Conor. "I've a flight to catch at eight. Gotta leave here around five o'clock, but I'm happy to help until my taxi comes."

Holly's eyes find Hunter, who is standing next to Conor, his arms stretched across his chest. Her gaze settles on him for a moment too long, taking in his beautiful face – though his striking eyes are hidden behind sunglasses. Her stomach flutters and she quickly looks away.

In her moment of distraction, the group starts to disperse. Holly's heart flips. "Wait, no, come back!" The last thing she needs is for them to make a mess of everything – for someone to pull up seedlings, or hoe a recently seeded bed. *Think, Holly. What would Grandad do? How would he use all of these hands?*

"We need to be organised with the jobs that need doing. Let me have a quick think about this. OK, so – who can do what?" She looks around the garden, then back at the group. With Grandad's voice playing in her head, Holly works out the tasks for the day. "Conor, Hunter – the compost heap needs digging over." She points to the back of the garden. "Transfer the left-hand heap into the empty compost pit next to it. Make sure you use the garden forks to separate it out as you go. Please." Everyone is looking at her as she calls out orders. Ignoring the slight burning of her cheeks, she continues. "Ruth, do you think you can brush the shelves in the greenhouse, please? Here, use this." Holly passes Ruth a small hand brush.

Ruth nods eagerly, a big smile on her face. She hobbles over to the greenhouse.

"Do you need any help, Mum?" Bex calls after her.

Ruth waves the brush dismissively in the air. "No need, Rebecca. I've got this, as you young ones say! I'll be fine, thank you, love."

Bex turns back to Holly and grins at her, mouthing a silent "thank you".

"Who can wash the glass of the greenhouse? The outside needs a really good clean, and I've not managed to get to that yet."

"We'll do it," two young women call out in unison, giggling gleefully to each other. "What will all our followers think when they see photos of us washing a greenhouse?" one of them squeals, and they both collapse laughing. Everyone smiles indulgently at them.

"Ask Dee for a bucket of soapy water – don't use too much soap, though. Oh, and see if she has a couple of sponges." The two young women vanish into the kitchen.

Holly continues passing out jobs and before long, the kitchen garden is a hive of activity. As tasks are completed, she finds more work for people to do. Audrey and San are harvesting from a list Dee has supplied. The inseparable married couple are pushing canes into the ground and tying beanstalks to them. Hunter and Conor get on with the heavy lifting, moving big pots, taking full wheelbarrows of weeds to the compost heap and digging over raised beds ready for planting. Bex follows on behind with a garden fork and hoe, flattening the top surface, so that Holly can draw drills in the soil and plant seeds for late summer and early autumn vegetables. The young women washing the greenhouse glass make a game out of it, and are like children who've just been let out of school for their summer holidays. Ruth is singing a song about Maud and a garden as she works away in the greenhouse, walking stick in one hand, hand brush in the other, systematically cleaning the shelves. She's working slowly, but Holly doesn't mind, as long as Ruth feels like she is doing something useful.

"I've got to hand it to you, Holly," Bex says, pausing in the middle of hoeing a raised bed, looking over at Ruth who has moved on to washing terracotta pots and putting them out in the sun to dry. "You've worked wonders with Mum. She hasn't moaned about anything for at least an hour."

"It must be really hard for her, becoming so reliant on you."

Bex looks at Holly and blinks. "Honestly, I only ever think about how hard it is on me. But yes, I suppose you're right. Before COVID she was really independent – super active, did everything for herself. Still had us all over for Christmas dinner, worked in a local charity shop."

"Maybe this garden will remind her that she can get back to being independent. She needs that as much as you do." Holly flashes a broad smile at Bex, who looks over at her mum, singing away to herself as she works.

"I hope so. It's amazing to find something that she can do – something that doesn't tire her out too much and makes her feel like she's part of the team."

"It's the jobs I used to give Nan once she became unsteady on her feet. She hated sitting on her bottom, doing nothing. All her life she'd been busy." Holly smiles, wistfully.

"Where are your grandparents now?" Bex asks.

"They went into a care home after Nan had a bad fall. She needed nursing care, and insisted it wasn't my job to look after her. I wouldn't have minded though. They'd done so much for me, and I thought it would be good for me to look after them for once. But Nan wouldn't hear of it. Said I was too young to spend my life looking after her. So we moved Nan into the home for rehabilitation, and Grandad went with her. They were inseparable. Anyway, the care home had been clear of COVID through the worst of the pandemic and we thought they'd be safe there, but they'd only lived in the home a little over a month when the whole place was riddled with COVID. Grandad survived Nan by a few days, but I think his heart was broken. He couldn't keep going without her."

Bex gives Holly a hug. "I'm sorry. That's tough."

Holly's eyes sting and she squeezes them shut, forcing back the tears. Nobody has hugged her over her grandparents' deaths.

"Thanks, Bex." Holly fills her lungs with the clean garden air. "Come on, let's get on. This garden isn't going to sort itself out."

* * *

By late afternoon, the garden is in a far better state. Holly starts putting tools away in the shed, Hunter brushes up and the two young women call everyone together for a photo to upload to their socials. Everybody gathers around Ruth, who is sitting on a kitchen chair that Conor brought out for her a little earlier on.

"Tea up, everyone," Dee shouts from the kitchen door. "Conor, your taxi will be here in about ten minutes. And a special treat for you all: black bean chocolate brownies to give you some energy." She holds up a plate of brownies as if she is showing off a coveted award. There's a hum of friendly conversation as everyone files along the garden paths, and gathers around the proffered plate.

"Can I take one for Mum, please?" Bex asks.

"I'll take it over to her," Dee says, smiling at Bex. "You stay with your friends. It'll be nice to have a little natter with Ruth about her day."

Bex sits on the bench at the back of the house next to Conor, and not for the first time Holly sees the two of them exchange a flirtatious look and a smile. San joins Holly and winks at her nodding her head towards Bex and Conor.

"Sure, your mam's had a grand old time of it today," Conor says. "She was telling me tales of bringing up four boys and a girl, and how those brothers of yours teased you rotten."

"Oh god, what's she been telling you?" Bex laughs. Holly feels a little like she's eavesdropping, but it's lovely to see her friend looking so happy.

"Ah, nothing too incriminating. Except for the story of you getting into a toy crate, and the lads locking you in it before sending you off flying down the stairs."

"I didn't think she knew about that! Did she tell you how they'd put me in goal and then fire all the balls straight at me, one after another? I had bruises to show for it for months after."

Conor smiles. "Yeah, we've probably all done that, at some time or other."

"A sister's rite of passage, huh?" Bex smiles back at him. "You'll be glad to get back to Ireland tonight, will you?"

"Kind of, yes. I'll miss you lot, though. I've had such a grand time here." Conor's knee touches Bex's, and Holly feels the butterflies in her stomach do somersaults for her friend.

"I've never been to Ireland. Is it as beautiful as they say?"

"Around Killarney where I live, yes. Truly God's own country. You should come and visit."

"Really?" Bex blushes.

Holly nudges San's arm with her elbow, and the two smile at each other as they pretend not to be snooping.

"I'd love to show you around. Maybe get one of those good-for-nothing brothers of yours to have your mam for a long weekend, and come on over to stay." Conor flashes a broad smile at Bex.

"I'd love that. Thank you." Bex giggles like a teenage girl, and takes a bite from her brownie.

"Look, I'd best be getting myself that taxi or I'll miss my flight. Give me your phone and I'll put my number in it." Bex digs her phone out of her back pocket and passes it to Conor. "Text me," he says. She nods enthusiastically. "And remember, everyone, you can find me on socials as @frogandtoadfanaticsGBI."

Conor says his goodbyes to everyone, with hugs all round, and, as he walks back into the house, he turns and gives Bex a little wave. Bex waves back, and when she spots San and Holly gawping at her, she does a little dance on the spot.

HOW I FEEL: 9/10. Maybe even 10/10. Today was a really good day

SLEEP: Six hours. Sleeping is becoming a bit of a habit. I could get used to this

WEATHER: A bit of a wind got up from nowhere at the end of the day today, but it's been lovely all day, with big fluffy white clouds against a perfectly blue sky

WEARING: New shorts, pink blouse with the Peter Pan collar, flowery pumps

PROMPT: What surprises me most?

I had a huge surprise today, finding everyone in the garden waiting to help me. I've been feeling like I belong in the garden – and having everyone there with me today made me feel like I belonged to a community too. It was such a lovely feeling. We got loads done, with so many people pulling together. Hunter even joined in, and so did Conor, even though he had a flight to catch.

People kept telling me how much they were enjoying helping,

and they were asking me for advice like I know what I'm talking about. I suppose I do, when it comes to gardening. I was also surprised at how easy it was for me to instruct everyone on what needed doing. Can you believe I did that?

Hang on, the question is what surprises me _most_. I think the answer is my panic attacks. I mean, the fact that I'm not having panic attacks. I've not had a single one since I got lost on my first day here. Goodness, was that only last Friday? Feels like it was weeks ago. With so much going on, like all the stuff with Dylan, I'd have thought I might have had a few panic attacks. But I haven't. That's pretty amazing.

This whole week has been pretty surprising — in so many ways. Yeah, Pinewoods is definitely working its magic on me.

20

CANES, THORNS & PINE CONES

THE howling wind rattles against the window in Holly's room, waking her from a deep, dead-to-the-world, sleep. Something in the garden is banging, and Holly reluctantly pulls herself out of bed, throws on a sweat-shirt and her wellies, and takes herself off outside to see what's going on.

The banging is coming from the back of the garden. *Damn, is the shed door open?*

She weaves her way along the garden paths, buffeted by the wind, and pushes the shed door shut. As she pulls across the bolt to secure it, Holly has the sense that she isn't alone. She holds her breath and hears something moving over the gravel path. And again – it sounds like feet crunching on the gravel. She peers into the darkness. *Crunch, scuffle, crunch.* It's over by the greenhouse ... *Bang!* Holly's skin prickles down her spine, and her heart thumps. Surely it's just the wind, playing tricks on her?

The trees around her creak and crack as they are buffeted from side to side. Holly peers into the darkness again, just as the moon comes out from behind a cloud, throwing a dull grey light over

225

the garden. There's someone stooped down near the greenhouse. *Bang!*

"Who's there?" Holly shouts into the wind. No response. "Hello!" she shouts. The fierce wind snatches her breath, and knocks her off balance. Holly picks up a cane, clutching it tight in a vain hope it might give her some protection as she takes a few steps closer to the greenhouse.

"What are you doing?" Holly says, closer to the figure now.

"Holly!" comes a familiar voice. *Is that ...*

"Ruth?" Holly shouts into the wind, dropping the cane.

"They'll get broken!" Ruth shouts back.

"What are you doing, Ruth?" Holly is shocked to see the woman out in this strong wind. "Come on, let's get you back inside."

"No, I can't leave them." Ruth stands as straight as she can, and Holly sees her arms are full of terracotta pots. Ruth had washed them earlier in the day and left them out to dry. "I've closed the cold frames to protect the seedlings, but these will all get smashed to smithereens if I leave them out in this wind."

"It's OK, Ruth," Holly says, her voice a lot calmer than she feels. The wind is whipping up a sense of anxiety in her, though nothing like the way she feels on the build up to a panic attack.

"I need to put them away in the shed. If I don't, they'll cause all sorts of damage to the greenhouse."

Holly shakes her head. Ruth will do *herself* all sorts of damage, out here in the wind. "OK, let me help. We'll get it done in half the time." Holly gathers armfuls of pots, cursing herself for not putting them away earlier. "Put them inside the greenhouse, Ruth, it's closer. I can put them all away in the shed tomorrow, when the wind drops." The two of them move the pots to safety, and Holly can't help but notice how different Ruth is as they work together. Her movements are assured, and there's a determination about her. It's like being needed is giving Ruth a new lease of life, like it's recharged her batteries. Perhaps everyone is better for being needed.

"Mum! Mum, are you out here?" Bex's shouts can be heard through the wind.

Holly steps out of the greenhouse. "It's OK, Bex! Over here. We're nearly done."

Bex runs over. "Mum, have you lost your mind? Get inside, now."

"It's OK, Bex," Ruth says.

Holly stops mid-stoop. Ruth didn't call her Rebecca – she called her Bex. She smiles to herself and adds to the pile of pots in her arm.

"I need to help Holly," Ruth continues. "She can't do all this on her own."

"You'll make yourself ill, you old fool!" Bex sounds concerned for Ruth as she rests a hand on her mum's arm.

"Really, love, we're nearly finished here." Ruth stops what she's doing and looks at her daughter. "I know the damage that wind can cause. Just one of these pots could get blown against the greenhouse and shatter the pane. I don't want that to happen."

"We're done," Holly says, out of breath. "Come on, Ruth, best get you inside now. Thank you for thinking of the garden in this weather."

"Glad I was awake and could help you out."

Ruth retrieves her stick that she'd left leaning against the greenhouse as they worked, pats Holly on her arm and winks at her. She leans on to her stick and shuffles back to the house. As she vanishes indoors with Bex, the telling-off is shut away with the closing door.

After checking that the doors and windows of the greenhouse are all safely on their latches, the lids of the cold frames are secured in place and the shed door is locked, Holly takes herself back to bed. Despite the adrenaline pumping through her veins, she's soon back in a dream-filled sleep.

* * *

In the morning, Holly is woken early by an eery silence. The wind has dropped. Still in her pyjamas, she opens the back door on to the garden, keen to survey any damage. Her heart sinks.

Supports for peas and beans have been yanked out of the ground, flattened by the force of the wind. Branches, pine cones and leaves from the surrounding trees litter the raised beds. A rose arch and trellis that separates the garden from the hut Simas stayed in is in pieces on the ground. The garden is a complete mess.

"Well," she says to the lettuces, "at least you survived."

Holly picks up some twigs and fallen branches which will do for supports. She gathers them up in her arms and stores them down the narrow gap at the side of the shed. After her third trip, she squeezes back out through the gap and walks straight into Hunter.

"Oh! Sorry," she says.

"'Sorry?'" Hunter repeats, before smiling and raising his hands up in front of him. "No, my fault. I shouldn't have crept up on you like that."

Holly's hand goes to her hair. Oh lordy, what a state she must look. The wind made a mess of her hair last night, and she went straight back to bed with it all over the place.

"Can I help?" Hunter asks.

"Help?"

"This," he waves a hand around him, expansively, "the garden."

"Erm – well – yes, please. I, er . . ." Holly looks down at her pyjamas, suddenly painfully aware that she is *not* wearing a bra under her pyjama top.

Hunter grins. "Hufflepuff PJs. Nice. More of a Slytherin man myself." The sides of his eyes crease with laughter lines as he smiles at her.

"I'll get changed," Holly says, squeezing past Hunter and scurrying quickly back to the house with rosy cheeks. Back in her room, she pulls her hair into a messy bun – the best she can do without washing it – throws on a bra, a pair of shorts and a T-shirt, and is soon back in the garden.

Hunter is bent over, pulling up cane supports heavy with beans that the wind blew on to the ground. His T-shirt is ridden up, showing a slither of smooth skin. God, he's gorgeous. The butterflies in Holly's stomach crash into each other. Seeing Hunter here, so close, helping her, being kind, caring, sexy as hell – and more than that, flirtatious . . . it all makes her want him so much. Holly strokes her neck, her fingers coming to rest on her chest.

Hunter straightens up, his arms full with the beans, his muscles bulging.

"Holly? You able to help?" Hunter turns his head and looks straight at her. Neither moves, their eyes locking.

Holly thrusts her hands into her pockets, her skin tingling with desire.

"Earth to Holly. Any chance you could lend a hand over here?" Hunter says again.

Holly nods. "Yes, sure." She joins him, grabs hold of the middle section of the bean supports and pulls it all up off the ground. Their arms nudge against each other in spark-filled touches as they work, pulling the bean stalks upright and pushing the supports back into the ground. When the beans are secure, they move on to the peas in the next raised bed, so much sexual tension in the silence that hangs between them.

They finish securing the last of the supports and stand back, side by side, looking at the peas.

"It's a mess," Holly says, surveying the garden.

"After everything you've done to bring the garden back to life," Hunter says, shaking his head.

"That's the force of nature. Sometimes the weather is kind to us. Sometimes it's cruel."

"A metaphor for life." Hunter laughs, and as Holly shoots him a glance he adds, "My life, anyway."

Holly wonders if he really meant his own life, or if he was making a clumsy attempt to delve into her own. She scoops a stray bit of hair up into her messy bun.

"What made you want to help sort the garden out in the first place?" Hunter bends down to pick up some twigs from the path.

Holly shrugs. "I couldn't bear to see how it was looking. It didn't seem like Dee and Lorraine had the time, so I thought I'd help."

"There's more to it than that, surely?" Hunter looks at Holly with those soft, kind eyes, and she is hit once again by how much she's attracted to him.

"It's good to be useful, I guess. Needed. And gardens are my happy place."

"And you need your happy place because . . .?"

"Here comes Doctor Hunter again." Holly tilts her head and raises an eyebrow at Hunter.

"Ah, hey, that's not fair. I'm genuinely interested." Hunter bends again and picks up a few more twigs. "But yeah, I guess I did sound a bit like a therapist. Sorry."

Holly laughs. "Well, you're better looking than my last one." She immediately regrets saying that. Feeling a blush working its way across her cheeks, she looks away and clears her throat. "Anyway, thanks." Steadying herself, she lifts her eyes and looks straight into his, speckled with gold.

"What for?"

"Helping. This morning. With this." Holly waves her arm out towards the garden.

"No problem." Hunter holds Holly's gaze for a moment, before looking away to the back of the garden. "The rose arch. We need to sort that out."

"Right, yes." Holly's voice is husky, the familiar butterflies fluttering in her stomach. There's no settling them. Holly follows Hunter over to the trellis and arch, which lie in pieces on the ground.

"Not sure we can save this," Hunter says, with a low whistle.

"No, I doubt it," Holly agrees.

"I could make one."

Holly's heart leaps in her chest. He would do that? "That'd be nice."

"I'll do it. I'll make you one." Hunter nods.

Holly blushes. "Oh, well, make it for Lorraine, I suppose. It's her garden."

"Oh, right. Yeah." For a moment, Hunter looks crestfallen. He bends down and pulls at the climbing rose, now clinging to the ground. "Ouch! Bloody thorn." He holds out his hand to show Holly a small thorn sticking out of his finger.

"Oh! Here," Holly says. "Let me." She steps in closer to Hunter and takes his hand in hers, her thumb resting on his palm. As she leans in towards him, her head over his hand, she feels the warmth of his body, his breath whispering past her ear. Holly stops breathing. Carefully, slowly, she pulls at the thorn, and as it releases its hold, she looks up at him and breathes. "Done." She holds on to his hand, still, and as they stare at the offending thorn, his thumb strokes hers.

"Morning, you two." Their heads shoot around as one, like two naughty children who've been caught doing something they shouldn't be doing. Dee is standing at the other end of the garden holding up two mugs. "Tea's up. And I'll bring you some toast out too."

Holly drops Hunter's hand. He coughs, and kicks a pine cone down the path, watching it roll.

"Thanks, Dee," Holly calls back. She walks down the path after the pine cone, and feels Hunter's eyes following her. There's something between them, surely? He feels it too, she knows he does. OK, so she's not exactly experienced in matters of the heart, but she can't be wrong. There's definitely something going on, it's not just her. These moments between them are real.

Holly takes a mug from Dee, who gives her a playful, knowing look. As she settles herself on the bench, leaning against the wall of the house, the rain comes. Big, heavy plops of rain. Holly laughs and holds out her arms, letting the raindrops gently stroke her skin. Hunter looks at her quizzically from the other end of the garden.

"It's only Mother Nature doing her thing again," she calls to him. "She's helping to heal the garden."

Hunter smiles back, watching Holly as she lets the rain soak her.

Sunday 20th June

HOW I FEEL: 9/10. Taking a point off for being so exhausted!

SLEEP: Two hours, got up because of the wind, then another four hours

WEATHER: Started off dry, then heavy grey clouds, stair-rod rain. No breeze, not even the teeniest hint of last night's strong winds. Warm, very humid, and that wonderful, earthy scent of wet soil in the summer, when it's been dry for a few days and then it rains. There's a German word for that - petrichor. I love that smell. I love that word, too

WEARING: I've forgotten why I started to write down what I'm wearing. Was it just to fill up lines in my journal? Anyway, wearing jeans and a T-shirt today

PROMPT: What is my purpose in life?

This is an interesting prompt. Watching Ruth last night in the wind, I realised something. Ruth is a better person for being needed. She is kinder to Bex. Happier. I think we all need to be needed. We all need a purpose.

Where have I heard that before? That was it - my counsellor. He told me to find my purpose in life. Well, as much as it pains me to admit it, he's right. We do all need one. I need one. Working on the garden has felt like having a purpose. I know I've made such a difference already, and in a short time too. And it's making a difference to me, as well. Like Nan and Grandad's old saying, "every day, in some small way, I'm getting better and better". At least, I feel better in myself.

I've really enjoyed feeling needed here, by the garden. I don't think I've ever felt needed like this before. I loved Nan and Grandad, but I suppose they didn't really give me space to be needed. I needed them, though I'm not sure they ever needed me. Even when Nan could have done with my help after her fall, she wouldn't let me. Here, I am needed.

Last week, Lorraine gave us the prompt about what we're ready to welcome more of into our life. I know the answer now. This. More of this place. Pinewoods. More gardening, too. As the old saying goes, "the glory of gardening is having your hands in the dirt, your head in the sun and your heart with nature". I wish I could stay on here at Pinewoods. If I could do this every day, I'd be happy.

I feel safe here. I belong. I'm ready to welcome more of that.

My counsellor has brought up many times about how much I live with anxiety. I am constantly on edge, experiencing perpetual stress. It's no wonder I have panic attacks. Like he said, my body's been living in permanent flight mode.

But here, I haven't been feeling like that so much. I haven't been living in fear of . . . I don't know. Fear of what, exactly? Everything, I suppose. I was always scared of everything. I don't feel so scared of everything here.

PS. Hunter's cancelled tomorrow's training session on me. I need the rest, so it will probably do me good, but he didn't even tell me himself. Left word with Lorraine. What's that all about?

21

LOG HOPS &
WOODLAND WEIGHTS

REPAIRING the storm damage sets Holly back with her work on the garden. When Bex joins her, she's ready for a well-earned break.

"Anything I can do? Mum's helping Dee with the breakfast dishes."

"That's good of her."

"Don't be fooled. She's got some ulterior motive, I'm sure of it. Probably helping out to get attention – you know the kind of thing."

"Do you really think that?' Holly stretches her back, her spine clicking with the change of movement.

"Oh, yes." Bex plonks herself down on the side of one of the raised beds. "Everything she does is for attention. Or to annoy me. That's how it feels somedays."

"Have you thought that maybe she's lonely? I doubt she wants her only companion to be someone in her thirties. In fact, I doubt she wants to have just one companion."

Bex sighs. "Possibly not. But you can't take away the fact that she's horrid to me."

"I hate to say this, but there's times you're horrid to her too."

Bex shoots Holly a look. "You're supposed to be my friend!"

"I am your friend." Holly sits down next to Bex and takes her hand in hers. "Look, I'm not used to having friends, and maybe I'm getting this all wrong, but I know I wouldn't want you to agree with everything I say and do, just because we're friends. I'd want you to be honest with me. And I'm being honest with you."

Bex rests her head on Holly's shoulder. They sit quietly together for a few minutes, and Holly hears Bex sniffle.

"Are you crying?" Holly asks, laying her head on top of Bex's.

Bex rubs her sleeve over her cheeks. "Uh-huh."

"I'm sorry. I didn't want to upset you."

"It's not you who's upsetting me. Everything you say is right. I am horrid to Mum, just as much as she's horrid to me. I don't like who I've become; that I resent her. I sometimes even wish she wasn't here. That sounds awful – I don't mean I want her dead. I mean that I want to be here, at Pinewoods, on my own, to be able to spend more time with you and San. Do you know, sometimes even her breathing makes me want to scream?"

Holly nods sympathetically. "Like San said, you two need some space from each other. Have you sent that message to your brothers?"

Bex shakes her head. She pulls a tissue out of her pocket and blows her nose. "I keep meaning to, but I know they'll ignore it, so what's the point?"

"You know, my counsellor once told me to talk to my parents even though they weren't in the room. Out loud. He said my brain wouldn't know the difference between them being there or not, that the important part is me telling them how I feel."

"Did you do it?"

"I'm ashamed to say that I'm telling you to do something I never bothered to do myself. But he said it's a really good way to release negative energy. Maybe it's worth you giving it a try."

"Mum, you do my head in!" Bex turns to Holly. "Like that?"

Holly resists the urge to laugh. "I don't know. Maybe a bit more specific?"

"OK, I'll give it a go, even though it feels daft." She pushes herself up from the raised bed. "Let me know if she comes anywhere near the greenhouse." Bex goes to the far end of the greenhouse, and turns to face the tomatoes. Holly watches her mouth move, and hopes that all those negative feelings don't have a bad effect on the plants.

* * *

By the time Wednesday comes around, Holly's second week at Pinewoods falls into a relaxed routine. Breakfast is with Dee in the kitchen, early on, before most of the guests have stirred. She loves her time alone with Dee, talking about their plans for their days ahead: Holly in the garden, Dee cooking up the day's delights. When it comes to midday, Holly takes lunch in the garden, sometimes with San, once with Lorraine, and today Ruth and Bex joined her for a salad and sourdough.

The work on the kitchen garden is more manageable now, particularly as San, Bex and Ruth have become regulars alongside Holly. Ruth, in particular, happily potters about in the greenhouse.

She's made herself a little area where she pots seedlings for Holly, who then places the trays and pots in the cold frame.

"You're quiet this morning, Holly," Ruth says, passing her a tray of seedlings she's just thinned out.

"Mmm. Got something going around my head."

"A problem shared is a problem halved, as they say."

Holly smiles at Ruth. Something about her reminds Holly of Nan again, and it's not just the white hair and wrinkles.

"I'm worried about that journalist."

"Conor? Why would you worry about him?"

Holly laughs. "No, not him. He's lovely. No, the other guy. Dylan."

"Oooh, I didn't like him, not one bit. Tried to be all charming with me, thought his winks and smiles worked on me, but I saw straight through him, I did. No, not a nice man. Glad he's gone home. Sent shivers down my spine." Ruth shook herself.

Holly's not sure Ruth did see right through Dylan, having seen her nattering to him on more than one occasion, but she welcomes the sisterhood from her friend.

"You're right, Ruth. He's not a nice man. He's threatening to write a story about me for his magazine. Been on at me since our first night here."

"A story about you, love? No offence, but why would he be interested in you?" Holly is relieved that Ruth doesn't wait for an answer. "Anyway, I wouldn't stand for it. I find a strongly worded email does just the job."

"I was thinking that, but it won't change anything. Besides, he's not actually done anything yet." Holly walks out of the greenhouse with a tray of seedlings in her hands and places it in the cold frame.

"Maybe it won't change anything," Ruth calls through the glass. "But the important thing is, you'll feel much better for making your feelings known. Write to the editor of his magazine, and let him know what his horrible weasel of an employee was doing whilst he was staying here."

"Hmmm, maybe. I'll think about it. For now though, Ruth, it's time for you to have a sit down, and I need to get myself ready for personal training."

"You go on ahead, love. I'll finish up here. I'll be OK for a little bit yet."

"Are you sure?" Holly looks around and sees Bex is on the other side of the garden, sitting on the edge of a raised bed. Her phone is planted firmly to her ear. She's twirling her hair, and smiling. A lot. She must be talking to Conor. Holly grins at the exact moment that Bex looks over and catches her eye. Bex waves and grins back.

"Never been more sure." Ruth says, puffing her chest out. "I can look after myself, thank you, love. It's good to have something to do, to get dirt under my fingernails again. Now, run along."

Holly returns to the house, taking one last look to check on Ruth, and knows she's left the planting on and thinning out in the right hands.

* * *

As she changes into her gym gear, Holly knows she's too tired for personal training. Her legs and back ache, but she wants to spend time with Hunter. She hasn't seen him, except from a distance, since they rescued the storm damage. He cancelled Monday's session on her, without any explanation, and then San told her that he suggested she could join them today, without even asking Holly. Thankfully, San already has plans, but it feels very strange. What's going on? Is he avoiding her? Getting changed into her gym clothes, Holly notices a mix of excitement and nerves at seeing him again.

When Holly steps out on to the front porch, Hunter's chatting to a group of women at one of the cafe tables. Surely he's not planning to ask this whole group to join them today as well, is he? As she walks over to him, she thankfully hears Hunter say his goodbyes to the women.

"Afternoon. Come on then," he says abruptly, and without looking at Holly he turns on his heels.

"Afternoon," Holly replies to the empty air around her. She follows Hunter, and feels a fluttering of eyes track her.

"Right. Log hops and woodland weights today," Hunter says, directing Holly along a path through the pine trees. "Helps your core strength. Allows your body to function properly." Hunter's tone is business-like, like the first day she met him. "Strong core, strong body. Laid out some logs in a clearing in the woods."

They walk on in silence for a few minutes, Holly wondering about the change in Hunter. It's like they don't even know each other. Every now and again, Holly glances sidelong at him, in the hope he will look at her and smile, but his eyes remain fixed on the path ahead.

Eventually, Hunter stops abruptly in front of four logs, varying in size and distance apart. What torture has he got planned today?

"Where did you get these?" Holly laughs, nervously.

Hunter stares at the logs, his hands resting on his hips. "Neighbour of mine. Works for Woodland Trust. Tree surgeon," he says. He puts his foot on to the largest log. "Right!" His tone is full-on sergeant major. "Warm up. Run, on the spot. Five minutes."

"I think I'm warm enough, thanks. I've just marched for five minutes to keep up with you getting here." Holly smiles at Hunter, hopeful she can coax him back into their flirtatious ways. She knows she didn't imagine that spark between them – surely he felt it too.

Hunter walks up to Holly, puts his nose close to hers and stares right into her eyes. She blinks, surprised at the lack of his usual warmth towards her.

"Did I ask what you think? On the spot, now. No more excuses." She swallows hard, aware of the spark of tension that flashes between them.

"Really?" She struggles to hold the intensity of his gaze.

"Now is not the time to stand up for yourself. When I say run on the spot, what do you do?"

"I tell you that I'm already warmed up and I don't want to do it." The corner of her mouth twitches upwards. She dares to be gutsy with Hunter in a way that she has never been with anyone before. With Hunter, she can stand her ground. Push him. She feels a pulse of . . . what? A pulse of desire. And she likes it.

"Run on the spot. Now. Six minutes." Hunter takes two steps back.

"You said five!"

"That was before you argued back. You'll get seven minutes if you don't move. Now!" Hunter looks at his watch.

Holly rolls her eyes and runs on the spot.

The six minutes drag, but she says nothing. She watches Hunter move logs around the clearing, creating a ladder shape, two long branches placed alongside. At the end of the allotted time, he barks orders for her to jump side to side over a narrow log. Reluctant to have time added to the task, Holly does as she's told and delivers twenty side jumps. The first ten are relatively easy; the next five are exhausting; and by the last five Holly's legs scream at her to stop. She pauses between each of the final jumps to build herself up for the next one.

"Get a move on, Holly, or you'll do another five."

"Leave me alone. I'm doing it, aren't I?" Holly purses her lips. What a pain Hunter is being. Well, if he's going to be mean to her, then he can darn well see how mean she can be when she's pissed off. "Seventeen. Eighteen." Holly jumps sideways over the log, one leg lagging behind the other. "Nineteen." She glares at Hunter and almost trips over the log with her trailing leg. "Twenty." She flops to the ground. "I'm dying."

"You've only just started. Two minutes rest, then on your feet and follow me." Hunter strides off to the side of the clearing and picks up a long, thick branch, about the size of a weightlifting bar. He holds the branch in front of himself and twists from his waist, back and forth. "Time's up," he snaps, glancing at his watch. "On your feet."

Holly hauls herself up. "You're being particularly mean today," she mutters under her breath.

"Yeah, yeah, heard it all before." Did his mouth just twitch into the start of a smile? "Rest this branch over your shoulders and hold on to it with both hands. Ladder workout." He carefully places the branch across Holly's shoulders, pausing for a moment. She feels his breath on her neck, the warmth of his hands resting on the branch next to hers. "In three, two, one . . . go." His voice is thick and gravelly.

Holly steps one by one over each of the branches laid out like a ladder on the ground. She predicts the military-style orders she'll be given, and picks up her pace, not giving Hunter the chance to shout at her. Turning, she makes the return journey back along the ladder, and repeats the exercise.

"Back over here," Hunter yells when she's done. "Bunny hops!" He marches back over to the four larger logs. "Five reps, starting now!"

Holly drops the branch to the ground and starts on the bunny hops. Hunter picks up a large log and lifts it above his head, lowering it down to his shoulders, back up into the air and out in front of him, all in one smooth motion, repeating it as Holly hops over the logs. On her fourth bunny hop repetition, her tired legs trail behind her. Her left foot hits the largest, and last, of the logs as she jumps over it. Knocked off balance, she's sent flying and lands in the sand on her hands and knees.

Hunter immediately throws his makeshift weight on to the ground and strides over to Holly. He holds out a hand to her, and pulls her back to her feet with such force that Holly falls into his chest. She looks up at him.

Holly holds her breath. Their hands are clasped, their eyes locked. Neither one of them moves. Then, Hunter's face moves closer to hers. His warm lips almost touch hers, and she parts her lips in response. As his top lip gently grazes hers, a spark passes between them.

Suddenly, Hunter blinks. He drops her hand, steps back and clears his throat.

"Two more reps," he says, his voice thick.

What just happened?

Holly turns her back to Hunter and takes in a slow, deep breath. She touches her mouth where his lip stroked hers.

"Two more reps," Hunter says again, quietly this time.

Holly shakes her head, arms and legs, like athletes do as they line up for a race. "Two more reps," she repeats, her voice husky, unfamiliar. She jumps over the log that tripped her up. *What happened?* She jumps over the next log. *Did he mean to kiss me?* And the next. She looks at Hunter. His eyes are fixed on her. She leaps over the last two logs.

"Last rep," Hunter says, kicking a pine cone into the nearby shrubs. His eyes follow it as it rolls to a stop.

At the end of the session they walk back to Pinewoods in silence, Hunter slowing his pace to match Holly's. Every now and again his arm brushes against her. There it is again – that spark that passed between them in the moment of the nearly-kiss. She risks a side glance at Hunter. His jaw tightens and he rubs a crooked finger under his nose – back and forth, back and forth. He looks the other way.

"Come on, you need an Epsom salts bath within fifteen minutes of finishing exercise. We need to get back to Pinewoods." With that, Hunter picks up his pace to a jog, and Holly matches his stride.

* * *

San and Bex are sitting on Holly's bed as she dries her hair.

"Oh my god, Holly!" Bex says, with a little squeal. "Are you serious? That is hellishly sexy."

"Yeah, but we didn't *actually* kiss – it was a nearly-kiss."

"Lovey, you've a lot to learn," San says, laughing. "There is no way you can be mistaken about that kind of close contact. I reckon he meant to kiss you."

"I don't know that he did. He's been acting odd since Sunday. I mean, he cancelled Monday's training session, and then it's been like he's avoiding me – leaving the kitchen when I walk in, that kind of stuff. And then he invited you to join me on today's training session, San."

"Seems to me like it was handy I already had plans." San laughs again.

"But why's he acting so strange around me?"

"Awwww," Bex says, placing her hand on her heart. "Hunter's got a crush on Holly. That's why he's acting all weird around you." She pouts at Holly.

"Did you want him to kiss you?" San pulls her legs up on to the bed and crosses them in front of her.

Holly looks dreamily into the mirror. Her cheeks burn as she recalls the moment of the nearly-kiss, and she gently touches the curve of her top lip. The butterflies in her stomach rise up and flutter, and she feels something else, too. Desire. Longing. "Yes," she says, breathily, and groans.

Bex squeals again. "I knew it! Oh Holly, how exciting. This is the best holiday of my life. Ever." She claps her hands with delight and San laughs.

"Bex, you are adorable. Ever the romantic. And what about you and Conor, too?" San gets up, takes the hairdryer and brush from Holly and takes over the blow-dry. "Have you been in touch with him yet?"

Bex lies on her front on Holly's bed, kicking up her legs, the way that Rose used to. "Might have." Bex grins, her cheeks glowing. "But this isn't about me. Go on, Holly, spill the beans. What else happened?" Bex rolls on to her side, her arm propping up her head.

"That's it. There's no more beans to spill."

"So what'll you do when you see him again?"

"Run away and hide?"

"You can't do that," San says, teasing Holly's hair into soft curls. "You need a strategy."

"That *is* my strategy." Holly laughs. "No, that's what old me would have done, before I came to Pinewoods and met you two. I need to do something different."

"Go on then, what would new you do?" San asks.

Holly pauses to think for a moment. "If I can muster the courage," she hesitates, "I think I need to be cool and collected around him. I'll have to act like I'm . . . I don't know, sure of myself. Confident. Not convinced I'll be able to do that, though. I'll probably be a nervous wreck when I see him again!"

Journal entry
Wednesday 23rd June

HOW I FEEL: 6/10. If Hunter had actually kissed me,
it would be 10/10

SLEEP: Seven hours. All this gardening and fresh air is
helping me sleep

WEATHER: Dry and hot, not a wisp of wind

WEARING: Shorts and pale blue blouse with the tiny flowers
on it

PROMPT: If I could change one thing in my life right now,
what would that be?

Hunter.

Oh. My. Goodness. He nearly kissed me. He very nearly
kissed me. I could feel his breath on my lips. The heat of
his body against me. It was . . . electric. It's all I can think
about. I feel . . . what do I feel? Awake. Alive. Excited.

But, he didn't actually kiss me, did he? He came to his
senses before he actually did it. He clearly remembered who
I am. Saw the great, big, ugly scar down my cheek.

If I could change one thing right now, it would be that Hunter did actually kiss me.

I wrote that email to Dylan's editor like Ruth said I should. Ruth's right, I do feel better for writing it. But I'm not sure if I'll actually send it.

22

WATER BUTTS, NOTEBOOKS & GANGS

HUNTER is at the back of the garden, leaning against the shed, when Holly walks out of the back door.

"Hello." She feels a surge of nerves and doesn't know where to look.

"Dee said you need a hand." He coughs.

Holly raises an eyebrow. He's already been helping in the garden. He knows there's loads to do.

"Is that OK? I'd like to help. Again. I can spare an hour." He rubs his thumb back and forth over his top lip, like he's recalling the moment of the nearly-kiss.

Holly nods and steps into the shed, hoping he doesn't notice how nervous she suddenly feels around him. Why is she embarrassed? It wasn't her who nearly kissed him. He's the one who made a move.

"You OK in there?"

"What?" Holly turns too fast and knocks a rake off its perch. Hunter's head is poking into the shed. He sticks out a hand and catches the handle of the rake. "Yes, I'm OK. Just working out what jobs we need to do." She gives her head a little shake, picks up the watering can and a trowel, and walks back out into the bright sun. "Here, take this. Everything needs watering before the heat of the sun gets too much." Holly holds the watering can out to Hunter, still not meeting his gaze.

"Can we not use a hose?"

"No. I'd really rather you didn't, please."

Hunter nods. "You're the boss. I'll fill up the watering can then." He walks down the path towards the back of the house.

"Don't use the tap. Use the run-off from the water butts until they're empty. There's two. The one by the greenhouse has the least in it, so start with that one first." Hunter gives Holly a salute. "I need you to start on the peas and beans in this row, here," Holly shouts after him, and he gives her a thumbs up. "Each raised bed will need at least three watering cans full." Another thumbs up. "And don't waste the water. Keep the nozzle close to the soil."

As Hunter gets stuck into his task, Holly inspects the garden for what needs harvesting. She meanders around, and pinches out the tops of some plants to encourage bushier growth. Her next task is to plant out seedlings into the cold frames. Propping the lids open with a cane, she feels the soil. Warm and slightly damp – perfect.

"What next?" Hunter is leaning against the frame of the greenhouse, watching her.

"Have you watered the tomato plants in the greenhouse? And whilst you're there, fetch the seedlings that are on the shelf on your left. You'll see they're all ready for planting on." Hunter does as she asks, and returns with one tray precariously balanced on his forearm, holding another two in his hands. "Please don't drop those. They're for harvesting in the autumn."

Hunter looks directly at her. "Who's going to do that then?"

Holly takes the trays, one by one, and lays them on the ground. She sighs. "Good question. Not me, sadly. I won't be here." She smiles at Hunter, in the hope he will smile back. "You?"

Hunter lets out a short laugh. "I don't know the first thing about gardening. I only know what you've told me."

"You better make sure you remember it all then, because there's nobody else to do it."

"Hunter," he says, tapping the side of his head, "remember to water plants using the run-off in the water butts. I reckon I can remember that." He smiles at her and the butterflies in Holly's stomach rise as one with elation.

"Go and get a notepad and pen from Dee," Holly says, calming herself. "I can at least tell you things that you can pass on to whoever will be doing the garden after I've gone."

"Don't you trust my memory?" Hunter says, a glint in his eye.

"No, I don't, actually." She smiles back at him. "Dee said that Simas told her things she had to do before he left, but she couldn't remember it all. We need to start keeping a journal of what's planted where, and when everything needs to be harvested." As Hunter wanders off to get a notebook and pen from Dee, Holly feels a wave of sadness lap over her. She can't imagine not being here, in the garden. *Pull yourself together, Holly. You knew you were only doing this to help out.*

When Hunter returns, she explains how to plant the seedlings out, what is in each row and how many weeks they need to be in the cold frame before being moved on to the raised beds.

"Why don't we plant straight into the raised beds?"

"If we get any heavy rain it will flatten these seedlings. They're not strong enough to survive a downpour yet. And you know how the weather can change in July and August. If we get some bad weather, we can put the lid down, and prop it open a bit to allow the air to circulate. Like this." Holly gets a small block of wood and places it between the lid and the cold frame, leaving an opening of about two inches.

"OK, got it." He scribbles something down in the notebook. "I hope the new gardener knows all this stuff."

"They will. Someone just needs an idea of what we're growing and what jobs are next. You need to water these, by the way, but turn the rose on the watering can so that it's facing upwards, and hold it higher so that you don't flatten the seedlings with water. You're creating a light shower, not a downpour."

Hunter does as he's told and Holly moves on to the next cold frame, filling it with more seedlings. She continues to instruct Hunter as she goes, and he dutifully jots down notes.

When they move on to hoeing, Holly explains how to keep weeds at bay. Hunter copies her on the other side of the raised bed.

"Careful, be gentle. Plants are tender little things. Do it more like this." Hunter watches and copies, and Holly smiles to herself. He's a quick learner. If the garden did need to be left in his hands, at least it won't get back into the state she found it in.

"Never thought I'd find myself in a garden." Hunter laughs to himself.

"No?"

"Gardening's for wusses." He shrugs. "I know it's not, by the way. That's just how I used to think. But it's good for the soul, isn't it? Getting close to nature, and all that."

Holly nods, and watches him. "Hunter, do you mind if I ask you something?"

He rests his hands on top of the hoe. "Depends." His face gives nothing away.

"No, it's OK, never mind." Holly hesitates. There's something she remembers Hunter saying the first time she met him that she wants to ask him about, but looking at him now, she regrets saying anything.

"Go on."

"It's just – I mean, you said . . . your panic attacks."

Hunter bends and pulls a few weeds out of the soil. "I don't get them now. Not often, anyway."

"But when you did . . . what started them?"

He tosses the weeds into a nearby bucket. "I don't talk about it. Men like me, coming from my background, we don't get panic attacks. Don't own up to it, anyway."

"You mean your army background?" Holly lifts her foot and rests it on the edge of the raised bed. Hunter walks around to where she's standing and bends down to pick up a pile of weeds by her foot. He throws them into the bucket.

"No, not that. You get close to your mates in the army. Know pretty much everything about each other." He sits down on the raised bed behind him, his back to the house. Holly sits next to him. "No, back when I was a teenager. I was a bit wild, I guess. Got mixed up in all kinds of stuff. Bad stuff. Gangs and whatnot."

"Whatnot?" Holly stifles a laugh. 'Whatnot' is not a word she expects to hear from Hunter, and definitely not alongside the word 'gangs'.

"I was trouble, Holly. Like I said, did stuff I'm not proud of." Hunter pulls at a weed poking out from the side of the raised bed by his feet. "Gangs target lost kids. Give them somewhere to belong. The gang I was in kind of became my family. Wasn't an easy life. I knew it wasn't right, the kind of stuff I got caught up in." He laughs flatly. "It was even more obvious when I was up in front of the judge. Lucky that he gave me a chance – he offered me the choice between youth detention or the army."

"You chose the army."

"You're quick." He smiles at Holly and nudges his shoulder up against hers.

"What does all this have to do with your panic attacks, though?"

Hunter pauses for a moment. "We were on a job. Taking stuff out of a warehouse that had no security, or so we were told. They must have had CCTV, I guess. Me and a few of the other lads were picked up by the bizzies. I went into a bit of a meltdown when I was in the cell. My first panic attack. Had a few after that. Not many. But they came on proper after I left the army. Bonfire Night's the worst, even now. Anyway." He pushes himself back up to standing in one smooth move, and picks up the bucket. "That's it. I'll put this lot on the compost heap, then."

Holly watches as Hunter zigzags off down the paths to the far corner of the garden. She didn't expect him to open up like that, and feels touched that he shared something so personal. He comes across like he's got his life together, like he's all confidence, but he's not so different from her, after all. There's something about knowing that he is vulnerable too, just like her, that makes Holly even more attracted to him. Right now, she'd love to run after him along the garden path and hug him. Damn it. He's so gorgeous. What she wouldn't give to be in his arms right now. She watches as he empties the bucket on to the compost heap and turns back to face her. He starts to smile, but in a split second, his whole demeanour changes.

There's a crunch on the gravel behind her. "All right, Holly."

It's Dylan.

Holly bites down on her bottom lip. *Not him, please not him.* She pushes herself up from the raised bed, turns around and finds herself inches away from the one person she least wants to see at Pinewoods.

"What's going on here, then?" His grin is unnerving.

"Gardening. And what are you doing here, Dylan?" She doesn't even attempt to hide the contempt from her voice.

"Oh, you know. Had a few loose ends to tie up for my article." Dylan lifts his notebook up and taps it with his knuckles. "Checked out some facts. Took a few pictures. You know the kind of stuff." He grins at her, a broad, frog-like grin that sends ice-like shivers down Holly's spine. "It's going to be a good'un, this article of mine."

After a few moments of silence, Dylan continues. "Right, I'll be off then. This story won't file itself." He taps his knuckles against his notebook again. "Good to see you again, Holly." Dylan winks and walks off around the side of the house.

Holly is fixed to the spot, watching him go. His appearance has unsettled her and she jumps when she feels the warmth of Hunter's body next to hers.

"What was that about?" Hunter asks.

Holly rubs the bridge of her nose in an attempt to calm herself. "He . . . nothing. Forget it. Let's get on."

"You're on your own, I'm afraid. My hour's up. Got a bootcamp group to train in five." He doesn't look at her as he marches off in the same direction as Dylan, his arms swinging back and forth by his side, like he's on parade.

JOURNAL ENTRY
Thursday 24th June

HOW I FEEL: 6/10

SLEEP: Six hours, and it felt like proper sleep too

WEATHER: Bit of a grey day, but warm and muggy

WEARING: Denim shorts, white T-shirt, nothing on my feet

PROMPT: What is a promise I want to keep?

What was Dylan doing coming back? I know I stood up to him, but it completely threw me to find him standing there behind me. Thought I'd seen the last of him. He gives me the creeps. I know I shouldn't let him get to me, but he really does make me feel uncomfortable. He's probably one of those people that just picks himself up after a knock and dusts himself off, always smelling of roses, as Nan would say. And meanwhile, I'm left worrying what he'll write about me in his article.

Hunter was so calm to be around today. Which is odd after how he's been this week. I mean, he ghosted me, in a way. Then yesterday, we nearly kissed, for goodness' sake. Oh, that nearly-kiss. It was so ... romantic. Then he went cold on me.

And now, today, he's been really nice again. It's lovely that he shared some stuff with me from his past, but really? It's like he runs hot and cold. One minute we're getting really close, and then the next, he's all formal and distant with me.

I'm falling for him. I know I am. But the feeling can't be mutual. If it was, he'd surely not change like the wind on me.

OK, enough about men. Promises I want to keep:

· I promise I'll do my best to keep in touch with San and Bex, when we all go home.

· I promise to try and let go of controlling every inch of my life.

· I promise to find something that gives me purpose.

23

HAND-HOLDING & TOE-TICKLING

HOLLY and Bex have claimed the best table in the Pinewoods front garden cafe, the one that gets the best of the morning sunshine. They made sure to arrive early, knowing it would soon get busy, being a Saturday.

"Can you believe we've only known each other for a couple of weeks?" Bex says. They are waiting for San to join them for coffee and cake, before she catches her train back into Liverpool. "I can't remember a time when I've made friends so quickly. Ever."

"In recent years, I can't remember a time when I've made friends," Holly replies, laughing.

"We're the misfits together," Bex says, gently squeezing Holly's hand. "Forever friends. Mum's so confused." She laughs. "On the one hand, she really likes you and San, but she's also moaning that I've less time for her."

"You're putting yourself first, and that's a good thing. You deserve time away from her. And I don't expect Ruth truly wants you to give up your life for her, you know."

"Morning." Jess smiles at a man with a large bullmastiff

settling himself at the next table as she approaches Bex and Holly, two coffees in her hands.

"Hello, love," the man says. "I'll have a strong, milky tea with two sugars, and—"

"I'll be with you in a moment, sir," Jess responds in a cheery voice, walking past his table and ignoring the loud *harrumph* escaping his mouth. "There you go," she says, placing the drinks in front of Holly and Bex. "Two oat-milk lattes, ladies. And San asked me to tell you she'll be out shortly. She's settling her bill with Lorraine."

Holly and Bex smile their thanks as Jess turns to the man at the next table. He's staring at Holly's face, and she feels a chill run down her spine.

"Now, sir," Jess says. "How can I help you?"

He coughs and turns his attention to her. "Strong, milky tea, two sugars, and I'll have one of them posh BLT bacon sarny things you've got, but you can hold the bloody L and T." He snatches a glance back at Holly, patting his dog's head.

"Absolutely. We're a vegan cafe, by the way. We don't do actual bacon. It's tofu BLT."

"What do you mean, you don't do bacon?" He laughs, picks up the menu and jabs at it. "Look! It says here you do a BLT. That's bacon, lettuce and tomato. I'll have one of them, but like I said, hold the bloody lettuce and tomato."

"It says here," Jess points at the menu, "tofu BLT. We don't do bacon."

The man isn't listening. "How can it be a BLT if it's got no bacon in it? The clue's in the name, girl!"

"I understand, sir, but it does say—"

"Oh, forget it." The man stands to leave, mumbling abuse. His chair falls backwards and the dog scrambles to his feet as his master tugs his lead. "Come on, Barney."

"Are you OK?" Holly asks Jess. She encountered so many customers like him over her years at OO-TO Travel. Ones who got angry with her because their card was declined for the final payment on their holiday, as if it's her fault, insisting she try again; or the abusive customers who were not impressed that the cruise to New York sets sail the week after their anniversary – they want it to leave the week of their anniversary.

"Oh yes, I'm fine. That's a regular conversation, unfortunately, particularly in the summer months when we get out-of-town visitors; people staying at the caravan park. There's always someone who doesn't read the menu before ordering, and doesn't notice that we're a vegan cafe." She shrugs and smiles, before moving to the next table to take their order.

"I wish I had Jess's confidence," Holly says to Bex.

"Or San's. What I'd give to be like her," Bex replies.

"Hello, you two!" San says, right on cue. "I can't believe I'm going home and leaving you both here. I'm going to miss you." There's cries of "me too!" in unison from Holly and Bex as she sits down at the table.

"This has been the best two weeks I've had in ages," Bex says.

"It won't be the same without you," Holly adds.

"I wish I could stay but my annual leave's up. No more holidays. And my editor's chomping at the bit for my piece about

Pinewoods. I can't come up with any more excuses to be able to stay with my two new besties." San grabs hold of Holly and Bex's hands. "Honestly, you two, you've been lifesavers for me."

"Stop, you'll have me crying at this rate," Bex says, using her free hand to fan herself in a weak attempt to stop the flow of tears.

"It's been perfect, spending time with you both. I'll feel very lonely when I get back home and won't have you to natter with."

"We'll have to meet up in town sometime soon," Bex says.

San nods. "And promise me, any more action from Hunter-the-nearly-kisser, and you'll message me straight away. Do you understand, Holly?"

Holly does a mock salute. "Aye, aye, captain. Though I doubt there's going to be any new developments. It was quite obviously a mistake on his part that he's not going to repeat."

"I doubt that," San says, one eyebrow raised. "I want a blow-by-blow account of anything that goes on here at Pinewoods Retreat once I've got on that train. Bex, I'm relying on you to tell me everything. Plus, I want an update on you and Conor, too."

Loud chatter takes over the garden cafe. Three women in gym gear walk through the gate and choose a table on the other side of the garden. They talk with the unabashed confidence of people expecting to be heard.

"Another great session with Hunky Hunter," one of the women says, as they take their seats.

"He's the only reason I exercise," another says. "Who'd bother if you didn't have him to look at as you train?"

"Did you see the way he looked at me? He is so coming on to me."

Holly lowers her head. Of course he wouldn't be interested in her when he can have any woman he wants. She's a fool for ever hoping that he was.

"Would you . . . you know?"

"Would I?" The woman guffaws. "I'm ready and waiting." She pulls her T-shirt down to show off her ample cleavage, and her friends squeal with laughter.

"Christ, have you seen the woman with the scar who fawns all over him?"

At this, Holly's stomach plumets. Her cheeks burn red as San grabs hold of her arm and gives it a gentle squeeze. "Ignore them, lovey," she says, her voice quietly icy. "They're bored housewives who need something to gossip about, that's all."

At the other end of the garden there are more shrieks of laughter. Holly missed what was said, but as she looks at the woman who was talking, she sees her eyes settle on her. Holly can't breathe. For a moment, the woman freezes.

"Ignore her." Bex rests her hand on Holly's arm.

The woman turns back to her friends and says something quietly to them. They all look across at Holly and smirk.

"Don't lose yourself in what others think of you," San says. "You'll miss the small things in life that you could be enjoying."

Suddenly, the women let out a squeal, and shout out "Coo-ee!" as one voice.

"This'll be interesting," Bex says, nodding over towards the garden gate. "Hunter's arrived."

Holly watches as he walks over to the women and rests his hands on his hips.

"How can I help you, lovely ladies?"

"Take a seat, join us," the ringleader says at a volume intended to be heard across the cafe.

Hunter's far quieter response is only just audible from the other side of the garden. "No, no. I'm fine, thanks."

"Any plans for the weekend, Hunter?"

"Working," he says, crossing his arms over his chest.

"Ohhh," one of them chimes in, "poor you. I could think of something much more exciting for you."

Hunter laughs. "A hazard of life. If I don't work, I don't earn."

The ringleader stands up and rests her hands on Hunter's arms. "Well, if you need a break from your clients, you know where I am," she says in a baby voice.

"God, get a room," San mumbles next to Holly.

"So, Hunter," another of the women says, "what do you know about the girl with scar? How did she get it?"

Hunter shrugs, and stuffs his hands into his pockets. Holly's sure she sees his shoulders tense up. "Nothing."

"Come on now," another woman continues. "You must know something."

Holly stands up. Before she can stop herself, she strides over to the women.

"I'll tell you what happened." Her heart thuds in her chest. "I got this scar when I fought off a guy with a knife who attacked a colleague. Now you know." Silence descends over the garden

267

cafe, all eyes on Holly. She glances at Hunter. He's staring at her. Feeling her knees weaken, she turns and strides, less confidently, back to the table where San and Bex are sitting.

"Wow!" Bex hugs Holly as she sits back down.

"Proud of you." San holds a hand up to high five Holly. "Don't leave me hanging, Holly." With a mix of adrenaline and embarrassment coursing through her veins, Holly slaps her shaking hand against San's. Did she really just do that? She lets out a belated giggle, and realises that she feels a little bit proud of herself.

"Morning." Hunter is standing near their table. He looks straight at Holly and nods at her, giving her that twitch of a half-smile he does, before turning to San. "I've come to say goodbye, San," he says. "Hope our paths cross again. Given me a little faith back in journalists, you have. And I'll not forget your quick wit on the dune runs." He laughs. "Now, promise me you'll keep at it? The exercise, that is, not the wit."

San grins. "Thankfully, there's no dunes around the Albert Dock, so I'll never need to run up another one in this lifetime," she laughs. "But yes, you've got me over the pain point, and I promise I'll keep working on my fitness. Thank you."

"Great." Hunter puts out a hand for a handshake, but San stands up and goes in for a hug.

Hunter turns to Holly again. "Morning," he repeats, his voice soft.

"Hi," Holly says, breathily. She picks up the spoon nestling on the saucer and stirs her half-drunk coffee.

"Right – er – well." Hunter shifts from foot to foot. "Bye, San." He gives Holly a weak smile and walks off. Holly watches as he leaves through the garden gate. He waves at the flattering of females as he disappears from view, their eyes following him as he walks away.

"See you later, gorgeous," baby-voice calls after him. The women laugh loudly.

"Come on, you two," San says, "drink up. Let's go for a last walk down the cinder path."

They wander out on to the path which, at this point, is straight as an arrow pointing down to the sea. For a length of about one hundred metres it is tree line, with the branches of the trees on either side holding hands over the top of the path. As the trees peter out, and the dunes gradually rise up alongside the path, San links arms with Bex on one side and Holly on the other.

"We need to talk," San says. "You both need to listen up."

"I'm listening," Bex says.

"Me too," says Holly.

"Bex, your brothers. Have you sent that email yet?"

Bex shrugs, but she looks embarrassed. "I've not had time."

"Yeah, you have. Nearly two weeks. Do it. I know you're making excuses in your head."

"Well," Bex stretches out her free arm. "You don't know my brothers like I do."

"I don't, but I know you give in to them to the point where you lose out. Send that email today and tell them they're picking up some of the load for looking after Ruth."

"You have to write to them, Bex," Holly agrees. "We can both see how being with your mum challenges you. It's time for you to have a break from her now and again, so that you can look after yourself. Then, when you're with Ruth, you won't be snapping at each other all of the time."

"Holly's right, Bex. Please, send that email." Then San turns to face Holly. "And you," she says, squeezing Holly's arm closer into her body. "Stop putting yourself down."

Holly wants to say that she doesn't put herself down, but she knows she does. Instead, she smiles weakly at San.

"You're a beautiful woman, Holly," San continues, "and a brave one. I'm so proud to be your friend. It upsets me that you put yourself down so readily. Look how you've helped me and Bex. Both of us are in a better place – because of you."

"Agreed," Bex says. "And Mum. You've worked miracles on her. And on the garden."

"Thank you," Holly says quietly. Inside she is beaming. It feels so good to be appreciated, particularly by her two friends.

"And you too, San," Bex says. "You're amazing. I love how you see through all the crap for us." She laughs.

"That's years of being a journalist. Believe me, I've seen and dealt with a lot of crap." San smiles, and then sighs.

Holly gives San's arm a little pull towards her. "You're beautiful, too. And funny. It's time for you to get back in charge of your life. So are you ready to sort out your own crap?" Holly asks.

"Hmm, I'm ready," San says. "But you know what? I'm going to need my two wonderful friends at times to keep me on the straight and narrow." San squeezes both their arms close into herself.

When they reach the beach, the tide is in. They take their shoes off, and let the gentle waves tickle their toes, making plans for meeting up soon.

Saturday 26th June

HOW I FEEL: 7/10

SLEEP: Another six hours

WEATHER: Big, fluffy, white clouds like the opening credits for The Simpsons, the kind that never seem to block the sun. Hot, like, properly hot, in a way that makes your skin prickle

WEARING: Shorts that I cut from an old pair of jeans (my new gardening shorts), mucky grey T-shirt, black pumps now covered in a sandy dust from doing the garden

PROMPT: What triggers my emotions - positive and negative?

For the prompt, Lorraine said to be careful not to write about the outcome of my emotions being triggered - for example, my panic attacks. I should focus on the things that cause my emotions to come about.

So, what triggers my positive emotions?

The garden. Being in a garden, and working on a garden - that definitely triggers positive emotions. There I feel alive, calm, happy, needed.

Being part of a community. I loved the community down the allotment – it was good to be doing something together that we all loved, and, of course, Nan and Grandad were loved by everyone. We've got a bit of a community going here in Pinewoods kitchen garden now, too.

When it comes to negative triggers, I know I get triggered by meanness. Like the flattering of females at the cafe this morning, like the girls at school, like Tasha at OO-TO Travel. That's a huge trigger for me. I feel so small – or at least I did, until today. Wow, I know I was shaking when I went over to those women and told them how I got my scar, but I really did stand up for myself.

I have another negative trigger that I'm fully aware of: not being in control of what's happening around me. It usually results in my body going into panic mode.

I remember, once, my counsellor told me about these three parts of our brains we have. I think it was a monkey or chimpanzee brain, and that's the reactive bit of me; my human brain, me, the person I am; and then there's a computer, or something – my memory banks. He told me that my human brain needs to programme the computer bit so that the monkey knows what to do. Is that my problem? Have I not programmed my computer brain?

Or maybe I have: I've programmed it with the same old story, that my life is filled with one bad thing after another, and that the appropriate response is to panic. I'm so focused on the bad stuff that has happened to me, that now whenever anything bad happens — and even sometimes when it doesn't? — I resort to panic mode.

Well, I've had enough of that. I need let go of what happened to me at OO-TO Travel, and all of the other bad stuff that has happened to me. What is it my counsellor says? "One incident doesn't define you". He's right. It's time to let go of the past and to start looking forward, to good things. Oh, here we go again. That's something he asks me at the start of every counselling session, too. "Tell me something good that's happened since we last saw each other." Looks like he was right again.

I'm going to add that to my journal from now on, to remind myself to think of good things. I won't let my life be defined by what happened in my past.

So, something good that happened today: I went on a lovely walk with Bex and San this morning. We paddled in the sea, and made plans for catch ups very soon. Plus we had a good chat. Bex has promised to write to her brothers. And they both said such lovely things about me.

Perhaps the best thing that's happened to me today is knowing that I'm ready to let go of the past.

24

AN OUT OF THE ORDINARY DAY

IT was an ordinary day, like any other ordinary day, when Holly's life changed again. It wasn't actually her day to work, but then she'd worked every Saturday since Christmas, what with one or other of her colleagues wanting to do a swap with her. This time it was Donna. Holly didn't mind. Not too much. It wasn't like she ever really had plans for her days off.

That morning, Holly set about gathering the dirty mugs from everyone's desks. Her own desk was neat, tidy and clean, as she left it before she finished work every day. She knew she deserved the Employee of the Month award for being the tidiest member of staff, but that never seemed to be a criterion for getting the award.

By the time the rest of the staff arrived, the mugs were washed, kettle on, and Holly was busy changing the signs in the window that advertised the holiday deals of the day. She couldn't leave that job for Cat to do – she always managed to get finger marks over the Perspex, and creased the sheets of paper as she put them in place.

The day started off slowly, as it often did. With people booking holidays online, it wasn't nearly as busy as when Holly first started work at OO-TO Travel, almost fifteen years before. The phone broke the silence, simultaneously ringing on everyone's desk until someone chose to take the call.

"Out Of the Ordinary Travel, how may I help you?" Cat's sing-song voice rang out like she was rehearsing for *The X Factor*. Holly stepped back from the window to admire her work. Time to sort out the post.

Joel wheeled his swivel chair over to Tasha's desk, using his heels to pull himself along. "Got any paracetamol, boss? My head's cracking."

Tasha laughed. "You should have drunk a pint of water before bed, you daft sod. Better still, you should have stopped drinking well before you got on to those shots. How many did you have?"

"Ugh, don't remind me. Too many."

"No kidding. I can smell your morning-after-the-night-before breath a mile off."

"You weren't exactly a saint, boss. Hey, Hols, you got any of those mints you keep in your drawer?" *Holly*, she felt like saying. *My name is Holly.* And could he never say please?

She opened her drawer and picked up the tin of mints, neatly positioned between the pack of tissues and the glasses cleaner. She held the tin up for Joel to take from her, right at the moment that he launched his chair back to his own desk, expectantly. Holly sighed and walked over to his desk. Joel accepted the tin, opened the lid and took a handful of mints out.

"One for now," he grinned, popping a mint into his mouth and passing the tin back to Holly. "And one for every customer that comes in, just in case." Joel lined the mints up on the top of his keyboard. "You missed a corker of a night out last night, Hols."

"Don't be daft, Joel," Cat said, putting the phone back in its cradle. "Our Hols was tucked up in bed well before we even got to the bar. Weren't you, Hols?" Holly's cheeks burned, and she was relieved that the door of OO-TO Travel opened and a couple walked in.

Tasha switched personality in a heartbeat and presented her best saleswoman-self to the customers. "Hello, Mr and Mrs Thomas. Here to pay our balance, are we? Come on in. How exciting, not long to go now! You'll soon be jetting off to the sun." Tasha's smile didn't make it to her eyes as she motioned to the couple to take the seats in front of her desk.

A few more customers floated in, some to browse the brochures, others to pick up tickets or pay their balance. After half an hour or so, the shop went quiet again.

"Your turn to make the drinks, sweetie," Tasha said to Holly.

Obediently obliging, she walked from desk to desk, matching drinks to people. Coffee, three sugars for Tony, his bald patch frowning at her as he focused on crucial phone-scrolling. "Just-show-it-the-teabag", black, no sugar for Jane, who grunted and peered around Holly who was standing in the way of a good gossip with Tasha. Builder's tea for Joel . . .

The door flung open, wobbling on its hinges from the force.

"Good morning," Holly said, still holding the tray with the last three drinks on it. She smiled at the tall, broad man filling the doorway. His face was red with anger as he looked straight through her at Cat.

"My vinyl," he shouted at Cat, the muscles in his face twitching as he stood for a moment, fixed to the spot. The shop fell silent. "You smashed up my whole vinyl collection when you left me. My fucking vinyl, for Christ's sake!"

The blood drained from Cat's face. She stood up, her chair swivelling like a playground roundabout.

"Not here," Cat snapped back at him.

Holly spotted a knife glinting in the man's hand and swallowed a gasp. He stomped straight towards Cat, lifting the knife in front of him, pointing it at her. "Yes here, bitch." Spit flew from his mouth. He raised his arm and moved as if to thrust it towards Cat. Without thinking, Holly threw the tray at the man, the hot drinks flying through the air towards him. The tray and its contents landed with a clatter at the man's feet, scolding fluid seeping into his crotch.

The man growled, deep in his throat. He reacted so quickly that Holly had no time to protect herself. It didn't hurt when the knife sliced through her cheek.

The door slammed behind the man; Cat crumpled to the floor; Jane shouted "oh my god" on repeat, and ran over to Holly; Tony jumped up, mid-doom-scrolling, as if he'd only just noticed something unusual had happened; Tasha screamed, high-pitched and ear-piercing; Joel shouted down the phone: "Ambulance. Police. I don't know. Both. There's been an attack."

Holly's legs shook. She sat down at her desk and tried hard to concentrate on controlling her breathing.

She wiped the back of her hand across a damp patch on her cheek. That was when the pain hit her. Blood dripped down on to her clean desk, soaking into her crisp, white work shirt. She watched as the blood seeped into the fabric, creating a pattern like one of those ink blot tests. She squinted, and thought maybe she could see a butterfly. The stain grew and got fuzzy, and Holly drifted out of consciousness.

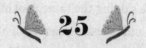

25

MOCKTAILS & MAGAZINES

IT'S Tuesday in her last week at Pinewoods and, after a long day gardening, Holly sits on the bench outside the greenhouse and closes her eyes, letting the sun ease her weary bones. In the trees above her, the crows chatter away to each other. Seagulls cry out in the distance. A bee buzzes nearby. There's a crunching of gravel under someone's feet, and she opens her eyes.

"Here." Hunter is standing in front of her, a newspaper tucked under his arm, carrying two iced drinks. He holds one out for Holly to take. "Dee said it's a mocktail. Pink lemonade kombucha with frozen raspberries and ice." He smiles at Holly, a glint in his eyes. A blush gathers in the hollow at the base of Holly's neck, working its way up her throat and face. Hunter clinks his glass against hers. "Cheers."

"Mmm, thank you," Holly says, taking a sip. She holds the glass in front of her neck to hide the blush.

"Can I join you?" Hunter nods at the space next to her on the bench.

Holly smiles, shyly. "Of course."

They sit in silence, sipping their mocktails. Holly takes a side glance at Hunter. He's doing the same, looking right back at her. He clears his throat and takes another sip of his drink.

"You've worked hard," Hunter says, nodding at the garden.

"I ache. Everywhere."

"You need a bath to ease those muscles."

"You're always telling me to take a bath." Holly lifts her arm and exaggerates smelling her armpit.

"I forgot," Hunter says. "Have you seen this?" He holds the newspaper out to Holly for her to take from him.

Her heart leaps into her throat, and she almost chokes on her drink. "Is it Dylan's article?"

"Dylan?" Hunter furrows his brow. "No. It's San's piece about Pinewoods. It's in the magazine inside. I thought you'd like to read it. You get a mention – kind of."

"Thanks," she mumbles, placing the newspaper on the bench between them.

"Aren't you going to look at it?" Hunter asks.

"I've had some bad experiences of articles that mention me. Makes me a bit . . . nervous, I suppose. Even though I know San will have been kind about me."

"Nothing to be nervous of here, I promise you. It's a lovely piece. Done us proud, she has."

Holly looks straight into those beautiful, hazel eyes with the gold flecks, and finds a gentle, caring kindness. Her butterflies rise up, like a cascading fountain.

"Honestly," he says, holding her gaze. "You'll like what she's written."

When Holly doesn't respond, Hunter pulls the magazine out from the centre pages of the newspaper and opens it on a page with a beautiful photograph of the pinewoods filling half of it. He clears his throat. "We all need a bolt hole," he reads, "and I found mine at Pinewoods Retreat in Formby." He reads on as the article poetically describes a place that Holly recognises, written in a way that makes her want to be here even more – if that's possible. San definitely knows how to paint a visual picture of the place, and it evokes the warmth and kindness that brought them together over such a short time. As she listens to Hunter reading through the piece, she starts to relax, feeling assured that San will have taken care in any mentions of people at the retreat.

San has written of a woman who came to Pinewoods for some healing, and found herself nurturing not only herself but other guests, too, bringing them together through the curative powers of the kitchen garden; a woman who connects to others through intuition, helping them find what they need from working with the soil; that San hopes she has found a friendship that will live on well beyond her time at Pinewoods. No information that identifies her and yet, hearing the words Hunter is reading out loud, it's obvious that the woman San is writing about is Holly. San's subtle use of language means there's nothing that tells anyone it's her – Holly Bush, the Boffin Bop Kid.

"Wow." Holly leans forwards, rests her elbows on her knees and covers her face with her hands to hide the threatening tears from Hunter.

"Told you it was a good piece," Hunter says.

Holly is taken aback by how overwhelmed she feels. It's so good to be described in a positive light. "That's . . . that's beautiful. Such a lovely article. San's written me as a person others would want to know. Heck, I'd like to know this person." She smiles and shakes her head in wonder.

"I'd like to know this person too!" Hunter laughs.

"Ever since my sister's death, I . . ." Holly pauses. Something about this moment feels right to tell Hunter who she is. After all, he told her about his past. "Well – I . . . when I was younger, I became known as the Boffin Bop Kid." Holly's eyes brim with tears. She's avoided telling people her connection to the Boffin Bop campaign for so long, that to speak openly to Hunter like this is a relief.

Hunter nods. "We had a Boffin Bop. Well, my younger brother did. Blew up. In the garage. Nobody got hurt, but my dad supported your mum's campaign. He wrote to her about our Boffin Bop."

Holly straightens up and looks at Hunter. "You knew?" Tears plop over her eyelashes and run down her cheek.

"That you're the Boffin Bop Kid? Yeah, I knew."

"You didn't say."

Hunter shrugs. "What's it to do with me? Like you say, you've lived through a lot. You don't need everyone you meet reminding you of all that." He gently wipes a tear from Holly's cheek with his thumb. "Besides, you're not the Boffin Bop Kid. You're Holly. Like San said, you nurture people, you're there for them. You're kind, and you're caring and . . . you're beautiful." His voice is almost a whisper as he stops talking, his eyes resting on Holly's lips. After a moment, where the world seems to pause, he leans in towards her, hesitating mere inches away. Holly feels herself lean in closer, lifts her chin and lets her lip graze his. They stay like that for a moment, like time has stopped. Then, his mouth covers hers, a hand on the back of her neck. Holly's skin tingles as he gently tugs at her bottom lip with his mouth, pulling her in closer, his fingers stroking her cheek, her scar, her neck. He kisses her sensually, passionately, fully. Holly follows his lead and when his tongue searches for hers, she joins the dance. Her fingers tease through his hair and she melts, putty in his hands.

Hunter stops. He pulls away, sharply. "Shit, sorry. Shit."

"No, it's OK, please." Holly's voice is unfamiliar – her whole body aroused, alive.

Hunter is on his feet now. "I shouldn't have done that. I mean . . ." He looks down at the ground, runs his hand through his hair and turns away. "Sorry." And with that, he strides off.

Holly holds her breath. Tears cascade down her face as she watches Hunter vanish around the side of the house.

Tuesday 29th June

HOW I FEEL: 3/10

SLEEP: Seven hours

WEATHER: Blue sky, light breeze, warm in a nice way

WEARING: Gardening clothes

SOMETHING GOOD THAT HAPPENED: San's article

PROMPT: What are three things I hope for over the
next year?

Hunter kissed me. It was amazing. And then he ran away.

I can never look at him again. More than that, I can never
be in the same room as him. Or the same garden. This is
totally and utterly, horrifyingly, horribly humiliating.

He kissed me, and immediately regretted it.

But that kiss. It was tender, romantic, passionate . . .
like it was straight out the pages of a romance novel.
Of course it was too good to be true.

At least San's article was nice. She's a good writer. She made Pinewoods sound amazing, which it is, and she wrote lovely things about me. I've never seen myself as the person that San wrote about. It's so nice to discover what someone else thinks of me.

OK, time for the prompt. Hope. That feels difficult to write about after Hunter kissed me and ran off. But I promised myself I'd work on being more positive, so let's give this a go.

I hope I can hold on to the sense of peace that Pinewoods and the garden give me.

I hope I can get to know myself the way that San wrote about me.

I hope . . . gosh, three things, this isn't easy. I hope I can learn to value myself, the way Nan and Grandad used to encourage me to.

26

A PROPOSITION, AN IMPOSITION & TWO SMASHED AVOCADO ON TOAST

HOLLY, Lorraine and Dee survey the kitchen garden in the fading evening sun.

"I need to do a harvest for you before I go home on Friday," Holly says. Lorraine and Dee nod. They look at her, and then at each other. "The problem you've got is that if I harvest everything that's ready for picking now, you'll have a glut. Do you have time to turn all of this into food, Dee?"

"I don't, no. Even if I did, I haven't got enough freezer space to store everything I'd make. They always say 'pick for today, preserve for tomorrow', but things like the pickling and fermenting all take time, and I don't have enough of that in the height of summer. At least it's not jam season yet." Dee sighs, shaking her head. "You're right, Holly. I definitely don't have time to turn the harvest into food to eat."

"Seems a shame to put all of this into the composting bin, but I guess that's all that's left for us to do." Lorraine says, with a frown.

"We could sell some of it." The words are out of Holly's mouth before she has a chance to check herself. She can feel Lorraine and Dee's eyes boring into her, and she blushes.

"Now that's a thought." Lorraine crosses her arms and nods slowly.

"Sell it where?" Dee asks.

"Um . . . at the front, by the gate?" Holly looks down at the ground as she speaks, digging the toe of her shoe into the gravel.

"Oh, genius, Holly. What a great idea," says Lorraine. "It's a captive audience, what with all of the walkers who go past every single day."

"We need someone to do the selling, though," Dee says. "None of us have any spare time. Or do we set up an honesty box?"

"I'm happy to do it," Holly says, eagerly.

"I can't ask you to do that," Lorraine says. "You've only got a few days left."

"It's OK, I'd like to help. It'll be a nice way to spend my last day here. I can do it on Friday?"

"Are you sure?"

"Totally." Holly smiles at Lorraine and Dee, happy that they like her idea.

"Right, let's start small and see how this goes," Lorraine says. "I've a couple of old apple crates in the Shepherd's Hut, and we've already got paper bags for the spa. You work out what you can harvest tomorrow, Holly. Dee, you tell Holly what you need to keep for the kitchen and whatever meals you've got planned. Let's give this a try."

"Perfect," Holly says.

Dee hugs her. "This is so good of you. And after everything you've already done! Thank you."

"Let's look for those crates," Lorraine says, "and you can put the veg straight in as you harvest it." She leads Holly and Dee down the central garden path to the end of the raised beds, and to the building at the bottom of the garden.

As she follows Lorraine and Dee to the hut, Holly feels a beat of excitement. She's already had a few sneaky looks through the windows, when no one was watching, and immediately fell in love with the place. It's built half in brick, half in wood, with a tiled roof and ivy growing up over the top of a window that faces the garden. A few flagstones act as a mini patio, with a bench pushed up against the hut, giving it a view of the kitchen garden. Pushed into the far corner, an old steamer chair gives the area the feel of a secret garden.

Fishing a key out of the back pocket of her jeans, Lorraine unlocks the door and holds it open for Holly to walk into the hut ahead of her and Dee.

"Welcome to the Shepherd's Hut. I don't know why we call it that. There are no sheep around these parts, so no shepherds either," Lorraine says, with a laugh. "But the name's stuck over the years. It was probably a coal shed, but that doesn't sound as idyllic, does it?"

"It's beautiful." Holly sighs.

"Simas helped do the place up last year. He did the plastering. Plumbed in the little bathroom. A friend of mine ran electricity cables from the house for heat and light. No need for a kitchen, of course. Simas took his meals with us."

The hut looks even better on the inside than it did when she peeked through the dusty window. Painted white throughout, it is sparsely furnished. Pegs adorn the walls, some with old wooden hangers dangling from them, in place of a wardrobe. Along the back wall, a queen-sized bed is covered in a patchwork quilt. Next to it, an old Bentwood chair, the kind seen in French cafes, serves as a bedside table, with a lamp sitting on top of it. A small wingback chair faces the compact log burner, and next to that is a narrow chest of drawers. The room can't measure more than ten-foot square, yet clever use of the space makes it work perfectly. Holly peeks her head around the single internal door and inspects the bathroom, also painted white and containing all the necessaries.

"It's heavenly," Holly says, turning back to face Lorraine with a big smile on her face.

"Knock, knock. What's going on here, then?" Hunter is standing in the doorway.

Holly's heart plumets to her stomach, crashing through the butterflies on its way. She tucks her hair behind her ear, feeling unusually shy in his company, particularly with everyone else around. She had hoped to see him earlier in the day, for personal training, but he didn't get back to her when she left a message with Lorraine that she was up for another session.

"Hello, Hunter." Lorraine smiles. "I was grabbing some apple crates, and showing Holly our lovely Shepherd's Hut." She stoops down and pulls two old wooden crates out from under the bed.

"Here we go, these will do you for selling the veg, Holly."

"Selling veg?" Hunter asks.

"There's a glut," Dee says. "Like Holly said, it's a shame for it to go to waste. We thought it's worth selling some of it out on the cinder path. You know, give it a go."

Holly takes the apple crates from Lorraine and squeezes past Hunter to put them outside on the bench. She glances at him and gives him a nervous half-smile as she passes.

"Talking of giving things a go," Lorraine says, carefully. "Would you like to stay longer, Holly? Beyond Friday? You can sleep here, in the Shepherd's Hut, if you like. Nobody's using it until we fill the gardener's position."

"Really?" Holly and Hunter speak at the same time.

Hunter raises an eyebrow. "Huh, you never offered the hut to me," he says, a smile playing on his lips.

"Give over, you big oaf. You've got the caravan," Lorraine says.

"You can't ask Holly to do that," Dee says. "She's got her own life to be getting on with on the other side of Liverpool."

"I know, I know." Lorraine holds her hands up. "But it's worth an ask." She flashes a broad smile at Holly. "What do *you* think? You could stay a few days, a week if you like. Only if you want to, of course. It's just, well, you seem to love it, that's all. And you'll be right here in the garden. That's if you're OK doing a bit more work rescuing the place for us."

"Of course I am." Holly answers without hesitating.

"Are you sure?" Dee asks.

Holly nods, a grin slowly spreading across her face.

"Brilliant! You're doing such a great job," Lorraine says. "Every little helps until we can get a gardener. We'll fill the job soon, I'm sure, but if you could help us out for another week, that would be great."

"I'd love to. Thank you." Holly doesn't trust herself to say more, feeling happy tears pricking her eyes.

She looks back at the one-room living space and soaks in a sense of belonging. Yes, she wants to work on the kitchen garden, stay in the Shepherd's Hut for a few nights, take long walks on the beach at sunset and spend more time with her new friends.

There's nothing for her to rush home for. Except maybe job hunting, but that can wait. For now. She's got enough money from her redundancy payment to last a few months yet. One more week here won't make a difference.

"That's that, then!" says Lorraine. "You can move in on Friday. That'll give me time to give it a quick clean and airing. Hunter'll bring your bags down here for you on Friday morning, won't you?"

Holly glances over at Hunter, unsure how to be around him. "S'pose so," Hunter says, his raised eyebrow becoming a permanent feature. He looks over to Holly, gives his head a little nod, and walks away.

As Lorraine and Dee follow him, Holly hugs herself and spends a moment staring at the tiny dwelling. She can't remember when she last felt as much at home as in that moment when she walked over the threshold of the Shepherd's Hut.

* * *

The rest of the day, and all of Thursday, is spent working out what to harvest ready for selling on Friday, and what Dee needs to keep for cooking. Bex uses her graphic design skills to make a poster advertising the veg sale, which Lorraine uploads to social media and prints off for the noticeboards, and then lends Holly a hand searching the internet to find out how much the organic veg can sell for. Holly organises a float using takings from the cafe, and then turns her attention to the garden itself, with a little help from Bex and Ruth. Hunter is on the opposite side of the garden to Holly, working on his notes for the new gardener so that he can pass on all the instructions for keeping the garden in the best state possible. Every now and then, Holly checks in with him and he responds, curtly, before returning to his work. There's no hint of the teasing that usually passes between them, no half-smiles, no accidental touching. Finding it all too confusing, Holly gets back to the main jobs she needs to do before the harvesting starts in earnest later in the day.

As the day draws to an end, Hunter having gone off an hour earlier to do personal training with a client, Holly wanders down the garden path towards the kitchen to wash her hands and update Dee on progress. She's about to push the back door open when she hears her name from inside. "But we didn't ask Holly, Dee. She offered."

"I know, but I feel like we're taking advantage of her. Like I said, she's got her own life to live, and we're imposing on her with everything that needs doing."

Holly freezes on the back step, listening through a crack in the door.

"We need to get that gardening job advertised again," Lorraine sighs. "It won't take long to get overgrown again, and all Holly's efforts will be wasted. Wouldn't it be lovely if she just stayed on for ever as our gardener?"

Holly finds herself nodding from behind the door. It *would* be lovely – more than that, it would be perfect. She'd love the job. But Lorraine and Dee can't seriously be considering giving it to her, can they? She's not got the experience they're looking for.

"She fits in so perfectly with us. You're right, it would be lovely. But no, she's got her own life, away from here."

Holly bites down on her bottom lip. It's not been much of a life this year – until she came to Pinewoods, anyway. She wants to push open the door and shout out "I'm here, I'll do it! I'll be your gardener". But her feet won't move; like they're stuck in mud.

"What does she do for a living?" Lorraine asks.

"I don't know, but she lives in South Liverpool, so it's too far away . . . and you can't ask a young woman like her to live permanently in the Shepherd's Hut. It'll get dreadfully cold in the winter."

Lorraine laughs. "But you were OK asking Simas to do just that?"

"It was his idea to do the place up and live there in the first place. This is different. No, I don't think it's fair to put Holly on the spot like that. She's here on holiday, and she's been really good to help us out. We've imposed on her too much as it is. We can't ask her to stay on as the gardener."

"Two smashed avocado on toast, one ginger tea and a

peppermint tea, please." Jess's voice interrupts the conversation with an order from the cafe.

Holly sighs with disappointment, all hope that they'd offer her the job gone. Waiting a moment or two after the conversation ended, Holly wills her legs into action, pushes open the back door and stumbles ungainly into the kitchen, trying desperately to act as normal as possible.

"Any chance of a cuppa, Dee?" Holly says. "And when you've got a mo, Lorraine, I can take you through the pricing I've come up with for the veg sale."

27

COOKIE PINCHING & PREGNANT PAUSES

HOLLY'S up early on Friday for her veg-selling venture, setting out a mini stall on the cinder path by the gate to Pinewoods. It's not yet seven, but she hopes to catch some of the early dog-walkers and runners on their way back from their daily exercise.

Lorraine has given the old wooden apple crates a quick clean, and Holly places them on their sides, one on top of the other, on a slightly rickety stool. She carefully arranges the vegetables to make them look appealing to passers-by, and settles herself down on another stool that Dee's given her.

She waits. There's a slight chill in the early morning air and Holly's glad she put her cardigan on. There are grey clouds above, but it looks like they will burn off when the sun makes an appearance. As people walk past, Holly says a friendly "good morning" to them, the way she used to when customers walked into OO-TO Travel. Selling veg surely isn't going to be that different from selling holidays – she simply needs to put on a friendly face, and show the customers that she knows what she's talking about.

Within thirty minutes, Holly has sold a small bag of tomatoes, a large bag of kale, a pot of lavender and a couple of leeks. It's working. Maybe she could sell some of Dee's jams and preserves, next time? She'll have a chat with Dee about that later – assuming it's something they do again. Holly smiles to herself, realising that she's getting a little carried away with ideas, considering she's only been set up with her veg stall for half an hour.

Customers and passers-by are kind, and one elderly couple stop for a natter for a good five minutes before continuing on their walk. They don't buy anything, but Holly enjoys the chat. One dog-walker asks for her to hold on to two pots of herbs until her return loop, so that she doesn't have to carry them with her over the dune paths. Two people stop to see what she's selling, notice that Pinewoods has a cafe, and sit themselves down for a coffee and toast. Who would have thought that her idea to sell veg at the gate could be a draw for the cafe too?

"What have we got here, then?" Holly recognises the man from the cafe who wanted the BLT – hold the L and T – along with his lively bullmastiff, who is yanking on its lead to follow a scent it's picked up.

"Homegrown vegetables from the retreat's kitchen garden."

"Waste of time, if you ask me. You can buy it all from the supermarket for half the effort, and half the price."

Holly attempts a smile, but already knows it's lost on this man. He picks up a leek, throws it up in the air, catches it and dumps it back in the veg box. The dog jumps up on to his back legs. "Down, Barney. Down!" Barney jumps up at Holly and she half-heartedly pets him, not wanting to rile man or dog. Barney yanks again on his lead, almost pulling his owner over. The man rights himself, pulling Barney back towards him, and, as he does, the dog knocks into the rickety stool, upending everything.

"What the heck!" Holly shouts, scrabbling to save vegetables from under the dog's paws.

The man pulls at the lead, yanking a reluctant Barney to his side.

"Hang on a second. I've seen you before," he says, his lip turning up in a sneer.

"Last week, in the cafe." Holly picks up the crate and glares at the man.

"Yeah, I remember that. I saw you there. But I also saw you online, this morning. I recognise that scar on your face, from the photo of you."

Holly goes cold. Dylan must have published his article already. She feels a slight tightening in her chest and gives her head a little shake. "So," Holly says, wishing the man would just leave; take his dog on his walk.

"So, I know who you are." The man stares at Holly. Neither says anything. As Barney pulls on the lead again, the man says, "Anyway...", shrugs, and marches off, leaving Holly to pick up the veg that's scattered across the cinder path.

"Here." Hunter hands Holly some of the veg.

Where did he pop up from? He has an irritating habit of appearing at the most inopportune moments. Holly's cheeks burn and she coughs to clear her throat.

"Thanks." Her voice is quiet and low. "Can you . . ." she pauses and looks away from Hunter. "Can you put it in the crate, please?"

Hunter puts the veg back into the crate, brushing off some of the dirt from the path as he does so, before turning and picking up a few more bits, and putting them into the crate too. He stands and looks at Holly, and then to the crate, and then back at Holly.

She takes in a deep breath, picks up the crate and walks back towards the house.

"You're not giving up because that dog knocked your box over, are you?"

"I'm not giving up." Holly snaps more than she intends to, and sighs. "I need to wash some of this. That dog was sticking his nose on it. Goodness knows where that's been." Holly carries the crate back into the kitchen.

A few minutes later – all the veg washed and sorted through, damages passed on to Dee for making soups with – Holly walks back out on to the cinder path, carrying the crate. Hunter is putting a board across two chairs, creating a makeshift table. He takes the crate from Holly and places it down on the board.

"There," he says, standing back as if to admire his handiwork. "That should be a bit more secure."

"Oh, right, yes. Thank you."

"And there's a couple over there," Hunter points through the gate to a table in the garden cafe. "They want to buy a few bits. I said you'd be back."

"Well, here I am." Holly smiles half-heartedly. At least she still has customers, despite the dog incident.

By early afternoon, Holly has sold out of everything she harvested to sell. Dropping the money on to the kitchen table, she counts it out, making columns of coins, stacked in neat lines.

Just then, Hunter walks into the kitchen from the garden. "Oh," he says, like the word is a full sentence. He pinches a cookie from the cooling rack, something that Holly has noticed him do with regularity.

As Holly pushes the last of the coins together into a small pile, she looks up and sees him staring at her. She matches his stare. If pauses truly can be pregnant, this one's carrying twins. The pause reaches the embarrassing, uncomfortable, squirmy phase when Lorraine walks into the kitchen.

"Wow, look at all that cash! Is this what you made today? Is there any veg left?"

"I sold all of it – everything we harvested. That's £61.55 there." Holly nods at the lines of coins. "And one Euro."

Hunter takes another cookie from the rack, his eyes not moving from Holly. There's a hint of something on his face that Holly can't place, like the cookie doesn't taste right – or he's annoyed about something.

"Fantastic." Lorraine fingers the coins as if they're precious gemstones. "Well, that was worth a try, wasn't it? You've done really well, Holly. I can't thank you enough for breathing new life into the kitchen garden, and then coming up with this great idea too. I'm proud of you." Lorraine beams at Holly, and pulls her in for a hug. "And now you're moving into the Shepherd's Hut! Hunter, did you take Holly's bags down to the hut?"

"Yeah," he mumbles through the cookie in his mouth. "First thing this morning." He still hasn't taken his eyes from Holly, and it's unnerving.

"Stop eating the cookies, Hunter – you know they're for the café." Lorraine raises an eyebrow at him and retrieves a key from a dish on the Welsh dresser. "Here," she says to Holly. "This is yours for the next week. I love that you're doing the garden, but I also expect you to do other things too – enjoy yourself."

"Thank you," Holly says, nodding eagerly. "I am enjoying myself."

"And you've still got a couple of sessions left with our lovely Hunter, too. I know you didn't get around to using all the sessions you booked. Hunter, get that sorted for Holly, please."

"Yes, Lorraine." He licks crumbs off his thumb, and wipes his hands on his cargo pants as he walks out of the kitchen.

Holly fiddles with the coins in front of her, wondering whether she even wants to have the last of her personal training sessions with Hunter. She's not sure if she can stand any more of this awkwardness between them.

After a few more minutes talking with Lorraine about the veg sale, and how well it went, Holly takes the key and lets herself into the Shepherd's Hut. The sun is streaming in through the side window, filling the living-room-cum-bedroom with light. The door is one of those stable doors, and Holly opens the top half to allow fresh air in, and some of the heat out. She leans over the bottom half of the door and surveys the kitchen garden. Like her, the garden is in far better shape than it was two weeks ago.

As her eyes follow the lines of the raised beds, Holly spots Hunter standing in the kitchen doorway looking back at her. She wants to go over to him and tell him what an arse he's being, ask him what the hell's going on.

Instead, she turns to her new home for the week and starts to unpack her things.

Friday 2nd July

HOW I FEEL: 6/10

SLEEP: Seven hours

WEATHER: Started with grey clouds that later cleared up,
light breeze, warm and humid. Looks like it might rain later

WEARING: Striped shorts with the embroidered bees, blue
T-shirt with 'Be Kind' across the chest, my flowery pumps
with the yellow laces. (Thought I'd make a bit of an
effort today with setting up the veg stall)

SOMETHING GOOD THAT HAPPENED: Made lots of money
selling the garden veg

PROMPT: What am I proud of?

Funny. Now I've decided to look for the good in each day,
it's like Lorraine made this prompt for me.

I'm proud of selling the bumper crop of organic, homegrown
fruit and vegetables (I still sound like I'm selling to the
public, hehe). It was a huge success. I sold out. Everything
that I'd harvested has gone.

I'm proud that I came up with the idea, and proud of what I've done to the garden. I reckon Pinewoods could sell fruit and veg once a month, with homemade pickles, preserves and jams too. I'll have a chat with Lorraine and Dee about it later.

I'm proud of Nan and Grandad. They were good people. They knew how to be kind - not just to me, either, but to anyone - stranger or friend. Anyone who called around at teatime was offered a place at the table, even if it was the guy who dropped off the freebie newspaper. Nan would force food on people even if they said no thanks. I remember once, a poor DPD delivery man had a packed lunch thrust at him, because Nan had just finished making sandwiches for us to take down the allotment. I hope he liked ham and Piccalilli on white Hovis.

For the first time in my life - I think? Yes, for the first time - I am proud of me. I've overcome so much in my life, and it's easy for me to forget that sometimes. I pushed myself out of my comfort zone and came here, to Pinewoods, and I'm proud that I did that. It would have been so easy for me to wallow in front of the TV or under a duvet with my books - I can still do that when I want to, but now I know I can do new things even when they make me nervous. I'm getting my shit together, I'm getting fit, and I'm getting to know people that I like and can call my friends. I'm honestly proud of myself today. I am.

I feel at home in the Shepherd's Hut. My own little space here at Pinewoods for the next week. Note to self: Ask Lorraine about using the washing machine to do a load of washing. I'm running out of clothes to garden in.

Need to look online to find out what Dylan's written about me. God, it's going to be awful. I just need to get it over with. I can do this. Remember, I am proud of myself today.

28

HOLD THE
FRONT PAGE

AT first, the article that Holly finds after mere seconds of looking on the internet is all about Pinewoods. Quickly scanning the article, there's a bit of history about the area, along with background about Lorraine and Dee. But as she scrolls down, just as the man with the dog said, there's a photograph of Holly. It's a side profile, with her looking off at something, her scar in full view. There she is again, plastered all over the internet, like all the other photos of her from the time she was the poster girl for Ban the Boffin Bop campaign.

Holly puts her phone down and hides her head in her hands. Her nerves are on edge, the butterflies crashing violently around in her belly. She paces the small room in the Shepherd's Hut – seven steps, turn around, seven steps, turn around. She sits down, stands up, sits down again. Taking a few deep breaths, she steels herself to read the rest of the article and see what Dylan has written about her.

Starting back at the beginning of the article, Holly reads about the history of The Lost Resort where Pinewoods is based, then there's a paragraph that describes Pinewoods as a place for misfits and miscreants – not exactly painting it in the best light. There's mention of Dee and how she had a failed chain of restaurants across the region. There's even a bit about Hunter and how he's ex-army, coming from a street-gang background. Holly's surprised Hunter shared anything about himself with Dylan – she felt he was revealing something quite private when he spoke to her about it. It's not as if Hunter had any time for Dylan, either. In fact, if anything, Hunter seemed to really dislike him.

The next two paragraphs in the article are devoted to her. They start with a reminder of the Boffin Bop Kid, before linking her to the travel-agent slasher, with Dylan saying he got to spend a week in the company of the "oddest woman" he's "ever encountered". Dylan drops in a bit about her mother's meltdown on TV and muses about the effect on Holly of being brought up by someone who "perhaps should have been sectioned", suggesting that there are sure to be long-term impacts. He describes Holly as being "more than a little unhinged" and suggests that she is perhaps "not all there", leading on to describe her as having got in the way of a madman with a knife.

As she reads, Holly goes cold. The things that were written about her when she was younger were bad enough, but this diatribe that dares to describe her so nastily is something new. How can such a thing be published? It's not even supposed to be about her.

Holly's emotions are all over the place. She feels crushed by the article, furious at how Dylan has portrayed her, and weary with her life getting more media attention again.

She throws her phone across the bed and it slides down the other side, on to the floor. Letting out a scream, she pulls the bed away from the wall, retrieves her phone and, as she pushes the bed back into place, she stubs her toe.

After rubbing her foot for a moment, she clambers under her duvet, pulling it over her face, and cries.

* * *

The next morning, having barely slept and when she thinks she's run out of tears, Holly knows what she needs to do. She picks up her phone and calls San.

"Have you seen it?" Holly just about holds it together at the start of the call.

"Oh, lovey. I haven't. You talk, I'll see if I can pull it up on my laptop."

Hearing San's voice, Holly squeezes her nose in an attempt to stop the tears that are welling up behind her eyes. "He's written a long paragraph about my past."

"Here it is." San pauses. "Bloody hell, he's not pulling his punches, is he? This has nothing to do with the retreat. He really shouldn't be writing about you at all, Holly. What a bastard."

Holly sniffs and swipes a hand over one cheek and then the other. "I just don't understand why he needed to do it."

"Because it's sport to the likes of him. He smells blood, and sniffs after it. And then there's Dee and Hunter, too! Can't imagine those two are happy either."

"You think he's been digging into their pasts as well?"

"It seems like it," San says. "I doubt either of them will have sat down with Dylan and spilt their life stories. They both seem . . ." San pauses, "private, even though they're both really friendly."

Holly takes in what San has said, and nods to herself slowly. Dylan is the type of journalist who digs for dirt – of course she's not the only one whose life he was digging into. "I know, I know, you're right. They won't have told him anything. This is all Dylan, digging about to find out whatever he can to create a story that sells." Holly lets out a shaky sigh. Dee and Hunter won't be happy with Dylan either, she's sure of that. What Hunter shared with her was private; not the type of stuff he'd want to see in print. "Thank you." Her voice wobbles, and then the sobs come. Noisy, wet, snot-filled sobs. "And Hunter kissed me." The sobs come louder.

San squeals down the phone. "Oh, lovey, that's fabulous!"

"No, it's not. He ran away, and then he was horrid to me, and now I just don't know what's going on."

San gasps. "Bloody hell," she says, sounding exasperated. "I . . . I just don't get it! What is that man doing?"

"What should I do, San?"

"About Hunter or Dylan?"

"Both."

"Dylan is easy. Just email his editor. I know you said you were going to do that, but I bet you didn't actually send the email, did you?"

Holly shakes her head, and then remembers that San can't see her. "No," she says, in a near whisper.

"Well, after this article, you're going to have to do it. I expect Dee will, as well. We were all given a brief for what we were covering in our articles for a free stay at Pinewoods, and Dylan has broken that agreement."

"OK." Holly sniffles and hunts for a hanky. "And Hunter?"

"I've no idea if he'll email."

"No, I mean, what do I do about him?"

San lets out a gentle laugh. "Oh, that," she says, her voice warm. "Stand up to him."

"I can't."

"You can. When's your next training session?"

"He's been avoiding having them, but I've got one this afternoon. Lorraine pushed us to book my final ones in. But I'm not going."

"Yes, you are."

"I can't go." Holly is sobbing again now, angry with herself for feeling so weak.

"Come on, of course you can, lovey. I've seen you in action, remember." Holly smiles wanly down the phone. "Hold your head up high, show him that whatever his problem is, it's *his* problem."

"It doesn't feel like it's his problem. It feels like I'm the problem."

"It's bound to feel like that, lovey, but I promise you, it definitely *is* his problem. Look, if he meant to hurt you – and I'm not so sure he did – well, don't give him the satisfaction. Be the warrior woman you are, Holly."

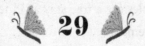

29

YOU CAN'T CALM
THE STORM

AFTER lunch, here Holly is – tears wiped away, face washed, hair pulled back into a ponytail – walking down the hall to meet Hunter, who is standing in the porch with his back to her, surveying the empty garden cafe. Talking to San was just the tonic she needed. If Hunter says anything mean to her – anything at all – she's giving him a piece of her mind. Same if he tries to kiss her again, too. If she can stand up to Dylan, to those horrible women in the cafe, she sure as heck can tell Hunter what she thinks of him messing around with her heart.

Holly stops next to Hunter and looks out at the drizzle. Hunter glances her way, before immediately turning his head away again.

After an uncomfortable few seconds, Hunter says, "I didn't think you'd come."

When Holly doesn't reply, Hunter stiffens and pushes his hands into his pockets. "Ready?" he asks.

Holly throws a tight-lipped smile his way. "Yup," she says.

"Let's go then. We'll walk at pace for a warm-up." Hunter stomps off out of the porch and into the drizzly rain.

The continuing uncomfortable silence is wedged between them on their long, brisk walk. Eventually, Hunter sprints up a steep dune covered in marram grass. There are no barked orders this time. Simply an expectation that Holly will follow. She does. At the top, there's a huge circle of dunes that surround a deep depression, like a teacup. An undulating path leads off in both directions along the top of the dunes.

"Right," Hunter says. "Run around the top of the blowout."

"Blowout?"

"This." He points off along the direction of the path. "The circle of dunes."

Holly nods.

"Full circuit. Three times. First time – fast, next time – pick up your pace, last time around – as fast as you can. I'll be behind you, timing your pace. I want to see an average of eight-minute kilometre pace the first circuit. We'll up that pace on each circuit. Going for negative splits. No slowing down, no complaining, no moaning. Ready?"

"I don't moan," Holly snaps.

Hunter raises an eyebrow. "OK." He sets his watch. "Three, two, one . . . go!"

Holly takes the path off to the left.

"Pick those feet up. You can go faster than this." Hunter is right behind her.

Holly picks up her speed. Wet sand clings to her trainers and her feet feel heavy. She runs on. The rain comes down faster. Halfway around her second circuit, Holly stops.

"For crying out loud, what have you stopped for?"

"My trainers. They're clogged up with wet sand. I need to clean some of it off." Holly rubs one foot on the marram grass, then the other. Hunter watches, hands on his hips.

As Holly starts running again, the rain comes down heavier still.

"Is this all you've got? You've slowed down. Negative splits, remember."

Holly pushes herself, despite her legs and lungs screaming at her. Gradually, she increases her speed.

"Come on. Pick those feet up."

For goodness' sake, what does he think she's doing?

"Take charge of yourself, Holly. Make the decision to give this your all."

How dare he push her like this? She made the decision she was giving it her all the moment she pulled on her trainers, and anyway, after the way he's treated her, he's got no room to be lecturing her about giving it her all. Holly purses her lips and puts in a further burst of effort.

"Push yourself, Holly. Come on. You can do better than this."

She stops abruptly and Hunter ploughs into her back.

"Shut up, Hunter! Just shut up." She turns to face him, fists clenched, rain running down her face. Hunter takes a couple of steps back. Sand gives way under his foot, and his leg slides a little way down the dune. He rights himself and wipes rain from his eyes.

"What now?" Hunter snaps.

"You're on at me all the time, that's what . . . and I've had enough."

"I'm getting you fit. You've paid me to do this, remember?"

"That doesn't mean you need to boss me about all the time!"

"I'm a personal trainer. It's what I do."

"No, I'll tell you what you do. You flirt with me, get close to me, kiss me. And then you run away like I'm your worst nightmare." Holly lets out a long breath as the rain batters against them.

Hunter lifts his T-shirt and wipes the rain from his face. "I'm sorry." He shakes his head. "You're right. I shouldn't have done that. But you didn't have to go and shoot your mouth off, did you?"

"What?" Holly is thrown by Hunter's reaction. "I haven't done anything!" she shouts with indignation.

"You know exactly what you did, Holly – and it pissed me off. I saw it this morning."

"I have no idea what you're on about, Hunter."

He throws his hands up in the air. "You told that guy. The idiot journalist. Dee showed me the article he wrote. It's online."

"I saw it." Holly shakes her head. "But I'm lost. What am I supposed to have done?"

"You told him about me. About my gang life." Hunter's nostrils flair with anger.

"What?" Holly shakes her head, incredulous. "No, I didn't."

"Oh, come on, Holly. You're the only person I've told. And I saw the two of you, whispering. Not two minutes after I told you."

Holly's eyes are wide, the heavy rain causing them to sting. "Are you serious?"

"I trusted you, Holly. It wasn't for you to share."

Holly pushes ringing-wet hair back from her face. "I wouldn't do that. Especially to you. How could you think I would?"

"You didn't want him writing about you. You thought you could deflect his attention by telling him about me."

"You really think I'd stoop so low?"

Hunter brushes his hair off his forehead, and wipes more rain from his face. He sighs. "Well then, who else did it?"

"I've no idea, but it wasn't me. I would never do that. And I can't believe you think I would." They glare at each other through the rain. "But anyway, this is about *you* and what you did to me." Holly jabs a finger in Hunter's direction. "You kissed me and ran off! How do you think that made me feel? You *actually* did that." She turns her back to him.

"You're changing the subject. But yeah, I wanted to kiss you. I've wanted to kiss you since the first day I saw you."

Holly explodes, whirling round to face him again. "So you did! You kissed me, and then you ran off like . . . like . . . like I'm diseased." She waves a dismissive arm at him. "That's it. I've had enough. You flirt with me. You tease me. You get close to me, open up to me. You take me for a smoothie in the cafe. In training sessions, you challenge me to be better, like you care about me. And now, now you're accusing *me* of sharing your private life with Dylan. What do you take me for? Of course, I'm fed up of my life being plastered all over the press, but . . ." She pauses and throws her arms up in the air. "*Argh!*"

"I'm helping you to get stronger, Holly," Hunter says, calmly. "It's what I do."

"I've always been strong – here," she prods her chest, "on the inside. How else do you think I survived everything I lived through? This is me," she yells. "I've done this. Me." It feels good to let all the years of anger out, to stand up to Hunter, to give him a piece of her mind. "Being here at Pinewoods, I've been able to find myself again. And you know what, I don't deserve to be treated the way you've been with me. I deserve better, Hunter." Rain streams down their faces, and a gathering wind batters into them. "And do you know what else? It's not right that you act like you're so much better than me, when I can tell you've got things to sort out, too. You're not perfect, you've got your own stuff going on, but you make it all about me. When are you going to deal with *your* baggage, huh?"

Hunter stares at her for a moment before replying. "OK, you're right. I've got my own shit." He shakes his head slowly. "And I've let it spill over into this."

"You have, yes. My guess is you're not dealing with whatever went on in your life."

"Do any of us properly deal with what goes on in our lives, Holly?" Hunter thrusts his hands into his pockets, and let's out a long sigh. "Fine. You wanna know what happened?" His voice is quiet. "Watched my mate get shot in front of me on patrol. Should've spotted the sniper, and I didn't. He died. That was my fault. It's on me. I'll carry it with me for ever." Hunter steps closer to Holly. She watches in silence as Hunter bites on his top lip and then his bottom one. "I'm sorry, I messed up. I'm proud of you, Holly. Of what you've pushed yourself to do during these last few weeks." He takes another step towards her, his voice calm and measured. "Look at you now. You stand tall, chin up, and you're taking back control of your life. I'll always help you to do that, if I can."

"Well, maybe I don't want you to." The shock at Hunter's revelation about his friend barely touches her through her anger and frustration. She notices the damp creeping up his cargo pants, and the splattered specks of sand. "I don't need anyone's help," she says, quietly. "And definitely not yours."

Hunter puts his hands out to his side in question.

"I'm done. I've had enough." Holly turns to walk away, before turning back to face him once last time. "Please, leave me alone. No more flirting. No more kisses. And do not follow me now. I want to be alone." She turns and sets off along the path, breaking into a run.

"Holly, wait!"

Holly runs along the top of the dunes and when a narrow path appears to her left, she veers off in the direction of the beach. Ignoring Hunter's distant calls, his voice carried along by the wind, she slides down the wet dune on to the beach. She picks up speed, surprised at how fast she's running.

A wide expanse of sand stretches out left, right and way off in front of her. As the rain pelts down, Holly splashes through puddles and rivulets, pushing herself harder and harder, putting as much distance as possible between her and Hunter.

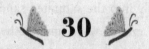

30

THE EDGE OF
THE WORLD

AFTER ten minutes, fifteen, maybe longer, Holly stops on a sandbank, raised slightly higher than the rest of the expansive beach. Looking out into the gloom ahead, she opens her mouth, takes in a deep breath, and lets out a long scream. A loud, lung-emptying scream, her arms out to the sides, like angel wings. Filling her lungs again, she lets out another scream, and another, and then another.

Holly peers through the rain. Where's the sea? Why can't she see it yet? Her legs shake from the exertion of running, but she's not finished yet. She wants to get to the edge of the water – to stop and look out across the vast Irish Sea. She runs on. She feels strong. Invincible. She stretches her arms up above her head as she runs, unshackled.

The sand becomes wetter and soon her trainers are soaked through, her feet squelching inside. The splashes continue to get bigger. Finally, a gentle wave laps at her feet. She has reached the sea. She looks out towards Ireland. There's nothing there, except rain and ocean. This is the edge of the world.

Another wave slaps over her trainers, and splashes up her legs.

Her feet sink slightly into the saturated sand. She takes a step back, getting hit by another wave, and another. A rush of waves. The tide has turned and it's coming in fast. Holly whirls around towards the dunes.

The wind hits her full in the face, suddenly strong. It grabs hold of her wet hair and flings it across her face, stinging her cheeks. She peers into the distant gloom, half-expecting to see Hunter waiting for her. Visibility is poor in the heavy rain – but no, he's definitely not there.

Holly puts her head down and pushes against the wind, trying hard to break into a run. She needs to get away from the incoming tide. Her drenched trainers slap into the wet sand. The wind takes her breath away, and her tired body screeches at the effort. The poor weather has reduced visibility and it's almost impossible to make out the coastline ahead. With the sea behind her, advancing fast, she's sure she's heading in the right direction. The dunes must be out in front of her – somewhere.

How could she have been so stupid? She should never have got herself into this kind of trouble. She feels for her phone . . . *No, no, no.* She didn't bring it – she never takes it out on her training sessions with Hunter. No one knows she's here, and she has no way to contact anyone. Holly feels panic rising. She will be lost – like one of those iron men, the Gormley statues in the sea, for ever gazing longingly at the horizon.

A sob escapes from Holly's throat as she pushes on, head down, leaning into the wind. The sea keeps pace with her, nudging her, snatching at her feet as she runs, splashing around her legs; the wind calls to her – *fool, fool, fool* – slapping rain into her face. Then there's something else: a hissing, sploshing sound. She lifts her head and wipes rain from her eyes, peering into the gloom ahead. There's something there.

Whizzing along the beach, spray and sand thrown up in its wake, is a Land Rover.

Holly waves her arms wildly above her head and shouts as loud as her aching lungs will let her. The wind catches her words and throws them back into the sea. She jumps up and down, splashing as she lands back in the rising waves. Holly watches as the Land Rover drives swiftly on in the direction of the Mersey, straight down the coast. The lights fades into the gloom, as she drops her arms by her sides, a final, weak plea hanging on her lips.

Part Three

Part Three

31
TIME & TIDE

THE sea is soon above Holly's knees. She wades through, her legs heavy in the water, feet sinking into soft sand. She holds on to a small shaft of hope – she can make it; she will make it. The wind blusters and batters her, rain pelting into her face. And still she moves forwards, yanking her feet now, as they're swallowed by sea and soft sand. One slow, heavy step at a time.

Holly looks down. The sea is up to her thighs now. Cold. Dark. Menacing. She stops for a moment to calm herself, closing her eyes, breathing deeply. This is no time to panic. She can do this.

She pulls on her right leg to continue on. It doesn't move. Her foot is trapped, the sand sucking her in and refusing to release its hold on her. She pulls on her left leg. It doesn't move either. The sea swirls around her. *Oh god, oh god, oh god.* Holly lowers herself into the freezing water and feels around with her hands. With her chin in the water, her fingers just make contact with the sand. She digs and digs, scrambling with her fingers as best she can, yanking at her feet. Nothing changes. Except the sea is now slapping against her closed mouth.

Holly straightens herself up, gazing towards what she thinks is dry land. Towards safety. The rain lets off a little, and there's a hint of lightness in the sky ahead. Holly peers ahead, spotting the merest hint of the dunes in the distance. And then she sees it. There's someone there, on the beach.

"Help! Help!" Holly shouts into the wind. She raises her hands above her head and waves. The wind gusts into her and, unable to steady herself with her feet stuck in the sand, it knocks her backwards into the sea. She swallows a mouthful of seawater as she collapses back into the incoming waves, her head fully submerged. Holly fights to pull herself back up to standing, gasping for air, coughing. She looks towards the dunes again. The figure is still there.

Holly shouts again and, leaning forwards into the wind, she waves her arms above her head. The figure doesn't move. She takes off her hoodie and waves it wildly above her head, screaming at the top of her voice.

Then it spots her. It starts coming towards her, waving its arms in response, before stopping for a moment. Do they not realise she's stuck? Holly waves more frantically now, and then the figure moves again towards her. As it gets closer, and the shape morphs from a blob to an actual person, Holly breathes with relief. It's Hunter.

He splashes through the sea, running towards her.

"Are you OK?" Hunter shouts as he gets closer.

"I can't move," she shouts back. "I'm stuck."

"It's OK, we'll get you out of this. I just called the Coastguard. They should be here soon." Hunter reaches Holly. He grabs her, pulls her in close to him, holding her tightly in his arms. "You're

OK, Holly. I've got you." She wraps her arms around him, allowing herself to be held, and lets out a loud sob.

"Here," Hunter says, thrusting his phone into her hands. "Hold this." Holly grabs his phone and watches as Hunter disappears under the water. His hands scrabble around her feet and she can feel him digging at the sand. He comes up for air briefly before vanishing again, only his feet making a kicking appearance above the water.

"Try and move now," he says, standing next to Holly as he pants. She pulls and yanks at her feet.

"My left foot – it's moving a little," Holly says, the sea pushing into her back.

"Great. Let's try again." Hunter makes to dive under the water again. "Shit! My foot's stuck." He takes in a gulp of air and goes back under the water anyway, digging and pulling at Holly's left foot. She yanks on it, and the sand frees its hold, leaving her trainer behind to be fossilised for future generations to dig up in years to come. Hunter reappears, takes in another lungful of air, and submerges himself. He frees her right leg, and Holly treads water, scared to plant her feet back into the soft sand. As Hunter comes back up, he's gasping for air.

Holly dives under the water without a word. The water is murky, and she's forced to go by touch. Grabbing hold of Hunter's leg, Holly follows it down to the seabed and his trapped foot. She claws at the sand around his ankle, digging desperately with her fingers until her lungs are ready to explode. She surfaces to take in air, and sees the waves lapping around Hunter's mouth, despite him tilting his head back. Hunter holds her arm.

"The lifeboat, over there." Hunter splutters as his mouth fills with seawater.

Holly treads water, keeping her head above the waves, and turns herself around. The lifeboat is not far from them. She raises one arm above her head and calls out. "Over here! Help!" She turns back to Hunter, whose head is nearly submerged. "Hold on, Hunter. I'm going to try one more time. Keep waving your arms." She dives below the surface and claws desperately at Hunter's foot. He pulls and pulls and yanks and pulls, as she digs and digs. Suddenly, his foot comes loose, kicking Holly in the chest, knocking the wind out of her lungs and forcing her to take in seawater.

Holly scrambles to the surface, spluttering and gasping for air. Hunter bobs next to her, his head just above water.

"I need to hold on to you," he says, taking hold of Holly's arm. "Done something to my leg. Can't tread water properly."

The lifeboat comes to a stop about ten metres away. "Holly? Ray?" Holly nods, almost sobbing with relief. One of the crew climbs out of the boat and swims over to them.

"Help him first," Holly says, panting. "He's hurt."

As the crew heave Hunter into the boat, he cries out in pain, grabbing his calf. Next, it's Holly's turn. Once she's in the boat, she retches, her body desperate to rid itself of the seawater she's taken in. Someone wraps her in a foil blanket and she holds it tight around her chest, the boat picking up speed, skidding across the surface of the sea.

"What have you done to your leg?" Holly shouts across to Hunter, who is on the other side of the boat, the engine noise and slapping of the bow against water almost drowning her out.

Hunter slowly shakes his head, shivering and pale beneath his foil wrap. "Pulled a muscle? I don't know. Did something when I slid down the dune, earlier. And then, when I yanked my leg out of the sand, something snapped." He coughs and then winces, tightening his hold on the foil hung around his shoulders.

"I'm sorry." Holly shouts over the boat's engine. She holds her hand out to Hunter, closing the gap between them. He takes hold of it, and she feels his body shaking. "Thank you for rescuing me," she says.

"You rescued me, too. Thought I was a goner." Hunter gives her a weak smile as the lifeboat slows down and taxis into land.

* * *

An hour later, following a thorough check over by paramedics, Hunter is taken off to the hospital in the back of the ambulance, and Holly is bundled into a Land Rover and driven back to Pinewoods.

"You're lucky Ray called it in," the driver says. "You were a long way out to sea."

"Ray?" Holly repeats, through chattering teeth.

"Ray Knight. The guy you were with."

Holly's brow furrows in confusion. "Hunter?"

"Oh, I didn't realise he was still using the name Hunter." The driver laughs, cranks up the heating to full and wipes her sleeve over the windscreen to clear the mist. Holly wants to ask what she means, but exhaustion and uncontrollable shivering take over both her body and her mind.

As the Land Rover comes to a halt outside Pinewoods, Bex runs out with a blanket hung over her arm.

"God, Holly! Are you OK? I've been worried sick. What happened? You look dreadful. Oh my god. Where's Hunter? Are you OK?" She bundles Holly up in the blanket, puts an arm around her and ushers her inside. Between Bex's persistent questions and the chattering of her teeth, there is no space for Holly to respond.

"Now then," Dee says, pushing a mug of hot chocolate into Holly's hands. "Drink this. Bex, here's the key to our apartment. Go and run Holly a hot bath. You won't be disturbed with me down here, and Lorraine's gone off to the hospital to be with Hunter."

Holly follows the instructions thrown at her over the next hour, her head fuzzy. When she returns to the kitchen an hour later, dressed in a mix of her own clothes and some extra-warm ones that Dee has provided, Bex is waiting for her.

"Dee has made you some soup," Bex says. "Sit yourself here, by the range. You need to keep warm."

Holly laughs weakly. "You're mothering me."

"I was worried about you." Bex tilts her head, her face full of concern.

"We all were," Dee says from the other side of the room.

"I'm sorry I gave you all a fright. I can't believe I was so stupid."

"What actually happened?" Bex asks.

Holly feels herself blush. "I was an idiot. We had an argument in the middle of my personal training session, and I ran off. Told Hunter not to follow me."

Bex nods in understanding. "He came back here, thought you'd already be back. Then he went off again, looking for you."

Holly hides her face behind her hands for a moment, feeling a mix of embarrassment and shock at what happened. "I caused such trouble, didn't I?" she says, quietly.

"The tide was out," Dee says. Her voice is kind and gentle. "It's easy to be caught out. Many people have been caught by the tide before you. Many will be caught after you."

Holly swallows a tear, along with a mouthful of too-hot soup that burns as it passes down her throat. She coughs, still able to taste seawater.

JOURNAL ENTRY
Saturday 3rd July

HOW I FEEL: I've no idea. My head is all over the place

SLEEP: Six hours

WEATHER: Torrential downpour for hours now, howling wind that's making itself known in my little Shepherd's Hut. Feels cold with that wind

WEARING: Lounge pants, T-shirt, sweatshirt. Cardy belonging to Dee, and Lorraine's thick walking socks. You could also say I'm wearing a hot water bottle and a warm mug of turmeric, lemon and ginger tea that Dee made for me

SOMETHING GOOD THAT HAPPENED: I didn't die today

I thought I was done for. I know people say that the sea comes in fast at Formby Point, but I didn't realise how fast until today. It was like one moment the sea was miles away, far off in the distance, and then suddenly the waves were lapping around my feet. Having to run so fast away from the sea was bad enough, but then getting stuck . . . Crikey, what would have happened to me if Hunter hadn't turned up when he did? And thank goodness for the lifeboat. If only I'd stopped when he called out to me as I flounced off, we'd never have got in this mess. At least we're both safe now.

Bloody hell, I was scared! But you know, I coped with it. Fear took me in a completely different direction when I was stuck in the sea. When faced with difficult situations, I'm so used to my panic attacks making me freeze in time. Yet when I was in danger of losing my life - in one of the most panic-ridden moments of my life - I didn't freeze. I didn't give in. I refused to give up. What better lesson that I can actually cope in life? Whatever is thrown at me, I can survive it.

I just need to remember that next time I freeze and want to give in. I have the strength to get through whatever happens to me. If all of that had happened to me three weeks ago, I'd have had one of my worst ever panic attacks, I'm sure of it - and then who knows what the outcome would have been? But today I stayed in charge of my body, and in control of my thoughts. That's pretty miraculous.

Really worried about Hunter. I hope he's OK. Lorraine's with him now, at the hospital. We should hopefully hear what's wrong with his leg soon. Waiting up for news.

32

CONSTELLATIONS & MURMURATIONS

THERE'S a light tap-tap-tap on the door of the Shepherd's Hut. Lorraine's standing under a large golfing umbrella. She looks drained and worried.

"You're back," Holly says, relief flooding through her veins. She holds the door ajar for Lorraine to escape the heavy rain.

"For now, yes. Came to get some food, and Hunter needs some warmer clothes."

"What've the doctors said?"

"He's not been seen yet. It's a long wait in A&E. At least another couple of hours. And that's just for him to be called through." Lorraine pulls Holly in to hug her. "Thank God you're safe. You gave us such a fright, Holly."

Holly holds Lorraine tight for a moment, relishing the loving warmth of the hug. "I'm sorry," she says, squeezing her eyes tight shut.

"Don't be, please. It's my fault. I didn't impress on you enough that you can get caught out by the tide." A puddle gathers on the flagstone floor where Lorraine has leant the umbrella against the wall.

"We had a fight," Holly says, biting her lip in an attempt to hold back the sobs that have been stuck in her throat since she got back to Pinewoods. "Will he be OK?"

"I'm sure he will. As long as he rests, lets himself recover, he'll be fine." Lorraine takes Holly's hands and holds them tight, like she's scared to let go. "What was Hunter thinking, taking you out in this weather?"

"It wasn't raining heavily when we went out, and the wind wasn't that bad to start with. Really, it wasn't."

Lorraine frowns. "He should have checked the forecast. I knew there was a storm coming in. I've given him a ticking off as we've been waiting in A&E. He shouldn't have put you in danger like that."

"It's not his fault, Lorraine. I ran off. I was angry."

"He said." Lorraine sits Holly down in the chair, and perches on the end of her bed.

"What's he done to himself?" Holly asks.

"He thinks he's torn his calf muscle, right across. Hopefully nothing broken. His biggest worry is that he's torn his Achilles tendon. Hunter'll be a nightmare to look after. Can you imagine, someone as active as him having to sit around for a few weeks to recover?" Lorraine shakes her head. "One of us will have to look after him at his caravan. Probably me, though how I'll do that with this place to run, I have no idea. And just as we go into our busiest weeks!"

"He can stay here," Holly says. "I'll look after him for you. He'll be able to get about easier, and the bathroom's just there."

"You can't do that, Holly. It's too much to ask."

"Honestly, Lorraine, it's the obvious solution. You said it yourself: someone has to look after him. You've far too much to do with the guests." Lorraine opens her mouth, but before she can protest, Holly continues. "Let me look after Hunter. You can rest then, and tomorrow you can get back to your guests. They come first."

"Well, if you insist," Lorraine says, reaching out for Holly's hand again and giving it a little squeeze. "It would be a great help. I've got an airbed somewhere. Not used it in years. I'll get Dee to dig it out. There's enough space on the floor to put it up." Lorraine stands and picks up her umbrella by the door. "You're a godsend, Holly. First you rescue our garden, and now you're going to look after Hunter. I always say that Pinewoods finds you when you need it most. But with you, maybe Pinewoods found you when we needed you most, too."

* * *

It's dark when Holly hears crunching outside. Lorraine is pushing Hunter's wheelchair across the gravel with some difficulty, the front wheels scooting off in different directions. One of Hunter's legs sticks straight out in front of him, and Dee is carrying crutches. Holly watches them from the doorway of the Shepherd's Hut. The rain mercifully stopped an hour or more ago, the wind calmed to a light breeze, and there's not a cloud in the starlit sky.

"They've insisted on bringing me here," Hunter says to Holly as they get closer to the Shepherd's Hut, "but you can't give up your bed for me."

336

"It's a done deal," Holly smiles, "so you've got no say in the matter. Besides, it's late, and you're tired." Hunter looks like he's had the life sucked out of him.

"Where will you sleep?"

Holly shrugs. "On the floor. Dee found an old air bed for me."

"You can't do that! Let me sleep on the air bed."

Holly laughs. "You'll never get up from it. I'm sleeping on it tonight. Tomorrow, we can work out what we'll do until you can go back to your caravan."

Lorraine and Dee help Hunter out of the borrowed A&E wheelchair and into the Shepherd's Hut. As they fuss around him, Holly steps outside, welcoming the opportunity to hide her flushed cheeks. Her heart is pounding and she feels a strong pull of desire for Hunter, despite everything. Looking up at the stars, she attempts to get hold of her emotions – torn between her earlier anger towards him and the ordeal they went through together. She's still angry with him for the way he has been treating her, for thinking she would share his personal story . . . but oh god, is she thankful for him turning up on the beach when he did, and for the fact he is now safe. Holly walks over to a lavender bush, rubs some leaves between her fingers and brings her hand to her nose to take in the aroma. It does nothing to calm her.

When Hunter is settled in bed, propped up by three pillows, Dee passes him a bowl of stew she's brought from the kitchen. "Here, eat this up before you go to sleep. It'll help build your strength back up after today's ordeal."

Hunter eagerly takes the bowl from Dee and devours a few

mouthfuls. "Dee, you're my saviour. This is exactly what I needed. Thanks."

Lorraine and Dee reluctantly leave, with instructions that Hunter is due his pain meds in three hours. For a moment, Holly and Hunter look at each other, neither speaking. They haven't spoken to each other since they stepped out of the lifeboat, hours ago, and neither of them mentioned their argument before they parted ways.

Holly breaks their gaze, taking a glass into the bathroom and filling it with water, giving herself a few seconds to collect her thoughts. She passes Hunter the glass, and as she turns away from him, he grabs her other hand and gives it a squeeze. "Thank you," he says. Pain is etched across his face.

Holly switches on a table lamp and turns off the main light. The room immediately takes on a warm cosiness in the low light. She smiles at Hunter as she settles herself down in the single chair in the Shepherd's Hut and puts a blanket over her knees. "Let me know if you need anything," she says, picking up her book.

"I'm OK for now. Thank you. How are you?"

"I'm OK. Well, despite swallowing a few pints of seawater." Holly laughs and pulls a face of disgust.

"God, me too. I can still taste it."

"I'm sorry. Sorry that I ran away and left you. Sorry for getting trapped by the sea. Sorry for everything I put you through. And before you tell me off for saying 'sorry', this is an actual apology, not a habit." Holly winds a tassel on the blanket around her little finger. "I didn't realise you'd hurt yourself when you slipped down the dune."

"Apology accepted." Hunter smiles gently at Holly, a yawn taking over mid-smile. "It's not just your fault, you know. We were both angry with each other. Ever since . . . shit!" He winces with pain as he adjusts his position in the bed, and sucks in a sharp breath through closed teeth. "Ever since . . . you know . . ." he runs his hands through his hair, "since that day I kissed you." He leans his head back against the pillows and closes his eyes. "I didn't mean to hurt you, Holly. God, I so wanted . . ." His voice is almost a whisper. "I know I hurt you. I'm sorry for that."

"I don't get why you did it, though. Why you kissed me and then ran off."

Hunter shakes his head and takes in a deep breath. "There's so much mixed up in this." He pauses.

"I'm sure there is," Holly pushes, not prepared to accept half-finished explanations. "But I think I deserve to know."

Hunter clears his throat. "Well, for one thing, I could tell you'd been hurt in the past. I like you, Holly. A lot." He pauses. "I didn't want to cause you any more hurt. But being a clumsy idiot, I did that anyway."

Holly's heart misses a beat. She remembers what San told her: that she isn't the problem. Listening to Hunter now, surely this is exactly what he's telling her. Did he really want to be with her all along?

Holly leans forwards, her elbows resting on her knees. He's right, he was a clumsy idiot. But she can't help but feel like there's something else going on.

"Come on, Hunter, there's more to it than that. Tell me."

Hunter rubs the palms of his hands into his eye sockets. He shakes his head. "You don't want to be associated with someone like me, Holly. Like I told you, I was mixed up in the gang life. I'm not a good person, not deep down. I've done stuff in my past I'm not proud of."

"You're not in a gang now, though."

Hunter shakes his head. "Not for years now."

"And you're not doing *stuff* now, are you? Whatever 'stuff' is."

He shakes his head again.

Holly stays quiet for a moment. "You said 'for one thing', as if there's more to it."

Hunter sighs. "I have a rule. I don't get involved with clients. It's not right. I have to keep professional boundaries. I keep my personal and professional lives separate." Holly nods, waiting for Hunter to go on. "That first day I met you, I could see that you were vulnerable. And as my feelings for you deepened, I knew I needed to stick to the code, even though I didn't want to."

"Well," Holly says, about to tell Hunter that he could have told her that sooner when he jumps back in.

"I know, it sounds pretty weak now I say it out loud. And I could have just told you that. I really don't know why I didn't."

"That would have made things a whole lot easier, Hunter." She gives him a small smile.

"And then when I saw that article that prick Dylan wrote . . ." Hunter takes in a deep, slow breath, "I genuinely thought you told him all about me. Since leaving the army, you're the only person, other than Lorraine and Dee, that I've talked to about my gang life."

Holly is touched by his openness. "I'd never do that, to anyone. Not after all I've lived through with the press," she says.

"I know that now. I really am sorry for thinking that of you. I still don't know how Dylan found out about me."

"Is there anything online about you? Or maybe he found someone who used to know you. That woman who drove me back here in the Land Rover remembers you. Perhaps Dylan found someone like her who was happy to tell your story."

"I thought I recognised her from somewhere. I doubt she'd have told him anything though. How would Dylan have found her, anyway. It's pure coincidence that you came across her."

Holly nods slowly and yawns. "Do you think maybe he overheard us talking? In the kitchen garden. I don't know how long he was standing behind me when he came back to Pinewoods."

"Yeah, maybe. Anyway— *Argh!*" Hunter winces again.

"I'll set my alarm for when you need to take your painkillers. Get some rest now." Holly takes a couple of pillows away from behind Hunter's head and pulls the duvet over him. "I'll be right here if you need anything."

She lies down on the air bed, adjusting her position to get comfortable, pulls a blanket over herself and listens for Hunter's breathing to change. Just moments later, he's asleep.

Holly expects to fall asleep with ease herself, being so tired, though admittedly the air bed is not the most comfortable thing to sleep on. She closes her eyes and waits for sleep to descend. The happenings of the day play over and over again in her mind: their snappiness with each other, their big fight, running away, getting trapped in the sea, Hunter rescuing her, her rescuing Hunter.

After a while, she shifts her position, and as she does, the telltale sound of air escaping the air bed valve gives a stark warning of what's in store for her for the rest of the night. Giving up on sleep, she eases herself up from the now squidgy mattress, quietly opens the door and stands outside. With one hand in her pocket, loosely holding her rose quartz heart, she looks up at the stars and marvels at the sight, until gradually the dawn starts to creep in.

"Are you there, Holly?" Hunter calls, a little while later.

"I'm here." Holly walks back into the hut. "What do you need?"

"Can you pass me my crutches, please? Dee left them leant up by the window. I need to go to the bathroom. What time is it?"

"A little after three. You managed to get a couple of hours sleep. I was just about to wake you for your painkillers. You can have them after you've used the bathroom."

"Yeah, I thought it might be time. The bloody pain woke me up." Holly helps Hunter up from the bed, and cringes for him when he yelps with pain.

When he returns to the bedroom, Hunter looks around the small room. "You're not seriously telling me you've been trying to sleep on that sorry thing?" He points one crutch towards the now flattened air bed, wobbling a little on one foot as he does it.

"Yes." Holly laughs. "Though it did start out with air in it. Leaky valve."

"Shit. Not much good for sleeping on, then."

"No, not really. I couldn't nod off, so I went out to look at the stars. I like making out the constellations. And then I've been watching the light change just now. Dawn is a beautiful time of day."

Hunter balances on one leg as he leans his crutches against the wall. Holly rests her arm under his elbow, and he turns his head, resting his chin in her hair.

"Lie down next to me," he says, quietly. "You can scoot in to the side by the wall. We'll both fit."

"I can't get into bed with you," she says, not meeting his eye as she helps him lower himself down on to the bed.

"Don't worry, I'm in no fit state to do anything about it." Hunter grins, and for a moment, Holly can imagine the cheeky child that he must have been. "At least if you're lying on the bed you might get a little bit of sleep, and I won't feel so bad about inconveniencing you." He pats the bed. "Come on, be sensible."

Hunter lifts his damaged leg on to the bed, and beckons Holly into the gap between him and the wall. She hesitates, suddenly nervous. There's definitely something between them, she knows that, but this isn't what she expected to happen when she offered to look after Hunter.

"It's OK, Holly," Hunter whispers. "Relax. Your safe."

Gingerly, stepping over Hunter, Holly lowers herself on to the bed. A light dip in the middle rolls her a little closer to him than she intends to get. She shuffles herself to the other side of the bed, as close to the wall as she can.

As the night draws on, aware of the warmth of Hunter's body close to hers, Holly finds herself wanting to reach out and touch him, but not daring to.

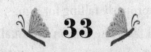

33

FINGERTIPS & SOFT LIPS

THE next morning, Holly kicks the stable door open with her foot, her hands full with a tray laden with food. "Dee's made us a morning feast," she says, laying the tray next to Hunter.

"Great," Hunter says, carefully pushing himself up to sitting in the bed. "I'm starving."

"Well," Holly says, "that's just *your* breakfast, so eat up. Dee's made up another tray for me," she laughs. "She's invented some saying about Epsom salts healing *sore* muscles and food healing a *torn* muscle." Holly rolls her eyes before going off to fetch her own tray of food with a skip in her step. Despite the events of the previous day – and having got very little sleep – she feels strangely happy.

When she returns with her food, they eat in silence. Holly's thoughts drift to the few hours of sleep that she had next to Hunter, as she glances over at him between mouthfuls. Every fibre of her tingles, the butterflies in her tummy flying all over the place. Ever since she lay down next to him, it's like an explosion of excitement has waved over her. She knows that she's falling for Hunter – properly falling for him.

"I never get breakfasts like this on a normal day," Hunter says, taking a mouthful of sourdough toast loaded with some of Dee's homemade strawberry jam. "I guess that's one good thing that came out of yesterday."

"Dee's breakfasts are good," Holly agrees.

"And sorting things out between us, that's good too."

Holly nods and thinks for a moment, a spoonful of granola halfway to her mouth. "What you told me on the blowout," Holly says, putting her spoon back down into her bowl. "About your friend being killed. I'm sorry."

"I shouldn't have told you that. You're here for yourself, trying to heal from your own stuff. I shouldn't have put that on you."

"Yeah, I get that, but you hurt, too. And that's OK. I know what hurt like that does to you."

Hunter rests his toast back down on the plate in front of him. "Yeah, I had a hard time." He pauses. "Really tough time, actually."

"I'm not asking you to tell me about it. I know how annoying that can be – you know, people wanting to know what happened."

Hunter nods. "Thanks. This felt like a good place to hide out for a bit, sort my head out." He laughs and shakes his head. "Never realised there's a bloody firing range nearby. You'd think I'd have checked."

"I remember you flinching that day you came out to find me. Is it something from your army days?"

Hunter nods. "You were close by the firing range, with the

guns going off. I sometimes get panic attacks when they're shooting."

"And that's why you were moody with me."

"I wasn't moody."

Holly raises an eyebrow. "That's like me saying I don't moan."

Hunter laughs, loud and full. "Hmm, yeah, that's fair." He nods, serious again now. "I'm not as bad as I was last year. This place rubs off on you after a while. And Lorraine's been a great help, like a favourite auntie. Dee, too. Look after me, they do. Really helped heal my scars. And talking of healing – time for my medication, please. I've eaten my breakfast, like you told me, and my pain needs its reward."

Holly passes Hunter a glass of water and the bottle of pills, their fingers brushing. Surprised by the touch, she quickly pulls her hand away, spilling some of the water on the floor. Clearing her throat, she bends to pick up one of the trays, letting her hair fall across her face to hide her flushed cheeks. "Take your tablets. I'll take these back to the kitchen."

Walking down the garden path back to the kitchen, Holly breathes in slow and deep. She's relieved to have a brief moment to herself, to gather her thoughts. Being so close to Hunter intensifies her desire for him. She wants to kiss him, wants to show Hunter how ready she is to be kissed. But it's really not who she is. With Will, her ex-boyfriend, she never made the first move – she was too fearful of possible rejection.

Hunter isn't Will, though. With Hunter she *knows* he likes her – that he wants to kiss her as much as she wants to kiss him.

As she puts the tray down on the kitchen counter, Holly's mind is made up. She turns, and, without saying a word to Dee, she marches back up the garden, straight in through the door of the Shepherd's Hut, and over to the bed, where Hunter is hauling himself up to standing with his crutches. She stops right in front of him, their bodies almost touching. She rests a hand on his chest, and Hunter hops back away from her.

"It's OK," Holly whispers. "I want this." For a moment, she's unable to look up into his face. Then she lets a cheeky smile spreads across her cheeks. "Besides, I'm not going to be your client for much longer."

Slowly, Hunter takes hold of her hand, a crutch dangling from his arm, and lifts her fingers to his lips, kissing one, and then the next, and the next. Holly lifts her gaze, and traces his top lip with the tip of her finger, sending a tingle down her spine, before leaning in.

She kisses him gently at first, as if it's his soft lips he injured, not his leg, and pulls herself in closer to him, feeling her body contour around his. Hunter responds, tenderly at first, his mouth exploring hers as his kisses become more urgent. Holly kisses Hunter more fully now, harder. She weaves her hands through his hair, strokes her thumb along his jawline, down his neck, across his chest. Hunter's hand rests on Holly's waist, his thumb stroking bare flesh where her T-shirt has ridden up. He lifts his other hand from the crutch, slipping his fingers under her top, stroking the skin under her breast and . . .

As Hunter wobbles, the crutch bangs against Holly's leg.

She flinches, pushing into Hunter who collapses backwards on to the bed.

Hunter shouts out in pain. Then they both burst out laughing.

Sunday 4th July

HOW I FEEL: It's probably fair to give myself a score of 10/10, for once

SLEEP: Five hours, maybe more

WEATHER: Another beautiful blue sky, no clouds. Air still clear and fresh, with a light breeze, and warming up again

WEARING: Pyjama bottoms and Hufflepuff T-shirt

SOMETHING GOOD THAT HAPPENED: Kissing Hunter

PROMPT: What are three simple pleasures that make me happy?

This one's an easy prompt for me today.

1. Being in the garden and getting dirt under my fingernails.
2. Seeing smiles on other people's faces. It's such a pleasure to see Ruth singing to herself in the greenhouse as she potters about. I didn't even ask her to do any work with me today, but there she was, whilst Bex did a trip over the water back to their house, checking how the repair works are coming on. It makes me happy to see her happy.
3. Lunches in the kitchen with Lorraine and Dee, and the

laughs we have together. That kitchen is becoming one of my happy places.

4. (I'm giving myself an extra one) Kissing Hunter. Spending time with Hunter. Teasing Hunter. That's making me very happy.

There's a Japanese word I came across a while back, for repairing broken pottery and making the repaired item more beautiful than the original: kintsugi. It means something like "golden repair". Pieces are put back together with gold. I looked it up on the internet - it's about beauty being in the imperfections. Hunter has worked a bit of kintsugi for me. Hunter's helping me see some of my beauty, despite my scar.

I can't believe I've actually been sleeping next to him?! I know nobody reads my journal, but I feel the need to write "and reader, nothing actually happened, he is being a complete gentleman". I kind of wish something would happen, though . . . Can't believe how much I want him. But it's unlikely anything will happen until his leg is better.

I also can't believe I was the one who kissed him. Decided I might as well . . . it's not like he could run off if he'd wanted to. Haha.

P.S. I've sent off that email to Dylan's editor. It's been sitting in my drafts folder for days. I've done what I can now.

34

THE SCARS
THAT MAKE US

WHEN Holly wakes the next morning, the Shepherd's Hut is flooded with light. Hunter insisted that she sleep on the bed next to him again, promising to be a gentleman, so that she could have a reasonable night's sleep. She's curled up towards Hunter now, her arm flung across his chest.

"Morning, beautiful," Hunter says in a low voice, gravelly with sleep. "I've been watching you sleep."

Holly's hand swiftly moves to her scar, suddenly aware that it's on show. Gently, Hunter takes her hand in his and moves it back away from her face, resting it in the middle of his chest.

"Both sides of you are beautiful, Holly. Our scars are what make us – the hidden ones, as well as the ones that are out there for everyone to see." He reaches across and touches her cheek, gently. "*Argh!* Shit, shit, shit! I keep forgetting about the pain. I need my next lot of tablets. Could you . . .?"

"I'll get you something to eat before you take them," Holly says. She checks the clock on the makeshift bedside table. "Six thirty. Dee's always in the kitchen by now. I'll get you some breakfast." As she shuffles down to the end of the bed, Holly looks back at Hunter.

"I've been meaning to ask you. Who's Ray Knight?"

Hunter raises his eyebrows in a look of surprise. "Who told you about that?"

"The lifeguard. The one who drove me back here when you were taken to hospital."

"Ah, right, yeah." He lets out a small laugh, and pushes himself up to sitting. He extends a hand towards her "Ray Knight. Pleased to meet you, Holly Bush."

Holly eyes his hand but doesn't take it. "Repeating your name doesn't answer the question."

"What question?"

"If your name is Ray Knight, why do people call you Hunter?"

"Goes back to my army days. We all had nicknames. Hated mine."

"How can you have a bad nickname from being called Ray Knight? At least you didn't get called *Holly-bobs* or *Red Bush*," Holly says. "Go on then, what was yours?"

"Sunny." Holly looks blankly at Hunter. "From ray of sunshine? It started out as Sunshine in my first week but inevitably got shortened, and I was known as Sunny for years."

"That still doesn't explain why you're called Hunter, though. The lifeguard said it was something to do with your street days."

"Yeah, I remember her – knew her way back. We lived on the same estate. She's right, I became known as Hunter when I was on the streets. Cos I could hunt anything – or anybody – down," he says, with a hint of pride. "I liked being called Hunter – the one

353

thing from my gang days that I did like. So I changed my name to that, when I arrived here." Hunter shrugs, and then grins. "Don't start calling me Ray or Sunny now, whatever you do. It could be the early death of a blossoming romance."

* * *

Shortly after breakfast, Holly is tidying the shed when there's a rap on the open door. "Only me!" Bex says.

Holly puts the garden rake on to its hook and turns to Bex. "Come to help?"

"I wasn't planning on it," Bex laughs.

Holly walks back out into the garden and waves at Hunter, who gives her a thumbs up. He's perched on the bench at the back of the house with a makeshift table in front of him, planting up herbs into pots ready for selling.

"He seems to be recovering from his ordeal," Bex says.

"He's bored. Not used to doing nothing, so I'm giving him jobs he can do sitting down."

"I can't imagine Hunter being the kind of person who does nothing well. Mind you, you're not much good at relaxing and doing nothing either. You came to Pinewoods for a break, and then spent most of your time turning the garden around." Bex smiles at Holly. "Anyway, the reason I wanted to chat is that I'm the bearer of bad news, sadly."

"Oh?"

"You know yesterday I went to see how the repairs are coming on at home? Well, they're done. Finished. And we've got a date for moving back into the house."

Holly feels her heart sink slightly. "When are you going? I'll miss you." She isn't sure she's ready for everything to change around her. Everything about Pinewoods Retreat has become her new way of life; she doesn't want reality to sneak back in and take them back to their normal lives.

"Friday." Bex gives Holly a tight hug. "I'm going to miss you, as well – so, so much. You're the best friend I've ever had. And you work magic on Mum, too."

Holly shakes her head. "No, Bex, you're the one working the magic – on yourself, as well as your mum."

Bex smiles. "Well, she's definitely loads better in herself. I've not seen her looking this well since before she had COVID. Two of my brothers have agreed to help, as well. San was definitely right in pushing me to message them all. And Mum's even saying she's ready to do more when we get home. Wants me to start looking for a job." Bex beams at Holly.

"That's amazing, Bex." Holly smiles back at her friend, knowing what a huge difference these changes are for her. "I'm so proud of you. And Ruth, too. You've both come so far in just a few weeks."

"We really have, haven't we?" Bex smiles to herself. "Anyway, enough about us. How are you feeling after your little escapade?"

"A bit better. My stomach is still a bit unhappy after all that seawater I swallowed, and I can't even face the thought of going down to the beach at the moment."

"I'm not surprised. God, Holly, you must have been scared out of your mind."

Holly nods. "I was. But when Hunter got stuck too, I knew I had to help save him. The water was up to his mouth."

Bex shakes her head. "Well, no more excitement for you pair for a while."

"Erm, actually . . ." Holly bites her lip.

Bex gasps. "You haven't!"

"Kissed, only kissed," Holly says hastily, holding her hands up in front of her. "And cuddled, a lot. And I slept on the bed with him. But that's all. Nothing more." Holly's cheeks burn, but she can't help but smile.

Bex squeals and jumps up and down on the spot, like her shoes have turned into springs. "I'm so pleased. You *have* to WhatsApp when I'm home. I want all the details."

"And I expect to hear all about you and Conor, too!"

"You will, I promise," Bex says. "What about you? When are you due to go home?"

"I've only a few days left. I'll have to speak to Lorraine and Dee about when they need me out by. I don't know yet if it's Friday or Saturday I need to leave."

"Let me know when you find out. But right now, I told Mum I'd show her how to do an online shop so that she's a bit more in control over the food we buy. She's going to get herself a mobile phone too, so that I don't need to worry when I go out without her. We'll both feel happier knowing she can contact me if she needs to."

"That's amazing, Bex. You two are taking strides forwards to a totally different way of being together. I'm so pleased for you."

As Bex wanders back to the house, Holly looks into the shed.

She's impressed with herself that she's kept the neatness and order that Simas set up for the tools. A place for everything, and everything in its place. Though she must tell Lorraine that some of the tools need oiling, to keep them in the best condition.

Closing the shed door behind her, she surveys the garden next. There's a patch in front of the greenhouse that will be ready to plant soon. She'll mention it to Dee. Maybe the new gardener could plant some lavender there in the spring. Lorraine could use it in those eye pillows they give out to guests.

Holly sighs. Will the new gardener care as much about the kitchen garden as Simas did – as she does? This place deserves someone who's simpatico, just like Dee said.

35

WHERE FLOWERS
BLOOM, SO DOES HOPE

THE late-morning sunshine kisses the bench outside the Shepherd's Hut. Holly tilts her head back against the wall and closes her eyes, relishing the memories of another night sleeping next to Hunter, laying in his arms, breathing him in.

The now familiar clicking of crutches in the hut announces that Hunter is making his way out through the stable door to join her.

"What are you doing sitting here?" he asks, leaning on to the doorframe.

"You were busy with your exercises. I didn't want to disturb you."

"I wouldn't have minded."

Holly shrugs. "I was just thinking. About stuff."

"Is it OK if I join you?"

Holly scoots across the bench so that Hunter can sit down without having to navigate around her legs. For a big man hobbling on one leg, he lets himself down on to the bench with ease and grace.

"I should let you have your Shepherd's Hut back," Hunter says, leaning his crutches against the bench.

"It's not mine. I'll need to give it up in a matter of days."

"You're really leaving? I hoped you'd stay longer."

Holly looks out across the garden. "I don't want to go. I love it here. I feel . . . like I belong." Before the retreat, she never would have thought that anywhere other than the house her grandparents left to her could feel like home – but she's found somewhere that really does.

"You do belong." Hunter picks up Holly's hand and holds it in his. "Who's going to look after the garden when you go? It's like it's your garden now."

"That's how I feel, but Lorraine and Dee are looking to fill the job permanently and I don't have the right skills that they're looking for."

"Did you ask them about it?"

Holly fiddles with the hem of her shorts. "No."

"Why not?"

Holly shrugs. "They're placing an advert. If they thought I was good enough to do the job, they'd ask me."

Hunter shakes his head. "You don't know that. Talk to them about it." He nudges Holly with his elbow. "Go and ask."

"You're bossing me around again." She laughs.

"I'm not being bossy. I want you to ask because you're good here. And I want you to stay." His amber-flecked eyes look straight into hers.

"I want to stay too. But I don't think the job is mine, sadly."

They sit together in silence for a moment, looking over the garden, now with neat rows of vegetables and soft fruits, free to grow without being strangled by weeds.

"Thank you," Hunter says.

"For what?"

"Coming to Pinewoods when you did. Staying this extra week. Letting me move into this place for a few days. Looking after me. You must be sick of me by now."

"Never," Holly says, her voice almost a whisper.

Hunter smiles at her and her skin tingles with desire in response – like her body is an electric current, and Hunter clicks the switch. He leans towards her and presses his lips to hers. The crutches clatter to the ground, and Hunter cups Holly's face in his hands. He stops abruptly and pulls away.

"Shit," Hunter groans. "I'm twisting the wrong way into my sore leg. It's killing me."

Holly stands and gently lowers herself on to Hunter's lap. "Better?" she asks.

Hunter nods with a grin. "Better."

She smiles at him. "Can you believe we haven't even been on a date yet?"

"We've had plenty of dates!" Hunter mock-protests. "Three weeks of personal training sessions."

"They weren't dates, Hunter!"

"OK, OK." Hunter laughs and pulls her in towards him. "I better put that right then, hadn't I? I know just the place. There's a lovely little cafe not far from here – a hop, skip and a jump from this very spot – or a hobble on crutches, in my case. Might I take you for afternoon tea later? I'll book a table. Half-past three?" He leans in and gently kisses Holly's eyelids, her nose, her cheeks, and finally, when Holly thinks she's ready to explode, her lips.

* * *

Lorraine is thrilled when she hears the plans for Holly and Hunter's date in the garden cafe, and offers to help Hunter to get ready. She takes him into the house to help him change for their date, a little like it's wedding preparations that are underway. Holly takes her time getting dressed, with help from Bex who irons her favourite cinched-in-at-the-waist, emerald-green tea dress with the white collar – the colour complements Holly's green eyes and auburn hair. The dress is teamed with cream ballet pumps and a cream cardigan. Holly's wearing a little make-up, and her hair is pinned into a soft up-do with tendrils framing her face – Lorraine sent Jess over to do it for her because, as Lorraine said, teenagers like her are a whizz with hair.

Holly's stomach butterflies are doing acrobatics when she walks around the side of the house, past the yoga yurt and the takeaway trailer, and into the garden cafe. Hunter is already settled at a table laid with a white table cloth and a jug of garden flowers in the centre. Holly approaches the table, relieved to see that the flattering of females is nowhere to be seen and the cafe itself is relatively quiet. She notices Lorraine and Dee standing in the doorway, before spotting Bex and Ruth at a table on the other side of the garden. They give her a little wave.

Hunter laughs. "Go on now, everyone. What did I tell you all? This is a date! We don't need the whole family here, chaperoning." He winks. "I'm sure Holly will give you the low-down when we're done."

Holly leans in to him, planting a gentle kiss on his lips. Bex lets out a whoop before helping Ruth to her feet and, full of chatter, they scuttle indoors behind Lorraine and Dee.

"A bit more public for our first date than I expected," Holly says, rolling her eyes. She settles herself into the chair next to Hunter. For the first time since she met him, he's wearing something other than cargo pants and a fitted T-shirt. Now, his always-outdoors tan is shown off by a white linen shirt and a pair of navy shorts. On one foot – his good one – he wears a boat shoe, the other foot resting on a velvet cushion, placed on a stool. He looks heart-stoppingly handsome – and here she is, on a date with him.

Hunter leans forwards and pulls a flower from the jug. Breaking off the stem, he pushes it behind Holly's ear. In the distance, Bex can be heard saying "awww!".

"See you later, Bex," Hunter says, smiling and not taking his eyes from Holly.

Holly giggles. She picks up the edge of the tablecloth and traces the hem with her finger and thumb.

"Nervous?"

"A little," she admits.

"I could make you do star jumps or run on the spot, if you like? You know, something more familiar."

She laughs. "In this dress?"

"Why not? You look . . ." Hunter pauses, as though he is taking her in.

"What?"

"Breathtaking. Absolutely stunning."

Holly blushes, running finger and thumb over the same small section of the tablecloth hem in front of her.

"And you look very handsome." Holly is all a-flutter with nerves and excitement. Hunter takes her hand, lifts it to his mouth and kisses each finger. And *whoosh*! With that, every part of Holly's body sings with pleasure and desire.

"So, let's get some of the important stuff out of the way," Hunter says, a glint in his eye. "You know, to make sure we're compatible."

"And what if we're not?"

"We could ignore the results." He grins.

"Go on then, what stuff?" Holly asks, squeezing his hand.

"You know the kind of thing. Star jumps or press-ups; cats or dogs; city apartment or cottage in the country; the Maldives or the Lake District."

"Let me see." Holly taps her chin, the way Grandad used to. "Well, it has to be star jumps – I hate press-ups."

Hunter cringes. "Oh, shame, and there was me thinking we were going to be a perfect match."

"Well, I actually hate both, so you could teach me how to do better press-ups, maybe? And I could learn to put up with them. Does that give us a bit of a chance? Unless the rest of my answers hand you the hammer to put the rest of the nails in." She raises an eyebrow, a cheeky grin spreading across her face. He leans back in his chair and waits for her to continue. "OK, so the other answers are non-negotiable for me." Hunter crosses his arms, one eyebrow raised, and gives her a lopsided smile. "The Lakes win hands down, every time. And I'd have to say cats *and* dogs, I like both."

Hunter nods. "And living arrangements?"

"Goodness, you're pushy for a first date. Hmm, that would be the Shepherd's Hut, as a starter home. Though I'd need a small extension out the back, and I'll probably have to widen the door for your muscles to get through when you come to visit. How did I do?"

"You did just fine. Perfectly fine." His eyes lock on hers. Hunter picks up her hand again, and strokes it with his thumb. "Despite you being Team Star Jumps, I promise to take you on another date."

"Shall we get this one out the way first?" Holly teases. "We may yet discover a lack of cake compatibility."

"I think you know by now that it's Dee's cookies for me, particularly when they're still warm out of the oven."

Holly laughs. "Yes." She nods. "I've noticed." She leans forwards and kisses Hunter, her fingers gently stroking his jaw. She soaks in the happiness and excitement she feels being close to him.

Yes, she could get used to this.

* * *

Lorraine helps Hunter back to his feet at the end of the afternoon tea, leaving Jess to clear the table. "Holly, can Dee and I have a quick word in the kitchen?"

Holly's heart sinks. This is it, then. Lorraine and Dee are going to tell her that it's time for her to pack up and go.

"You two go ahead," Hunter says, clickety-clacking his crutches across the grass. "I can get myself back to the Shepherd's Hut."

In the kitchen, Dee and Lorraine sit on one side of the table, Holly on the other.

"We need to talk," Dee says.

Holly lowers her eyes. She takes in a deep breath and fixes her eyes on the old, handwritten recipe book that sits between them in the middle of the table. The pages are crinkled and marked with splashes and drips from years of use.

"We want to ask you something," Lorraine continues.

Holly steels herself to look up at them. These wonderful women have been her friends for nearly four weeks. They've opened their hearts and home to her, and she owes it to them to be kind and polite as they ask her to pack her bags. She takes in another deep breath and looks up, meeting their eyes, a forced smile on her face.

Lorraine clears her throat. "You've been here for – what? A few weeks now. Can you believe it's that long?"

"Feels longer to me," Dee says. "In a good way," she adds quickly.

"You've done amazing things here over these weeks," Lorraine continues, looking at Dee. Dee nods and smiles back at Lorraine. "The garden is back to how Simas left it. Better, even."

"And look how you've brought everyone together through the garden," Dee says, butting in. "And selling all the veg!"

"Well, we wondered," Lorraine looks at Dee again, before

taking in a deep breath, "have you ever considered a job as a gardener?"

"A job?" Blood rushes in Holly's ears, and her heart thuds. They're not asking her to go home?

Dee looks at Lorraine, her brow slightly furrowed. "I knew it was a bad idea."

"It's OK, Holly," Lorraine begins kindly. "We understand you have a life elsewhere. We don't expect you to take us up on—"

"Yes, I have." Holly says, her voice a whisper. Lorraine and Dee both look at her in surprise. "I've considered a job as a gardener. I saw an advert for one a couple of weeks before I came here, but they were asking for an experienced organic gardener."

"That was us!" Lorraine clasps her hands in front of her. Dee nods enthusiastically, a smile spreading across her face.

Holly desperately wants to grin back at them. She's pretty sure she knows what they are asking, but until she hears them say it . . .

"Will you come and work here, Holly, in our garden? We would absolutely love to have you. Shepherd's Hut and meals here in the kitchen included. Weekends off."

Holly leans back in her chair. A powerful sense of relief and contentment washes over her. This is the job of her dreams, in a place she belongs. She lets the grin she's been holding in spread across her face. "I'd love to."

"Perfect!" Lorraine says, laughing and clapping her hands.

"Wonderful!" Dee says, joining in with Lorraine's laughter.

As she thinks about the job and the freedom she will have to improve the garden, ideas whir around Holly's mind. She could set up a beehive, and plant a plum tree, and ... She looks earnestly at Lorraine and Dee. "Perhaps we could offer gardening therapy? You know, for people who want to lose themselves in the garden – guests staying at Pinewoods, maybe even locals?"

Lorraine and Dee look at each other, smiles plastered across their faces. "I told you," Lorraine says. "She's perfect for the job."

Dee raises an eyebrow. "And I agreed! It wasn't all you, you know." The three of them burst out laughing and link hands across the table.

"Start next week?" Lorraine asks, squeezing Holly's hand. "Monday, maybe?"

"I'll need to go home and sort a couple of things out, but Monday should be fine." Holly says. "Hunter will have to take me on a second date now, to celebrate!" She laughs.

She can't believe how perfect the day has been – and now topped off with getting to stay at Pinewoods. Knowing that she will be working here makes her feel free again, like she's fourteen years old again, before everything changed.

She truly couldn't be happier.

Monday 5th July

HOW I FEEL: Can I have a score of 100/10?

SLEEP: Eight hours

WEATHER: Big fluffy white clouds, high up in the perfectly blue sky. Breezy, giving a slight cool edge to an otherwise hot day

WEARING: My favourite green dress

SOMETHING GOOD THAT HAPPENED: My new job as gardener, my date with Hunter, Lorraine and Dee's kindness (and Bex and Ruth's too), my lovely hair, the flowers on the table . . . Basically everything that happened today!

PROMPT: What can I do in the next week to bring change into my life?

Lorraine's prompts keep getting easier and easier. In the next week everything is going to bring change into my life. I'll go home, sort the house out, maybe see what I'd need to do to rent it out – but that's not urgent. I'll pack up some more things to bring back with me, and I'll move in properly to the Shepherd's Hut. Then, next week, I'll start my new job.

Hunter says he'll be OK to move back into his caravan at the weekend so that I can settle myself in here, but I'm sure he will still be around a lot . . .

That's a lot of change in one week! Dee said she's going to call me the Head Gardener, even though there's nobody else working with me. Haha.

I still can't believe they offered me the job. Working here, at Pinewoods, in the garden. It's going to completely change my life. I'm so happy - happier than I ever thought I would be again. I get to stay here at Pinewoods, I get to have my lunches in the kitchen, and I'll potter about in the garden. Plus, I've got my lovely little home in the Shepherd's Hut. It's a shame that San and Bex won't be here, but we'll be able to catch up. Oh, and the pay is the same as I got at OO-TO Travel, with my meals included, which is good.

Hunter is chuffed to bits too. This gives us a proper chance to get to know each other and see how our relationship grows (gardening pun not intended!). We talked about making sure we have space, but agreed that at the moment we just want to be with each other all the time. Being away for a couple of days will feel odd, as we've been spending so much time together recently, but I suppose it'll help him get back on his feet a bit. He's still got lots of exercises to do, for his leg. That shouldn't be too difficult for the man who's always dishing out the orders in personal training sessions!

We also went on our first proper date today. My first date in years. OK, so it was only to the garden cafe at Pinewoods Retreat. But it was a full-on, official date. With Hunter. Oh my god!

I have another date in my diary, too: I'm meeting Bex and San in Liverpool for lunch at an Indian street food restaurant. I've never been before, but they've both told me I have to have the tamarind treacle fries and the chaat bombs. I can't wait to see them.

I've got my rose quartz heart in front of me as I write. I feel like it's brought me all the luck I needed. Lorraine told me it's the love stone, and helps us to love ourselves. I've found love in so many ways being here. I have so many people in my life who I love now. And yes, I do love myself more, too.

Nan was right, about needing to nurture the garden of my heart. I was like a sunless garden, where little could grow. I didn't care for myself, and I let all the flowers in the garden of my heart wilt and die. If anything, I became a weed. Mind you, as Grandad always said, a weed is simply an unloved flower.

Here, at Pinewoods, I've definitely cultivated the garden of my heart.

And now I feel like a flower, not a weed.

EPILOGUE
WHEN AUTUMN LEAVES START TO FALL

HOLLY puts the last of the autumn harvest into the old apple crates, ready for the last veg sale of the year. The garden is in a mix of raised beds laid fallow, ready for the spring sowing, along with winter veg like Brussel sprouts, kale, cabbage and, her latest favourite, kalettes. Leaves on the trees are just starting to turn orange and yellow, giving the garden a golden glow.

Hunter comes up behind her, running a hand around her waist, and kisses her on the cheek. "Here," he says, passing her a copy of *City Magazine* – the October issue. "Dylan," he says.

"More rubbish for the compost heap?" Holly asks, laughing. She takes off her gardening gloves and plants a kiss on Hunter's lips, hugging her arms tightly around him.

"After you've read it, maybe."

Holly pushes the magazine away and sits down on the bench outside Pinewoods' back door. "I'm not really interested in what Dylan's got to say. I've got the garden therapy group arriving in an hour. We're going to do some winter prep work today."

"Are you changing the subject?"

"No . . ."

"You'll want to read this. Believe me. It's closure, Holly." He looks at her steadily for a moment before bending his head and nuzzling her neck. "Do it," he whispers into her ear.

"You're so bossy." She laughs and snatches the magazine from his hand, opening it up on the page with the turned-down corner. "I hate you, by the way."

"Apparently. You've said it before when I take you out on dune runs," Hunter replies, a glint in his eye. "I'll make us some tea. See if I can pinch a couple of Dee's cookies, too."

Holly puts one hand into her pocket and rubs the rose quartz resting there. She takes a deep breath, before scanning the page in search of Dylan's name.

> APOLOGY
>
> *City Magazine* apologises to the people of Liverpool for the actions of reporter, Dylan Brown, who no longer works for this publication. Mr Brown acted independently of *City Magazine*, and his actions do not reflect the ethos or values of our publication. The editor unreservedly apologises to victims of the recent Birkenhead Tunnel disaster who were hounded by Mr Brown in the name of *City Magazine*, and to victims of other tragedies in and around Liverpool. *City Magazine* is proud of Liverpool and its people, and significant donations have been made to the following local charities . . .

Holly closes the magazine without finishing the article. She puts it down on the bench next to her.

"Wow."

"You did it, Holly," Hunter says, returning with two mugs of tea and a chocolate chip cookie for each of them.

"Just wait until I see San and Bex tomorrow. I wonder if they've seen this. I'll take it with me."

Hunter nods, too busy munching on his cookie to speak.

Holly lets out a long, slow, even breath. "I'm glad I wrote to the editor. And I'm glad San wrote her piece in the *Liverpool Standard News* about ethics and journalism." Holly smiles. "Can you believe the number of people who came forward? Over eighty. All with complaints about him hounding them."

"You stood up to that nasty piece of shit." Hunter sits down on the bench and puts his arm around Holly's shoulders. He pulls her in to him, planting a kiss on the top of her head. "Proud of you, love," he whispers into her hair.

Holly smiles. "I'm proud of me too."

PEACE AT PINEWOODS

Come, sit, rest your tired feet.

Let the trees wrap their arms around you.

Let go of your worries, your cares.

Let the sand warm your toes.

We've no interest in where you're from,

Where you thought life might take you,

Who your friends are, or what you do.

Your past, your job, your education:

None of that matters at Pinewoods Retreat.

We're here to feed your belly, your heart, your soul.

Open your mind to the freedom to be you.

At peace,

At Pinewoods Retreat.

ABOUT THE AUTHOR

Zoë Richards was inspired to write *Garden of Her Heart* by being a suicide survivor from which she learned the healing that worked best for her, which is not the same for everyone.

Dog walks around the Formby pinewoods, not far from her home, gave her the location, in an area known locally as The Lost Resort, a town that never came into existence, close to the sea. In the woods there is a sole Victorian house, standing alone on a cinder track, and this is the inspiration for the location of Pinewoods Retreat.

She lives in Southport, near Liverpool, has been married to Rob for 34 years, and they have a grown-up daughter and a cockapoo who will never grow up.

She worked for the NHS as an improvement programme manager, reforming how children and young people with special educational needs and disabilities are supported in healthcare. Writing gives her an escape from the intensity of work and from caring for her elderly mother.

ACKNOWLEDGEMENTS

I'M an overnight success following a lifetime of hard work – or more realistically, with 4 years of properly doing the work of writing behind me. There is no way that a short acknowledgement section can recognise the village that has supported me along the way, but I'll try.

I'm grateful to the team at Jericho Writers who have been constant supporters. I found out about Jericho Writers from Lucy Atkins in her lockdown lunchtime lives on Instagram. Thank you for being so open with your knowledge. I was fortunate to get a place on the ever-popular Jericho Writers Self-Edit Your Novel course in September 2020, where I learned so much from Debi Alper, and I met wonderful friends in my fellow students – particular mention goes to fellow alumni Sarah J and Fiona who I know will be forever friends.

The novel I used for the exercises we did on the Self-Edit course is the one that led to me meeting my agent, Clare Coombes of The Liverpool Literary Agency – though Clare didn't sign me at that point. She rightly said that my novel wasn't ready. That led to me writing this novel that you have in your hands, and when Clare read my submission that I'd sent to her, she was very quick to say she wanted to work with me. Thank you Clare – your never-ending belief in me carries me along, and I feel incredibly fortunate to have the perfect agent.

Thank you to Stephanie Butland and her writing retreats at Garsdale and at Gladstone's Library. Stephanie is my writing coach and mentor, from whom I've learned so much. Holly would not be the rounded character she is without Stephanie's support. And my wonderful Garsdale Retreat crowd, thank you Sarah L, Ashley, Hilary for being beta readers – and with extra special thanks to SJ and Kathryn who were beta readers, continue to be supporters extraordinaire, and who I've been lucky to work with at both of Stephanie's retreats that I've attended. Then there's the Gladstoners – Em, Erika, Cat, Tessa, Mo as well as SJ and Kathryn.

My wonderful group of alpha and beta readers – thank you for believing in my novel. Special thanks to Sarah Gorst for showing me where Holly wasn't working as a character in my first scribblings through your initial reaction to her, and to my mum, Joyce, for being an alpha and beta reader. Thanks also to Becky Chilcott, Jane Sinclair (still miss working with you – oh dear, I didn't say that about Sarah G. Of course I miss working with you, Gorsty!), Jane M, Julie, and Hannah. Every word of encouragement from your beta reading has helped me along my way.

Thank you to my incredible editor, Jasmine Dove, who totally got what *Garden of Her Heart* is about, and helped me do the final and thorough shaping of the novel so that it works on every level, and to Jo Spooner for such a beautiful and eye-catching cover. I had no idea what I wanted the cover to look like, but what you created is exactly what I wanted! And thanks, too, to Hazel Holmes of UCLan Publishing for taking on my novel for the launch of your women's fiction list. I knew you were the right choice when you said that you wished Pinewoods Retreat exists in real life. Thanks also to Becky Chilcott, Karen Stretch, and to all the team at UCLan Publishing, including the students who have worked on my novel as a live project during their studies.

I think every writer would say that there's a village that's been there for them as they write a novel, and that's true for me. There are so many authors along the way who I have learned from and have been supported by – and to name just a few, thank you Amanda Brooke, Caroline Corcoran, Philippa East, Kira-Anne Pelican, Lucy Atkins, Anna Burtt, Amanda Berriman, Dani Owen-Jones, Sarah Moorhead, Rob Parker, Mark Stay and Mark Desvaux of The Bestseller Experiment, and all the guest authors who have appeared on my podcast, Write, Damn It! generously sharing their knowledge and experience. Thank you, all. When I say it takes a village to write a novel, I truly mean it because my writing would be nothing without these amazing people, and more. I know I've missed people – but if you've supported me even for a moment, know that I am forever grateful.

And then there's my amazing colleagues at Lancashire and South Cumbria NHS – we were an incredible team together, and I thank all of you for us being able to be there for each other during the pandemic and beyond. The way we worked together meant I had the time and energy to write, despite the high pressure we worked under. There are too many to mention, so know that I mean all of you in my thanks, but particular thanks to Helen K, Helen M, Sarah G, Anna, Lisa, Anne, Clair, Sue, Alex, Becky,

Claire, Vic, Alison, Julia, Hilary, Sarah C, Helene and Jane S. Thank you for being wonderful people. Miss you all.

Special mention is reserved for Ellie, my wonderful and inspirational daughter who I'm so proud of and who has supported me on my writing journey in many ways, and to Rob, my husband, who kept out of my way whenever I had a writing stint, made me plenty of cuppas, and put up with me suddenly coming out with 'great ideas' for my writing on our dog walks and hill walks. Thanks for putting up with me through everything we've gone through together.

SOUTHPORT OFFSHORE RESCUE TRUST

In *Garden of Her Heart*, Holly and Hunter are rescued by the lifeboat. Along the coast in Merseyside, there is no RLNI – the station was closed back in 1925, despite the issues of people getting trapped in the sands by the incoming tides.

In the 1980s, following accidents resulting in the loss of lives, a campaign was set up and Southport Lifeboat – run by Southport Offshore Rescue Trust – was created with donations from the public. Southport Lifeboat still runs today as an independent Trust responsible for all its own financing and fundraising.

The crew respond to callouts from the coastguard, and have brought over 250 people to safety since it was set up, including 40 people who were stranded by the fast incoming tide in 2020.

If you would like to support Southport Offshore Rescue Trust, you can find out more by visiting:

www.southport-lifeboat.org.uk/